GHOSTS ON THE PRAIRIES

A SACRED LAND STORY

GHOSTS ON THE PRAIRIES

A SACRED LAND STORY

TANYA REIMER

Elsewhen Press

Ghosts on the Prairies
First published in Great Britain by Elsewhen Press, 2014
An imprint of Alnpete Limited

Copyright © Tanya Reimer, 2014. All rights reserved
The right of Tanya Reimer to be identified as the author of this work has been asserted in accordance with sections 77 and 78 of the Copyright, Designs and Patents Act 1988. No part of this publication may be reproduced, stored in a retrieval system or transmitted in any form, or by any means (electronic, mechanical, telepathic, or otherwise) without the prior written permission of the copyright owner.
Use of the Ringbearer font by kind permission of the designer
Peter Klassen.

Elsewhen Press, PO Box 757, Dartford, Kent DA2 7TQ
www.elsewhen.press

British Library Cataloguing in Publication Data.
A catalogue record for this book is available from the British Library.

ISBN 978-1-908168-43-6 Print edition
ISBN 978-1-908168-53-5 eBook edition

Condition of Sale
This book is sold subject to the condition that it shall not, by way of trade or otherwise, be lent, re-sold, hired out or otherwise circulated in any form of binding or cover other than that in which it is published and without a similar condition including this condition being imposed on the subsequent purchaser.

This book is copyright under the Berne Convention.
Elsewhen Press & Planet-Clock Design are trademarks of Alnpete Limited

Designed and formatted by Elsewhen Press

This book is a work of fiction. All names, characters, places, religions and peoples are either a product of the author's fertile imagination or are used fictitiously. Any resemblance to actual places or people (living, dead, fictional or in spirit-form) is purely coincidental.

Ford is a trademark of Ford Motor Company. Use of trademarks has not been authorised, sponsored, or otherwise approved by the trademark owners.

CONTENTS

For Wendell.

He breathes with me when I can't do it alone.

–PROLOGUE–

November 1918—

The three of them rushed from the rundown shed toward the cemetery. Tiny beads of snow stung their skin and blinded them, yet no one complained as they hurried past the few headstones. Antoine knew it wouldn't be easy to vanish on the open prairies of North Dakota with Emma and her son.

"Here." Antoine Depaix fell to his knees to rummage under the cold dirt for the entrance to the tunnel that would lead them across the border. It was marked by the headstone that read *Here Rest the Ghosts of the Earth.* The humour was lost on him tonight.

He tossed open the trapdoor and reached for Emma. "Climb down."

Emma hesitated, pulling Charlie against her.

"Dark bad," the boy mumbled not looking in the hole.

Antoine's jaw tightened with determination. "This dark good."

"Someone's coming." Emma tried to hide her face, ready to run, but Antoine grabbed her hand. His fingers were covered in cold mud and she slipped from his grip. Or had she pulled away? Dammit.

With a deep breath, Antoine focused on speaking with a gentle tone, so his panic didn't spread. "It's fine. The priest will help us."

"Do not let him see that I am a slave."

You aren't! he wanted to scream but Antoine didn't have time to debate, he scooped Charlie up and headed down the hole. Emma would follow her son into the dark despite her fear of tunnels.

Antoine set Charlie on the draughty floor and reached up to help Emma.

The priest called down after them. "I expected you sooner. You did well. Sacri would be proud to call you her son." Antoine looked up at the priest, his comforting eyes gleamed in the dim light.

Antoine watched his lips curve down in what Sacri used to call a sad smile. "Some things are worth a fight, " Antoine reminded him with a tight jaw.

The priest slammed the door and the sound echoed as dark settled on them like a frosty blanket.

The three stood still in the frigid tunnel facing their route to Saskatchewan, searching the dark for shadows or sounds.

Something scurried over Antoine's moccasins and he pulled back to protect Emma and her child. "Just a mouse," Antoine lied, as they huddled close for heat. He'd never tell Emma it was a rat, not after the horror she'd seen them inflict on her friend. "They tickle, nothing more."

Emma's gentle hand gripped his forearm. She was always touching him. Maybe she would forgive him. Antoine fought the urge to take her in his arms, to whisper against her long dark neck as if they had all night. Would they ever have that kind of time?

"I vowed that Charlie would get his happy forever, and I won't break that promise, Emma."

Somehow, Antoine assumed running would actually involve running. Not this painful slow pace. Standing still was harder than running, than fighting.

The chilly air tasted like dust as dirt turned to mud in his mouth. He should have expected it, yet every time he travelled these tunnels, the taste surprised him.

"We're gonna walk in the dark, Emma," Antoine whispered as he lit the old lantern. It was better to warn her. "I'll just make sure Charlie is fine. Take a minute to rest. Water is on the shelf, help yourself."

Antoine knelt in front of the boy. "You ready to run again, Charlie? It'll be dark, but carvings on the walls guide me. You're safe on Depaix land, I promise."

"Dark not safe."

After setting the lantern on the shelf, Antoine picked

Charlie up. The dirt on the lantern made shadows dance around them. "I'll teach you to read the markings on the walls with your hands so you can see in the dark."

"Like Hoolie?" Charlie asked.

Antoine's gut twisted when he mentioned Hoolie, but he took Charlie's tiny hand in his and ran it over the stones where Sacri had carved symbols many moons ago. Antoine read them with his fingers as he showed the boy. Each one dug deep into the stone, long lines carved with a blade. "Feel the markings my mother made? It means, *Where the Crow Flies*, we go that way."

"This means you know where to go?" Emma asked, an edge to her voice.

"Only one way to go, *ma belle*—home." After two years, he was finally taking them home.

Home. Then what? Antoine cleared his throat but he couldn't voice his new fears.

Charlie touched the wall then met Antoine's eyes. Unlike Emma's rich deep brown, Charlie's sparkled green. The green made Antoine uncomfortable, yet he took a moment longer to meet the tiny boy's eyes as he gently set him down. They might be green, but like Emma's, Charlie's eyes revealed his fears, his hopes, and that he trusted Antoine completely.

Antoine grabbed the lantern and ran the light over him one more time, making sure he hadn't been hurt in the journey. The gold cross peeked out from his jacket and glimmered in the light. That simple twinkle was enough to give Antoine the push he needed. "Gosh, he looks like you, Emma, even his smile." He wouldn't fail this child. Not again.

Emma stood with her back to the wall, eyes closed as she held her growing belly. Antoine shone the light on her face. Her swollen lip angered him. He glared at it, wishing she'd never had to live the pain of it. "Our boy is fine," he reassured her.

She opened her eyes to study Antoine. They were bright and alive. Trusting. Slowly, her cold hand went to Antoine's cheek. "You aren't." Her voice gave away her love.

Antoine dimmed the light and backed up before she could see the damage. He didn't need her worrying about him.

When his shoulder rubbed against the freezing rock, Antoine winced, the wounds still tender.

They started their journey. One step, then the next. Side by side in the dark.

"I'd ask you to forgive me, but I'm not sorry," Antoine broke the chilly silence. "I admit, things didn't go the way I planned, but I regret nothing."

She tensed as they walked. "We are different then."

The silence was deafening. One of them needed to speak, but neither got the chance.

A scream tore down the tunnel in a blast that forced him against the icy wall and Antoine made the sign of the cross, to summon his courage. He couldn't afford to make one wrong decision.

"Ghosts found your sister," Emma whispered, stealing the thoughts from his mind as a second scream rushed at them; a terrifying reminder of the war he'd brought home.

PART ONE

TWO YEARS EARLIER

"When earth and sunlight blend, the entire world is blessed."

–Sacri

–ONE–

April 1916, North Dakota—

Antoine and Franklin lifted the wooden barrel into the back of the wagon. They were about half a mile from the main part of Clement's Ranch. The orchard was to the left, the pastures to the right. The sky was clear except for a hawk soaring above them. Antoine felt like king of the world out on the prairies and he took it all in, seeing land he would eventually be at one with.

From the sturdy wagon, Antoine noticed Emma hanging laundry on the line not far from the large two-storey house. Her dark skin was a beautiful contrast compared to the white of the house as she stopped to hug a large towel against her. She shook out the towel and twirled with it... was that his towel?

It might be.

He took a step as if to see it better. He wanted to twirl her like that. Gosh. He couldn't wait to talk to her again.

"You done daydreaming over there, churchboy?" Franklin pulled him from his reverie. Franklin was the farmhand who had found Antoine four towns away while he searched for work last week. He was always eager to have Antoine around, as if he had some big secret to share.

Franklin's hand shook when he placed it on the last barrel, leaning in, his shoulders slouched inward awkwardly. "Listen, I wanted to talk to you about something."

"Spit it out."

"I need me some land to impress Clement, and I hear you have some. Could I buy it from you? I mean, I don't have much but you're welcome to it all."

Antoine frowned. Tommy had asked him the same thing yesterday. "It's not for sale. I work it, in hopes that it blesses me with food to share."

"Well, let me work it."

Antoine sighed. He couldn't explain to guys like this that Depaix land was sacred. "Not gonna happen. Why do you want to work land in Canada?"

He shrugged. "Why do you? Give me a hand with this."

"What are in these things anyway?" Antoine asked, as he jumped from the wagon to help him with the last barrel.

"Liquid magic." Franklin knocked on the barrel twice with a silly smirk. The dirt on his cheek made him look like a young boy.

"What the heck does that mean?"

Franklin took off his cowboy hat. His grimy curls were plastered to his head, but his grin extended so big, it lit up his eyes. "You drink?"

"Pa told me to stay away from booze, it wouldn't help my obsessing, and my sister made it clear I wasn't allowed in our house if I got stupid."

Franklin frowned. "So all this talk about prohibition, you for that?"

"Don't much care either way. My pals, they curse it, though." Antoine rubbed his hands on his slacks and grabbed the sides of the barrel. "You *not* saying that this is booze in these barrels?" No wonder Clement could afford to pay his hired hands so well, and why these boys were so eager to please him.

Antoine felt like he was crossing lines he shouldn't. What had he gotten himself into? Why hadn't they told him sooner? In his thoughts, he heard Sacri reminding him that a butterfly was just a caterpillar. He never understood what she meant by her weird sayings, but he assumed it meant that he should let fools be fools. This wasn't his problem. He'd do his job and go home with a bit of extra cash to pay some debts. He'd go back to his quiet life. No worries. Yet he looked at the barrel nervously.

Franklin's grin grew as they carried the barrel to the wagon. "Why not? A man like Clement, he knows how to make the best of these times." Franklin always smelled like whiskey so it didn't really surprise Antoine that he was all for a dumb idea like this. "Speaking of making the best of these times, you wanna cover for me again tonight so I can slip away with Mable?" Franklin did an awful lot of slipping away with the boss' daughter, yet Antoine nodded. He didn't see the point in telling Franklin to behave again. Last night, it just got him teased about being an innocent churchboy.

The wind picked up and Antoine enjoyed the cool breeze that eased where the sun heated his arms. They walked the barrel to the wagon. It was just as heavy as the other four but Antoine pretended his muscles weren't straining. "Those crates we hauled yesterday, that wasn't booze. And I'm annoyed that you boys dragged me out here for this without filling me in."

"Well, you see, Tommy mixes what's in those crates with the magic in these here barrels and makes dreams that will make you forget your own mother." They heaved up the last barrel, and Franklin licked his lips as if tasting this dream he spoke of.

Antoine climbed in the wagon to slide it back beside the others. "Where did Tommy get to anyway?" Antoine's long hair was normally in his face but his new hat kept it back, which was nice.

Tommy was about ten years older than Franklin and Antoine, but like Franklin he had pale skin, and like Franklin, Clement called him 'son', as if these boys stood a chance at marrying one of his six daughters. Well, the way Franklin was always pawing at Mable, he might actually wiggle his way into Clement's family.

"He was yelling at the dog about stealing his cookies and chased after him that way." Franklin pointed toward the slough.

His cookies? The other farmhand—the one with darker skin who Clement didn't call son—Philip, had warned Antoine not to eat Tommy's cookies because they made a guy puking-dizzy.

Antoine adjusted his cowboy hat and searched the fields for Tommy. He spotted Tommy on the open prairie easily but the dog wasn't anywhere in sight.

Suddenly, Franklin jumped in the wagon almost knocking

Antoine over. "Sorry. Bloody snake almost got me." Franklin cleared his throat and tried to look tough.

Chuckling, Antoine jumped from the wagon and tossed the snake aside. "No worries, *petit bébé*, I'll protect ya," Antoine teased.

"Not funny. Those things are bad omens."

"Whatever, I'll check what Tommy's doing. I don't like the idea of sitting out here with illegal barrels of magic in a country that confuses the beans out of me." Antoine walked toward Tommy who stood like a statue, watching the slough with his arms crossed. His hat was beside him, his boots were off, and the cuffs of his pants were wet.

Ah cripes. Antoine groaned when it clicked in what Tommy was doing. That prick had threatened to drown the dog all morning. Antoine tossed his hat toward Franklin, dug his bare feet in the loose soil and sprinted for the water. He dived in without a glance at Tommy. He'd deal with him later.

Cold, grimy water greeted him. Antoine swam downwards searching the slimy weeds for the dog. Movement to his left, closer to the shore, caused him to break the surface.

The dog moved weakly in the reeds. The water wasn't deep along the edge and Antoine shoved the cattails aside to see Beast tangled in the mess of weeds. He growled when Antoine approached and snapped at him half-heartedly.

"Shh. It's me, Beast. I'm gonna keep ya safe."

The dog let out a whine and snapped at a water spider. He struggled again, tangling himself even more.

Antoine knelt beside the dog. "Beast." Antoine waited for him to meet his eyes. It took a moment and Beast whined, pleading him to help. "Shh..." Antoine expected the dog to be afraid and fight him, but when he ran his strong arms around him, he fell limp against them. He was heavy but Antoine hauled him to shore, not looking at Tommy.

"What did you do to this dog?" Antoine laid him on the ground, keeping his voice even. Any anger on his part might set the dog off. His fur sopped into the dirt and made mud. Antoine watched his breaths. They were shallow but went down easily enough. Still, the image reminded him of Sacri when she took her last breaths. "Is he drugged or dying?"

"Beast ate my cookies. Not my fault. He wandered in himself like a cranked fool." Tommy's hanky was on the ground and sure enough, crumbs lined it. "Kinda funny. Never seen a dog get high before. Deserves him right. Not like I was gonna let him die or anything."

The sun was warm against him and Antoine slipped his suspenders down and undid his wet shirt. He tossed it on the ground.

Tommy stepped back and said in his raspy voice, "What? You gonna beat on me because some dog ate cookies he shouldn't have?"

"My Pa used to say some things were worth a fight, so yeah. I'm thinking this just might be one of them things."

"You think I'm scared of you?" Tommy looked around for help, but Clement was in town. Franklin ran toward them, and in the distance, Antoine saw Philip jump on a horse and head their way. They were far enough that he could get in a few swings to set Tommy straight.

Tommy stepped back. "It's just a dog. Not worth the effort."

Antoine charged and dropped Tommy in a tackle. They rolled together to the water's edge and the cold mud covered Antoine's back.

Tommy hit his left shoulder, and Antoine used his right arm to push Tommy off him. Tommy flew into the weeds along the edge and scrambled to his feet, but Antoine dived for him.

Tommy rolled out of the way, and Antoine slid. He felt Tommy's bare foot against his neck, pushing his face in the sloppy mud. "Your life means about as much to me as that dog's so don't tempt me, you bloody half-breed." Tommy spat on Antoine and let him go, but Antoine grabbed his leg and hauled him back into the water for another round.

"Dang it. Here comes Clement," Franklin hollered as Antoine took a hit to the face that knocked him under the water. Tommy was on him, pinning him deep down.

–Two–

Clement was waiting for Antoine when he returned to the barn. It had been a long day and the last person Antoine wanted to see was a disappointed boss.

Clement glared at him. "Minding your business now, mutt?" Clement's voice was deep and crackled when he called him mutt.

Antoine set down the saddle and faced him, ready for another fight. "*Ouais.*"

"No French on my land." Clement's piercing green eyes bore into him, as if reading his soul for the truth. "You remember where you are? Or did I hit you too hard this afternoon?"

"Yes, boss, this is your ranch. What you say goes. I respect that 'cause you pay pretty decent and you got yourself real nice fillies I like to chat with."

"Always with the mouth. I see you're stuck with night duty again. You don't go to town for fun? There are your kind in town." Clement stared out the barn door at the town in the distance.

Your kind? It was meant as an insult. Everyone was put into categories on this ranch and since he'd arrived, Antoine found himself doing the same, and it annoyed him. He wanted to head home where there were no *his kind* and *my kind,* and where everyone was just proud to be himself.

Breathe, don't take the bait. "I'm here to work your ranch, boss. Don't need trouble." Antoine clenched his fist but didn't take a swing. He'd promised Philip to stop fighting and keep out of trouble for the rest of the week.

"You'll never fit in with the others around here."

"I'd fit in better if I knew what the hell you idiots were

really up to."

Clement rubbed his jaw, flashing the strange tattoo on the back of his hand. Antoine kept his eyes on it. Reminded him of a black teardrop. He wracked his brain to remember Sacri's teachings. What did a symbol like that mean? It angered him. Was it a *Cîpay* symbol? Why would Clement and his crew have tattoos on their hands from his mother's tribe? Surely they weren't studying to be Ghosts of the Earth.

Antoine rubbed the *Cîpay* symbol tattooed around his upper arm as memories of his sister Josée's death haunted him, but Clement's rough voice pulled him from his failings. "Does your kind plan to fight in the war?" Clement watched Antoine's eyes.

His kind? What class was he in now? Did he mean French Canadians? Farmers? Métis? Cree? Why didn't this guy ever say what he meant?

Antoine settled on the truth. "Pa told me to stay out of that mess. He wouldn't even let me read about it. Said I did enough fighting without someone putting a gun in my hand and giving me a cause. I was too young anyway, and now, I have a farm to pay for."

Clement faced Antoine as if he thought of something. "You won't find a woman if you never go to town. Aren't you interested in girls? You ain't one of *them* are you?"

Antoine wasn't sure what the heck Clement accused him of now. "I'm only nineteen. No rush. Besides, there's plenty to do here." He smirked. "Nice looking gals, too."

"We don't have your kind on my land." Clement tightened his eyes and his jaw firmed. His hand came around his belt buckle as if thinking about whipping it off. Antoine noticed that it was already undone.

Weird guy. Who walks around the barn with their belt undone? Is he just fishing for a reason to use it?

"I expect each to stick to their own," Clement said. "No mixing on my land. And I thought I got rid of that cross around your neck."

Antoine pushed it under his shirt.

"I remember specifically throwing that pretty necklace in the slough while you bled all over my boots this afternoon. You have a short memory?" Clement tilted his head. "Didn't

I make it clear you were gonna have to follow my rules while on my land?"

"Yes, boss."

"Did you swim in that slough and fish out your pansy good-luck charm?"

Antoine would never tell him that Philip retrieved it. "It was my sister's. After she died by a wolf, my father gave it to me, to remind me that there are things worth fighting for, despite how tough it gets." He bowed his head, remembering Josée and how solemn his pa had been when he handed it to him. "All I have left is my older sister, and I promised her to behave while I search for my happy forever. I always keep my promises, so step aside."

Clement's thick eyebrows shot up. "Even if it means breaking them to me?"

"I only promised you that I'd work hard. Even with my sore ribs, I didn't break that promise."

"Your mouth is asking for another good whopping."

Antoine pulled the saddle up and cleared his throat. Everything he said pissed this guy off. "I better get back to work then."

"What ya doing in your spare time?" Clement demanded.

With a sigh, Antoine set the saddle back on the cement floor. *What now?* "Not much for spare time. Franklin works me hard. Tommy keeps me busy hauling illegal crap around that just seems to materialize in your pasture over night. Philip always needs help with the horses."

"I saw you talking to the girls in the house."

Clement's daughters wore the same strange tattoo on the back of their hands as Clement and Franklin. Antoine knew that meant hands off. He didn't need anyone smacking a message like that into him.

"Not your girls," Antoine admitted. "Just Emma, and we were outside. I didn't even glance at your daughters, swear."

The belt flashed out. Antoine stepped in so most of it slapped across his arm. He caught it, and wrapped it around his hand and pulled Clement so they were eye to eye.

"I warned you not to do that." Antoine glared. "If I ain't working hard enough for ya, cut my pay, send me off, but stop fishing for reasons to use the belt. I'm not your dog to discipline and no amount of beatings will change my beliefs."

"No girls here for you."

Antoine raised an eyebrow. Now this prick planned to tell him who he could talk to? "Screw you."

His lack of fear clearly angered Clement more. "I don't like mongrels on my land."

Antoine let his eyes wander up and down Clement before he settled on the belt between them, waiting for him to break free from Antoine's grip so they could fight like men.

"So why did Franklin offer me this job if I offend you so?"

Antoine relaxed his body, ready for another hit, but instead, Clement laughed and pulled away.

"You have some fire in ya." Clement slapped him on the back. "You have no idea why he invited you, do you?"

Antoine's body tightened on its own. He was dang sure he wasn't sticking around to find out why.

Clement smirked. "Get rid of that cross and stay away from anything that belongs to me and we'll be fine." Clement came closer. "I see you're as confused as a 'pecker in a tin shed. What is bothering you now?"

"I told you I didn't want trouble and I meant that. I don't know your rules and frankly, some don't make a lick of sense to me."

"I shouldn't have to tell you that a dog is off limits. Don't see Franklin talking to a dog like Emma, do ya?"

Antoine felt his anger rising. Why did this guy always have this effect on him? "Don't call her that."

"What you gonna do, mongrel?"

Antoine could almost feel his pa's hand on his shoulder, keeping him back. If he were here, he'd say something like, *"Antoine, there are fights which matter to your next breaths, and fights which end them."* The problem was knowing which was which.

"I'm going back to work if you're gonna talk like your head is shoved up your ass." Antoine reached for the saddle again and walked past Clement.

"What? You ain't gonna swing at me this time?" Clement's wine breath pulsated against his face as he grabbed Antoine's arm and pulled his body toward him. "I want your land, name your price."

His land? "I'd like to breathe without you in my face, thanks." Antoine tightened his grip on the saddle. "And Depaix land is not a possession. It just is."

"You pricks annoy me." Clement rubbed the tattoo on his wrist. "This is my land, and I set the rules. Repeat the one I just gave you."

"*All* gals are off limits, boss."

"Dogs too. Repeat that."

Antoine ran his tongue over his teeth, looking straight ahead.

"Say it."

"Can't." Antoine kept his jaw firm. "Franklin made me sleep with Beast last night. I might end up next to your poor dog again tonight."

Clement chuckled. "Yeah? You learn anything by sleeping outside with the dog?"

"*Ouais*, Franklin's a prick when he's drunk, yet your daughter spends the night with him, making him moan like a hungry stallion."

"My Mable?" Clement stepped back and shook as if Antoine nailed him in the gut. He pulled himself together with a few quick breaths. "I didn't know Franklin was drinking again. Dammit. You fetching to take his place? Is this what you want? You want to partner with me, because I can arrange that?"

"Nope, thought never crossed my mind."

"Hmmm." Clement pointed to Antoine's arm. "We'll see. Check that arm, someone got ya good." Antoine refused to acknowledge the welt on his arm. He wouldn't give Clement the satisfaction.

He met Clement's stabbing green eyes. So green they sparkled, making him uncomfortable.

Clement leaned against the beam, thoughtful. "You see my gun collection?" Clement pointed to the guns on the far wall.

"*Ouais*, considered tossing them in the slough with my cross. I'm more a rock man."

"Your sister handles a gun nicely." Clement folded his arms, the belt dangling beside him. "Marie, isn't it?"

Antoine kept his features frozen, not giving his thoughts

away as he carefully placed the saddle at his feet. He felt his rage mounting. No one messed with his sister.

"You see, Antoine, I went to talk to you. Wanted to offer you a fair price for that useful land of yours, but much to my surprise, you weren't home, and I was greeted with a shotgun. You've been gone a long time from that farm of yours in Canada." He spat out the *Canada*. "Took Franklin a while to find you and bring you to me." The threat was mild, yet Antoine shifted, uncomfortable. Why bother Marie about Depaix land? "Franklin said you jumped on his cash like an animal. How much you need? I'll pay you off. Even build you a nice new house in town. What's that town of yours? Clear Water?"

"Eau Claire, and I'd rather earn it fair and square. Don't like the idea of owing you. As it is, now you owe me. Chew on that while I finish up."

"Oh you dirty prick." Clement was in his face again. "Is this your plan? I should pay your sister another visit."

"I've taken on a wolf for a sister before, and I'd do it again. With pleasure." Antoine knew he should keep his anger quiet yet he'd never been one for keeping his opinions to himself.

"You have useful land, Antoine. No reason for you to work for me, anymore. A million reasons for you to work with me. Let's change the rules, right here, right now, and I'll show you how to make real cash." Clement put out his hand to shake.

Antoine looked at his peaceful hand, remembering Uncle Silver's warning. *"When a white man puts out his hand for you to shake, run like the devil is after you."*

Antoine shoved his hands in his pockets, forcing Clement to pull his hand away. "So it's not money... hmmm. What is the one thing you can't live without?"

Antoine studied his bare feet as his cheeks grew warm with thoughts of Emma. That wasn't any of Clement's business. That was between Emma and him. "I'm good. Thanks."

"So let's try this another way. Keep your land. All I need is to travel it a few times a month. It'll be dark and no one will know but you. Give me a number, a fee, a token I can give you to show my appreciation for you to look the other way."

Antoine could not have strangers on Depaix land. It was a

sacred burial ground for his mother's tribe but Clement wouldn't understand. "I doubt my wife or sister will like scum like you hanging around."

"Wife?"

"Yeah, I plan to ask Emma to come home with me, ya know? The idea has me a bit giddy inside, but I think she might say yeah."

Clement's head snapped up and his eyes bore into Antoine. He was still gripping his belt. "No."

No? He really didn't see what gave Clement the right to say no.

He eyed Antoine up again as if deciding what to do with a guy like him. "Remember where you are, mutt. As long as you're here, you belong to me, and so does your sister's shotgun." Clement pointed to his gun collection, and sure enough, Pa's shotgun was the second from the bottom. How had he missed that?

Clement looked Antoine up and down before saying, "Don't waste your time with the girls around here, they won't be interested in a mongrel." He left Antoine alone in the huge barn.

Confused, Antoine took his time in the backroom, putting the saddle away. After his rounds, he'd have the place to himself. It'd be late before Franklin and Tommy returned, and Antoine wanted to sleep before he was forced outside again.

Maybe he'd ask Franklin for his pay and head home tonight. He should have left this afternoon but Emma had been waiting for him when Philip hauled him back to the yard and well... he wanted one more moment with her. Would Emma come with him? They'd had some nice conversations these past few days but could he just blurt that out? He needed to build up to it. Take her for a walk or something. He just needed a bit more time.

A gentle sob came from the stalls that made him reach for the lantern.

–THREE–

Antoine peered in the last stall cautiously. Emma was coiled up in the straw, clutching her skirt when his shadow swept over her.

"What ya doing out here?" Antoine glanced around. If Clement walked in... *screw him*. He could talk to anyone he wanted.

Antoine took off his hat and hung it on a nail by the lantern. It grew gloomy in the barn as the night shadows crept on it. Yet his focus was so intense on her, that when Emma turned, a shine on her cheek forced him to his knees beside her. "You hurt? Emma, look at me."

The panic in her rich brown eyes made him pull away.

"I... damn. I mean..." He didn't know what to say. Her eye was swollen. Yet she wiped it on her sleeve and tried to stand, but fell back holding her stomach.

"Let me help you up," he offered. "What the heck happened? Gals aren't supposed to be out here."

She curled up, pain making her let out a whimper she hid along her arm.

"What hurts?" he asked gently. Her silent tears fell in streams he needed to put out, as if they were a fire eating up his entire soul. Kneeling beside her, Antoine tenderly wiped them from her face with his hanky. "Let me help you."

"Just go. I'm fine. Please, just leave me alone. Sometimes he comes back." Her eyes darted over Antoine's face as if explaining the horror of it.

Antoine sat on his heels and watched her for a moment. "Did one of the boys do this to you? That Tommy had better not be behind this. I'll tell Clement. He won't tolerate this." Antoine rubbed the welt on his arm. "He'll—"

She glared at him, cutting him off with her intense eyes.

Antoine swallowed. "Cripes. You not telling me that Clement hit you? Why? Because you talked to me this afternoon?"

"I deserved this. I know better. Just go."

Antoine knew Clement sported a short fuse, but why would he hit Emma? "I'm leaving at the end of the week, come with me."

"Leave me alone." Her eyes bore into him, making his breath catch.

"That ain't gonna happen. I'm not letting him touch you again."

"You can do that?" The desperation in her voice made him eager to do something. Anything.

"I'll..." He had no idea what he'd do, but it had felt like a smart thing to say. Like yesterday, Emma kept her eyes on his lips while he talked. Antoine had never seen eyes so full of love. He wanted to scoop her up and whisk her off to safety and just... *protect her*. "I'll carry you to the bed up in the loft."

She grabbed the folds of her skirt and curled up tighter.

"Don't be afraid of me." He brushed another tear off her cheek and to his surprise, she rested her head against his hand. Why was he always touching her? No... maybe she was touching him. He couldn't tell. It felt like both. "I hope to protect you like the last grain of wheat on the planet. Please let me bring you someplace safe."

"Your bed is not safe."

He pulled away. He shouldn't be touching her. "I didn't mean it like that. I just want to make sure you're safe. I'll tear Clement apart. I will."

"Clement is a good man," she said in a rehearsed voice, as if telling herself something she would never believe. "I know my place."

"Clement is far from a good man."

"I just..." she mumbled to the stall, not looking at Antoine. "Leave me."

He studied her, not sure what she hid. When Marie wanted a secret, she'd tell him a secret first. "A secret for a secret?"

Emma kept her eyes straight ahead, ignoring him.

"Those idiots who work here, they're gone to see their gals."

She took in a deep breath. "Why tell me this?"

"It's my secret, and as secrets go, it's hard for me to say, so will you let me do this my way?" She hugged her knees, so he kept talking. "I didn't go, because truth be told, I hoped I'd find you and take you for a walk. They go see their gals, but I didn't have to go anywhere. You see where I'm going with this, right?"

Her lips were puffy and chapped, calling out to him as she smiled briefly. She rested her head against the straw, a dark beauty. He thought about touching her cheek again, but nervously rubbed his hands together instead.

"I can't walk. My legs are like jelly." Straw fell from her short messy curls. "I need a bath."

"Then a bath it is. I only get sponge baths in the loft, but I can haul you out to the slough for a dip if ya like. I'd even skinny-dip with ya," he joked. "Bet it'd be more fun than the swimming I did with Tommy today. Man, he's a prick, eh?" Antoine grinned, his goofy grin, hoping to make her smile again.

While Emma thought about this, her eyes ate right through him. "I like you." She didn't smile. "Your eyes are golden, like when the sun hits the crops while they reach for warmth."

He raised his eyebrows, pleased that she thought of him this way. "So is that a yes?" he asked, hopeful.

"I have to head back." Emma stood, but then bent over sucking in air in painful moans.

"Just let me help you. Ten minutes in fresher air and a comfortable bed and you'll feel better. I'll make tea. My pa made the best tea. The secret is brown sugar." Why was he rambling?

"These boys who have girls, do they spend the night or will they be back?"

"Don't know," he admitted. "Last few nights they came back late, drunk, and stupid."

"Why are you so nice to me?"

"Can't help it, *ma belle*." He scooped her up and she leaned into him, spent. "Besides, think about the bragging I'll do tomorrow.”

“About what?”

“The gorgeous woman I hid in my bed while they were in town getting dumber. That’ll get the rumours flying around, no? Me being an innocent Catholic boy and all.”

“Shh...”

“Why?” he asked. “I was kiddin’ around. Franklin ribs me about it all the time.”

“Flashing that cross will summon ghosts.”

“Ghosts?”

“Very bad.” She shivered and hid the cross that peeked out again.

“This is harmless. Why does it make everyone around here crazy?”

She took several breaths, focused on the pain again.

Antoine lightly kissed her forehead while he carried her. Her thin eyebrows curled up even more. He’d never laid his lips on a woman in his life, yet it was the most natural thing he ever did. Still... should he apologize? It didn’t feel wrong. In fact, it felt pretty dang right.

Her hand came up as if she might slap him, but instead, it rested lightly against his cheek. “Am I heavy?”

Antoine felt invincible. “Gosh, no. Light as a feather. I’m tough. Ploughed Depaix land by hand.”

“Why work for Clement if you own land?”

“No one owns land. They owe it. Still… I inherited a few debts I can’t afford.” Despite himself, he smiled because he liked her. She was real and it was easy to be himself with her.

He walked through the barn as if he had every right to carry this forbidden gem up to the room he shared with the other boys.

“Do you have slaves on your land?”

He almost dropped her. Why the hell would she ask that? “Slaves?” Antoine felt dirty saying the word. Sacri let him swear but a word like slaves she would have whacked him a good one for saying. “Heck no, no one has slaves. Do they?” She glanced away so he kept talking. “Just me and my grumpy sister. Soon her husband. When I was young, my mother made it very clear that no one owned living things.”

Antoine laid her in his bed and brought over a lantern.

While he waited for the water to heat, he wet a cloth from the basin and placed it gently on her swollen eye. Then he went to prepare clean water.

Warm water in hand, he paused in front of her. She was breathing better but the cloth he'd placed on her eye was gone. He scanned the area for it. Where had Emma put it?

Antoine sat beside her and wrung out another cloth, then placed it against her cheek. She didn't move, letting him wash her face. Her short hair needed a good cleaning, too. The straw and mud in it made him want to take care of her. He picked them out the best he could, then washed her incredibly smooth dark neck. "I never met a girl with short hair before."

A tear welled in the corner of her closed eyes.

"It's pretty," he added quickly. "I like it. Makes your neck that much yummier." *Dang.* He didn't say something that stupid, did he? She'd think him a fool.

"I hate it."

He pulled away to rinse the cloth. "Then why'd ya cut it?"

"Gracie cut it."

"The cook? Philip's wife? Why'd she go and do that if you didn't want it short? I wouldn't let my sister cut mine, even if she swears I'll never get a girl running around wild like this."

Emma looked at him. "Your hair is nice. I like it. I watched you ride yesterday and it flows behind you, makes you look..." She swallowed as if the word she was about to say was stuck in her throat. "Free. Can I touch it?"

He nodded but she never moved.

"If you like long hair, why did Gracie cut yours?"

"She said I was too pretty, too hard to refuse. She said the long hair was too easy to grab. She said lots of things while she cut it." She let her fingers gently brush the tips of his hair. "Is it wrong that I like you touching me?"

"Doesn't feel wrong." He ran the rag over her arms, working on the places he saw, not daring to sneak under her clothes. She could wash there when she was ready.

He held her arm as he pulled the cloth over it lightly. She rested peacefully. "Man. Are you ever dirty. I might have to take you to the slough, after all. What the heck did you get into?" he teased, but his gut locked in knots by what he saw.

Each arm told a different story. Scars from childhood, recent ones. Mud and a light golden dust caked her skin. Her hands weren't soft and delicate like the rest of her. They were worn and rough, with burn marks along the knuckles.

He talked while he worked, in case she wasn't sleeping, telling her about his sister and how she planned to marry when he returned. Antoine couldn't wait to meet her fiancé. "He must be something special because my sister was considering being a nun when I left. She told me love didn't exist, just compromise. I hope she found her happy forever." Antoine told Emma about how he kept saying the wrong things to Clement. "I'm pretty sure I'll tick him off even more, because I'm planning to steal his housekeeper to boot since she's the prettiest little thing I ever did see."

Emma never even cracked a smile. Just lay perfectly still in her tight ball, letting him wash her. Her feet were bare like his. He ran the rag over them slowly, wondering where she'd walked today. He wiped the dust from around her ankles. Her legs. Not pushing higher than her knees.

"Is it possible?" she asked, eyes closed.

"What?"

"For you to steal me."

He eyed her thighs. Like her arms, they screamed for attention. Love. Still she lay, quietly. So peaceful now. Beautiful like a blade of wheat in a field of thistles.

"I think you're stealing me. Does that make sense? I feel brilliantly stupid all of a sudden." Antoine ran a hand against her cheek and kissed her forehead again, pausing when her poignant fragrance drew him in for a second kiss. "Come home with me," he whispered to her full lips.

Her eyes opened and she sat up. Before Antoine had any clue what she was doing, Emma had her blouse undone, and he stared at her bare chest. Womanly curves. Firm breasts.

He swallowed and met her eyes.

Scars. A belt mark across her breast was new. He saw the pain of each one in those eyes.

Burn marks on her chest. Even a knife wound.

Her stomach was swollen, but untouched, sacred. Antoine ran a finger lightly over it before he realized what he was doing. Why was he always touching her? He pulled away but she grabbed his hand and held it.

Her eyes searched his for God only knew what. "Do you understand? I can't leave."

"I have no idea what you're showing me," he admitted. "My mind is numb with your impossible story. It hurts me to see these scars yet they can't be unseen. Who did this to you? Clement?"

"Clement takes care of everyone else, but the Missus, he says, is my problem." She studied the back of their linked hands as if that explained everything. "Today was my fault. I know better. It hurts less if I give in."

Antoine was incapable of moving as he tried to control his rage. He was getting her out of here. "You'd better do up your blouse. I probably shouldn't see these things until we're married."

"Married? We must be married for you to see me?" She looked confused.

"See this much of you, hell yeah." He moved in to help her do up her blouse because she wasn't moving fast enough. When he was close to her, he forgot about the blouse and rested his head against her, breathing with her. Would he ever be able to breathe alone again? "This is a promise I made to God. I don't break my promises, especially to God." He sat beside her, sick inside. What had Clement done to her? "The thought of anyone hurting you drives me mad. Why did Clement hit you tonight?"

"It's part of being with a man. I know this."

"What?" His anger exploded in a blast that shot him to his feet. He was ready to storm out and knock the coins right out of Clement.

She reached up and touched his arm, stopping him. He couldn't leave her here. Antoine paced in front of the bed.

The urge to ram Clement's head into a pot of hot grease came over him. "He's a married man with daughters your age. He's..." *a dead man.* "He's not touching you again," he snapped with no clue how he'd ever do that. He didn't care.

"No one touches Gracie 'cause she's married," Emma offered as he paced. "Gracie says it's because no man wants what another man owns." She tightened her skirt and curled up. "Philip doesn't touch her unless she asks. A smart girl won't ask. He's safe and Gracie says a gal should find safe."

He paused to look at her, confused. "Philip doesn't own Gracie, that's his wife. They're equals."

She shrugged. "Doubt that, Gracie's a slave-digger, like me. Philip is a servant. He can own her if he wants and since, really, Clement owns him, it's all the same to him."

"What the heck is a digger-slave?"

"Slave-digger. It means we belong underground, digging tunnels for land owners—"

"What!" Slaves... *Oh heck*. Why hadn't he been paying attention? "No one owns you. That's over." Truth was, even though Sacri had talked to him for hours about the types of slavery around them, he never actually thought he'd face a problem that absurd.

"I am a slave-digger. I will always be this. Gracie says. Philip says if I do my job I'll keep safe. No worries here."

"Your job? Housekeeping?"

"My job is to please Clement." Again, her words sounded rehearsed to him, as if she couldn't believe them but had to say them.

Antoine felt bile rise in the back of his throat. He had no idea this was going on around him. "What kind of monster buys people so he can... *use* them for his own pleasure?"

"It's not like that. I am not people. I am a slave-digger. I was not bought, I was saved. I am safe." She looked away from him. "He talks of buying you off. That does not sound safe."

"Gosh." He climbed on the bed and pulled her toward him. He just needed to hold her. "No one buys me off."

"I wish someone else owned me. Someone like you."

He shook his head. "Emma, never, ever, would I own you."

"Never?" She looked devastated. "You don't want me now?"

"A wife and husband, they're partners. Happy forever. This is what I want. Equal."

She was silent.

"You disagree?" he asked.

"I... I only know what I see."

"What do you see?"

"Clement and the Missus are not happy. He did a lot of

crying when she broke his heart. He talked of killing himself and not much helped with his pain at all. Not much at all. That doesn't sound like happy forever to me. It sounds like the Missus owns him."

"Clement was crying?" Antoine let out a puff of laughter. "Seriously? Like tears and all?"

"It's not funny when a man cries."

"Sorry, I can't picture it. The guy is a tight-ass. What did she do to make him cry?"

She shrugged. "He told me that life is a journey we survive alone. I know what that means—find safe. Gracie showed me what Philip did to protect her. It's a deep scar she calls a tattoo. It means mine; touch and die. Right across her hand like Clement's, only not so well done since all he had was a knife. Philip told Clement an eye for an eye. If anyone touches his wife, he'll go after his. Once he does something like that, it can't be undone."

"Maybe I should talk to Philip. Nothing you say makes sense."

"Sorry if I'm stupid."

"I'm the stupid one." He felt like a blind fool. "I had no idea this was happening."

Emma pulled away completely and pushed into the corner, her skirt tight around her. The cloth was left behind, having fallen from under her skirt. Antoine picked it up. "Blood? Are you bleeding under your skirt? Why?"

"I'm not supposed to talk of these things," she said to the wall.

"Dammit." Antoine tossed the cloth in the water bucket and stared at her. No idea what was going on. "We talk about *all* things. I might know nothing 'bout girls, but I know that much about us."

"I should go. I know better than to talk to you." She glanced at him but didn't make an attempt to get up which made him think she wanted to talk to him, despite her words.

"Yet here you are." Antoine shook his head, frustrated. He held her hands and took several breaths to get control of his rage. "Tell me why you came to the barn when you know you shouldn't."

"I asked Clement for a tattoo so I would be safe like

Gracie, and he said I have to do something first. That's why I was coming to see you, because I do not know how to do what he asked, but you might."

"You were coming to see me?" His anger vanished.

"I want to know what your mother was like."

"Sacri?" Why would she need to know that? Still, if it was this important to her... "Well... I guess she was tough." Antoine smiled, remembering her gentle way with him. "Yet kinda mushy on the inside. Like all women of her tribe, she was very in touch with the earth, and she taught me incredible things about the world around me."

"Tough?" She sighed. "So your father roughed her up to make a boy like you?"

"*Quoi?*" he asked 'what' in French, too confused to filter his thoughts to English. Antoine's frown deepened as he tried to figure out what she was asking him.

She rubbed his eyebrows, as if eager to work the frown out. "I have to be tough. But how? I feel un-tough." Emma had her hand on his chin. "I mean, I know my place..." Her finger lightly traced his bottom lip and Antoine closed his eyes enjoying her touch. "But something inside me wants..." Her voice trailed off.

"Wants what?" Antoine tasted her fingertips.

"Your golden eyes to see all of me. You make me want things I have no need to want."

"Good. I don't like you here. You belong with me at Eau Claire." He was doing this all wrong but he was too frustrated to think straight. "Sacri, she taught me how to handle situations like this. Well not like this exactly." She'd talked about Chinese slavery and Native American slavery, he wasn't sure what the heck a digger-slave was. If only he'd been paying attention and not goofing off.

His eyes swept over her. "Now I know the real reason for my journey. It was to find you." He could hear Marie give him a sermon about how he was a foolish boy who had no idea what kind of trouble he was getting into now.

"I have to be in my room at sunset or I get a whipping and no supper. The Missus is always looking for a reason to belt me a good one." She bit her bottom lip and made an attempt to stand, but sat on the edge of the bed.

She was too tense. Something hurt.

"Let me grab my jacket for you, it'll be chilly." His jacket was on the hook over the bed and he reached for it. She didn't move so he slipped it around her.

"I've never seen a jacket like this."

"My uncle Silver gave it to me years ago. He made it from deer hide, during a winter storm. Even stitched this warrior emblem along the breast pockets. He did a good job, given he's a hunter."

She slipped her arms in. It was excessively big on her but she'd be warm.

"It's soft." She ran her fingers along the fringes.

"Takes work to tan a hide this perfect. I'll show you how when we get home." Already he saw them together on Depaix Farm.

He slipped a hand around her waist and pulled her to her feet, but she squeezed his arm in a panic as footsteps resounded up the steps to the loft.

–FOUR–

The Missus stormed in and Antoine let Emma go when she tied into Emma. "There you are, no good filth. I suppose you're giving favours for cash. As if I didn't already give you everything, now you turn to mutts for money. Don't you ever tire of me whipping you? Who hit you? I thought Clement kept Tommy off his nightingale."

Clement's wife was a plump, unpleasant woman but Antoine had no idea what her name was. He wasn't supposed to talk to her either, but the tattoo on her hand was cut off, leaving a deep scar.

Her hair was in a bun, and her cheeks were rosy with her anger. She completely ignored Antoine and got right in Emma's face. When she raised her hand to slap Emma, Antoine grabbed her wrist without thinking.

"She's hurt. I was helping her to the house." Antoine let the Missus' wrist go. "It's your stupid husband who does this to her. Get him on a leash or I will."

He expected her to yell or have a fit, but she pulled away shocked. "What did his precious nightingale do to deserve that? Suppose he caught you with this mutt?" She turned around and snapped, "Ten minutes or I tell Clement that I caught you with Philip."

Emma panicked. "Hurry. I have to get back."

Her panic pushed him into action and Antoine scooped her in his arms, dashed down the steps of the loft, and almost ran her to the house. He saw Clement's wife at the front door as he rounded the house. She glared at them, but then went inside with a smug smile.

Antoine brought Emma to the backdoor where he set her down before they went inside. He found the lantern on a hook and lit it, leaving it there. "I'll carry you to your room and you can pack your things."

"No. He might be there. I'll walk. It's not far." Emma started to remove the jacket but he stopped her. He wasn't letting her go in alone if there was a chance of Clement being in there, waiting for her.

"I like the idea of my jacket keeping you warm while you get your things."

She closed her eyes and leaned against him. "I'm tired." She looked exhausted. He couldn't force her to travel like this. She needed sleep. Dang it. He'd have to let her sleep first.

"Which one is your room?" He scooped her up.

"Third door."

He carried her there, and was relieved to see moonlight filtering into the small room from the large window over her bed. In the corner, the dresser held a lantern. He laid her on the bed and shut the door before he lit the lantern.

Slowly, he unknotted the corner of his hanky and sat beside her.

Intrigued, she watched him work the knot. Finally, the ring came loose and fell between them on the bed. Antoine picked up the simple band and handed it over, eager for Emma to wear it.

She eyed the ring without touching it. "You give me a ring?"

"Not any ring. Sacri's ring. My mother was brave like you and no one told her what to do. Ever. I saved this ring for years to give to the only woman I'll ever dream of marrying."

"I'm not sure what this means. Would you own me? Is this 'cause you wish to see more of me?" She started to undo the buttons on her blouse again and he reached over to stop her.

"No owning. Stop with that. I just want you to know how serious I am about you. No matter what, I promise to keep you safe."

"Clement will not allow this, not now." She bowed her head, shamefully.

"I'll tell Clement he can't touch you anymore because you're married to me." He sounded bitterer than he'd intended because he knew that conversation wouldn't end well.

She twisted her skirt, her eyes darting over him; even the swollen one stared deep into his soul.

He studied her warm brown eyes; her cheeks pushed downward, making them that much more innocent. "You keep me safe, I keep you safe," he promised.

"You safe from what? Are you in trouble?"

Pa had called him a trouble hound. "I tend to obsess over things, need to be reminded to focus every now and again. Think you can breathe with me when I can't do it alone?"

She stared at the door, her jaw locked shut.

"Emma? Say what you're thinking. I want to hear it. Always, we talk." He set the ring on the bed between them, troubled that she wouldn't take it.

"Breathing with you is nice, this is all I think about."

"*Holy horses all in a line*. Is that a yes? Will you come to Eau Claire with me?"

She covered the ring. "What I want will not work."

"It worked for Philip and Gracie, didn't it? Don't let Clement scare you into saying no if you don't want to."

"We are not Philip and Gracie." She peeked at the ring then covered it again quickly. "They are both black and they are both Clement's."

"What are you afraid of? Don't you feel our souls all happy about this idea?"

She shrugged. "It doesn't matter what I feel, it is what I know. I am not allowed to want. I am a slave-digger. I told you this."

"To me, all that matters is what you feel. Always. It makes me happy when you're happy. Like we're connected or something."

"Yes. I feel this." She smiled quickly and looked away. Tears fell and she closed her eyes. "But Clement said no one would want me now. I am his now."

Antoine rubbed her wrists. He couldn't make out her features in the dim light and brought up her face so he could touch his lips to hers. She tasted salty, but all she allowed was a brush and she pulled away to wipe her tears on her apron.

"I want you to come home with me as my wife," he

whispered, but she wouldn't let him near her.

With her face in her apron, she mumbled, "He said he'd toughen me up to make sure I gave him a boy." She said it all in her apron. "I told him I no longer wanted a tattoo and he corrected me. After all he's done for me, I should want a tattoo. I should want to give him a boy. Yet I don't. How can I know what I want when I am a slave-digger?"

Antoine pulled her against him. Images of her swollen stomach held a new meaning all of a sudden. She'd been showing him something important but the scars had distracted him. "Are you saying you're gonna be a mama?" Antoine ran his hands around her to stop them from shaking while she nodded against him. "You'll make an excellent mama." He focused on that and not the urge to snap Clement in two. Their next conversation would be deadly.

"You do not want me though?" Her tears flowed silently.

Antoine softened. "Well, now instead of just you and me, I see a rascal with us, that's all."

She looked so tired.

Unexpectedly, her lips came on his. Hard. Demanding. Antoine pulled away confused.

"You don't want to smooch me?" she asked, shocked.

"I do, but..." He slipped a hand along her hips and pulled her on his lap while he met her eyes, teasing. "Kisses should be like butter melting on toast and tenderly pouring into the cinnamon." His lips brushed hers as he spoke.

"Show me what this means."

He saw it in his mind, but had no idea if she'd allow this. He came in gently, his lips found her neck. Leisurely, he massaged her skin. She tightened a fist around his shirt, gripping him, but she didn't pull away. He journeyed along her neck, faster, addicted. Eagerly, he explored up to her tiny ear where once again he took his time. Her head fell back into the cusp of his hand, letting him have his way. He used his teeth to excite her, praying for another reaction. When her chest pushed against him, his hands pulled her in by the small of her back so they kissed with their entire bodies.

"What are you doing to me?" Her breath tickled his neck.

"Melting into you." He licked her playfully along the jaw line and she didn't move, enjoying the attention. Finally, he was before her lips. "Buttering your beautiful dark skin with kisses." He took the bottom lip between his in a silent hug. He needed to taste her a little longer, but he paused before her mouth to breathe the same air as her.

"I had no idea such kisses existed," she said.

Their lips met and he relinquished control to her. He was a puddle desperately soaking in as much of her as possible. Never in his life had Antoine imagined kissing would be so wonderful.

"You need to rest." He pulled away lightly and searched the bed for the ring. He slipped it on her finger. "So you can make the trip to Eau Claire in the morning." That would be safer. "We leave at dawn."

She touched the cross on his neck. So close to him. "You make me desire things I shouldn't."

"It's not about wanting forbidden things, but things that are right for you," he told her, his face against hers as he spoke, wondering how he'd ever leave her.

"And... what does your church say about marrying a woman with a baby inside her?"

He placed a hand along her cheek and looked deeply in her eyes. "God will be happy if we raise His child in the warmth of our love. Don't you think? I mean... he was fine with Joseph taking care of Mary when he found out she was gonna be a ma. The way Pa told it, He was all for it."

"I do not know them. Are they friends of yours?"

Antoine smirked. "It's a nice story. You see, Mary was blessed with a child who a ghost fathered, a holy one, and so when she tells her betrothed she's sure that he'll turn her away, yet he doesn't. Not 'cause Joseph is happy about it— he's not, it ticks him off something fierce—but because God asked him to care for her and her child."

"Joseph was safe?"

"Very safe," he assured her.

"Is this a real story?"

"Depends who you ask. Pa said every word of it is true, but Sacri claimed it was a legend meant to teach. They had interesting debates about it."

"Fights? Kicks and screams? Did he toss her down the stairs?"

"*Quoi?* Gosh, no. I never heard of such things. No fights between husband and wife, nothing but butter kisses."

"Everyone fights." She touched the welt on his arm. "I watched you fight today."

His face warmed but he didn't explain his actions to her.

"You gonna behave?" she asked.

"With you? Probably not. I'm dreaming up all sorts of ideas that feel naughtier than heck, but now that I thought them, there is no way we ain't gonna have us some fun with them."

"I meant with Clement."

"Oh." No. That wasn't gonna happen and he didn't want to lie to her. "Don't worry about the wolves. I can handle them. Can I kiss you one more time?"

"Antoine. I didn't tell you that so you could go off and get dead. Be smart. I trust you to be there for me so we can kiss again."

He took a big breath. "That is a good reason. I'll talk to him somewhat nice. Rest up. It's a long trip home, *ma belle*." He tucked her in.

"Will you be far?" She clutched his arm.

"No. You're safe." With an effort, he pulled away. He needed to beat some sense into Clement. He dimmed the lantern and left her, sure she was already sleeping.

From the veranda he'd be able to cut Clement off when he went to her room so he leaned against the rail with the lantern lit. He stared through the screen door. Her kiss lingered with him and he closed his eyes for a moment reliving it. Maybe he should sleep beside her tonight.

~~

Antoine was shocked out of his fantasising by his uncle's voice. "*If you're waiting for that scumbag to show his ugly mug, he took off with Tommy to harass the countryside.*" Antoine spun around when the deep voice he loved fiercely caught him off guard. There stood Silver, his face covered in mud so he'd blend into the earth. "*Debating following him, I was, but then I catch you pawing my target. What the heck are you doing, boy? Didn't you see the mark of judgement on this ranch? This is my problem, not yours."*

The moment his uncle Silver said it, Antoine remembered Sacri showing him the black teardrop tattoo. Judgement. It meant his *Cîpay* ancestors delivered the marked to God for judgement. It was the most dishonourable tattoo anyone wore. God would take away the marked once they were worthy, until then, *Cîpay* shadowed their life. Antoine had no idea how real such a curse was, but he imagined guys like his uncle Silver took shadowing scum fairly seriously.

"Why is his family marked?" Antoine wondered. *Cîpay* wouldn't do such things.

"He did this to mock our beliefs. Pretending that others support his beliefs and therefore he's safe from God's judgement."

Antoine peered in the shadows of the trees for the outline of his uncle Silver. Antoine hadn't seen Silver since Sacri's funeral, and even then, he'd only been a shadow.

"I thought you were dead."

"So did I. A few too many times. Turns out a ghost ain't that easy to kill. Figures. I have to earn my paradise like all the others."

It warmed Antoine inside to know Silver watched out for him. His tough uncle was days from his home. For him. "I wanted to be just like you."

"Yet here you are. Being nothing like me. Worse than your mother you are. It was her, you know, who marked Clement. Should be an interesting test for you, eh?"

If Sacri marked Clement for judgement, it meant Antoine was forbidden to kill him. That part of her teachings he remembered very well. It meant Clement had a lesson to learn and *Cîpay* were to shadow, not to interfere. The moment Clement learnt the lesson, he would die. "What if I kill him?" Antoine didn't see any other option.

"You mean before he learns what he came to learn? You know that answer. Then you shall bear the weight of his schooling until your death. He would become a shadow haunting your soul, forcing you to learn the lesson for him. That could not be undone and is a great responsibility to undertake. Do you really want a guy like him shadowing your life? Didn't you learn after the wolf?"

Silver knew the wolf was haunting him? Antoine bowed his head shamefully. He still didn't understand why it had been wrong to avenge his sister Josée's death by killing her murderer. Why wasn't that worth fighting for?

"I want him out of Emma's life. Vanished."

"Do not jeopardize your soul for my target." Silver's eyes gleamed, highlighting the urgency of his order.

"Target?"

"Next digger I was to vanish. I'd been holding off 'cause she seemed happy enough the last bit. Not sure what happened these past days to upset her."

"You mean since I showed up? Nothing happened. I talked to her." He'd dreamed of her, but Antoine didn't admit that to his uncle.

"Whatever, it's clearly time to help her move on. That one, she's seen enough pain for ten lifetimes."

"You vanish them or kill them?"

"Ones I vanish get freedom—paradise." Silver sighed. "Ones Clement vanishes get the hole—hell. You can look at that how you want. Some say I give them life, others call it death. Really, it's nothing more than a shift of energy. This has turned into a battle of wits, though, and I ain't fairing so well these days. Now you just complicated things for me. I had to threaten to vanish his girls if he don't lay off you, and I hate doing that shit."

"Silver. What am I gonna do? I want to marry that woman."

"Then I guess you'll marry her. I've never known you for the type to do anything other than what you want. Sleep. I'll wake you when the scumbag returns." Silver melted into the shadows.

Emma screamed as if in pain and Antoine rushed through the screen door. Gracie met him there. "Back off." She glared at Antoine and he let her pass.

He paced the hallway trying to hear what they were doing. Things shuffled. Something banged followed by a long silence.

He swung open the bedroom door.

It was empty.

-FIVE-

Philip was by himself brushing a horse so Antoine pulled a mare from the stalls and dragged it behind him so he could talk to Philip while they worked.

Philip glanced up at him. "Ya been stormin' around like a bull. What I tell ya about that? Keep a low profile. Why ya gotta keep drawing attention to yerself?"

"Philip, I need to talk to you about Emma." Antoine felt his stomach tighten. What if Clement did something to her?

"Ya finally calm enough to talk, are ya? When I hauled you outta her room, you hit me." Philip glared at him with his wise eyes, well not at him, at the cross around his neck. "Leave her alone. She might actually be the first one of us to amount to somethin'. Clement promised her a tattoo."

"Yeah right. We both know that's not an honour."

"Just leave her be. Stop messing yer nose where it don't belong."

"Where is she? I'm leaving tomorrow and she's coming with me. I'm going crazy." Antoine couldn't help it, the pain shook his voice and crept on his features. Would Philip understand?

Philip paused for a moment and licked his bottom lip. It was split in the middle. "You talk to Clement 'bout this?"

"He's still breathing, so no, not yet. I don't want to make things worse for her. Where the heck is she?" Panic came over Antoine and he felt as if his chest crushed in. He wanted to hit something but he took a deep breath as Pa taught him, trying to use his fear to push him forward, not down. "Philip, what if he's hurt her?"

Philip sighed. "Gracie says she won't stop throwing up."

"Dang it. I have to see her."

Philip clenched his jaw and flared his nostrils. "Listen Cowboy, walk away from this one. Clement wants your land and he's gonna take it."

"It's not something he can have. I'm here about Emma. If you won't help me find her, I'll find another way, but she's coming with me."

Philip glanced at the cross around Antoine's neck and whispered, "Will ya take Gracie, too?"

"You want me to bring your wife with me?"

Philip brushed in his even rhythm as if they were discussing the weather. "Tell me what it's like in the promised land."

Not once, not ever had Antoine thought of Saskatchewan as the promised anything, yet Philip kept talking about it as if it was paradise.

Antoine said, "Nothing but farmers making homesteads. Look around. What you see here, we ain't got."

"Ya mean Blacks?" Philip asked.

"I mean all of it. No running water, no beautiful stables, heck even the train is miles out of town. We got nothing. We're still breaking land."

"So are there Blacks or not?"

"Not many," Antoine explained. "Mostly Natives. French. Some British folks. One Chinese family who Sacri brought home and told me to keep an eye on, like they were in danger. Métis like me. Quite a few cultures coming together. We had all sorts of coloured folk in our house back when Sacri was alive, and she swore her pa brought countless slaves across from the states, but mostly, they passed through and settled in the cities. Said we were much too close to the border for their liking. It's a world where no one fits in, so everyone does. Make sense? Come with us."

"Diggers like Gracie? Servants like me?" Again, Philip's eyes fell on the cross.

Antoine tucked it in his shirt. "I have to be honest, I spent all week here and still have no bloody clue what that means. It's beyond me why you don't pack up your crap and hit the fields. Walk off. What could he say?"

"Can't do that, Cowboy, I got Gracie to worry about, and she's safe here. We walk out of Clement's reach and we have the whole world to contend with."

"You telling me you stay because Clement is safe?"

"Why else?" Philip creased his brow, thoughtful. "He teaches me things, just doesn't look at me. As if I offend him or something. I'd say it's strange but I knew his old man, and to be honest, I'm surprised Clement turned out half as decent as he did. I saw him take a few upside the head when he was a squirt. Must have knocked a few bricks 'round in his old noggin'."

"So you're staying?"

"Not much choice if you won't help me. I got no monies, no education. I'm safe here. Got me a pretty wife who loves me to pieces and I work with horses. It's not much of a life, but I'm kinda partial to it."

"I could sit and hash this out with you all day, but I want to see Emma. Where is she?"

"You bringing us or not?"

"Us? So you're coming?"

"A man follows his wife to hell, no?"

"One minute you're telling me how good you got it, and the next you're leaving?" Antoine frowned. "Walk off. What ya need me for?"

Philip rubbed the horse. "I was a boy when I heard the first tales of the girl wearing the golden cross. They called her a prairie ghost. Young, beautiful, a dream. *Sacri*." He spoke her name as if it were forbidden. "She sneaked onto farms to help servants who wanted to leave but didn't know how, escorting them to the promised land. I used to dream of her coming for me. When I was a teen, a swarm of these ghosts raided one of the buggies belonging to Clement's old man, Edgar. He hauled diggers around, was selling them— illegally, of course." Philip held the brush and looked at it. "Now that was not a good man. Edgar caught this dream and tortured her. It was Clement who freed her after a long battle against his old man that ended with Edgar dying." Philip met Antoine's eyes.

"You saying that Clement killed his own father to save my mother?"

"Yer mother?" Philip tilted his head and frowned. "She gave him that tattoo on his hand and told him that he had to learn the secret between a father and son. Something weird like that. Clement won't talk about it anymore, but for many years I had to listen to him whine about it." Philip sighed and patted the horse. "Cowboy, you walked on this ranch like ya had a plan. I was ready to drop my good life and run the minute I laid eyes on ya. Freedom. Every time I look at that cross around yer neck, it's all I see. I have no idea what that would taste like, but it leaves me a curious taste, nonetheless."

Antoine's skin itched with worry.

Breathe. Breathe. He sucked in air until he was dizzy.

Finally, Philip said, "They have her out back in the shed, the brown one. We stay there when we're not well so Clement doesn't find out."

"Doesn't find out about what? How much did she tell you?"

"Nothin', but I ain't stupid. If a man sits silent long enough, he hears things."

"Then shut up about what you hear. I'm handling it." Antoine left the mare with Philip and marched off to see her.

~~

Moments later, Antoine knocked on the door to the back shed. It blended into the trees, yet he glanced around nervous that someone might stop him.

The door opened slowly and Gracie peeked out. "Get outta here, Cowboy."

"I have to see her." Antoine felt desperation.

Gracie glanced around and pulled him in quickly. It took a minute for Antoine's eyes to adjust. They had a lantern lit, but there were no windows to bring in natural light.

Antoine's eyes gravitated to the limp Emma on the old mattress. She had clean sheets, but he wasn't impressed with this place. Storming Pete, the bloody goat, had a better home than this.

"If she's sick she shouldn't be in here." He glanced around the tiny shed, disgusted. "She needs air, light, dirt under her feet to give her energy. What the heck is this hole you got her in?" It smelled like vomit. The walls crowded him. "Open the door, I'm taking her outside."

"It'll pass. She's fine." Gracie was close to his mother's age. The lines on her forehead screamed that she'd seen hard labour most of her life.

Emma didn't look fine. She snuggled in his jacket so Antoine scooped her up, the jacket tight around her, and marched her to the door. "Open it. Now."

Used to taking orders, Gracie flung the door open, allowing Antoine room to pass with Emma. He took her out to the orchard and rested her against a tree. Gracie followed, glancing over her shoulder.

Antoine grabbed Emma's frail hand. It had only been a few days since he'd seen her, but it was clear she wouldn't make the trip to Canada anytime soon. She was weak.

"I'll stay with her," he said. "Gracie, she needs tea. Mix it with brown sugar."

Emma opened her eyes but she was clearly too weak to talk. She took a deep breath.

"Feel the earth under you? It's full of life. Steal that energy to heal yourself." Antoine rubbed her hands on the soft grass, then pushed them into the soil like Sacri had taught him.

Emma leaned against Antoine.

"Breathe with me. It's the most important part." He took a deep breath, prepared to fight, like Pa had taught him.

Antoine stayed beside her all afternoon so Gracie could do her chores, and Emma's. Beast found them and curled up beside Emma. They listened to Antoine tell stories while Antoine helped Emma sip the tea, hidden away in the trees and bushes.

Gracie returned. "Can we get her back? What if someone finds her?"

"I'll deal with it," Antoine said. "She looks much better, no?"

She still hadn't said much, just held him. He rubbed his forehead, feeling the weight of his new responsibility. He had to bring Gracie and Philip with them, which wasn't quite as easy as walking off with one girl he was forbidden to breathe next to.

Philip's shadow came over them. "Cowboy, you gotta be either the biggest fool I ever seen or the bravest. Clement is on a rampage for yer sorry ass."

"So?" Antoine asked.

"He finds Emma sick, she eats a bullet or worse—the hole. He don't tolerate sick servants infecting his family."

"What? Everyone gets sick."

"Yeah, and when a digger does, they vanish. Got it?" Philip pulled Antoine up. "Go. He's crazy. Even had Franklin searching for ya. Not that he's doing much hunting. Mable stepped in his path before he could search the orchard, but she'll only buy you so much time, Cowboy."

Antoine didn't plan to leave Emma.

"I'll carry her to the sick shed," Philip offered.

"The sick shed? Cripes. Burn that hellhole down." Antoine shook his head. "Even the name screams death." He kissed Emma's forehead. It was sweaty and he didn't like that. "I'll come back as soon as I can, promise." He took off his chain and placed it around her neck. "For protection while I'm gone." He squeezed her hand gently and took off.

He needed to do something with his built up anger before he faced Clement.

–Six–

Antoine busied himself, obsessing by the woodpile, chopping wood angrily. One swing. Then another. Not breathing properly in his rage. Praying Emma was better by morning so they could leave.

He still wasn't sure if he should talk to Clement about it or not. What if he said no? Screw him. He didn't need Clement's permission to do anything.

He wasn't thinking straight. Antoine ran his hand against his forehead. What was he doing? Could he look after a family?

Clement found him about twenty minutes later. "You avoiding me? You think I like running around this blasted ranch looking for mutts who should be reporting to me?"

Antoine shouldered the axe, wondering how deep he could embed it in Clement's head. One swing. Then another. Then he wouldn't have to tell him squat.

"Working. It's my last day. Earning that pay before I swing this axe at the devil." Antoine wiped his brow on his sleeve. "Why? You need something only a mongrel can give you?"

"There's a goddamn priest asking for you. You escort that prick off my land or I ain't paying you a dime."

"Is this how you normally work? You promise all this cash then drop the ball?" Antoine glared.

He expected Clement to throw one of his fits but he dug in his pocket and pulled out a wad of cash that he tossed on the ground. "Get him out of here, and I don't want you coming back. We're through. I'll do things the hard way." With a finger, Clement moved Antoine's collar. "Oh." He blinked and tilted his head in that way he always did. "You got rid of it?" Their eyes met over the silence. Antoine waited for his question, curious what Clement thought as he stared intently.

Finally, Antoine shoved past Clement, stepping on the cash. If he couldn't hand it to him like a man, screw him. "I might stay awhile. Double it."

He went to see what had Clement so crazy, taking the axe with him in case Clement got a bright idea in that troubled brain of his.

~~

A priest he didn't know was on the edge of his seat in the salon when Antoine walked in. The priest jumped up and took a deep breath. "I'm Father Kilby."

"*Bonjour*, Antoine Depaix."

"But you're not French," the priest stammered.

Antoine looked down at himself. "Pretty sure some of me is."

"I meant..."

"Is there a problem?"

Father Kilby shook his head. "No, no, took me off guard to see someone like you in a place like this. Sorry if I offended you, I didn't mean to disrespect you. I'm a nervous wreck."

"Takes more than your mouth to offend me. Maybe I'll walk you to your buggy."

"I came by automobile, a Ford. Model T," the priest announced proudly.

"Really?" Antoine found it hard to believe that a priest needed a car he couldn't afford. "Well... let's look at your investment and return you to the safety of your church."

"Your sister sent a message through the church. One priest to the next until it found you. It's beyond urgent." He handed Antoine a letter.

"She went through all this trouble for a letter? What couldn't wait?" Antoine almost dropped it when he read the one sentence. "How long did this message take to find me?"

"No more than a month or two," the priest admitted.

A month was a long time, forget two. It would take him a few days to get home. Longer if anything went wrong. A whole week if he brought Emma sick like she was.

No.

He couldn't bring her. She needed to rest. He'd have to wait until she could make the trip. They'd go together.

He read it again as they walked to the car in the middle of the yard.

"Ain't she a beaut?" the priest asked Antoine.

Antoine glanced up, not sure what the fuss over a car was about. Father shined the brass plate along the front, but Antoine didn't comment, still partial to horses.

Clement watched them from the veranda, twirling the axe Antoine had left by the front door.

Antoine knew what he had to do. He'd take Emma with him, let her rest at this Father's church while he went back for his sister. Emma would be fine in the back of this car.

Out by the barn, Franklin and Tommy stood. Tommy had his beating stick out. *Great.* He wouldn't be able to sneak away for Emma. Screw them.

Antoine's eyes travelled the field when something caught his attention in the distance. Silver was on his knees, a shadow in the sunlight. An arrow was in his quiver, ready to shoot the priest.

Cripes. Antoine stepped away from him. *Of all the men here, the priest was the threat?*

Antoine took a second step away from Father Kilby. If Silver didn't trust him, then Antoine couldn't leave Emma with him.

"It's serious, isn't it?" Father Kilby glanced at Tommy by the barn.

If Silver was prepared to shoot a priest, *ouais*, it was. Despite himself, Antoine shivered. "Get outta here. Save your skin."

Father Kilby actually looked like he might hit the fields. Antoine waited, while Father Kilby rubbed a smudge from a bug on the large headlamp. "I'm not supposed to leave without you. You can get in right now, or I can pick you off the ground after they beat you senseless."

So that was it. Someone gave him a bloody fancy car if he brought Antoine somewhere. Antoine glanced around. "Who ordered this? How long did you hang on to this letter before asking around for me?"

"Just climb in before it's too late," the priest ordered, but

Antoine was on his knees. He put the letter in his shirt pocket, rubbed his hands in the dirt, and brought some up to bless his face with it. The priest kept trying to convince him to leave, but all Antoine saw was Clement who stormed toward him. Antoine got to his feet and with his fists in his pockets full of the earth that gave his tribe strength, he went to meet Clement.

Clement would have to hear him out. About halfway, Philip rushed from the barn to meet him. "What the blazes are ya doing?" Philip asked. "Go. This ain't up for debate."

"Not without Emma." Antoine refused to bend on this.

"You a bloody blind fool? Don't ya see? They're shoving ya to find out what you really want because they need yer land. Don't let them know Emma is yer weakness or they'll use that against ya. Go. Get outta here." Philip tapped Antoine on the head. "Use this." The men circled around Antoine and Philip.

Antoine shot the priest a glare. Father Kilby shined the FORD symbol on the front of the car with his sleeve, ignoring them.

Antoine pulled the letter out to show Philip. "My sister gave me this. It's the last sentence my pa said to me." He showed Philip the letter but Clement snagged it. "That's mine." Antoine tried to take it back. "I was showing Philip that."

"I can't read anyway," Philip said. "Clement taught me to write my name, but that's all I know."

Clement read it aloud. "This letter says, *The farm is haunted.*" Clement laughed as if that was a joke but it was serious. Dead serious.

Philip yanked the letter from Clement and gave it back to Antoine. "Leave him alone, he's just a stupid boy. Antoine, go see how your sister is. Go with the priest."

"Shut up, dog." Tommy swung his stick at Philip but Antoine stepped in front of him and took the hit on his shoulder.

"You protect servants?" Clement stopped Tommy from swinging again and some type of weird hope flashed across his face that made Antoine look long and hard at him.

"Philip stands on his own two feet, better than these fools.

Heck." Antoine shoved Franklin. "Franklin can't even take a piss without your permission. This is the servant."

Franklin swung and the others were on him, too, but Antoine was ready. He wasn't leaving without Emma and each swing he took exploded with determination.

PART TWO

MONTHS LATER

"Why must we constantly remind you to breathe?"

–Sacri

–SEVEN–

June 1916—

Antoine woke to a swirling world. Everything rushed at him. *Drugs*. He hated feeling like he wasn't connected to his body. He forced himself up, no idea where he was.

A crackling radio rattled off facts about the war that blurred in his mind. He hated that, too.

"Whoa, young buck. Sit back. Where you off to?" The man blurred in front of Antoine.

"Running water to soothe the pain." Antoine's words slurred. He focused on the unfamiliar face in front of him. "Where the heck am I?"

"You're in a hospital, in Pleti, North Dakota. I'm Doc Williams and this is Myles. You won't make the creek. Not today."

Antoine got up anyway. Strong arms came around him, holding him steady.

"Stubborn soul, he is." Myles had a smooth voice. The radio clicked off.

"He wouldn't have survived if he wasn't, Myles," Doc said. "Determination like this is impressive."

"What impressed me was the beast who walked him in. Never seen a soul like that. He was at peace with the earth."

"Sorry I missed it." Doc sighed.

Things cleared in his head a touch. Enough for Antoine to remember the fight at Clement's Ranch.

Silver. Where was he? Silver found him when the priest dumped him off in a field because he threw up in his stupid fancy car.

Antoine reached for the cross around his neck and

remembered it was gone. With Emma. He needed to get to her.

His throat was scratchy. He needed water. Running water to soak in.

Antoine studied Doc as he pushed him back into the bed. He was probably close to his pa's age, his hair greying a touch around the ears.

"My shoulder hurts," Antoine complained. Hurt was putting it nicely. Every time he took air into his lungs it sent a piercing pain flashing through his entire body.

"It will," Doc told him. "You took quite a beating."

"Think gophers feel bullets, because my fists went right through them?"

Doc chuckled. "I bet Myles has a gun that'll fit your fiery personality."

"*Aye,* but ye better rest up." Myles was non-negotiable. "I won't be handing off weapons to a fiery soul."

Antoine looked toward this Myles. He held a cane, a blur in the distance as he sat by a table with a reading lamp and radio.

"His eyes are clearing," Doc said.

"His soul isn't," Myles said, shaking his head. "He misses someone he linked to. A greyish thread comes from his soul that vanishes into the light and probably reconnects to another. They have an earthy connection. Like us."

"Can you see who he linked to?" Doc asked. "If we find this soul, he might heal quicker."

"Wish it worked that way. Let me worry about his soul, Will. Focus on his mind and we'll let him take care of his body. If he wants running water to sit in, we should get him outside."

"Still, makes me wonder why he was beat senseless," Doc said.

"Still stressing on that? Men wish to destroy each other," Myles told him. "Been that way since the dawn of our existence. It's our job to heal 'em up long enough to find peace between battles."

"I want outta here," Antoine mumbled, no idea what they ranted about.

"Tomorrow, if you stand on your own, we'll walk ya to the

creek," Doc offered.

Antoine nodded. He was tired anyway. "I need sun."

"We should have pushed his bed against the window the minute he arrived," Myles said. "Smart, this soul."

"How... I mean how long have I been here?" Antoine was parched.

Doc checked his chart and frowned. "Well. A bit. It's June 4th tomorrow."

"June?" Antoine tried to sit, shocked. "What kinda pansy takes weeks to heal?"

"Well, took more than my skill to save ya. Myles stayed to see that you received the best care. He even went to the local tribe and found a healer, because we thought you might be from a local tribe. You know, because Myles sees a wolf shadowing your soul and you clearly have Cree ancestry."

Antoine squinted at Myles. He had the Sight? He looked so ordinary it was hard to imagine this guy could see his soul. Sacri said *Cîpay* warriors were to protect those with the Sight. They were sent by God to guide. A part of him wanted to honour his ancestral beliefs and another part... He lay back, exhausted. "I gotta get outta here," he mumbled, too spent to fight.

"Then rest," Myles said. "Want the radio on?"

"The voices in that box rub me the wrong way. Sing to me, gifted one. Bless me with your wisdom."

"Wisdom? Ha." Doc chuckled. "You don't want Myles to sing to ya. Now lie back. Myles is right. If you don't listen I come with drugs, because you need to heal."

Antoine shot up.

"Why rant that way after I told ye not to?" Myles sighed. "All it does is upset him. Let him heal naturally. Now lie back, lad. I won't let Will use drugs, promise. Will, find that pretty nurse. She was fussin' over him somethin' fierce. Us all up in his face is annoying him. He needs a womanly touch."

Antoine relaxed and closed his eyes. He needed to heal quickly because the only woman he wanted to touch him was Emma. That much he knew.

–EIGHT–

A few weeks later—

From the corner, Emma watched Clement's family eat. She knew her place—to make sure no one went without, while she stayed out of sight. Invisible.

This was where she grew up yet nothing here was hers. These girls were all she knew and this was how things had been since Gracie dragged her out of the hole when she was young.

So why did she feel like a stranger watching people she didn't want to know?

Clement ignored her, yet he moved when she did. He wore a brown three-button suit that she'd pressed herself. No one else touched his clothes. Been that way for years. Now the idea sickened her.

His tie stuck out from his pocket and he had the top two buttons on his shirt undone. He hated ties.

Emma sighed. How could she un-know these things?

She thought about their first nights together, letting the memory relax her. Clement had sat beside Emma while she'd shelled peas. *"You don't mind me sitting next to you, do you?"* Clement had asked. *"It's mighty stuffy in there, all them girls yapping their gums and no one has the time of day for the old man."*

Without thinking, she had adjusted his tie. *"You aren't that old."*

"Hate these things. My old man insisted I dress up. Not sure why I still try to impress him."

"Mable said she never knew her grandfather." Emma had tried to talk to him, nervous that he might tell her to bugger

off.

"*He died because of Cîpay. They left me alive with a warning.*" He'd showed her the tattoo on his hand. "*Cîpay are very bad. One day, they might come for you, but I'll keep you safe.*"

She had nodded, adding them to the list of things she was not allowed to bring up with him. "*You should wear your tie properly. This rich green, it makes the green in your eyes that much brighter. I darkened it for just that reason.*"

He'd caught her hand and their eyes had met. "*The Missus said she whipped you. What was that all about?*"

"*Well,*" Emma had started, not sure if she should tell Clement this, yet he had asked and the Missus said she was never to displease Clement, which meant it was her job to please him so she confessed everything. "*It wasn't my fault, but somehow I get the blame for such things and Gracie says it is my fault and that's why she cut my hair.*"

"*Go on.*"

"*Not much to say. I didn't bring in any milk. When the Missus sent me back, I took a whipping instead.*"

"*Now why would you do that?*" Clement had looked genuinely curious.

"*A whipping was safer.*"

Clement had sat forward with a deep frown. "*Go back for a minute. Why didn't you get the milk?*"

"*Mister Jez wouldn't let me pass. He waits out there for me and I'd rather take a whipping than his crap. Sorry sir, I didn't mean to cuss.*"

Clement had gripped his hands in front of him. "*Go on.*"

"*He stank like booze. I still taste it.*"

"*Taste it? What? He do this to you often?*"

"*You mean get under my skirt?*" Emma had pulled her skirt around her knees. "*I guess I did deserve it yesterday, but today I didn't see anything. I swear.*"

"*You allow this? How old are you?*"

Maybe she wasn't supposed to let them do that. Then again, Emma didn't see how she could stop them from punishing her. Especially when Jez had been mad at her for catching him with his pants around his ankles the day before.

"*I can't count,*" she had lied, not sure if Clement would

approve of her working on her numbers at night.

"*What? That won't do. I like smart people around me. Don't you want to be smart?*"

"*No one ever thought to teach me such things,*" she had confessed. "*I... I try. I traced a number last night. It wasn't very good.*"

"*Hmmm. Let me get a notebook. You can show me.*" He had paused as he got up. "*You're definitely older than Mable.*"

"*She says so, too, sir. Gracie says I was born in the hole. She knew my mother, sir.*"

"*Clement. You always call me Clement, and you tell me when swine touch you. I don't want any of that going on around here. You're safe here, Emma. I pay your room and board, and keep you safe. You help out, it's a fair exchange. Right?*"

She had nodded.

He'd left without another word, but Emma never had trouble getting milk after that and their evening teaching sessions were something she looked forward to all day. He was smart. Clement knew lots of things. Too many things. She would never learn them all, yet she paid close attention to everything he said. Even Philip had come by to learn how to write his name, and Clement was as patient with him as he was with her.

These memories didn't help her, and the room rushed in, forcing her to lean against the wall as the real world and all its demands fell on her shoulders like a sack of flour.

Could she ask Clement to stop owning her? Gracie said no, it didn't work that way. She'd get thrown down the steps like he did to the Missus, and then where would she go? Nothing was safe but here.

Philip said to let Antoine handle things. But where was Antoine?

The banter around the table was about the war. Emma used to love listening to the lively discussions. She used to pay close attention to everything, remembering, answering in her mind. Many times, she'd even asked Clement about what she'd heard and discussed things with him afterwards.

Everything was different now.

Now, she... *wanted*. She wanted her baby to be safe. She

wanted a life where she was the Missus. Where she got to go to dances. Where she didn't have to know her place because it was her place.

And...

She touched her lips, remembering those butter kisses. She wanted Antoine to spread them endlessly on her.

Clement snapped a quick look her way as if reading her thoughts. She pushed into the wall.

She couldn't have any of those things.

Could she?

What if she could?

Emma rubbed her sweating hands on her skirt and stepped away from the wall.

When Clement set his empty water glass on the dining room table, she walked to fill it instead of rushing like she normally did. Standing near him made her nervous. Would he see the difference in her? Would he know she was going to leave with Antoine? What would he say?

She shook slightly as she set the jug down. Maybe she could vanish in the night. Invisible.

Clement grabbed her wrist with a snap.

So much for invisible.

His finger ran over her ring and slowly his eyes snaked up her body and settled on the cross around her neck. Clement reached for it, but she moved her hand to protect it. His voice crackled slightly as he stood. "Franklin, we have a problem."

Franklin glanced up from where he stuffed his face. When he saw Clement standing, he shot up and knocked over his glass of water. Mable threw her napkin over the spill.

"What?" Franklin asked.

Clement ripped the necklace from Emma's neck and tossed it at Franklin. "Look at the message he left us. *Cîpay* pricks want a war over land they don't even want. Well, they're gonna get one."

"I'll take care of it right now." Franklin walked around the table, picking up the necklace that had landed on the floor.

Clement still held Emma's wrist and he let it go after a gentle squeeze. "Turn up the heat for him. He thinks this is funny, doesn't he?"

"I'll put Vince on it. Come, dog." Franklin shoved Emma

toward the door with a nod.

"*Don't touch her!*" Clement snapped.

Franklin slipped his hands in his pockets. "Sorry, boss, I forgot."

"But Father, Emma is my servant." Mable stood. "You can't vanish her because someone displeases you. I need her."

"You're right, my sweet, loyal child." Clement stared at Emma, his dirty thoughts crawling over her.

Emma rubbed her hands on her skirt and looked down, fighting the urge to glare back.

"Franklin, leave her with your mother," Clement offered. "Close, yet out of his reach. Does this suit you, Mable dear?"

"Yes, Father. Franklin's mother is kind," Mable agreed. "She could use the help around her house. How decent of you to think of her. As always you show great compassion for those less fortunate than us."

Emma rolled her eyes. Why couldn't Mable say what she really thought?

"She won't be so offensive there," Franklin offered as they left.

"I must say good-bye." Mable rushed after them before Clement could argue.

Emma walked in front of Franklin. He wasn't following her but waited for Mable who threw herself in Franklin's arms. Tears streamed her face. He didn't push her away but kissed her frantically, his hands in her long wavy hair.

Emma stood still with her hands locked in front of her. She'd seen them together a few times and apart from Gracie and Clement, Mable was her best friend. Emma watched them closely as they kissed. It was eager, she decided. Not at all how Clement was with her. Clement's kisses were desperate and fearful. Almost guilty. She touched her lips, hoping to capture one, but all that came to her was Antoine's butter kisses. Eager would be fun. Something inside her leapt at the idea of kissing Antoine that way.

"How long will you be gone?" Mable whispered between kisses, taking the necklace from him.

Franklin glanced at Emma but returned to Mable almost instantly. "A few days. A week at most, I have to run an errand for Tommy."

"She'll be safe?" Mable demanded.

Franklin nodded. "Promise."

"Then hurry back." Mable pulled away and rushed to hug Emma. She slipped the necklace in Emma's skirt pocket, tears still hot on her cheeks. "Trust my Franklin, Emma dear. Gosh, I'm gonna miss the stuffing right out of ya. Be careful."

Emma stared coldly at Franklin, but he raised an eyebrow and met her eyes.

It was the first time that he met her eyes. Such a small thing but it gave her the smallest thread of hope. Maybe she wasn't invisible to him after all.

Clement opened the front door. "Franklin, I want a word with her, in case that mutt left me a message."

Franklin ran down the front steps and vanished into the barn.

"Leave her, Father. Franklin can handle her." Mable fluttered inside, pulling Clement with her but he shook her off, his eyes fixed on Emma.

The moment they were alone he stepped up to her. Emma kept her eyes down.

"Look at me." Clement ran a hand over her stomach and let out a long puff of air. "You better?" His hand rested on her arm. She pushed him off, but he was quick to return it. Did he still own her? Could two men own her? "Is my son growing?" he asked.

"This child is mine," Emma snapped.

"Emma." His voice was soft. "In order to keep you safe from my enemies, I have to send you off. I do this because he is mine. You're in danger."

"What do you mean?"

" *Cîpay* will come for him to make me pay for something I did a long time ago. Antoine was the first of many I expect to try and take this son from me. It's not a coincidence that he showed right after you told me. They are convinced that I'm to learn the secret between a father and a son, and they'll take my boy away the minute he's born to make me suffer. I can't have that. He's just a thought and already I love him. I'll be out to see you in a week."

Emma stepped back and threw his hand off again. "I'm married."

"Impossible. That mutt told you lies to confuse you. I take care of you and you know that." Clement leaned against the veranda railing, his arms crossed. She knew that pose. Talk. He wanted to talk. No touching. She calmed. "I treat Franklin like my son, yet he lies to me. What am I missing? What's the secret between a father and son, Emma?"

Franklin pulled up with the buggy but took his time, giving them space.

Emma looked at Franklin. She knew what Mable wanted. "Tell him to marry Mable."

"She's not old enough to marry that drunk." He rubbed his head. "She's seventeen."

"That's old enough to give you a grandson to run this farm."

"A grandson?" Clement smirked. "I never thought of that. It was mighty lonely around here without you."

"You're the one who hit me," Emma reminded him.

"For your own good. You don't understand how dangerous these people are. For the love of all these prairies, I don't see what he did to get you this annoyed with me. Did he cast a spell on you? Touch you?"

"Not like you," she admitted.

"Take that ring off. I got his message, no need to annoy me." Clement's hand shook when he rubbed her jaw.

"Married."

Franklin stayed back waiting to join them yet he shifted, looking mighty uncomfortable.

"Marriage?" Clement demanded. "Is this what you want?"

"You're married to the Missus," she reminded Clement. "Bother her with your needs. Antoine told me that a man waits until he is married to see a woman."

"That woman is dead to me, it's you who makes me feel special." Clement stepped closer. Emma shifted her eyes to Franklin and didn't move because Clement never touched her in front of others.

Clement sighed and stepped back. "What do you want, Franklin?"

"Really want me to bring her to Mom's? Or is that code for

the hole?" Franklin asked.

The hole? Emma tensed. Would Clement send her back to a hole? The idea had never even occurred to her.

"Meeting room in Pleti seems the safest place for her. Must I really say that out loud?" Clement turned to face him. "He'll come for her to piss me off. I want to be ready. I'll deal with her when I finish that gunpowder deal. I got a war to feed. You hear anything about the opium?" Franklin raised two fingers and Clement smirked. "Franklin, if you stay sober long enough not to screw this up, I might consider letting you date Mable. Would you like that, son?"

Franklin looked up at Clement towering over him as he peered down from the veranda. "I don't know what to say."

"You'd better say that you plan to stop drinking our profits away."

"Then yeah. Heck yeah. Come on, dog. We have to grab supplies." Then as they walked, Franklin said to Emma, "Wow. What ya say to put him in such a good mood? He should be ready to smack you. He was so flipping miserable these past weeks I was ready to shoot him myself. How do you do that? Ten minutes with you and he's happy for days."

"It's my job to please him." She followed Franklin across the yard.

"Well, you're damn good at it."

"What hole were you talking about?" Emma whispered to Franklin as they entered the barn. She kept pace with his long strides. Tommy was working in the corner and Philip was with the mares. "Where is it? Are there slave-diggers there?"

"Shut up. As if you talk to me in here. Know your place." Franklin was his usual silent, hard self and grabbed things, handing them to her but not glancing at her.

Afraid, Emma kept behind. Franklin whispered something to Tommy and made a gesture to Philip that she didn't understand. Philip hardly even glanced at her but he came back with a satchel and gave it to her. "Stick close to Franklin. He'll only give you one chance so take it. Run. God be with ya," Philip whispered and walked away as if nothing had happened.

Emma shoved the leather bag in her skirt without glancing at it.

When they returned to the buggy, Clement waited. As Franklin climbed in, she backed away from Clement.

"Get in," Franklin ordered, the shotgun beside him.

Clement said, "You climb in the back, and I'll put this blanket over you so no one sees you. If Franklin touches you, I have to know. No one touches you."

"No one? Even you?" Emma was surprised.

Clement frowned. "Franklin, give us a minute." Once he was gone, Clement asked, "Why wouldn't I touch you? Don't be stupid or I'll have to smack sense into you."

She wiped a tear. She had no idea why it came, but they flowed freely. How could she go with Antoine if she belonged to Clement? What if Antoine ended up hanging in the barn like that farmhand everyone said touched the Missus?

Why hadn't Antoine come for her? Maybe he changed his mind. Maybe Clement was right and this was a trick. That was the worst possibility of all.

"You're scared." Clement brought up her chin with his rough fingers. "I know you've never left the farm, but he'll bring you to a safe place. Just wait for me there." His body pushed against hers, too close.

Emma glanced away. "Married."

"Stop with that. He can't marry you. You're carrying my son. I plan to mark you as mine as soon as you deliver that boy."

Panic tightened her inside. She had no idea how to make a son. "And if it's a girl?"

"I have six daughters because of their curse, and this son I dream about; it's you who will give it to me, because they think I care about such things when they couldn't be more wrong." He studied her lips. "I want a son with you." Clement came in for a rough kiss but she pulled away. "It'll be a son, it has to be or those pricks wouldn't be coming for him. Now kiss me good-bye while we're alone."

Sadness crept up inside her. Would she really have to stand here while he kissed her? Something inside her screamed. She looked at the ground, wishing with all her might that Antoine would walk up to them right now and make things right.

Clement's voice pulled her from her nightmare. "Sometimes, when I look at you, all I see is a moment I don't deserve. Does that make sense?" He pulled away as if someone caught them together but Franklin had his arms crossed and was looking out at the field a ways away.

Emma studied her hands, used to his confusion about this.

"Know your place, woman." He balled up his fists. "You had no business seducing me. Evil is what you are. You cast some type of spell on me, you did. Even a son don't make this right." He turned his back on her and rubbed his eyebrows, working out the endless headaches she knew he fought.

Emma stepped in front of him. He had his eyes shut. Everything in her tightened. She had no idea what angered her but it exploded in her.

She slapped him.

It was something she'd never done before and she was sure he'd hit her back.

Clement caught her hand as she pulled away. His eyes were tight and he got right in her face. She could smell his sweet breath as his cheek grew red from the slap. "No one has to know I'm this weak but us, right?" His green eyes darted over her face.

Emma scrambled in the back of the buggy and curled up in a tight ball on the dirty floor. "I don't feel safe with you anymore," she mumbled. "And I want Antoine."

Diggers don't want. Gracie says.

~~

They travelled for hours and Emma was sore. Her breasts ached, her back throbbed. She needed a bed, so her body could get the rest it demanded.

Franklin pulled the blanket off her. She shot up but pulled back when she saw he held the shotgun.

She flinched, sure he'd hit her and get under her skirt.

"Really? You're gonna play that card? As if. I'm not Tommy."

Emma never had a problem with Tommy. "He gave me a cookie once."

"Don't take food from Tommy."

"So... you won't touch me? Are you safe?"

"Oh geesh, you really think that low of me?" he asked. Over the years, she'd given Mable many letters that Franklin dropped in the laundry basket. She had no idea what any of them said, but Mable always seemed delighted by them. Maybe Franklin wasn't so bad.

"Here, eat something. Mable says you haven't been well. You're quiet." He handed her a sandwich and sat on the edge of the buggy to eat his with her.

Surprised, she cautiously sat beside him.

Franklin stopped eating to say, "Should have told Clement that Antoine left that necklace with you before he took off."

"Antoine said he was coming back for me."

"Didn't look like he was coming back," Franklin argued. "Ever. You sure got a nice thing going with the boss. Why you wanna leave that?"

"I liked it better when you were too much of a coward to talk to me." Emma bit into the sandwich even if she wasn't hungry anymore.

What if she was stuck with Clement for the rest of her life? Her stomach turned despite the delicious food.

"You like it?" Franklin asked.

Her stomach lurched up. "Chicken. It's delicious." She took another bite to prove that she wasn't worried about Antoine. "Where did you steal the food?"

"I don't steal. My mother made it." Franklin smirked. "You were sleeping when we stopped there, but she left you that blanket." He pointed to it sitting on the front seat of the wagon. "I have to take a roundabout way to Pleti. Sorry, but I have a few things to check up on."

"I need to go to Canada. To Antoine."

"Antoine? I don't think so, Emma. Just be happy you didn't get the hole with the other diggers."

"What hole?"

"Clement has them digging us tunnels so we can move around quicker, especially in winter."

"Clement does this?" Emma was horrified.

"He does now. Antoine wouldn't cooperate so he has to dig his own bootlegging route."

Antoine would never find her if she was underground. "Please do not take me there."

He slid the gun on the seat. "Why pick Antoine over a guy like Clement?"

Emma licked her fingers. "He's safe."

"Doubt that," Franklin said.

She looked up and Franklin met her eyes.

"You have the most telling eyes," he said. "I'm sorry. I can't promise anything. Vince isn't someone I know, just the leader of things in Saskatchewan. Like me, he ain't got a dad and so Clement took him under his wing. Tommy says he's a pansy, but what does he know? Unless Clement sends me, my hands are tied."

"Get him to send you. Take me."

"I don't think so." Franklin shook his head. "You're not good for me to hang around. I promised Mable to keep you safe, and the boss wants you in Pleti. Honestly, that's as safe as it gets."

She stared at him.

"Damn you and those accusing eyes. You know how to burn through someone's soul. How about if Antoine shows, I point him in your direction. That work for you?"

"Tell me where he is so I can go there on my own," Emma said.

"You go to Saskatchewan? I doubt that."

Saskatchewan. That was where she'd go. She'd find Antoine.

-Nine-

Antoine examined the ticket Myles had bought him. To Eau Claire. He was on his way to the train station to exchange it for cash so he could find a ride toward Clement's Ranch when Doc sidled up beside him.

He wanted to tell Doc everything, yet he couldn't talk. He didn't want another person telling him to forget about Emma. He pushed past Doc and went toward the train station.

Doc followed. "I'm not sure what you're involved in, young buck, but I do know that sometimes, we get a second chance for a reason. But from my experience, there are no third chances. Think, really think about your next breath."

Antoine paused. If he stormed Clement's Ranch, what then? He'd get them both killed. He needed a plan, he needed to talk to someone deceitful, sneaky… he needed his sister.

~~

Antoine's house was the same as he remembered, yet... it was different. As if it had grown old while he was gone. The paint peeled around the windows, the steps were crooked. Were they always that way?

Everything was quiet, yet the silence was almost worse.

Antoine couldn't wait to tell Marie about Emma, yet his insides were in knots as he leapt up the front steps to the house they grew up in.

He was still sore everywhere, though mostly in the left shoulder. Myles gave him stretches to do that helped. Doc slipped him drugs for when they didn't. Antoine didn't like the drugs, but he knew that sometimes there was no other choice so he kept them in his pocket.

They were good guys, smart, too. Saved his life, they did. He owed them, and he wouldn't forget that debt. He couldn't wait to tell Marie that he met someone with the gift of Sight.

Antoine opened the familiar door, feeling like a stranger.

Two brutes blocked his path. "Heh, heh. Look at this guy," Brute One said.

"Get lost, savage." Brute Two shoved him.

Antoine pushed up his cowboy hat a smidgen and took in their serious faces. "I live here, morons. Who the hell are you?" No one was going to push him around. He'd ploughed every blasted inch of the soil around here until his hands bled at night and he could almost see the bone through them. He'd hauled the rocks off this land himself since he couldn't afford a decent horse and didn't want to exhaust the one he had. These thoughts fired him up and he felt ten feet tall as he faced the brutes.

"Antoine?" Marie called from inside. "Let him in. Don't be stupid."

Antoine pushed past them and Marie ran into his arms. Her tummy nudged him, and when she pulled away the bump under her apron was clear.

"Look at you. You bulked up," she said.

"Eh, seems you're carrying a little something extra yourself," Antoine teased in French since this was the language they normally used.

She ignored him and continued in English. "Glad you're home safe. That's a weird hat you have on. Where's your cap?"

He smirked. "You like? I picked it up in my travels. All the farmhands wear them across the border. Keeps the flying ants outta my face. Called a cowboy hat." He winked at her.

She let out a long-winded sigh. "You're home. Finally."

"Yup. So when do I meet the gem who stole you away from me? And who the heck are these idiots pretending you need protection in your own house from your own brother?"

"They are nobodies," Marie said, waving them off. "Here for a silly meeting, and I'm sorry, but you missed the wedding."

"You didn't wait for me?"

"I waited as long as I could, Antoine. Got married out on

the starlit prairies a while back."

"Not in a church?" He was surprised, that was something Sacri would do, not his woman-of-the-real-world-overly-religious sister.

"It was romantic, with the moon off to the side and the wind moaning in delight. You would have loved it." Marie forced a smile, unlike her usual scowl, and Antoine glanced around suddenly uncomfortable in his own house. "Mathew will be home any minute. He's setting up for the meeting with the boys."

"Mathew? French?"

She frowned. "No, and if he asks, neither are we."

Antoine casually poured himself a glass of water from the pitcher on the counter. "And what is this meeting about?"

"Not sure. But it's important to him."

Antoine leaned against the counter and watched the two brutes watching him in his own kitchen. Slowly, the anger built inside him. He'd been gone too long. "Where? I might want to see what's up."

"Right here."

Antoine just about spit his water out. They were having some sort of meeting on Sacred Land? That was one-step too far. "So you're fine then? Happily married?" He kept the edge from his voice, but Marie tensed and nodded, her golden eyes avoiding his.

"Of course." Her right hand shook as she pulled down her sleeve.

Antoine slammed the cup on the table and walked to her. "Well, nice to hear." He pulled her hand up and pushed the sleeve back to see what she hid from him. A purple welt across her arm. He met her eyes. "*Ouais*. Looks like a keeper."

A tall skinny guy stumbled in. He had his black hair slicked back and by the gloss in his blue eyes, he was drunk. Antoine checked his pocket-watch before eyeing him up. Two in the afternoon. Interesting way to come home to his new wife.

Drunky-boy stumbled to Marie and wrapped her in his arms. "Hey hun." He snuggled her neck and it took all Antoine's effort not to push the creep off his sister. "We let savages in the house now? Not enough room for them to romp around on these prairies? We discussed this last week."

"Ah." Marie adjusted her blouse and avoided Antoine's furious glare. "Mathew, meet my brother, Antoine."

"Oh." Mathew stood taller and ran his hand in his hair before offering it to Antoine. "Oh. I was joking. Didn't think you were a savage, it's just one heck of a tan you got there."

Antoine glared at his extended hand and didn't dare touch him, as if the drink might infect him, too. Unlike his own hands, Mathew's were smooth. *Clearly not a man of the soil.* Antoine let his eyes sweep over him casting a quick judgement. On his land, he had a different way to class people than Clement did. There were 'annoying gophers' and 'friends'. Antoine put this idiot in a class with Father Kilby and Tommy. *Too many gophers around.*

"We'll be out of yer hair in no time. Gonna do some travelling. Got myself a new job, I did." Mathew grinned but pulled back his hand, uncomfortable.

"You're not gonna farm with me?" Antoine shifted his eyes up, and Mathew took a step away from Marie. Antoine came between them. He wasn't nearly as tall as Mathew but Antoine had done a lot of scrapping on his way home, and his muscles were burning for this guy.

"I don't know much about farms, but I do like it here," Mathew said. "Um. Maybe we could talk about buying this useful section from ya, at a... more than fair price."

Useful. The word rubbed him the wrong way but he couldn't figure out why.

"*Ouais*, I see you made yourself right at home, didn't ya, *maudit p'tit chien d'prairie.*"

"Well—"

"That wasn't a question, gopher."

"Antoine." Marie grabbed his arm to calm him before he took a swing at the drunk.

Antoine snapped in French, sharing with his sister how he felt this loser was nothing but a gopher tearing the place up for his own benefit. Then he turned to Mathew and added, "We have clear rules on Depaix Farm and I'm gonna give you the first one. Come home drunk, spend the night with the dog. You meet her?" He turned Mathew to the door.

"What? I..." Mathew stammered.

"I assume you know your way without a savage escorting your royal drunken ass around." Antoine walked him to the door and the blockheads stepped aside with a funny grin. To the brutes he said, "No use smiling like cows lost in a herd. You're out too. If you two have a meeting, you'd better find whoever runs things and tell him to relocate. No meetings on Depaix land. Not ever. Find someone else to annoy. Nothing but pests, the lot of ya."

"Ah." Whatever dumbass number one wanted to say, he shut up when Antoine pulled the pistol Myles had given him from his pocket and shoved it in his gut.

"It only takes one of ya to pass my message to your boss," Antoine said. "You're trespassing and I'm within my rights to defend myself."

"Vince won't like this at all," Brute One mumbled to Brute Two as they left.

Vince. He had a name.

"A gun? Antoine, what's gotten into you?" Marie looked shocked.

Antoine faced Marie. "Cripes, Marie. Where did you find that gopher? Under a blasted cow patty?"

"He's celebrating his new job. You can't make him sleep outside."

"Can and did. Wasn't it you who made that rule? Made me sleep outside plenty of times yet you're gonna let him get away with *merde* like that? What's wrong with you?"

"He won't like this," Marie said.

"You're welcome to sleep in the barn with him."

She smiled, despite her words. "Things are always easier when you're around. I'll tell him he's welcome to come in for supper if he pulls himself together and apologizes to you."

"To you. I don't give a flying fist if that gopher ever talks to me again." Antoine went to the closet for the shotgun. He hid the bullets in his room and was headed there when Marie stopped him.

Quietly, she whispered, "What happened while you were gone? Silver appeared to me and warned me that I might never see you again."

Antoine kept his eyes on the gun. Clearly, his sister

couldn't help him rescue Emma. She was in enough trouble. "What happened here is the question. A man shouldn't need a gun in his own house."

"You don't," Marie said. "I took care of things so you'd be safe."

What the heck did that mean? "So there aren't nasties haunting our precious soil?" He showed her the letter in her own handwriting. "I've seen you talk men into a hole, yet you let him treat you like that?"

"I made my choice. Where have you been?"

"Hospital. For gophers, they sure pack a punch when their fists hit."

She snapped the letter from him and tossed it in the stove. "Garbage. You left for months and bring me back garbage?"

"I found a wife."

Marie flung around. "*Quoi?* I mean... where is she?"

Antoine answered her in French, annoyed that she wasn't even comfortable speaking their language in her home anymore. "Sick. I'll go back for her after I clean things up here. I was actually hoping you could help me with her but I ain't bringing her home to a mess like this. She's seen enough hell. You gonna tell me what's going on?"

"Everything's fine. As perfect as can be," she answered in English while she scribbled something on her writing pad and left it on the counter. "Add this to the fire for me."

She pushed passed him, and he went to see what she'd written. It read: *What happens to gophers on Depaix land?*

Gophers were a touchy subject for Antoine over the years, not the annoying human kind, but the furry rodents that tore up his soil. In one of his obsession-fits, he blew a huge hole into Sacred Land to exterminate the pests. Antoine tossed the note in the fire. Did she want him to blow her husband up? Because, that sounded like a plan he liked.

Pay attention to what they don't say.

His eyes scanned the walls, the ceiling, the floor. He had no idea what he searched for, but little things unnerved him. One of the pictures was crooked. A plate was missing from the fine china in the cabinet. The cross was gone.

The cross was gone?

He rushed to the sitting parlour. That one was gone, too. Pa had hung a painting he'd made of Sacri on her white horse and that was missing. Instead, there was a strange photo of King George. Antoine took it down and studied it, as if it might tell him where the heck it came from.

Antoine had no idea what was going on, but he rummaged around the dressers to find the crosses. They were shoved under blankets in a trunk in the hallway with the paintings. He put them up.

Then he tossed the photo of King George in the trunk, not sure what to do with something that bizarre. Why look at a king he didn't know or have stories about?

There. Better. It felt like home again. Well, almost. Just missing Emma.

Antoine knocked on Marie's door. "Apparently, I have to walk this area tonight to make damn sure these nasties are respectful. Hopefully, I'll meet *Cîpay* and get us some help," he said, good and loud in Cree. "But in the morning, I'm off to see the priest for a visit. Maybe he can help me. You coming?" Marie was always eager to attend church.

"No." Her voice caught on the word.

"*Non?*"

Marie hated it when he couldn't restrain his anger, or he would have slammed his fist into the wall. Antoine took a couple deep breaths as Pa had taught him. *Focus. Calm. Feel the air in your lungs. Trust that you can do this.*

Marie opened the door a crack. Her voice was low. "I'm not allowed there."

"I'm sure God hasn't locked you out of church."

"We're to go to the Protestant Church if we must go. It's called fitting in, you should try it. It works for our cousin Bernoit."

Antoine wouldn't pretend he was something he wasn't and he was fairly sure Silver wouldn't want his son Bernoit doing that either. "I'll go to church here, thank you very much."

"Our new church is several towns away so I haven't made it there yet, but I would like it if you came with me."

"What the heck is a Protestant? You even know?"

"I'm sure it's fine," she told him. "We find God around us, in us. Sacri believed this and so do I."

"Yeah, but—"

"Mathew made good points I won't discuss with you."

"I'm sure he did." Antoine went to his room for bullets. He could make a few good points, too.

~~

Antoine never made it to church the next day. Or the next. He was going on little sleep, but he'd made his point. Mathew stayed out of his way and Antoine had caught a glimpse of a nasty and they'd had it out.

He was sitting in a pew beside Father Hillsdale, telling him about it. "He was wearing a white sheet with no markings, a long hole cut in it for his eyes. I swear. Dumbest thing I ever witnessed. He came out of the shadows. When I pointed my gun in his face and promised to expose him as the coward he is, he ran. That's their weakness. They know that if *Cîpay* find out who they are, they're dead. Only a fool makes fun of Ghosts of the Earth on Sacred Land."

Antoine thought of Emma and her worried eyes. "But that's not why I'm here. I have a gopher problem I can't see a solution for."

Father Hillsdale groaned. "From what I heard, you and gophers are not a good combination."

Antoine told Father Hillsdale about Clement; all of it.

"So far they haven't hurt anyone," Father Hillsdale said. "There's good in everyone."

"I have a few bruises that say otherwise. I don't like them making fun of *Cîpay* by dressing up as ghosts. It's insulting." Antoine took a few deep breaths and his mind cleared.

"Sounds like he wants Depaix land. I'll ask around. Maybe that land is worth more than you thought. No gold there, eh?"

"Heck no. I ploughed that sucker myself. Rocks, skeeters, and a heck of a lot of dirt. Land not even suitable for horses. Gonna grow me some kickass weeds, that's about it."

"We have bigger problems than Clement. Unless he's behind the strange things going on with our government."

"Like what?" Antoine asked.

"Oh, someone whispered an idea to those idiots in charge to pass these ridiculous one language laws forbidding other languages being taught in our schools. It's very possible this is going to be a reality."

"What? You telling me that a school my pa built won't be teaching in Cree?"

"Or French. English only. Or so they say."

Antoine shot up. "Why? *Non. Non.* I will not have my children taught in only one language. That's..." He knew three languages yet was at a loss for words. "*Merde,*" he swore in French.

"You might not have a choice."

"I always have a choice." Antoine stormed to the door but Father Hillsdale chased after him before he got outside. "Leave me alone."

"Why? I'm used to your fits. Besides, this is too important. Focus, Antoine. Don't let him rile you up. You wanted my help, come back, sit with me. We'll talk about this, get your gal to safety. What are you hiding from me?"

"Loser brother-in-law waved a lot of cash in my face, like he's a big hero. I took it, told him I was donating it to the church, so here, do something useful with it."

Father slipped the cash in his pocket. "You calm enough to handle him? Sounds like he's working with Clement. You realized that, right?"

The back door to the church flew open and Silver appeared. "*Iskotêw!*" he growled in Cree, then flew out the door, vanishing in his usual way.

"Dang." Antoine felt his world crumble with that one word.

"What?" Father jumped up. "What's wrong? Who did you see? Was it *Cîpay*?"

"Fire." Antoine knew exactly what would be on fire. He flew outside to look at his farm. The flames were high enough to see in the distance as they licked up the hope of a happy home with Emma.

He'd prayed over tiny Josée's body there. Then Sacri's. Not his pa's though. His body was still missing. Deep inside, Antoine hoped he'd return home.

Antoine's happy memories in that building outweighed the shady ones. His childhood had been one of laughter and filled with learning. This was where he'd lived and where his family would live.

He watched the flames as he got closer. Screw them. He'd

build Emma an even better home. He walked with a determined force, prepared to take on the world, only because they were telling him to sit back and take their shit.

A crowd gathered but Antoine ignored the sympathetic nods and comments. No one got in his way when he was like this. They knew that his tight jaw meant someone would pay. He searched the crowd for Marie.

Antoine asked around but no one knew where she was. Of course they didn't. He refused to believe she was in there.

Flames danced up the sides of the house his father had built for Sacri, even though she insisted a burrow was far easier.

Antoine went to the barn to collect a few things and let his old horse go, in case the fire spread.

"You want us to start a fire line?" His best friend from childhood was at his side. Henri was a good chap with curly flame-red hair. "Gilles is gone to gather his wagon and some pails."

"Nope." Antoine pushed Henri aside. "It's too late. This is nothing but a distraction."

"This old horse won't get you far. Take mine," Henri offered. "So what's the distraction for, because to me it looks like you pissed someone off something fierce."

"Huh?"

"A message was pinned to your wagon. I took it down before anyone else saw it."

"What did it say?"

Henri handed it to Antoine who read it aloud. "*Where is your cross now?*"

"Kinda creepy, eh? You know what that means?" Henri asked.

His cross. Emma. How could he be so stupid? What were they doing to her?

"A bunch of fools making fun of *Cîpay* want Sacred Land. They're using my girl to distract me while they steal my sister down a gopher hole to annoy me."

"Sons of bitches. What ya gonna blow up now?"

"What ya think, moron? You got any cash on ya?" Antoine asked.

"A few bucks, but I'm coming. No way am I missing you on a rampage." Henri passed him a knife.

It was small and Antoine held it up to the fire to get a better look. "This is perfect for making my point. Thanks."

"So where ya wanna start?" Henri asked.

Breathe. "You ain't coming."

"If someone took your sister, I ain't gonna stand for that, Antoine. We stick together in this town. Your pa taught us that."

Time to mark these buggers for judgement. "If you hold me back when I get my hands on one of them, I'll use your own knife to skin ya."

"I like it when you get all rammy. Always fun. Can't count the times Gilles and I hauled your ass home after a fight you had no chance of winning."

"I'm not stupid, only reason you boys did that was so you could catch a glimpse of my nasty sister."

"Ah, you got me. I hope to come off the hero. Plan to save your sister so someone decent can marry her, and by that, I mean me. How the heck did she end up with that dirtbag, eh?"

"I misplaced my priorities for one moment, left to earn cash, and somehow my entire life fell apart. I know better, Henri. Sacri made it clear that money was the demise of men, yet what's the first thing I do? Dang it." Antoine watched his home burn.

"This is a story I can't wait to hear. Where is your gal? Should we be saving her, too? I like rescue missions, makes me feel important."

Antoine examined the familiar faces as they blended.

He still had land to rebuild on, nothing a little wood and nails couldn't fix.

His insides twisted, torn in two.

Antoine ignored the flames as his life burned away and walked his horse out of the barn. His sister was missing. They had Emma. What more did they want from him?

~~

Antoine paced the train. They'd followed a guy who looked like Mathew, but he just vanished. "The guy doesn't even know how to tie his own shoes yet he took her right under my nose." Antoine complained.

"We talking about Mathew again? You're all over the place." Henri sprawled out on the wooden bench as if he owned the car.

No one sat near them.

They'd train hopped for four days. They were out of cash, needed a bath and a better plan.

"We checked this entire train. He's not here," Henri reminded him. "We need off. I tell ya, we lost them in Moose Jaw. We're going in circles, but it always comes back to Moose Jaw."

"I tore that city apart." Antoine sat, frustrated.

"We missed something. Trust me. I'm thinking clearly, you aren't even breathing."

A scrawny man in a light brown cap walked in the car and actually pushed Henri's leg off the bench and sat so he faced Antoine, staring him down.

"Oh, you must be the great Vince." Antoine glared at him.

"Something like that. Listen. I don't know what the heck you did to piss off some highdog down in the States but my orders changed and I'm *not really* here to find out why."

"Just a ghostly visit, eh?" Antoine studied him.

The rough hands told him he was a farmer. Early twenties. Ticked at the world. The shined shoes told a different story. He was lining his pockets.

"They took my sister and told me I couldn't marry my girl. You take crap like that at your place, because I don't even stand for gophers tearing up land I plan to seed?"

Vince smiled. "I knew I'd like you. Never met anyone who pointed a gun at a ghost."

"Should have pulled the trigger on your sorry ass. I'll know better next time."

"Ha. We're on the same side, Antoine. Come to the rally in Moose Jaw. You'll like what I have to say."

"Blind fool. Do I act like I want in? I want my sister and my girl. That's it." Antoine sighed. "I don't want a war, enough of that in the world without us killing each other. I want these gals safe and happy and you morons hurt them for no reason."

Vince rubbed his smooth jaw. "A good reason and you

might like it. I'm gonna buy yer land. Pay ya a fair price. Double its worth and with that, you walk."

"I protect Depaix land from those who wish to do it harm, and in return it feeds me."

"Regardless, I'll pay you nine for land that useful."

Useful. Again, that word he didn't understand. Useful to who? "Nine bucks?"

"Nine hundred for the home acre and the stretch that runs to the border. Rest you can keep."

Henri actually fell off the seat and sat by Antoine. "Take it and run. You don't even have a house, man."

Rage burned in Antoine. He wouldn't fall for that again. Money wasn't everything. It was useless without Emma and if Marie was hurt, he was to blame.

"Seriously?" Vince acted flabbergasted. "I see you lingering toward no. Let me sweeten the deal for ya. I can't do much about your sister since she's married and not your problem, but I will go one further and see what I can do about this girl you plan to haul off as your own. Some highdog's daughter or something?"

"His slave."

Vince sat back and glanced at Henri. "Slave eh? Sure that's not right."

"Saw it with my own eyes. Slave."

"Then buy her," Vince said. "Good land for a good slave. Course if it was me, I'd take the nine over some bitch slave."

Antoine leapt. His wild attack clearly took Vince off guard.

Vince pushed Antoine away only to receive a fist across the right jaw.

Antoine rolled with him to the dirty floor. Vince was clearly used to fighting and wiggled out of his reach, hitting Antoine several times in the gut.

Antoine took each hit, letting the pain feed his rage, then he got on top and his elbow dug into Vince's neck. When Vince broke free, Antoine rammed a knee into his gut several times, matching the clicking of the wheels.

"And Pow! The war comes to little old Saskatchewan." Henri put a hand on his shoulder. "Keep control, buddy, you make progress when you breathe."

Antoine didn't have time to breathe. "Henri, reach in my

pocket for the heroin."

Vince tried to break free but Antoine slammed his head into the floor.

Henri handed Antoine a metal case.

"Open it, and stick the needle in his thigh," Antoine ordered.

Henri said, "He's moving too much."

"Hand me the knife." Antoine clicked it open. "One more wiggle and you're gonna lose an ear."

Vince stopped as the cold steel sneaked along his neck.

Henri had the syringe with an ampoule attached that Doc had given Antoine for the pain.

"Touch me, your sister dies," Vince threatened.

"The sister I knew is already dead."

Henri jabbed him with the needle in the thigh through his grey slacks while Antoine sat with his knees on his chest and a knife along his ear.

While Antoine waited for Vince's eyes to gloss over he searched Vince's pockets and tossed his finds on the seat for Henri to check.

"What did you do to me?" Vince smirked.

Henri handed Antoine his pa's cap that must have fallen off in the fight. Antoine put it on and rolled up Vince's sleeve. "You hear me, Vince?"

Vince mumbled but kept his eyes on Antoine, trying to focus.

"Grab his stuff and wait elsewhere, Henri. I'll be a minute."

"What you gonna do to him?" Henri wanted to know. "We don't have dynamite here. Do we?"

"Just a mark on his hand so I can find him when he's under those sheets he hides under."

"I like that. Make them face up to the crap they do." Henri picked up the stuff from the seat and paused with the flyer in his hand. "Gee Antoine, maybe we're approaching this wrong. See the rally they planned. Why not play their game? Be one of them, blend in?"

"You're a free man. Do what you want."

"Then I'm staying. I wanna see you mark this bugger up." Henri sat on the bench. "I can't believe you turned down nine hundred dollars. Man. You shoot this heroin when I wasn't looking?"

–Ten–

"We're sleeping outside tonight." Franklin tossed a blanket at Emma's feet. The skies were turning pinkish as the sun slowly set for the day. "Under the open skies of the North Dakota Plains." He sucked in a deep breath of fresh air.

Emma was not enjoying this trip. She was itchy with the dust and dirt of travelling and her clothes were tight, making her uncomfortable. Everything felt wrong inside her. She ran out of water yesterday in the tiny flask Franklin had slipped her. None was around, ever. She was parched. Tired. To make matters worse, they hadn't made much progress because she'd gotten sick again and spent more time throwing up than travelling.

She'd lost track of the days, of direction. She had no idea where they were. She was weak and dizzy.

"Tomorrow we'll go underground. Well. You will. I hate that meeting room. Snakes come and go like they own the show." Franklin shivered.

"Is it close?" Emma asked.

"Yup, but I can't find it in the dark. I'll show you to your new home come first light and I'll be back with food. Trust me when I say that room is your safest bet. This is Drink country and these buggers don't like coloured folk."

"Drink?"

"Yeah, an experiment Tommy tried," Franklin explained. "His own form of magic. Made Clement his own army of *Cîpay* hunters in Pleti which is why he wants you here. Problem is that the Drink has a strange effect on a man's tolerance. Lately, they're distracted by something else. Tommy needs more opium to get things back on track, but Vince is being difficult. You're safe in the meeting room so stay there."

"Is it... dark down there?" Emma fidgeted with her skirt.

"I'll leave you a lantern."

"No. Take me to Canada."

"What the heck you wanna go to that hole for?"

"It's a hole?" She had no idea. Had Antoine planned to take her to a hole?

Franklin ignored her and took a slug of water, then handed her the flask. She looked at it shocked that Franklin was willing to share his water with her. "Drink, I don't need you fainting on me again. I can't deal with this. What the hell is wrong with you?"

She just looked at it. This was not allowed.

He glanced around. "You need it. Here."

Emma drank before he took it away, then she curled up on the blanket and watched Franklin pace. He checked the gun then paced some more.

"What's troubling you, Franklin?"

He stared off in the distance at the open fields. "That cross you're wearing, I watched Clement toss it in the slough. Fact that Antoine left it behind on a woman he shouldn't even sneeze near means he's using you, Emma, to make Clement panic. That's why Clement is sending you here—erase you from the equation. Forget Antoine, he's not coming back, and if he does, it won't be pretty."

"Wouldn't you go back for Mable?" She looked up at him.

Franklin stopped his pacing. "Don't move."

Emma glanced down. A black snake with a red belly curled up by her bare feet. "It's cold and I'm warm. It won't hurt you." She grabbed it, to show him it was harmless.

Franklin was ten feet back. "Devil woman, keep that thing away from me."

"He's harmless. Come see. He's kinda cute."

"Bad omen. Bad. Dammit. I'll be back in an hour. I need a drink. Get some sleep."

He got in the buggy and left. He left. Just like that, she was alone on the prairies.

Run.

~~

Emma walked the field, determined, resting when she was tired. She was headed to Canada. Hole or not, she had to find Depaix Farm. She came across a sign many hours later. If Franklin searched for her, he was nowhere in sight. She touched the sign, spelling out the letters. P-L-E-T-I. She sounded it out but it didn't make sense. What kind of name was that?

She came to a path that led to a farmhouse. It was two storeys with shutters along the windows. The veranda had a couple chairs on it but no flowers like the ranch. Horses were in the field, and in the dim light of the setting sun, she noticed that the barn door was open. Inviting. It tempted her to sneak in to spend the night. It grew cold, and she didn't want to stay alone on the dark prairies.

Not sure how to approach things, she debated between walking up to the house and asking permission or sneaking in unnoticed.

A man appeared in the kitchen window and waved to her.

Emma didn't wave back, just hurried down the path. When the door to the cute house opened behind her, she picked up the pace but her bare feet were sore and she stumbled.

A voice with a strange accent called to her. A man. "Hey lass! Hey!" He ran after her and she picked up the pace. "Stop. I won't hurt ye. Where'd ye come from? Don't run, it's getting dark, stop please. I can't run."

How dark would it get?

Emma faced him.

He leaned on a cane, breathing as if he'd ran a marathon.

"Why can't you run?" she asked.

"Ye scared me. Where'd ye come from? We don't see many pretties walking by themselves. Not now that an army of drunken saps haunt these prairies."

She rubbed at the fabric on her patched skirt and watched him. He was stalky, balding, but had a nice smile. Too nice.

Another man ran down the path with a lantern. "Myles? What's going on? Why are you running around out here? It'll be dark soon." He stopped beside Myles and stared at Emma while grabbing his suspender with his free hand. He was taller than the first man Stubble lined his dirty face. The blood on his sleeve made Emma step back. "Where the heck did she come from, Myles?"

"She don't talk much, this one," Myles said, flashing her a smile.

"I'm Doctor Abraham Williams, but call me Doc or Will. We were about to start our meal. You hungry? Myles always makes too much."

"I'm on my way to a hole called Canada," she told them.

"Um. That's a little hike," Doc said. "Popular place these days. I can't let you go that far alone. Come with us, we'll take good care of ya, right Myles?"

Myles glanced around. "Not sure that's such a good idea, Will. We got 'nough problems with ghosts and her soul is linked, means someone won't like her hanging with us, no matter how noble we are."

"Ghosts." Emma clutched her skirt.

"*Aye*." Myles sighed. "They think we're plottin' to destroy the world. Not sure we should invite more problems by adding a coloured lass to our nest."

"I'm married," she announced as if this might change their minds. "And with child."

Doc Williams grabbed her shoulder and turned her toward the house. "You look petrified, child. We can't leave her out here, Myles. Come in and eat. You're welcome despite what the big baby Myles says. You on the run?"

"I don't run, I fight."

"I like you," Doc said, and Myles nodded as if it was up for discussion.

Not a soul in sight, not even a bird to save her if these guys decided to attack.

–ELEVEN–

"Gophers are using her as bait," Antoine mumbled to Henri when he saw they sent Marie to pin the poster to the lamppost in Moose Jaw.

Marie walked off with a smile and a nod to a group of young men. She wore an elegant formal dress that Antoine was sure didn't come from her wardrobe. Even her hair was well done under a new hat.

"What are we saving her from again?" Henri asked. "She's so smoking I'm hot, and we're a block away. Only thing that bothers me with this is that I can't figure out how the hell a dumbass like you ends up with such a beautiful sister?"

Antoine whacked Henri on the back of the head and his cap flew off.

They watched from the train station window as she vanished into the shoe repair shop. It was the third time. Henri walked in after her the first time and said the place was vacant. Where the heck was she vanishing to?

"I hate this," Antoine said. "I should walk over there and talk to her. This isn't how I do things."

"You agreed to try things my way, since running around the country ain't working. This is how they do things. They pretend to be ghosts, you pretend to be them. Watch and learn my friend. I'll be in and out in no time. We'll meet up at the church around midnight. Bet I get more reaction by telling them I'm for their dumbass ideas than if you storm the place like the macho moron you are."

"This is still not a good idea. We should smoke them out, not blend among them. You don't hunt gophers by acting like one."

"Argh, trust me, Antoine, no one hunts gophers but you.

You're an idiot with that. Let it go. These aren't gophers, they're men."

Antoine's gut twisted. He had no idea who to trust, but this *felt* wrong.

Henri rushed off, excited about his plan. He walked to the lamppost and yanked down the poster. Casually, Henri leaned against the post, reading, waiting. Sure enough, out of the shoe repair shop came a young guy about their age, maybe a year older. He ran into Henri. Again, it was a scene they'd watched play out earlier in the day. This time, Henri was the victim. He hoped to learn what the decoy said to those who read the poster.

Henri nodded, talking wildly, his hands flailing around him. The other smiled and pointed to the train station. They grinned and parted ways. Henri rolled up the poster and left, turning toward the residential area.

Antoine held a copy of the poster in his fist. He'd taken it down earlier. He read the crumpled paper: *Need better wages? We fight for you. Voice your opinion in an open rally.*

"You going to that? I'm excited to hear what they have to say." A young fool in his early twenties smirked at Antoine.

"I have better things to do than listen to a bunch of bootleggers," Antoine grumbled.

"I can use more money. Coolies are stealing all the good jobs."

Coolies? The Chinese *almost-slaves* Sacri talked about? Antoine smacked him on the back of his head as Sacri often did to him when he was being stupid. "Respect others."

"Wow, are you cranky." He rubbed his head, eyed Antoine up, and decided he wasn't worth the fight.

~~

At two in the morning, Antoine opened the door to the church. He paced in the cold night. Every minute Henri was late made Antoine even more nervous.

A few moths fluttered around the streetlight while Antoine sat on the church steps to watch them. Streetlights. *Now the night sky wasn't bright enough for man to see, he put up lights that never went out.*

Sacri wouldn't have liked that. She believed nature provided. Pa would have liked it, though. He said if men could invent streetlights, they should. Why let nature have all the fun?

The light sure excited the moths. A bat swooped in and grabbed one, making its hunt that much easier. He liked both views, depending on his perspective. He liked the night sky showing him the way while he needed to blend in, but sometimes, extra light was nice for hunting.

Tonight wasn't one of those times. Like the moths, he was in the open, with light on him. He wanted to sit in the shadows and wait for Henri. Where was he? His gut was in knots.

A buggy whipped around the corner and Antoine leapt to his feet. Four guys in plain white sheets with no markings and holes for eyes were in the car. It was the oddest thing he ever saw. Geesh. What the heck was the world coming to? Henri would laugh himself sick when Antoine told him this.

The car stopped in front of him, a body rolled out and landed at Antoine's bare feet as the car rolled away.

"Henri?" Antoine flipped him over.

Henri looked up at him with lifeless eyes. "Tunnels." It was a great effort for him to speak.

"Henri." Antoine shook him lightly, but he wasn't breathing. "Breathe. Breathe. In and out. Focus." Dead. Henri was dead. Not breathing. "Henri, breathe. What did they do to you?" Antoine searched him for wounds but found nothing.

"Hey you there!" Someone came around the corner and Antoine shot up and ran for the first time in his life. He had no idea how to fight invisible forces. So he ran, waiting for answers to find him.

He ran.

And he ran.

~~

The morning light warmed Antoine as he stood along the river. He'd covered his body with mud to ease his pains and now Antoine knelt, waiting. Somewhere on these prairies would be the answers he needed. There always were.

A swan floated by. Peaceful.

Antoine had a hard time believing that inside him was this endless torment, yet at his feet was a world at peace. He sunk his hands deeper into the cold mud. A serene stream brimming with life called to him. He waded in, letting the energy heal the war invading his soul and wash off the mud that concealed him, so he could restart this life as someone new. A breeze picked up, and he welcomed it, pushing the troubles to the surface of his soul so the wind could free him of them.

A soft hum tickled his lips. Slowly, it blossomed as the song inside him fought for freedom and he called to nature, asking it to listen. *"Peh---taw. Peh---taw."* Another life given back to the earth and he sang of this.

He pulled from the loss, letting the melody consume him as The Song of Sorrow floated down the stream and lapped against the shore in gentle slaps.

The train rolled by, clicking and chugging.

He sang to the faces in the window as they blurred by, one after another. Short snaps of life. Faceless images. Possibilities.

It bothered him.

Everyone should have a face.

Of this, he lamented, moaning with the wind as if it could heal his torment. Telling the world he wasn't a faceless ghost. He wanted to matter. He wanted Henri's life to have mattered.

Exhausted, Antoine lay in the grass, but his song continued. Every breath he drew was a promise of peace, of one moment he foresaw but knew not how to obtain.

Happy forever. A moment that couldn't exist.

"Cîwêw." He drew out the word until his entire soul felt the burden of such a promise of peace for him.

Peace for Henri. *"Cîwêw."*

Peace for those he cared for, especially Emma. *"Cîwêw."*

The silence that followed was crushing, as if the world had no idea what to do with his grief. The sun warmed his face and so he closed his eyes and lay in the grass.

What was Emma doing right now? Was she thinking about

him? Where was she?

He knew where Marie was. Antoine had promised his pa never to let anything happen to her. Antoine was damn sure he wasn't keeping that promise right now.

"It won't be long, Emma." Antoine ached inside his soul, sure he'd left a part of himself behind to protect her. Still, he said a prayer as Pa had taught him. One for her and one for Henri, who he missed already.

A gopher ran up to him and when Antoine moved, the bugger rushed to his hole, hiding, reminding him of his obsession with the gophers back at Depaix Farms. He hated them, always tearing up the land he worked so hard on. After he'd blown up one of their holes with a stick of dynamite he'd stolen from the rail lines, Pa had shaken his head and said, *"When you get rammy, you don't think straight. Now breathe. I told you to work with them. You're running after gophers that hide when afraid. So your solution is to blow the whole place to bits? Breathe and give me a solution that doesn't involve you destroying the entire world."*

Antoine had no idea what the solution was. He'd pulled away and tore after them again, but Pa wouldn't hear of it. *"Breathe. Focus. Where do they go when you chase them?"*

The memory made his gut ache. No one to blame but himself. He'd failed to protect Henri. He wasn't breathing. He chased gophers in sheets, and it blew up in his face. Henri walked into a trap like some gopher led to... *Tunnels.*

Cripes. He shot up. He'd been blind.

–TWELVE–

Emma stretched in the big bed when the sun warmed her face. She'd never slept in a bed so soft, so full of blankets and pillows. She couldn't believe Myles gave her his bed and bunked with Doc. What a sweetie. She didn't know any men who'd do that for her back home. Nope.

She stretched again, enjoying the warm smells that greeted her. Mmmm. It smelled great, like bacon and eggs, coffee, too.

Emma washed up in the basin by the bed and paused before the mirror. She saw a free woman. Free. What would Antoine say to that? She tried to smile at herself in the mirror, yet she looked odd when her lips pushed up. Why couldn't she find happiness in her freedom? How did Antoine make those smiles appear on his face so easily?

She touched her lips, but the smile still felt forced. Maybe she wasn't made to smile.

This ache crowded it out. She hurt in her soul—if such a thing was possible. How did one heal a soul? She'd find Antoine, but the question nagging at her was why had he left? Why hadn't he come back as promised? Had he forgotten about her and found another wife? What would she do then? The idea was impossible.

These thoughts sent shadows in her features. What if she found him and he sent her off?

The ache deepened until she sat. She felt out of place.

Her baby kicked.

Emma ran a loving hand over her stomach feeling the slight bulge. A warm safe feeling crowded her like when Antoine's kisses were on her neck. For a moment, just then, she'd actually craved his hands sliding over her. His hands were full of safe.

Emma got up and was surprised to see a smile on her lips. She touched them again as her lips curved so naturally along the edges. Was happiness so simple? Just a memory?

She leaned on the dresser but pulled away swiftly; she shouldn't touch Myles' things. Yet it was dusty. Maybe these guys needed a housekeeper.

The room was spotless, just her fingerprints in the dust where she'd touched.

She heard Myles downstairs in the kitchen so she gently pulled out the top drawer. It was empty. What was going on? Didn't Myles own things? She'd assumed this was his room yet... Myles had never said this, had he?

There were only the two rooms.

Oh no. Images of Jez with his pants around his ankles flashed over her. She should have never stayed here. Now he'd beat her for sure. Nervous, she dressed and headed to the kitchen. "Myles, I am leaving. Thank you for the warm bed."

Myles was cooking and stopped to whisk her into the kitchen. "Eat first. You sleep well? Look what I made."

She sat at the table even though the eggs made her stomach turn. Myles talked, but everything swirled. Nauseated, she rushed out the door. On her knees on the damp grass, Emma threw up on the lawn. Horrified, she lay in the grass, her hands in the dirt as Antoine had shown her. Feeling the life of the earth.

Myles dropped his cane, plopped on the lawn, and lay beside her, as Mable would have done. "Didn't realize my cooking was that horrid."

She gave him a weak smile. "Sorry. I haven't been well."

"Yer body is hurt and yer soul is missing someone. Yer a physical healer so if ye want to cry on my shoulder, I'll understand."

It was exactly what she felt like doing, but Emma turned from him, afraid. Instead, she buried her hands deeper in the grass, remembering when Antoine held her hands like this and how wonderful it was to have him against her.

"I didn't mean to embarrass ye, Miss Emma. Some, like me, heal their soul with a simple breath, but a lass like ye, uses touch when afraid or unhappy. I noticed it last night, yer soul, it transfers yer emotions through yer hands. Doc does this, too, but more to heal others than himself."

Myles was right, of course. She was always in trouble because of how she touched things... people. "Is that wrong?" Emma asked the grass. "Am I casting spells with my hands?"

"Of course not, it's interesting to note that ye'll use yer body to express yer pains. Take what yer doing with yer hands right now."

She still had them against the grass, the blades sharp against her fingers. She could almost feel Antoine's warm skin against hers. She pulled them away.

"Don't let my observations stop ye. Go on, feel that grass until it helps. I recommend that Will check how that baby's doing, tonight. It'll help knowing all is right." He shrugged. "Maybe it's normal to spew yer cookies. I don't know much 'bout a pregnant lass."

"You don't have a girlfriend?"

"Nope." Myles pulled a leaf off the bush so he could pull it apart while they lay there. "Was married once. A mousy redhead with a bright soul. I was so amazed with her soul, I just plum right out started a life with her. I used to sit in awe and watch her soul dance when she talked. No idea what she ever went on about, but that soul, it was magical, innocent."

"What happened?" she asked.

He let the leaf go. "She got sick. Didn't want me to see her die and so she ran off. She was pregnant. He'd be sixteen this year if he would have survived. I knew the baby was to be a boy. Saw his soul shadowing hers."

"Did you go after her?"

"*Aye*, but the world is big, Emma. One day, I had to accept that she'd made a choice. Bothers me though; I'd like to know if my boy is safe." Myles' chin quivered.

This bothered Emma. If Myles had looked for his gal and the world was too big, would Antoine ever find her?

"You love this boy, even though you never met him?"

"*Aye*. There's a bond between a father and a son that I see in the light around them. Energy that works together like they... might be one." He studied another leaf. "I couldn't wait to experience that magic. Doc helped me look for him, but we never found him."

"You trust Doc?"

"*Aye*, he's a marvellous doctor when it comes to the mind, but he sucks at seein' what a person needs spiritually. Where I come in. I see yer soul longs for someone, too. Horrid pain that I hope ye remedy bloody soon. Seriously, I got a shoulder to cry on, use it, lass."

She thought of Antoine, and she refused to give into the tears until he held her.

"Do others see this soul you speak of?"

"My father had the Sight, and I'd hoped to pass it to my son. Bet he looks like her." He smiled.

"My husband, he said he felt my soul. But I don't know what that means. Can I feel a soul, too?"

"Perhaps you already have. A kiss is a perfect example of such a moment. A spiritual connection to another. It is expressed with touch, yet yer mind remembers it as healing to the soul."

Emma understood exactly what he meant. "I got a kiss that melted me inside here." Emma pointed to her stomach. "I want another one like that."

"Mmmm. I steal at least one kiss a day like that. But I am greedy that way."

"It's all I think about. I know nothing about kisses and love, even about souls or healing, but I know I want another kiss like that, even if I am a digger and should not want. I do." She glanced over. "But not from just anyone. Make sense?"

Myles smirked. "*Aye*. That's the secret right there. It's not the kiss itself, it's the soul that connects to yours." Myles sighed dreamily. "Thrilling."

She felt much better and sat. She touched Myles' hand to thank him. He didn't move and she pulled away in case he got the wrong idea. "What do you do out here? It's so quiet compared to the farm I came from. You work?"

"Mostly, I run this place and help at the clinic. Makes me a comfortable living. Got nice hens, a bit of livestock I brag 'bout. It's nothing fancy-dancy like them farms east of here, but I'm happy. No one hears my theories but the chickens. I used to teach at the university, but had to escape the rush, the crowds. Too many souls in need of healin' make me edgy. Had to find myself. Ever feel that way?"

"No. I never thought about it," Emma admitted.

"It's important to find yer place in the crowd."

Emma touched her necklace, wondering what her place was now.

Myles grabbed the cross from her, hovering over her. She froze, wondering if this was the moment he'd beat her. He returned to his spot on the grass. "Religion. Man's most horrid entrapment."

"My husband, he believes in God." She stretched the husband to remind him not to steal kisses from her.

"*Aye,* so do I. The churches have me confused. Men made 'em to shut out what scares 'em. I find no spiritual growth in those walls. Sad really. There are so many, because everyone's 'fraid of somethin' different. This is the mind playing tricks on us. Pathetic, really."

"I know nothing about churches except what my husband told me, and well... that was more about God than church. He had beautiful stories."

"Since when are stories 'bout God beautiful?" Myles asked.

"His are. His pa told him a story, then his ma said something different. So he twisted them together to make up his own stories. Made me feel better when I was sick."

"Tell me one."

"I can't."

"Try," he encouraged her. "Most times, it's in the retellin' that ye'll discover new elements, details to share. This is how the mind helps the soul heal."

"Well." She did want her soul to heal. "This beautiful woman named Happy fell in love. Not this easy love either, but the kind that can't be ignored. They fit together perfectly."

"Linked. It's a connection to another soul by a fine lifeline. I have no idea why or how certain souls link, but I study it carefully, because it always amazes me to see which souls are linked. Powerful stuff."

"Yes, linked, this is what they were, her and Forever. Now the problem was that Happy's father betrothed her to another.

She didn't like her fiancé and refused to marry the man named Moment, and so she ran off with Forever. Fools that they were, they stole a white horse."

"Why was that foolish?" Myles asked.

"On the prairies, in the summer time, the white stood out like a sunflower in a wheat field. So Moment charged after them like the warrior he was, determined to save his honour. The wind blew their scent to him, and his dogs tracked them easily. He killed the couple for betraying him, but instead of them being mad at the horse and the wind for giving them away, Happy let her soul mingle with the horse's and Forever let his mingle with the wind, and now, when the horse runs free, facing the wind, their souls unite, making them Happy Forever. Moment can't escape them and they haunt his every breath. Yet if it wasn't for Moment, they would have never experienced that type of eternal bliss."

Myles was silent for an awfully long time.

"Sorry, maybe I told it wrong."

"*Nae. Nae.* That was perfect." His smile grew. "I loved it. I was working yer story into my own life and trying to see how that was 'bout God."

"He said, it means God gives us the choice to be happy in moments or happy forever, but we might not like how we have to live out that choice."

"Yes, I see what he means. God allows every bloke the freedom to pick who to love without judgement, but he must pay for that freedom." Myles sat and met her eyes, seeing more than her. "Beautiful story indeed. Tell it to Will tonight."

"I would pick Antoine if I could pick anyone." She lay back, dreaming about him, forgetting Myles was beside her.

He blurted out, "Wait, not Antoine Depaix?"

Emma shot up. "Yes. Yes. You know him?"

Myles smirked. "*Aye,* I've had the privilege of watching his soul heal." His eyes swept over her. "I understand why he healed so quickly. Yer soul motivates him. Linked." Myles studied her as if looking right into her.

"We're not really married yet," she confessed, in case he could tell that with his beady eyes. "But he said I could pretend we are, for protection. I can't really marry Antoine.

Not now."

"But you want to run away with him on a white horse, like a fool?"

She nodded. "Every inch of me is thrilled with that idea. This is why I'm here. If Clement finds me, he'll marry me and I suppose that would be fine, but..."

"Forever without chocolate cake wouldn't be the same."

"What does that mean?" she asked.

"This is how I see yer story in relation to my life. Ye can eat carrot cake daily and being a hungry fool, well, you'd settle for that in the moment. I mean let's face it, carrot cake is delicious and the texture mildly intriguing. But once ye know that chocolate cake exists, well, a smarty-pants can't un-know that. I mean, it's chocolate cake and it's what ye really crave. If there's a choice to make... really I agree—one should go with what makes ye happy."

Emma thought about this while she followed him into the house and sat in front of the eggs again. Her stomach turned so she took a sip of water. She had to eat something.

"I've been thinking 'bout ye getting to Canada. Need cash?" Myles asked her.

She pulled out the satchel that Philip had given her and dumped the contents on the table. Two coins rolled out. Myles pushed them toward her. "Hmmm. That won't get ye far. I'll add to that."

"I can't take your money."

"What ye normally charge to help around a farm?"

She studied the coins. "This is all the monies I ever saw."

"Well then. Ye work for the week and I escort yer hinny to Canada."

"Is it a dark hole?" The idea terrified her, yet if Antoine was there, it couldn't be that bad. Could it?

"Canada? It's like here, I imagine. Anywhere in particular?"

"It was a long word. Sasky-something-or-another."

"Saskatchewan it is. Maybe ye could help with my studies, too. I'll show ye maps I'm studying so we'll memorize the names of the towns between here and Saskatchewan."

"I do not read well."

"Perfect. I was an excellent teacher. I'll find my books. Eat up. Yer body needs nourishment."

She pushed around her eggs. Eggs a man cooked for her. The world was so much more than she knew. What was her place?

Myles pulled up a chair and tossed a few books on the table. She ran her finger over the one closest to her. It had a picture on it of water. She'd never seen that much water.

"What's wrong?" he asked.

"I don't know my place." She clutched her skirt. "You ask me to help here but I don't want to be a nightingale." She looked away. "I am sorry, I shouldn't want. I should be grateful."

He frowned. "Your soul is terrified. Tell me what happened to you. What does a nightingale mean?"

"When I was at Clement's Ranch I stumbled on Jez with one of the farmhands. He had to prove he was into nightingales and I am one. The Missus says." The words poured out of her as the memories of him on her flashed over her. She pulled her skirt tight around her so Myles would have to fight it off her.

"Oh. Because I steal my kisses from Doc, you think I'll have to prove my manhood by attacking you?"

She curled up ready for him to hit her, but Myles looked back at her with the softest, kindest eyes she'd ever seen. He sighed, tragically. "Miss Emma, remember what I said about a special kiss? Well see, the kiss is the easy part, the hard part is accepting who you become after the kiss redefines your entire perspective." He leaned forward as if sharing a huge secret. "We can't hide in that moment, it's our most vulnerable breath, and yet the most freeing. Not everyone can make that leap, yet they yearn to, and so they fall victim to their own sabotage, and this is what you lived. I am sorry for you, but know that I am fine with it, even though the rest of the world turns a blind eye to me, I have found my place."

She thought about this. "If a kiss changed my place, how do I make sure it doesn't destroy me?"

"From my experience, give in. Settle into your new place."

It's easier to give in. "I never find it easier to give in," she admitted.

"It's not, but forget that. I plan to teach a smarty-pants

some real things she can use."

"You think I'm smart?" She sat up taller.

"Lass, ye already taught me more than most."

~~

Later that day, Doc didn't say much while he checked her. Emma had never been to a doctor in her life. He felt her belly softly, then listened to it. He touched the veins in her wrist and watched the clock. He studied her worn nails, touched her feet, and massaged them a bit. He even opened her mouth and stuck a finger in. It was strange, but she sat still and let him evaluate her while Myles watched anxiously.

"Well?" Myles paced around, his cane making an endearing clicking sound. "Is she fine?"

Doc pushed Myles in the corner and mumbled something that made Myles snap. Was he speaking another language?

"Myles, calm down." Doc glanced over his shoulder at Emma.

She pulled her patched skirt around her tighter and bit her bottom lip while she traced the red patch she sewed on last summer.

They came back and sat on the edge of the bed. "You said you were vanished. What does that mean?" Doc asked.

Emma shrugged. "At home, life goes on and no one knows where I am. To them, I vanished."

"So they won't hunt for you?" Doc asked.

"I hope Antoine finds me first. Actually, I hope to find him." She told them the entire story, about Antoine. They listened intently.

"Sounds like Antoine. Young buck didn't even know it was an option to be crippled. Nope. He was too bloody stubborn. I'm taking you to Canada to find this Antoine," Doc said.

"Not without me," Myles snapped.

"Why did he leave me?" Emma wondered.

"Why?" Myles was hysterical. "Are ye listenin'? They beat him senseless. He was in a wagon full of trouble that one. What if they found him again?"

"Myles, you're getting ahead of yourself. We don't know the first thing about crossing to Canada. We—"

A loud bang made them jump. Doc was the first to the door. He grabbed the shotgun and ran out, aiming.

He fired.

Myles kept Emma in the house.

"What's going on?" she whispered to Myles.

"We got fools haunting us. I have to man the back door. Stay low."

Emma nodded, her insides taut. She'd brought ghosts to these good people.

~~

"It's fine, Emma." Myles tried to calm her. "We're used to it, really. They're annoying, but no harm comes of it. We're big tough lads who take care of ourselves. They were doing this long before ye showed. Sleep." Myles shut the door.

Two nights in a row ghosts had visited.

It was her fault. She knew it was her fault and Emma wasn't about to let these good people fight off ghosts for her.

Emma waited until they stopped talking in the next room, then she dressed, put the satchel in her pocket minus one coin that she left for Myles for his kindness. Then she sneaked out the back door into the night. She had no idea where to go, but she walked through the field, heading north.

It was dark. She glanced around as if Clement might be near, searching for her body. She broke a long branch from one of Myles' trees and held it in front of her in case she needed to defend herself.

Then into the night she walked, until the rising sun highlighted a town in the distance.

In the heart of it was a church with a cross. It shone bright and alive, calling her. She touched the cross around her neck. Safe like Antoine. Much to her relief, the door opened freely and she marched in as if she belonged.

Curled up in one of the pews, Emma went to sleep, safe. Warm.

~~

Emma shot up when a sweaty hand came on her. Clement!

"Shh. I'm Father Kilby. What are you doing in my church, child?"

Emma took a deep breath and touched the cross around her neck. "I'm going to Canada to find Antoine Depaix."

He groaned.

Emma sat back from him, concerned. "Can you get me to Canada?"

Father Kilby's frown was so deep it made her uncomfortable. "I can only get you so far. If you wait, I'll send a message to Monsieur Depaix and have him collect you. That would be wise. Do you know where he was off to in Canada?"

She pulled the paper from her skirt that Myles had given her. She read the long word. "Sask-at-che-wan."

"I'll be back, child."

She waited in the pew. The sun sparkled down on them from the colourful windows and warmed her. This was a safe place.

Father Kilby returned with a slice of bread that he handed her. "It's all set. He'll be here in a few days. Would you like to rest? Come meet the Sisters."

"How did you talk to Antoine?" Her eyes grew wide with hope. Maybe she could talk to him.

"They don't have telephones in that part of Saskatchewan, but I called the closest priest and he'll find this Antoine of yours himself."

Of course, the priests would know Antoine. He belonged to their church. She should have thought of that.

"Can I wait here?" she asked.

He glanced around uncomfortable. "I'd rather you didn't. Come meet the Sisters. They will look after you."

"Will they teach me about your God?"

Father nodded. "If you like."

"I would like that very much. Antoine knows lots about Him, and I would like to debate with him. Be smart like him."

Father Kilby paled. "You're a good soul, Emma. I wish you understood what was good for you like I do. I really do."

–THIRTEEN–

The Moose Jaw train station was closed and the dark surrounded Antoine. He was sure a tunnel entrance was in this building somewhere. He'd watched the place all day. A few people stepped off the train and didn't leave the station. He'd seen a few step on the train without entering the station. Somewhere in this place, there was another way in.

Antoine found nothing in the basement and now he was on the second floor. Patient and determined, he tried every wall.

The panelling behind the shelf in the cleaning storage closet echoed when he banged on it. He pulled the shelf and it swung forward. *Huh. Who would have thought?* Sometimes, he was glad he obsessed over things.

With a glance over his shoulder, Antoine stepped into the corridor. He raised the lantern to look around. The room was small, with a staircase in the middle. He followed it down three flights and stood facing three doors.

He did it. He found the tunnels. Well. He found three doors.

Antoine had no idea where to go or what he'd find. What would he say to Marie? Would she listen if he asked her to help him get Emma away from Clement? Would she even care?

He hated these games. He wanted to march in and steal her to safety. Why was she going along with these idiots?

"Don't try to understand women, just love them. Whatever you do, don't ask them why they're insane, pretend you're insane, too, it's much safer that way," his pa had told him one night at the table and Sacri had tossed a bun at him. Pa had thought it was funny to get her riled up, but he'd told Antoine later that the truth was that Sacri was *Cîpay* and he

might not always understand what she did, but her actions were always to support those beliefs and he vowed to respect that. He loved her just the way she was.

Gosh.

He missed them.

Antoine pulled the handle on the first door, ready for a fight, but it was locked.

He tried the next one.

Locked.

The third opened to a storage room with several boxes. As he stepped in the room, the air paused as if an explosion was about to happen. He rubbed his bare feet into the dirty ground, trying to sense what was happening down here. It wasn't good, but that's all he could feel.

Antoine snooped around, careful not to touch anything. Nothing of interest and no way out. He even pushed on each wall to make sure they were real.

Voices caught his attention and he dimmed the light and stood in the middle of the room, ready to fight.

–FOURTEEN–

Hoolie kept under the steps, watching the entrance to the tunnels. He rubbed the Wanted flyer in his pocket, fairly sure that the Mister who just passed was the one. Big reward. Huge. Money like that, might get him out of this hole. He shook the dust from his hair and put his cap on so he looked trustworthy. Then he removed his shoes, since Mister didn't have any, he wanted to come off like him—keep them on even ground. They were too big and clumpy anyway.

Hoolie shoved them under the steps. He might fit in them soon. He was growing faster than he could earn clothes. The shoes were nice though and he didn't want to lose them, since it wasn't easy to slip shoes off a dead guy.

He shivered. Dead guys always creeped him out. They were so... empty. Not that the living were any better these days but at least their bodies contained light.

He wiped his nose with his sleeve. With this reward money, he might even buy himself a home. A real one, with a bed and everything. The idea appealed to him something fierce.

Before he could meet his next target, two brutes came down the steps. Busy night. By the shine to the shoes walking past, he recognized them as Vince's boys. *They all had shiny shoes,* Hoolie thought. *Can tell a lot about where a man has been by his shoes.*

Hoolie slipped against the wall, deep in the shadows. If they went near the gunpowder room he was gonna have to cut them off. He was not losing this mark. Big reward for Mister. He couldn't read numbers or the names on the flyer but they had two more zeros than he was used to seeing on these Wanted flyers Vince handed him, and lucky for him,

Mister walked right into his hole.

"Tommy says if he has to come, heads are gonna roll," one of the fancy shoes said.

Hoolie winced. He didn't want Tommy to come again. That guy had troubled clouds in the light around him that Hoolie just didn't like. He rubbed his head, not sure why Tommy's cookies made his crew so nuts, but he wasn't going that route again.

"Where are your new shoes?" someone whispered behind him. Hoolie looked down at the newbie tunnel rat. His light danced around him excited and Hoolie could make out every feature of his face as he looked up at him, hopeful. Poor squirt had no idea how much this life sucked.

"Shh," Hoolie said.

The boy slinked back into the shadows.

"We went too far. Vince is pissed," one of the brutes said as he unlocked the door to the main tunnel.

Hoolie peeked. One had a shadow behind him that made Hoolie nervous so he hid away again, hoping to heck he didn't have to deal with them. Shadows were worse than dead guys. Why did all of Mister Vince's guys have shadows behind them? Vince didn't. Vince was a good guy. His shoes were really nice, too; always dusty, but he let Hoolie polish them once. Hoolie had been careful, earned an extra coin from Mister Vince.

"Who cares about Vince? Tommy's taking over. Trust me, that bloody coolie got what he deserved. What a rush. We're making a difference and if Vince can't see that, he's gonna get eaten alive."

Hoolie hated how these idiots talked. Just once, he'd like to meet someone who had every bit of stupid knocked out of them. That would be swell. A light that just danced with life and made him forget how much all this sucked.

The voices faded as they walked in the main tunnel. *Good. Let them get lost.* He sighed. No, a lost idiot meant he'd have to haul another dead body out of this hole. Hoolie turned to the brat behind him. "Follow them, wait until they get lost. Shake them up, then ask for two coins. Two, and lead them out the way they came in."

"I can keep 'em both?"

"If you earned 'em, they're yours." Hoolie fished in his pocket and pulled out his hanky. In it was his last bloody piece of cake. His stomach grumbled as his fingers ran over it. "But remember, don't take food unless I give it to you. Too much scum kicking around." He handed the cake to the newbie.

This better go well, he couldn't keep feeding these boys on the crumbs he was getting from lost blokes.

"I want that hanky back," Hoolie called after him.

Hoolie waited until the boy was out of sight and opened the door to the gunpowder room. He slipped in, keeping against the wall, ready for anything. The only light was dim, from the middle of the room. Mister's light was not like others. It was greyish, amplified by the life in the earth that surrounded them. He liked the idea of light responding to the earth and reached for the lantern and lit it to get a better look at his mark.

Mister was in the middle of the room, arms crossed. He had light dirt covering his face and arms, and streaks of mud under his eyes and on his forehead. It wasn't a mask or a veil, it was as if he'd just stepped out of the earth a warrior sent by the Almighty to protect it. Hoolie had never seen his kind down here before.

He studied Hoolie. No hiding for this one, and Hoolie kind of liked that brass. His shirt was filthy, but Hoolie let his eyes take him in quickly, scanning his clothes for the familiar bulge of a wallet or a weapon. He had neither. It was just Hoolie and him—a wanted criminal. A breaker of the law. Hoolie had no idea what this guy did to warrant a reward with two more zeros, but if Vince was giving a reward this big, it was really, really bad. If it wasn't for his light, he'd believe it, since Mister had a savage look to him. But the light coming from him was... earthy and really, the earth was the one thing Hoolie loved.

His bare feet dug into the dirt floor as if sensing Hoolie. Hoolie copied the action, curious what he sensed. A movement to Mister's left caught Hoolie's attention. A wolf. Hoolie almost stepped back, then caught himself. It was just a shadow. The wolf paced around Mister, studying him, too. He'd never met a man with a wolf shadowing him. Never.

What did that mean? Was it good or bad when a wolf
shadowed you?

–FIFTEEN–

Antoine watched the scrawny brat walk in. Not at all what he expected. He wore his cap like Antoine, with grey suspenders that matched. His slacks were at least a size too big but his shirt was tight and his sleeves came halfway up his arms. The boy held up his lantern to survey the area and stopped on Antoine. "Hey. You the new guy I'm supposed to show around?"

"Probably not, since I'm not really here."

"Neither am I, Mister. Neither am I. What ya staring at?" He spoke with a French accent that reminded Antoine of his pa.

"I didn't know a French squirt would be here. How old are ya?" Antoine asked.

"Old enough to ask for the coins up front. I ain't leading you through these tunnels to get ripped off. Let's go, three of them."

"How old? Fifteen? Sixteen?"

"Your guess is as good as mine. Now three coins or I walk."

"Three? I only got a buck on me." Antoine pulled out his last dollar bill.

"Gee. I never saw one of those." He snatched the bill from Antoine before it came into the light of his lantern and it vanished. "That'll do. Let's go." He adjusted his cap and rubbed his nose along his sleeve.

"Can you give me a layout of how these tunnels work before we go through them?" Antoine asked.

"For a whole buck I'll even draw you a map." He set the lantern on the floor and shooed at something to move. Antoine wasn't sure what he was doing and knelt beside him.

With his finger, the boy drew a line in the dirt. "All tunnels are built the same, because some idiot wants to get from here to there. We call that the main tunnel. It can be straight, round, curvy, don't matter, it's the point of having a tunnel. Over the years, this main tunnel will need other exits." He made a bunch of lines that joined to the first one. "These connect and lead you around in circles so don't think you won't get lost under this city without me. You will."

"I'm Antoine. What's your name?"

"What you wanna know my name for?" The boy looked ready to run.

"Like to know who I'm gonna die with, that's all."

He smirked. "Hoolie."

"Hoolie?"

"Yeah, it's Chinese. You got a problem with that, Mister? Because I don't care what you buggers say, I'm not changing it."

"Hmmm. I'll bite. How did a mousey tunnel rat with dirty orange hair and freckles with a rich French accent end up with a Chinese name?"

Hoolie put out his hands. "What you see is what you get. Do I walk or are you coming?"

"Is there an interesting story behind a name like Hoolie?"

"Really? You want my story? What the heck for?" Hoolie paused and eyed Antoine up before continuing. "Well, when I was young, I curled up by some Chinese guy for the night. Cracked up on opium, he thought I was a fox. Woke up screaming that a fox was in the tunnel. Name stuck. Hoolie. Don't ask me to spell it, I can barely pronounce it."

Antoine chuckled. He liked this brat. "Fox is a fitting name for a guy like you. I like it. Hoolie."

"Other guys call themselves tunnel rats, but you stick with the fox if you wanna survive down here, Mister."

"You sneaky as a fox, too?"

"Can be, if you flash the right coins at me. Heck, I'll even speak Chinese or Danish in a pinch. Of course, nowadays, with them idiots running around, us tunnel runners, we stick to English or get a whopping instead of a tip. They sure are arrogant pricks. Most of them are from the States, not sure what they're feeding them boys down there, but it sure makes 'em thirsty, if ya know what I mean."

Antoine continued in French. "Why work here?"

"I need cash to feed my family. It's honest good work. I run donkeys from one end to the other and take them where they wanna go. I shut up about what I see and earn a tip. Never a whole buck though. Makes you my favourite donkey right about now."

"After my pa died, I left home to make extra cash for my family, too," Antoine told him. "Ended up getting the whole blasted world ticked at me. My best friend died while we were searching for my sister and I had to leave my sick girl on a farm that wouldn't even bat an eye if she died. All I can tell you, Hoolie, is that if you get a chance to go home, take it. Don't worry about money, just go home."

"Home? Gee Mister." The squirt raised his lantern. "Gee. Where you wanna go?"

"To bed."

Hoolie laughed. "You and me both. One of them soft ones, too. Here, look at our map again. This is where we are. If we travel this wing, we come across sweet smelling stuff."

"I don't know what that means."

"Listen, I list off the areas and if something does make sense to you, that's where we go."

"Fine." Antoine waited for Hoolie to continue.

"This end, sweet tasting stuff." Hoolie paused. "Gee, most everyone wants to see the distillers. More booze made down here than Saskatchewan will ever slurp up."

Antoine stared blankly at him. "Booze? Why is everyone drunk but me? Man, that bites."

"Well, if it ain't the distillers that brought you here, how about this area? Kinda dry in there and you wouldn't want to sneeze the wrong way or you might blow yourself up."

"Explosives. Hmmm. I'm supposed to stay away from those, kinda got myself in trouble with those before. What about this here?" Antoine pointed to the mid-section.

"Oh that's haunted. Doubt you want—"

"Yes. Haunted. There. Take me there."

"Ghosts it is." Hoolie wiped out the map. "If you got anything I can munch on, I'll tell ya about them on the way."

"No, I haven't eaten anything decent in days. I own a knife

you can have. It was my best friend's, the one who died, but I don't need it anymore."

"Gee. You annoy me. Don't you have any stories that don't make me feel like I'm living the high life down here?"

"Not lately," Antoine admitted.

"Keep it. I'll tell you dirt for free. Never met anyone like you. What you gonna do, walk in and steal your sister like some drunken fool?"

"Why not?"

"Not the brightest, are ya? Maybe we should hit the distillers first." He brought Antoine to the far wall and shoved the box aside revealing a hole in the wall. "After you. My own fox hole."

"Is it far?" Antoine asked.

"Far. Dark. Rats. Welcome to my hell. It's not like yours, but it sucks just the same."

Antoine crawled in.

Wriggling through the tunnels was a lot of work and Antoine never felt so dirty in his life. His knees were raw and his hands bled after twenty minutes of following Hoolie. "You do this for a living, Hoolie? You need a better job."

Hoolie chuckled. "I'm working on it. You can stand here."

Antoine felt the cold, stone wall and followed it up. His head bumped something. A lantern?

He lit it and surveyed the room. It had a desk in the middle and a cot in the corner. "Nice. What's this? Your home?"

"If I have to call this hellhole home I might as well give up. Nope, this is your new home. You remember how to get here? Now, the tunnel through that door leads to the basement of the shoe repair shop. This fake wall." Hoolie tapped the wall. "This runs to the tunnel with the big room. They call it a gathering room. That's where they put on them sheets and talk and do whatever it is they do. They scare the bee-gibers outta me. Pay well though, so I don't ask questions. Nope."

"I talked to one today and he told me they were stopping bootlegging. Find that hard to believe since I haven't seen my stupid brother-in-law sober yet. Everyone thinks they're doing something different. Truth be told, they're here because I told the boss to screw himself and he's making fun of my family by running around with sheets on. You see, we're Ghosts of the Earth and my ancestors are haunting him, so he figures he'll haunt me." Antoine shrugged. "I don't care."

Hoolie seemed to think about that. "You don't care? Really? Could have fooled me." He frowned. "Um... well if you change your mind and want to care, I can tell you about Mr. Young's story. Check behind that picture."

Antoine slipped the knife on the table, and took down the picture of a dragon from the stone wall facing the door. Hoolie never moved for the knife while Antoine peered through the tiny hole not able to see much. It was another tunnel or room. A Chinese man in suspenders and a cap passed by the hole rolling a barrel like the ones he'd hauled around at Clement's Ranch, hanky sticking out of his pocket. He had a horrible limp yet moved quickly. His clothes were patched. He slumped forward but pushed hard.

"If you wait, you'll see Mister Young," Hoolie said. "He works harder than anyone down here, dragging things from one door to the next. Never sees light and gets paid less than the blokes at the livery barn because he's Chinese, no other reason. He's trying to get enough cash together to bring his family over and open up a business. He explained it to me, but I have no idea what it is, but it sounds right swell. You still gonna tell me you don't care? Because there's a light around you that says what you see angers you."

A light? Antoine glanced at Hoolie. Was he a gifted one? Like Myles? Like Uncle Silver?

Hoolie continued, "No one wants to know what happens down here, Mister. Not even me, but it happens just the same, and so we put up paintings of scary dragons and help ourselves. You gonna be like everyone else who comes down here?" He handed the painting back to Antoine. "Let me know if you need anything. Poker game going down in thirty minutes with the best booze in the province. Heck, might even be the only booze in the country." Hoolie lowered his voice. "I even know where the good foxes hide, if you catch my drift. That will cost you more than a knife, 'cause them memories ain't cheap."

Antoine noticed the knife was gone but he hadn't seen

Hoolie move for it.

"I have to mingle with my other guests. See ya later, Mister."

Antoine tossed the painting on the bed, thoughtful. Maybe Hoolie was right, maybe he wouldn't be in this mess if he wasn't just looking out for himself. "Hoolie, wait. Your mother knows you're down here, right?" he asked before Hoolie got around the corner.

Hoolie paused to think about this as if it was the most important question he'd ever been asked. "My guess is that mothers think their boys work at the livery barn for one coin a month, but what do I know?" He smiled at Antoine. "I knew you cared."

Antoine sat on the bed after Hoolie left and took a few deep breaths. Fights everywhere he looked. Why couldn't it be easy?

A click made him jump to his feet. He peered out the door. A lantern was across the way so he had a good view of the tunnel.

Mathew carried a big box and vanished in the shadows.

Marie was moments behind him.

"Pst." Antoine opened the door and called to his sister.

"Antoine? What are you doing down here?"

"They killed Henri."

"What?" Marie approached him, but Antoine didn't dare repeat himself. He brought her in the room with him.

"You can't stay with Mathew, Marie. The nasties who hired Mathew did it only to get to me. If I go back and bring my fiancé home with me, they'll kill you." There. It was out in the open.

She sat on the bed, her hands in her lap. "Look how pregnant I am."

"So? It hardly shows yet."

"So? Use your brains, Antoine. I haven't been married long enough to show at all."

All the crosses were down. She wouldn't see the priest. *I waited as long as I could.*

Antoine rubbed his head, starting to understand.

"I met Mathew after. I slept with him, told him it was his, and he married me. Convenient. I explained this to you before, Antoine. This is what love is. Forget your dreams of happy forever and find someone who gets you through the rough moments."

He was ready to give her a speech on keeping her skirt down but thought better of it when she wiped a tear. He was basically in the opposite problem. She might understand why he needed to get to Emma. "Tell me about this baby's father," he said.

"I was dizzy that night. It didn't make sense so I went to bed early. Woke up in the middle of the night, and there he was on top of me. No idea how he broke into the house." Marie shivered. "You have no idea what it's like Antoine, to be that powerless."

He was feeling his own type of powerless these days. "No, Marie, I don't. But I know what it is to fight with all my strength and still fail." Antoine hung his head, ashamed that he hadn't been there for his sister.

Marie put her head up, her jaw tight and for a moment, she looked like Sacri. Just her posture, her pride, her determination not to let anyone tell her what to do. "I'm in their den as one of them, and when I pull the trigger it'll be to vanish that prick who did this to me."

"Revenge?" Antoine was surprised. "This is not our way."

"I want him dead." Her words echoed around him in a whirlwind.

"You'll know him when you see him?"

"He was marked for judgement and his voice was raspy."

Antoine closed his eyes. "Tommy. Bugger has a rough voice. Like he gargles gravel for breakfast. Means we have the same problem. Help me with Clement and I'll help you with Tommy." He was a dead man.

"Go home, Antoine. I don't want you involved in this. They're hunting *Cîpay* but I don't understand why."

"So Mathew is one?"

"Since I married, no one has been by to ask to buy Depaix land. Means they think they have an in."

Antoine glared at his sister. "I don't like this."

The door opened and Mathew stood there with a confused look on his face. "I thought I heard you in here, Marie. Antoine? What are you doing here?"

Antoine pounced on him and they rolled to the floor. Marie shut the door.

"You hit her, I hit you." Antoine smoked him one and went to pull out his knife but it was gone. "Damn. I wanted to mark him. You got a knife on you, Marie? I'd like to let the world know he'd rather be dead."

"You're the one marking ghosts with those horrible scars?" Marie leapt up. "They look like *Cîpay* marks of death."

"*Ouais.* Give me a knife."

Mathew squirmed under him so Antoine put his knee deeper in his gut.

"*Cîpay* are afraid of what the ghost hunter might do," she told him. "They say such a mark is for the dead. It is a ceremonial tattoo given to request a second chance for a loved one. Another life to try again."

"They are dead so I marked them as such. Fitting, if you ask me." Antoine glanced up, and Marie grabbed his arm.

"You marked Vince," she said.

"So?"

"He's not the same since you marked him. These tattoos are powerful, you must beware."

Antoine didn't care about Vince. "Boohoo cries the ghost hunter."

Mathew tried to say something but Antoine shoved his foot in his groin and pushed his knee in him deeper.

Marie was quick to whip out a paper from her skirt and scribble something. "I'm leaving you the address for the rally tomorrow. You should join us in our fight for better wages. Read both sides of this."

Antoine frowned. Was she serious? "Marie. I don't want to fight anyone or anything. I want my wife." That wasn't entirely true. He wanted Clement dead, too, but in the end, if he had to choose between the two, he'd take Emma.

Marie whispered in Cree, "Run, Antoine."

Her warning came too late. A man in a sheet was behind him. Antoine looked up to see a metal rod coming at his head. As he fell, the world swirled in, and he could have sworn that was Hoolie hiding under the bed.

–Sixteen–

Things were happening so bloody fast in these tunnels that Hoolie wasn't sure what was going on. Mister said he was looking for his sister so why talk to trouble like the Reward Hunter? He stayed low to the ground, looking for his chance to get Mister outta this mess. He was his mark and like heck was he letting that dame get the reward. She stole his last two marks from under his nose and made them vanish. She looked helpless, too, but he knew the truth. That light around her was mean and he didn't want it to ever touch him.

"Get Mathew up," she ordered to the weirdo standing there in a sheet. "And take that sheet off. Why are you wearing that down here?"

"What about the savage?" The sheet dropped on Mister.

"He just about killed my husband," she said. "You're a hero. Let's get Mathew something to drink."

They vanished out the door and Hoolie rolled out from under the bed. He laid the sheet out and rolled Mister on it and dragged him in the side tunnel. Wasn't he wearing a cap? Damn. Hoolie slipped back in from the hole under the bed and was ready to snag it when the dame returned.

"Antoine?" She crouched to pick up the hat and met Hoolie's eyes under the bed. "Give me one reason why I should let you live, rat." He watched her outreached arm; there was a tiny cross tattoo peeking out from her lacy sleeve. Who the heck was this woman?

Hoolie watched her light. It was terrifying. He lay back and closed his eyes. "My first memory is about a French bugger manning the boilers in this tunnel. I called him Papa and followed him around, learning things. At night, I'd wander into the Chinese opium dens to stay warm. Oh and there was a Danish fellow who I trailed behind for a spell. A guy like me is alive by a hand only a Higher Power understands. You kill me, what's that gonna do for yer beliefs, Madame?"

Her light calmed and she reached for the letter on the desk and flipped it over. It was a Wanted flyer for Mister. "See this man, rat? You send him home. One ticket to Eau Claire. I double this reward. No one needs to know but us."

Double? Could he trust that? Her light was steady with the promise. She dropped six bills into the cap she held. "When he's home, you get the rest."

"Home?"

"I assume you'll find your way around Eau Claire tunnels." She dropped the cap, and the bills spilled out. Each one had a zero on it. Cripes. He snatched one up. He had no idea they made bills with a zero on them.

She walked out as if nothing had happened.

"Wait, what ya want with Mister?"

"I want him out of the way so I can do my job." She shut the door.

Damn. Did he just get a job from the Reward Hunter? The one dame he swore on his mother's grave to avoid? He shot up from under the bed and went to follow her out, but she was already vanished. Who the heck was that dame?

–Seventeen–

Hoolie. Yup. That was Hoolie swirling around Antoine.

"Damn Mister, you scared me."

Antoine groaned. His head felt like a horse ran wild in it. Even his tongue was heavy, but he managed to say, "Did my sister leave an address?" He tried to sit but fell back. His head was too heavy.

Hoolie shoved something in a pack he had with him and Antoine touched his head. It was cold and bandaged. Had the boy cared for him?

"Your sister isn't down here, Mister. Nothing but trouble down here today. What you need is to go home."

"Can't. Doesn't exist."

"Great. Why not?" Hoolie helped him up.

Everything was blurry. "It burned."

"Build a new one."

"Even if I do that, it won't be home without my girl and my sister."

They walked into the light and Hoolie said, "Well that sucks. I'm supposed to get you home. How do I do that if you have no home?"

"Where am I? Train station?" The platform was crowded but in his blur, he saw a ghost standing there. No, not a ghost, just a fool in a sheet, mocking his family's beliefs.

"Yeah. Bunch of people coming for this rally because the threat of prohibition is suddenly real and what everyone wants, especially the guys down here making booze. Means more money. So everyone is curious what's happening. Look at that idiot walking around in a sheet in broad daylight. Can you stand on your own?"

Antoine let out a big breath as he studied the field behind

the train station. It was clearly where the rally was being held. Endless faces gathered. He wouldn't need the address after all.

Using a trick Sacri taught him so he wouldn't get lost on the open prairies he studied the crowd, picking out one thing from each face that made them memorable. Black hat. Feathers. Dimples. Bandaged hand. He smirked and nudged Hoolie. "I gave that guy a scar on his hand while he was strung out on heroin."

Hoolie's beady eyes grew and it reminded him of how Myles looked at him—as if seeing more than the fool standing before him. "You crazy? No one messes with Vince. He's fair, but damn, is he tough."

"Hey Vince," Antoine called.

"Shh. Don't call him over. What the heck is wrong with you? You just go around looking for fights?"

"Feeling better?" Antoine asked Vince.

Hoolie let his arm go and stepped back. Antoine wobbled for a moment.

Vince flashed a nickel at Hoolie. "Take a hike, brat, us grown-ups need to talk."

Hoolie shuffled his feet but didn't grab the coin. "I ain't been paid yet for helping Mister."

"I count to three and my nickel goes. One, two, three." Vince shoved the nickel in his pocket and turned away from Hoolie who was tight against Antoine again.

"You live," Vince told Antoine while he pressed a knife against his ribs with his good hand. "Looks like you've seen better days, though."

"Where is my sister?" Antoine demanded.

"Hit the fields." Vince met his eyes in his I'm-boss-around-here way. "Boss says if you get out of hand, she gets it."

"What does that mean?"

Vince shrugged. "I got this prick headed my way who plans to explain it to me. How I see it is that, if you work with me on this one, we both get this oaf off our asses. I like to do things my way. I don't need a mother hen pecking at me."

"Mister, you need a hand?"

"Nah Hoolie, you can scram. Vince and I understand each

other."

"I ain't been paid yet for getting you home." Hoolie pushed between Vince and Antoine, shoving the knife down.

"Brave. I like that." Vince took a long look at Hoolie. "I've always liked you. Step back, boy, and I'll hook ya up working for the boss. Earn you top dollar. I like your determination."

"Cash later don't make up for cash earned now. I need to feed my crew, too, Mister Vince."

"Here." Vince tossed the nickel at Hoolie. "Go shine your shoes."

"This Mister pays better than nickels and dimes." Still he picked up the nickel he'd covered with his bare foot.

"Oh, I see you need to buy some shoes. Here then." Vince pulled out a bill. "Don't say I don't take care of you."

Hoolie grabbed it and ran, dashing through the crowd.

While Vince paid off Hoolie, Antoine vanished in the crowd, too. If Marie was gone, he'd better hunt for her. No need to talk to a lost gopher like Vince.

Antoine got in line for tickets but left when he saw Vince talking in his suave way to the man selling tickets.

Dammit.

Antoine let his eyes travel the crowd, no idea what to do. Where was Marie?

He couldn't risk taking Emma off the ranch with Marie still within Clement's easy reach. He didn't like his odds. Torn, he faced the sea of faces that couldn't help him.

"Pst. Mister."

Antoine looked up.

Hoolie was on the station roof. "Check your pocket and don't worry about paying me, I took my own tip." He flashed the dollar Vince had handed him.

Antoine found a ticket in his pocket to Eau Claire. How the heck did that brat know where he was from? He was surprised to find he actually had a dollar on him and his knife was where it usually was. He examined the dollar, sure he'd given his last one to Hoolie.

He turned to thank Hoolie, but the boy was nowhere in sight.

PART THREE

MONTHS LATER

"Remembering is easy, knowing what to forget is hard."

–Sacri

-EIGHTEEN-

Months passed as Antoine searched for his sister. Antoine didn't even know what day of the week it was anymore. He finally stopped his search and stood looking at Depaix Farm, feeling the strain of this hunting. Judging by the chill settling in at night and the hum of the skeeters out by the creek, he guessed it was close to September.

The dog rushed to meet him. He was healthy. The barn stood steady, the old horse wandered outside as if waiting for him. Antoine stood in the ashes, remembering what was. It felt like another life. Like his house, Marie was gone.

Antoine went to investigate. It didn't really surprise him that someone from town had come to look after these things. Henri's sister hauled straw to the stall. He couldn't even remember her name, but she stopped when she saw him. "You're back." Her freckles danced excited as her smile grew. Like Henri's used to.

"You got big." Antoine's eyes swept over her. She was a woman. "How long was I gone?"

She giggled. "I'm sixteen. Grown-up with no time for a life of my own. You got big too, but you need a bath. I'll warm you some water."

He couldn't look at her. "Henri was a brother to me."

"That's why I take care of you while you're off on your rampage. He would have wanted that." She kept working and Antoine helped.

"You're a good kid, helping out around here," Antoine said. "I owe you."

"I might be young, but I know how it works in Eau Claire." She paused mid-action and stared at him with the same dark green eyes as Henri. When their eyes met, all he thought about was Henri and he had to look away.

"I better head home and tell Maman you're back. She'll want to talk to you. No one will tell us anything about what happened to Henri, just that he died outside of a church. Some are saying you killed him, but I don't believe that. Maman hopes you'll work the land out by our place this year, but she'll be too proud to ask. Without Henri..." She rubbed her sleeve along her nose and sniffled.

"I'll take care of it. No need to ask."

She took a deep breath and pulled herself together. "Are you home now? For good?"

"No. I have to..." Antoine had no idea what he had to do. His sister had vanished and if he went for Emma he risked her life.

"You could marry." She gave him a weak grin. A tiny angel.

Marry. Would Emma even look at him now? She was in trouble because he was so stupid. He was back to where he'd started, without a clue how to walk her out of Clement's grasp. Did it matter? He had to get to her regardless. "*Ouais*. That's probably the smart thing to do. I'll be gone for a bit longer to see my girl. If you keep watching this place like this, that horse will love you more than me." It was his way of offering her the horse she cared for.

"I gotta go." She pushed past him and rushed off. He watched her go. *Jill*. Dammit. Her name was Jill.

Searching the barn, he found the booze his pa had hid away for special occasions. With the bottle, he went to the cellar. Antoine tossed up the cellar door, then climbed down the easy steps that Sacri had insisted Pa build. This was where he'd stay while he drank himself into a stupor, obsessing about his failures. Seeing Jill had done nothing but bring back the pain of losing Henri. Seeing his house in ruins reminded him how he couldn't get Emma. Where would they live? He was nothing but a disappointment to everyone he loved. A failure.

It was a basic storm cellar. Nothing fancy, not a place he liked to visit, but now, it felt perfect. A hole he could bury himself in.

Yup home. Hoolie was happy enough underground, why

couldn't he be?

Antoine pulled up a chair and sat in front of a candle. Tomorrow would be for planning. Today was for drinking. He set the bottle in front of him and a draught put out the candle. He relit it and opened the bottle.

The candle went out again. *Odd.* He stared at the candle as if it could explain things to him. Where would a draught come from in his storm cellar?

Antoine lit the candle a third time. Sure enough, it flickered and went out again.

He had a lantern somewhere and got it going. Then he lit the candle again and watched how the flame danced.

A breeze teased it from behind the jam shelf.

Antoine investigated the strawberry jam his mother had made before she died. He checked the date on it but it was faded and he couldn't make it out. Had it been that long since he'd eaten jam? He opened the lid and went to stick a finger in it to prove to himself that he wasn't afraid to eat the jam. That he wasn't avoiding things that reminded him of his failings. Yet he couldn't do it.

Antoine leaned against the wall. He took the bottle in one hand and the jam in the other, debating which to down first. The booze was the easier of the two to swallow. He leaned against the shelf and it shifted before he'd taken a swig.

The wall actually moved.

Antoine left the jam and booze on the table and pulled back the shelf to stare down a tunnel. A chilly tunnel. Where the heck did it lead?

"All tunnels are built because someone needs to get from here to there," Hoolie said, so matter-of-fact, in his numb mind.

The lantern guided his way, confirming what he thought. A damaged moccasin was in the dirt. A skill game made of a long needle and bones that he'd played as a child to increase agility was hidden along the wall. He found an old pipe, arrow heads, a basket made of bark. *Cîpay.* So this was how they moved around unnoticed, vanishing in the oddest places. It wasn't a coincidence that Pa built his home here. He was protecting Sacri's secret. This was why Depaix land was sacred.

Could Antoine be like *Cîpay?*

Antoine walked for hours, not sure where he'd end up. *Probably in a collapse somewhere.*

They were nothing like the tunnels in Moose Jaw. These were carved in the dirt, possibly made by natural causes, yet beams made of trees held things steady.

Not enough beams, if you asked him. One little quake and this would come down. *Not many quakes in Saskatchewan,* he promised himself. Still. Would only take one. He examined the beams. They had things carved into them. Names. His family name. Words in Cree. Images of birds. Images of people running. He ran his fingers over the markers.

Some side tunnels were buried, collapsed, yet the main tunnel continued. Had his father ended up in one of those tunnels? He had an urge to dig through them, to find him. Yet Antoine pushed on, knowing it wouldn't change anything if he did find him, just bring up the pain again.

Better to leave that buried.

It ended at a ladder.

Antoine took several deep breaths. Where would he come up?

Slowly he pushed the trapdoor and peeked out.

He was in a cemetery. It was morning.

He'd walked all night?

Antoine shut the trapdoor and sat on the dirt floor of the tunnel to think.

Cemetery. What cemetery was near his house? It hadn't looked familiar. Underground he might have turned many times. It was hard to tell. Still, he knew the cemeteries by his house.

No. Not by his house. A night's walk.

Cripes. He'd crossed the border. If someone from this side needed to come up in Canada, Sacred Land or Depaix Farms would give them a secret, safe way to do it.

He looked up at the trapdoor as he realized the truth. *Useful.* They could use this tunnel to travel from Canada to the States and back again, unnoticed. This was why Clement needed him to cooperate so they could move their outside business across the line, underground.

What were they smuggling? Had Clement killed his pa to get his hands on these tunnels? They'd been watching him, leading him to Clement's Ranch. No wonder he couldn't find decent work. They were one-step ahead of him. They found Marie a hubby who would ensure he cooperate. With Antoine dead, Mathew would inherit the land and they'd be in business. That meant... Marie was safe enough as long as Antoine was alive.

Don't let them get this land.

Antoine climbed the ladder and walked into the sunny cemetery. It came up along a shack with a simple storm cellar trapdoor.

The town was small, unknown to him, but he found the church easily.

A Cree priest swept the steps and he dropped the broom when he saw Antoine. "*By the light of me*! You're Sacri's boy. She talked about you. I haven't seen her in years but her soul flashed through me when I saw you. Look at you."

"You knew my mother?" Antoine asked.

"That why you're here?"

"Sure, I mean... I don't know what I mean. Maybe. How did you know her?"

"Come in, Sacri's boy. I'm honoured. Would you like tea?"

He brought Antoine into a small shack with no furniture except a bed, a table, and two stools.

"I was at home, ready to drink some... and well, I stumbled on this tunnel that led me to your front door. You wouldn't happen to know about that, would ya?"

"I might. Sit." The priest sat across from Antoine, serious. "Things need to be built; railways, tunnels, roads. The cheaper these things are done for, the more we can do."

"Sure, I guess."

"So you agree with meager wages or room and board not fit for a cat in exchange for this hard and sometimes dangerous labour? Or would you say these are jobs that curse those who don't have any other options, for whatever reason?" He sat back as if that was an explanation.

Antoine thought about what he was skirting around. "You not telling me that my mother helped you free slaves through those tunnels? Which way?"

"Both ways." He sighed.

"That explains a lot, actually. Strangers always popping up out of nowhere around our place. I always thought *Cîpay* dropped them off to annoy Pa."

"By sneaking them across the border we're making sure they don't end up back where they don't want to be. Make sense?"

"*Ouais.* I wouldn't want to go back too badly."

"A slave who's found again is lynched as a trader, or worse, they are mysteriously vanished," he explained to Antoine. "I've sent many to search for them, but they are truly vanished to hell, and I can't access that place."

A few more years, maybe Sacri would have walked Emma onto their farm. Yet instead, God led him to her. They were destined to meet. This thought warmed him.

"Who built the tunnel from here to my barn?" Antoine asked.

"God. We protect them. Sacri and I grew up in those tunnels. Handy for travel in the winter, when the snow deepens. Like underground roads."

"Why didn't she tell me?"

His eyes swept over Antoine. "*Cîpay* hear when ready, see when prepared, believe when enthralled." Now he sounded like her.

Antoine rubbed his dirty hands over his face. He was fighting a war his mother started. So much for his happy forever.

He stood. Enough messing around. This changed the rules. "Point me to the closest train. I know where there are slaves who want to walk."

–Nineteen–

While the sun set, Antoine walked onto Clement's Ranch. His hands were sweating. He had no idea what to expect.

Beast growled. Nothing had changed. The place still pissed him off. "It's just me, Beast. It's been a while, but come on, we slept together, I saved your life." It was dark but he saw the shadow as the dog paced around him. Antoine gave him a sour look, then to his surprise, the mutt leapt at him and licked his face. "No one pay you attention since I left, or what? Now be quiet, I have to find Emma."

After his weeklong journey and a full day of waiting, Antoine was tired and starving but he couldn't wait to see her.

Not a soul in sight so Antoine sneaked around back and searched the servant quarters. He found his jacket tossed on a trunk and opened the trunk to find it filled with an aroma of Emma. He dropped to his knees, taking in the earthy fragrance.

By the dust covering everything, the room hadn't seen life in a while.

His gut was in knots. Where was Emma? What if she didn't survive?

Impossible.

He couldn't imagine the world without her. Yet he couldn't imagine her not taking his jacket. She'd been so pleased in it. He slipped it on, and was surprised to feel how snug around the shoulders it was.

Giggling echoed through the house from the second floor. Someone would know where she was so he followed the laughter.

Antoine walked into an upstairs room, quietly, shotgun

raised. Franklin had Mable pinned against the wall, her hands over her head in his one hand while the other ran over her naked body. Once again, he had his pants around his ankles.

"Just once, I'd like to see your face and not your bloody ass."

Franklin paused. "Haven't heard that complaint in a while. Thought you'd be dead by now. You got twelve lives or something?" Franklin turned around slowly, pulling Mable behind him, then he hitched up his pants. "What the heck are ya doing here?"

"Came for Emma," Antoine told him.

"She vanished months ago. I left her out by Pleti where she begged me to let her go on her own so she could get away from you."

"Clement here?"

"Hell no or we'd both be dead right now. I expect him home soon. Said he had a surprise for me. Kinda hoping I can marry his daughter. I've been on his invisible-list ever since I lost Emma. Of course, I told him *Cîpay* attacked us. That made him right crazy."

"With good reason," Mable corrected him. "Everyone should be afraid of them. They are the ones who vanish our servants and Mom."

Antoine tossed a paper on the floor, his gun still on Franklin.

"What's that?" Franklin gestured to it but didn't move.

"I want Philip and Gracie brought to that address."

Franklin chuckled. "Then you bring them there."

"This woman needs you to save her," Antoine told him.

"I don't care about anyone," Franklin said, but when Mable hit his arm, he added, "Except Mable, I mean."

"Oh, you'll care. It'll take Philip to save her, since you're afraid of snakes. Call it my twisted sense of humour, but I find this here little joke funny."

"Snakes? I ain't afraid of nothing. I'm smart, they're bad omens. Last one I saw was near Emma and she plum vanished after that." Franklin took a step. Antoine got ready to fire but Franklin bent to pick up the paper. "You son of a bitch."

"Oh it gets worse. Clement knows you were messing with

his daughter. Should you be here when he returns with his little surprise for you?"

Franklin grabbed Mable's dress and tossed it to her. "We gotta scram. I should have known something was wrong."

"You're taking Philip and Gracie," Antoine said.

Franklin shook his head. "They'll slow us down."

"You'd leave your own mother with them bad omens so you can escape? The woman who gave you birth?" Antoine hadn't done anything to Franklin's sweetheart of a mother, yet Franklin wouldn't know that. Once there, Philip could make them disappear on his own.

Franklin crumpled the paper. "Double-fence-twisted-frigging prick. You... Tell Philip to get his shit together. We're leaving in ten minutes. They ain't there, they're left behind."

Antoine had the name of a town. It was all he needed and he stormed out excited, because if Emma was in Pleti, Doc would know where.

-TWENTY-

Head down, Emma listened to the story the Sister shared. She had spent many months in the convent connected to Father Kilby's church and she felt much better. She was just tired all the time.

A shadow loomed over them, but neither woman looked up until a hand ripped away the Bible Emma clutched. The familiar teardrop tattoo forced her eyes down as Clement sat beside her.

"I see you've picked up bad habits." Clement flipped open the Bible. "Oh yes, I love this story. God tells the fool to sacrifice his son and he goes to do it. Idiot. I would send Satan himself back to hell for a son." His voice quaked a touch each time he said son and it made butterflies in Emma's tummy. "How did you end up here? Those pricks dump you off? You have any idea how hard I searched for you?"

Father Kilby stood in the distance. Emma got up. Determined to put distance between her and Clement, she went toward the Sisters' quarters. Men weren't allowed in there.

Clement was inches behind her. "Where are you going? You got things you need? Talk to me."

She walked, eyes closed tight, and prayed to God to make Antoine take his place. She couldn't tell him she didn't want to go back, yet she couldn't go with him. Not ever.

"Emma, look out." Clement tried to grab her arm, but she pushed forward quicker. She opened her eyes a moment too late. Her head caught on the open door where Father stored things for mass.

One of the Sisters stared at her, horrified. "I'm so sorry.

People don't normally fly around this corner."

Clement slipped his arms around Emma almost instantly. "She's fine. Nothing but a bruised cheek." His fingers lightly grazed her cheek. "Speak. Tell her you're fine."

She was not fine. The pain in her cheek was nothing compared to her broken heart as the truth invaded it.

Antoine had not come.

God would not save her.

She'd waited months for Antoine. Months. Did Antoine abandon her? Would she have to marry Clement after all? She wanted to yell for help from Father Kilby, but Clement carried her off and all she could do was lean into him, crying tears for herself, for being so stupid.

Antoine had not come.

"I'll pray for you, child," Father Kilby said somewhere in the distance.

She wanted to ask Father Kilby if he'd heard from Antoine, but... *I know what's good for you.* Was this what was good for her? Why did she still want? Diggers don't want.

"I'll pray for you, Father. I'll pray for you," she yelled as Clement hauled her off.

"You'll pray for him?" Clement chuckled and set her in his buggy. She curled up in the back and he flung a blanket on her. "The prick thinks I'm his god. All I see is a sissy-ass church girl. Don't worry, I'll knock that right out of ya."

"I'll pray for him to go to hell with you," she spat under the blanket and that made Clement laugh even harder.

"That's better. I'm not too worried about hell, seems *Cîpay* made a pact with their god that I'm not to stop breathing until I learn something impossible. Kinda makes me feel invincible."

The buggy still didn't move. Emma curled up tight. She was petrified. Gracie talked of diggers who'd gone un-vanished. They'd been shamed; one was burned alive. What would he do to her?

Clement moved in the front.

The buggy was still.

Even after he pulled off the blanket and stared at her, Emma stayed silent.

Clement's eyes softened for a moment. "We're gonna

surprise Franklin." He grinned his crooked teeth smile. "Lucky for you, what *Cîpay* haul off I fight for harder."

She waited for his verdict as he leaned over the seat and said, "How's your cheek?"

"Throbs."

He wet his hanky from his water container and handed it to her. "Put cold water on it, sometimes that helps."

"Can I sit up front with you?" She was uncomfortable in the back. Her stomach pushed wrong. Her legs ached. Even her back didn't like this.

He glanced at the blanket on the seat beside him, then around town. "Don't be stupid. Best snuggle under this blanket where you're safe." He handed it back to her, with the water.

Safe from what? But already he turned around and drove away. They rode for a while and Emma pulled her damaged necklace out of her pocket and held it tight. Maybe she needed to pray harder for God to save her. Would He hear her out here in the middle of nowhere?

~~

When they stopped, Emma crawled out, aching.

Darkness loomed.

"Dark enough, eh?" Clement asked.

Her belly pulled her forward as she stumbled from the buggy. Clement was there, blocking her path to freedom.

Too dark. She needed to see him.

"No one needs to know but us, right?" The blanket dropped around her feet. Hot hands clamped on her hips, pulling her toward him. "Let's start in the buggy." She smelled his breath against her. His lips, sloppy and heavy searched for hers.

Using the cross in her hand, she lashed out at him with all her force. It was instinct. She prepared for the hit that would follow.

"Dammit." He let her go. "How rough can we get?"

Emma rushed into the dark, sucking in gasps of cold night air.

She ran. Bare feet. Dirt and rocks pushed her forward.

Clement tight behind her, reaching for her arms, her skirt.

Then the blanket draped over her head and he pulled her back violently. She twisted, falling into his arms and he fell to the ground with her.

It hurts less if you give in. Why was she fighting?

She squirmed back when Clement grabbed her ankle.

"Stop fidgeting."

Kicking.

Crawling back.

She would not give in.

"What the hell is wrong with you?"

Hot hands yanked her back and Emma realized too late that her screams echoed over the prairies searching for Antoine like little beacons of light.

"Antoine?" Clement pulled away, but kept a hand gripping her ankle. "He left you. Is this what it's about? You think that fool is coming for you?" The grasp around her ankle remained firm but she felt the disgust in Clement's voice.

Emma ripped the blanket off her head. She could hardly see Clement in the moonlight. Why didn't he ever do these things in the day so she could look at him? Then again, maybe she didn't want to see him.

"Stay away from me. I'm married." She tightened her body, waiting for his grip to loosen around her ankle.

"You still believe those lies he told you? You're so stupid no wonder you need me. I'm the one who searched for you. Me. Pisses me off that you think he cares about you. He doesn't. He's the one who took you from me and hid you at that stupid church. It was a scheme to get to me. Now come here, let me keep you warm until it gets light out and you disgust me again."

As soon as his grip loosened, she kicked. She knew better. This time he swung, meeting her leg.

"Damn. You want it rough tonight? Because you're pissing me off." He pinned her legs down.

It hurts less if you give in.

Yet not a muscle in her body would let her lie back and take it. For the first time, in her mind, she begged Clement not to continue. Could she say these thoughts out loud? Would he stop? Before she could form the words, her skirt slid up and a sharp pain ripped through her stomach.

Clutching the necklace tighter, fright filled her. *Not tonight.* The cross slipped from her hand as the pain wrapped around her stomach.

"Clement!"

"That's better."

~~

Emma lay still, breathing through the pain. She couldn't take it anymore and got up. Clement clicked his gun but she didn't care if he shot her. She needed to walk. She stood against the buggy. It was freezing yet she was sweating.

She had to escape before the next pain hit. Before he wanted her again.

Emma reached for her necklace for strength but it was gone. Gone.

She was spent. Hurting. Dying as her insides tore her apart.

She couldn't remember when she lost the necklace. Where. Everything was a blur of pain she couldn't escape. She rubbed her back. It hurt everywhere.

Her dress was in tatters. Her feet frozen.

So cold yet she was sweating.

Her stomach tightened again. She tried not to cry out but it was impossible. It was too much. She was drowning in the pangs of hurt.

"Ahhhrgh." She crouched and a gush of fluid warmed her bare feet. She knew what that meant. What this pain meant. She'd seen enough childbirths. This baby was coming *now.* Emma searched the buggy for more blankets. There had to be more.

She fumbled in the dark.

Nothing.

She hated the dark.

She hated Clement. He made this happen. Why couldn't he leave her alone? Why did she think God would help her? Clement was right, she was evil.

It was cold. She searched the horses for their blankets. Suddenly, a rough hand was on her shoulder and she smelled him. Like wine. "If you're cold, why did you get up? Tell me these things." Clement whispered along her ear, making her grip the blanket in fear. "Mmmm. I missed you. Your smells. Your soft skin." His hands were inside her torn dress, touching her. "Not a doubt in my mind it'll be a boy." He ran a hand over her hair. "You'd better fix that dress before morning so I don't have to look at ya. I have to go for a spell, but I won't be long."

"Married," she choked out. She elbowed him and he pushed up against her roughly. Too close. She needed space.

"Soon we will be. Married in the night."

"Antoine." The word was barely a whisper but Clement tensed.

"You say his name to me one more time I'm gonna be forced to toss you in a hole to think about things." His hands slid over her torn dress, finding her tender breast.

A cramp knocked her to her knees as she gripped the blanket. Emma screamed, needing Clement to give her room. The horses came around her, as if offering protection. She fumbled for the ring on her finger but it was gone, too. "Antoine." It was over. He was gone. Left her. She was dying.

"You'd choose the hole over me? Fool is what you are. Pining for the dead. It's you and me, girl. Just you and me. Get used to it and if you say his name again around me, I take my son away after he's born. I'll find a real woman to raise him while you rot in that hole, thinking about what you had with me. I see now what my old man meant, ungrateful wench is all your kind are."

Crouching with her hands deep in the dirt, she laboured. Feeling the pain of her loss. She couldn't do this right now. It was too much, all coming at her at once. Why wasn't she dying?

Rope came around her ankles, binding them so she couldn't walk. Couldn't labour.

"No." Her word was lost in the ache. She could no longer argue, her fight was gone, her focus on her unborn child.

"Oh yes. Now behave. I won't be long." Clement pulled her arms behind her and tied them. Then he took her in his arms and laid her on the ground, wrapping a blanket around her. "Stay warm until I return to heat things up again."

On her side, Emma caught her breath between cramps. Working before the next one stole her focus again. She shook off the blanket and rolled on it. The horses crowded her. She heard them, felt their warmth but they were nothing but shadows hovering around her. Too close, yet... their presence was welcome.

She moved slowly, as she spread out the blanket. It crumpled around her.

The binds had to come off. *Now.*

She screamed for Clement. Prepared to do anything he asked. Anything. She needed her freedom to labour.

Had he left her alone to die on these prairies?

"ANTOINE!" Her scream ripped through the night.

–TWENTY-ONE–

It grew cold. Nights were always the worst. Antoine needed sun. He stood on the path to Doc Williams' house out by Pleti, when a terrible chill swept over him. It was more than cold. It was... pain. He rubbed his stomach where the ache rested, but it deepened intently. What was wrong with him? He'd never experienced sharp pains like this before.

Down on his knees, he ran his hands into the healing dirt. He focused on the uneasy feeling, breathing in the peace as Sacri had taught him.

Flashes of Emma filled his thoughts. What was wrong with her? Was the baby coming early? He hadn't expected it until the snow flew, at least another month.

He calculated how much time passed but he had no idea what month it was. He settled on September. Closer to the end of it.

Still. Her screams tore him apart. He could hear them in the distance, as if she was lost in the dark. "Emma?" He called out into the night. Antoine was on his knees, trying to hear in the dark. He let his eyes scan the horizon.

Shadows moved.

Someone knelt beside him. "Always yell into the night, young buck?"

Antoine ignored Doc and focused on the shadows around him. He'd heard her. He saw things. It was far away, but he'd heard her.

"Glad to see you survived. What are you doing outside my house in the dark talking to yourself?" Doc placed the lantern between them.

Antoine met Doc's eyes. "Did you hear anything?" Antoine wasn't afraid of much, but he was afraid right now.

Powerless. "Someone is hurting her. Please tell me you know where Emma is. How come I feel her pain like this?"

"Myles said you were linked. That happens sometimes."

"Why?" Antoine scanned the prairies again.

"Maybe so she doesn't have to feel the hurt alone."

Antoine took deep breaths. "Am I crazy?"

"Come inside. Myles is making tea, the way you like it, with brown sugar. He can explain these things better than me."

"The gifted one is here?" Antoine didn't know Doc protected him. Was he *Cîpay?*

"Of course." Doc frowned, looking annoyed with Antoine, but before he could say anything else, a shadow flew from the bushes. Antoine didn't hesitate, he fired the shotgun he'd left beside him, aiming low, but making dang sure he caught skin.

The blast echoed around them, and they watched several run off. Antoine shot a few more times, and a couple fell with a cry.

"You shot men on my land." Doc didn't sound too upset.

"Wounded, not killed. You're the doc, fix them up, or let them bleed out on the lawn. That's your choice." Antoine got up and clicked open his knife so he could mark each one.

Doc was quick to his feet and grabbed the lantern. "I'd better get Myles, you're a handful tonight. I almost liked you better when you couldn't walk."

Before he took a step, Antoine heard it again. His name. Damn. She wasn't far. "Get me a horse. Now."

–Twenty-Two–

She was not in the safest place but the horses were huddled tight and Emma couldn't move anyway. She was warm.

Exhausted.

She couldn't do this. The sharp pains were too close, not giving her time to prepare. She needed to open her legs more, use her hands.

Argh. It hit again.

She didn't know how to make this pain stop. This thought scared her more than anything. She would die out here and who would look after her baby when it was born in the cold dirt having torn her apart? *God, please help my baby.* Panicked, she screamed for Antoine again. This time, her voice was so coarse it came out as a whisper followed by sobs she couldn't stop. She was going to die giving birth.

Warm hands slid along her ankles and her legs were free. The relief was instant as they parted naturally.

She stopped crying when someone sat her up. Her arms were free. Warm hands against her stomach.

The sun?

"Antoine?" she mumbled.

"Emma."

Was she dreaming? Dead? Had the pain killed her?

She turned around and gripped his shirt. It was him. It was Antoine. A final dream before she died. He felt real. His heart pounded under her fingers. He *was* real.

Anger burned inside her. Where had he been? She pounded her fists into him. Panic. Fear. Anger... all her emotions escaping at once. "Get away from me," she yelled, the tears streaming anew, yet she was tight against him, wishing she could cry all over him.

She didn't care if he hit her back. It felt good to release her anger on someone.

His hands came around her gently. So gently, she stopped. Why wasn't he hitting back? He wiped her tear stained cheeks.

"What did he do to you?"

"You left me," she shouted accusingly. "You got me thrown from the farm and now I have to go to the hole because I can't marry him. I am a digger who wants. I must be punished." Emma clutched her stomach and screamed. The pain was deeper inside. "Make it stop," she yelled at him, frantic.

"Whoa, breathe. Cripes. You're in labour. Let me help you."

The pain eased off with the sound of his voice.

"Stay away from me." Her voice was distorted, even to her.

Antoine held her. "Emma, I would never leave you willingly. Ever. You need help, so relax against me."

"Ever?" She wiped her tears and searched his face for a promise. The moon shone bright enough for her to see him. It had been dark moments ago. She glanced at her bare feet and her ripped skirt. It was as if Antoine brought light with him wherever he went.

"Ever. Our bond is so strong that I found you in the dark. Let me help you. I know what to do."

He knew what to do?

Instantly, she relaxed.

He knew what to do. He found her. God answered her prayers. "Can you make the pain stop?" she asked.

"No, but I'll teach you how to use it."

She leaned against him, sure she was dreaming.

"Breathe with me." Antoine's voice was shaky, but it was him. He was under the horses with her. Warm. Safe. "Breathe with me, *ma belle*. Start this over again. Make this next breath our first one. Together." He wrapped his jacket around her. The one she'd left in her room. He'd come back for her.

–TWENTY-THREE–

Antoine created a sheltered circle for Emma with his legs, so her bottom wasn't touching the ground and he held her completely. Behind her like this, she rested against him and he could feel the baby move. He sat steady, like a wall for her to push against.

"Comfy?" he asked.

"I can't do this," Emma sounded weak.

"You are doing this. You're almost done doing this. You're strong. I feel the baby. Focus on that." Antoine moved her hands so they were low on her belly under his.

"I feel the baby move." Emma's voice was full of love, even in her panic, and through all this pain, that love was still there and it amazed him.

He had to help her through this. Antoine wracked his memories for guidance. Pa had taken him to watch a calf birth. *"Out on these prairies, son, there are no doctors for our women. We're all they got. So you're gonna learn to birth a baby properly."* They performed a caesarean on a horse and he had helped when Josée was born because Marie was too afraid to go into the room. *"Come in, son. Remind her how strong she is."*

Antoine had been afraid to go in, yet he'd followed Pa.

"When she can't breathe, I'll breathe with her. Sometimes, that's all anyone can do."

Antoine remembered every detail yet he had no idea what to do to help Emma as she leaned into him and pushed. He held her knees, pulling them back. She was too tense. "Relax your entire body, even your toes. Breathe with me. You're doing well. Just breathe. Feel my chest moving behind you? Focus on that."

She matched his rhythm, as if they were one.

Antoine rested his head against hers and she grabbed his arm and held him for a moment. "I can't believe I was this close to you and almost didn't find you."

"How?" she breathed the word.

This was good, she was talking. Even one word was a good sign.

"I thought the screams were in my mind, but I came anyway, and much to my surprise, the moment I headed into the darkness, the moon escaped the clouds and I saw the horses."

Emma tensed again and he ran his fingers along her belly. Antoine continued to talk, needing her to relax. Something had her afraid. "Breathe in and out with me. I'm here. You're safe."

"Not ready."

"Life comes. Sacri said a woman follows the cycle of the moon. Tonight the moon is strong and bright, when the clouds let it shine, that is. Trust your body. This child moves, trust your wee one." Still, Antoine thought about the babies Sacri had lost before Josée was born. So much could go wrong.

"If it's a girl... hide her."

"He's got you crazy with that. Our baby will be safe. I got you. Would you like me to share a story so you can relax?"

She rested against him. "The moon will bless this child. Tell me about the moon." Her breaths were still even with his.

Afraid, Antoine whispered the story against her cheek, trying to get her mind off her pains. "Long ago, there was no moon, only a glow ablaze in the sky, manned by a dying soul. He asked his children to keep the fire burning after he died. When he didn't return, the grieving children fought, as siblings do. The daughter believed that as the oldest, she should be responsible, but the son believed such a job was for a man to do. The world went a long time without warmth. Finally, a disappointed God flung them to the heavens so they could see why their father cared so deeply.

"From the heavens they looked down, amazed that the light their father had provided was used for so much. The son believed the light was for warmth and the daughter believed it was for guiding their way. So the siblings each took the responsibility of providing the world with light. The son, he exploded in the heavens, eager to warm the days and the daughter lit the dark skies at night, following a pattern that allowed her the freedom to return to earth and be a mother to her children. She looks down on us tonight with that motherly love and strength, and thanks to her, I found you. As a mother, she believes you can do this."

Emma hadn't whimpered through his entire story. He had no idea which parts were Sacri's teachings or Pa's anymore, the story made sense in this moment and so he told it for Emma, hoping it would help.

Clouds stole the moon from them again and the wind picked up.

Emma grabbed his wrists and leaned into him, but didn't moan or scream this time. Just a solid push. Things shifted under his fingers. "Catch our baby," he said.

"I can't."

"If you can't, I will do it for you, but you must try." Antoine moved his cheek so it touched hers. "This is what Sacri did. She pulled my sister, Josée, out while Pa held her like I got you." Antoine guided her hands. "My hands are with you, I'll be there when you can't. We'll do it together but a mother should be the first to touch the child she nurtured inside her. Only you know how to ease the pain. Guide our hands, if I do it alone, in this dark, I risk hurting you."

Emma put her head into his shoulder and without a sound, she pushed. She was sweating but he came around her, sheltering her from the cold night. Antoine didn't like this spot under the horses, but it was warm, and he wasn't sure how she'd ended up there.

The horses didn't seem to mind, in fact, Myles' mare crowded them too. Were they protecting her? Never again would he question the smarts of a horse. His respect for them deepened.

Emma took several quick breaths while she leaned forward, focused on what was happening. He knew that if he let her control things, it would go better. He didn't have to get involved if she was strong enough. Yet all of him was tense, ready.

"He's beautiful," she said, but Antoine had no idea how she could see anything. The moon hid and it was suddenly so dark the child was a shadow, yet he didn't question it. If she said they had a son, he was sure she was right.

"We have a son?" His hands guided the child up, warm around his tiny body.

"A boy. I did it. I made a boy."

It annoyed him that she was still worried about pleasing Clement but he kept his thoughts to himself. For now.

~~

Emma slid the child under the jacket, against her bare skin.

Antoine held her, waiting for more cramps. It wasn't over, but she relaxed against him as if it was and he kissed her hair—instinct. "You did it. I can't believe how strong you are. Relax, you'll experience a few more pains. It's normal. Is our boy warm?"

"Safe."

The moon came out again, enough for Antoine to see the outline of Emma's proud face. Their eyes met and he said a silent prayer for them.

~~

"Emma, you're tired, but I have to get you to my friend, he's a doctor."

She cuddled against him, the baby between them. He kissed her forehead and when she looked up, despite the darkness, he saw her perfectly. She was so beautiful. He'd almost forgotten about her beauty in his search for her. "*Je t'aime*." His love rolled out of him in French. "Can I get you anything?"

"No one gets me things."

"How can they if you never ask?" He placed his canteen to her lips and she drank eagerly. "Why are you out here alone?"

"Clement is probably asleep."

That prick was here while she laboured and he left her tied up and did nothing? He gripped his knife, and left her on the blanket with his jacket covering her. Time to face that son of a bitch. "Stay here, I'll make sure it's safe."

The moon peeked and a faint light tickled the horizon as the sun promised to give them another day. Between the two, the world came alive around him. Antoine walked around the buggy and found a messed blanket. Blood and semen stained it, but Clement was nowhere in sight.

He kicked at the blanket, frustrated.

A warm glow caressed things on the prairies as morning crept up. Antoine glanced around thoughtfully. Where could Clement go? Should he wait for him to come back or steal Emma and run? He wanted to wait, but Emma needed a warm bed, food, water, clothes. Their son deserved better than this.

They came first.

Antoine scanned the area, searching for anything to give him a location. They were in the middle of nowhere. Not a tree for shelter, not a rock for locating himself, nothing but open prairies. It was almost as if the void itself could be the marker of this area.

A gold speck glimmered by the blanket. He knelt and unearthed his cross. By the blanket, he spotted his mother's ring.

He threaded the damaged chain back together—though it was too short for Emma to wear—and he cleaned up the ring.

Had she taken them off? Ache in his stomach ate at him.

Fear.

This was his fear—that Emma didn't feel this connection. That his feelings were an illusion his mind created. What would he do if she didn't want to return to Eau Claire with him?

~~

Emma was under the horses, wrapping the child. She was awkward with him, not like Sacri had been with Josée. For some reason, this made Antoine smile. They could learn to care for the boy together.

Antoine ripped the blanket off his horse and tore it so it kind of looked like the wrap Sacri used. "I'll show you how to sling the child so he's tight against you. He'll be warm that way and safe." Antoine walked toward her.

"Clement?" she asked.

"Gone. Vanished. Either Clement left you to die or someone picked him up."

"I heard nothing. One minute he was here, the next he was gone."

"There isn't anything in sight. The closest farm is Doc Williams' and I can't even see it from here. Why would he leave his horses and buggy?" *Not to mention you.* "Did he go for help or something?"

"Myles?" Emma smiled at Antoine, hopeful. "Are we close to Myles?"

"You know Myles?"

"Yes, when Franklin left me, I ran to his farm and he helped me."

"This is where Franklin left you?" Antoine scrunched up his eyes again, trying to see what was different about this spot on the prairies. "This is where Clement picked for camp, too. Son of a gun. Gophers always run home."

"What?"

"Tunnels. There must be an entrance. It's why they camp here. So they can make a quick escape." Antoine knelt beside her. The horses left. "Your colour is good. I'm proud of you, Emma." Antoine held the blanket, prepared to show her how to wrap it, but she was lost in the child so he gave her a minute to enjoy her happiness.

She'd earned the moment.

"Come meet him." Emma glanced excited at Antoine. "He's perfect."

Antoine was scared to look at the boy, but her smile was so radiant he couldn't refuse, and he brushed her cheek where it wasn't hurt.

Clement was a dead man.

Antoine glanced down for a peek, but she shoved the boy at him. He fumbled, not sure how to hold someone so wobbly. So tiny. Naked. Antoine couldn't help it, he smiled, too. "He looks strong." How could someone this small be so strong?

"Charles," Antoine blurted out.

"Charles?"

"Of course. He's strong, he deserves a powerful name." He met her eyes. "I mean... I... call him what you want, it's the name that came to me when he looked at me."

"It's perfect. Charles it is. Our little Charlie."

Ours. Antoine cradled him in one arm and took out the chain. He slipped it over his neck. Antoine beamed as he looked over the boy he planned to raise as his own. "He's tiny. Tiny but powerful. I'll show you how to wrap him and we'll get you to Doc. Are you sore? Can you walk to the buggy? I can carry you." As he passed Charlie back to her, their fingers touched innocently and both paused.

"Can I sit in the front with you?"

"Where else would you be safe?"

Her eyes studied his lips. "Clement took the ring you gave me." Tears fell and Antoine touched his forehead to hers. "I know how important it was to you. To me. To us. I'm sorry, Antoine."

"The moon and sun were out for a second together and their combined magic brought it back."

Ever so slowly, Antoine moved in for a kiss. Just a light one, while they held the baby between them. He slipped the ring back on her finger and her kiss deepened.

–Twenty-four–

Myles paced. His cane made the most irritating noise. Click. Clink. Needing him to stop, Antoine tossed the cloth at Myles' fancy black shoes so he'd pick it up. There were times for pacing; this was not one of them.

"Will you two stop it," Doc snapped. "She's sleeping. Your worrying gives me a headache."

"It's that buggy." Myles picked up the cloth and tossed it back at Antoine. "We can't leave it out front. We have 'nough trouble with these fools. Now they were shot on our land and ye got them in our bloody clinic. I want that thing off our property."

Antoine went to take care of it, because the last thing he needed was Myles convincing Doc to kick them out.

"Where are you going?" Doc followed him out.

"To dump this buggy in a slough and let the horses go," Antoine said. "What ya think I'm gonna do? Just keep an eye on Emma."

"I'll help you. Myles is worried enough for us."

"You saved those guys?"

"I'm a doctor. I can't think about revenge. That never works. Besides, I believe everyone gets their own, eventually."

"They gonna live?"

"One won't walk the same. Not as much damage to his hip as Myles suffered, but enough that he won't be enlisting."

"Did you know them once you pulled the sheets off?" Antoine asked.

Doc studied his hands.

"Did you?"

"Yeah. My wife's brother was one."

"You're married?" Antoine scratched his head, confused. Where the heck was his wife then?

"Many moons ago. This young girl I caught throwing up behind the barn at the farm where I was working. She was ill and pregnant and needed a good father for her baby so I played the hero."

"You got a child someplace?" Antoine asked. "A wife?"

"Nope, they died a week after we married. It's what pushed me to study medicine. Turns out, if I had known then what I know now, and with the skills Myles has, well... we could have saved them. Frustrating to know I was that stupid."

"Did you know the others?"

"One is from a farm four miles that way." Doc pointed south. "He brought his daughter over one night for supper in hopes that I'd be interested. Think he took it the wrong way when I sent them packing. Shortly after that the attacks started." Doc took a deep breath. "The third one I don't know. He had a graze so I let him go this morning. I had to stitch a scratch he had on his face, but that wasn't from you. The fool looked like he fought a savage cat. Didn't want to see his ugly mug anymore. Told him to go back to the hole he crawled out of since he was a filthy mess."

"Want me to apologize for shooting them on land you think you own?" Antoine climbed in the buggy and pulled up the straps.

Doc got in beside him. "No. That won't be necessary. I ran into a pain medication shortage at the hospital, so really, they aren't in the best of moods. I've been having a hell of a time getting supplies these days. On top of that, they're withdrawing from some type of drug... It's the strangest thing."

"Ha. I meant to you. I ain't sorry for shooting them. Just sorry I involved a guy like you. Still, it's nice to know who the guys making your life hell are, eh?" Antoine started the buggy at a slow trot. "So you pissed one off, and they all came after you. They're acting like tribals."

"Except they won't let it go. They get a touch more daring each time. Nothing serious, at first. Burned words on our lawn to offend us. Last month, we lost a cow. Showed up branded with *Nancies* across it. Poor cow. I mean really, who would do that to a cow? Between the attacks and my missing medical supplies, no wonder Myles keeps to himself."

"How'd ya meet the gifted one?"

"At the University. I was studying medicine and he studied everything possible. The guy is a genius, fluent in seven languages. They called him the voodoo man. Anyway, day we met, I was in the library searching for a book on herbs when this banging caught my attention. This door in the top corner held the fan, and well, when I opened it, there was Myles, bound and gagged in his underwear. Someone had shoved him in, a prank I guess, to see if he could escape with his voodoo magic."

"And so you played the hero again?"

Doc chuckled. "I suppose I did. Glad I did, too, everyone deserves one happy moment, right?"

Antoine looked at him surprised. That's how he felt about Emma. "Sacri said it's normal for a protector to care deeply for those they keep safe. Pa said that we'll find our happy moments with those we care deeply for. So if I slam their beliefs together, it only makes sense that we find happiness with those we protect. The two become one."

Doc nodded. "I do seem to have a soft spot for people in trouble. I like how Myles sees the world, and it annoys him how I don't. Just enough so he sticks around to set me straight."

"What happened to Myles?" Antoine asked.

"About a dozen fists. Probably a few boots, too."

"He got a shit-kicking, did he?"

"A few too many. The fact that he exists seems to tick most people off. My theory is that the world isn't ready for a guy like him. He's not afraid of what he sees in himself, in others. Instead of looking at you in the hospital and having me medicate you, he said you needed nature to heal, and bloody hell if he wasn't right. The minute we brought you outside you improved. As I said, he's a genius. He sees the world so differently, that scares people."

"Gifted ones are usually outcast and misunderstood. But I like him. He's..." What was the word Antoine wanted? "A pissed-off happy."

"Ha. That he is."

"So... how long should we stay?"

"Emma will let you know when she's ready. No hurry, you're welcome to stay as long as you want. Myles adores Emma and I can tolerate a handful like you if I tolerate pissed-off happy day in and day out."

"Feels good to have her near me again. All perfect inside, ya know?"

"Like you were someone stupid before," Doc agreed.

~~

They rode the horses bareback to Doc's farm.

"If Myles don't want these horses, I'll bring them home with me," Antoine said. "Damn. She moves as if made for me. She knows this area well, too. I can't even imagine the work I could do with a horse this well-bred."

"Clement has nice horses," Doc agreed. "But I prefer my car, sorry."

Deadly silence greeted them as they pulled up to the farm. The usually inviting farm screamed at them to run.

"I'll settle these fillies in the barn," Antoine offered as he dismounted.

"I'll check on Emma and Charlie," Doc said.

Charlie. He liked that.

The horses pulled, not wanting to follow Antoine in the barn. Trusting them, he let them go out back and opened the door carefully to find out what had them spooked. He searched the ground for a wild animal and was so focused on the stalls he almost missed the feet dangling in front of him.

No. His entire world slowed down until he didn't feel like he was moving.

A sheet hung from the beam in the middle of the barn.

Antoine recognized the fancy shoes under it instantly and backed out of the barn for air. He needed air.

Breathe dammit.

"Hey young buck, there's no one in the house." Doc came toward him. "Weirdest thing, Myles left his cane. Where would they go?"

"Stay back. Stay back." Antoine rushed out, letting the barn door slam. He pushed Doc back. "Get in the house. I'll bring him in."

"Who? Myles? Myles. Let me see. I'll help."

"Get in the house. I will beat the hero outta ya to keep you back. Now is not the time for you to play hero. I'll bring him in. Find Emma. Focus, breathe. They could still be here. I don't need you dead, too." Despite his panic, Antoine turned Doc toward the house.

Doc swung and it took Antoine off guard. He almost didn't duck in time, but Doc caught his shoulder and Antoine tackled him to the ground. They wrestled for no more than a moment and Antoine pinned Doc face down in the dirt. Still, Doc had hit him hard on the shoulder. Exactly where it was tender.

"Nothing you can do or I'd let you in." Antoine wouldn't budge. "Now go home."

He let Doc go and stood back, guarding the barn while Doc walked to the house in a drunken silence.

~~

Antoine held the cane. It was heavier than it looked. He didn't know what to do with it. It made him think about what he'd done. How he'd lost a gifted one. How he'd climbed the beam to cut Myles down. How upset Doc was.

Some things needed forgetting, but as Antoine watched Myles lying on the bed so lifeless, he knew these images would forever be a part of his soul.

His gut twisted with the failure.

Doc stared at him in silence.

"Doc, I need to find Emma and Charlie. Can I make coffee or something for ya before I go?" He hated leaving him, but every moment he wasted, his family got further away from him.

"Sorry I hit ya."

"Surprised me," Antoine admitted. "Didn't think of you as a scrapper."

"There are some people in life who you'd die for, but Antoine, there are very few you'd kill for." The threat fell on Myles' body.

Antoine dropped the cane and the clamour vibrated his

thoughts. "Sorry." Antoine picked up the cane and placed it by Myles. "Sorry I made you eat dirt, but you didn't need that image. Remember your friend when he was happy." He prepared to leave, but Doc sunk to his knees by the bed. With a heavy sigh, Antoine sat beside him. If only there was something he could leave Doc with... with his hand on Doc's shoulder, Antoine began to sing his healing song. *"Peh---taw."* The sorrow rolled over him. *"Peh---taw."*

Doc laid his head on the bed so Antoine couldn't see his pain. Antoine's voice trembled with the melodies of grief. Until nothing was left to sing.

Doc clutched the cane in silence.

"Cîwêw... Cîwêw." The melody was a whisper that swept their pain out the door.

"What was that?" Doc's voice was soft as if afraid to break the mood surrounding them. "It was so... peaceful."

"The Song of Sorrow. It's how my soul heals itself when nothing else save death can."

"Yeah. Myles would have loved a trick like that."

"Better than those drugs you shove at people, eh?"

"Instead of making me numb, it forced me to feel. I had no idea pain like that existed in me. I feel so angry."

"This is normal when we lose someone who touched our life," Antoine told him. "Pa said the same thing when Sacri returned to the earth."

"Who is Sacri?"

"My mother."

"You didn't call her mother?"

"Ah no. *Cîpay* don't believe in titles like mother or son. Everyone is connected through the earth with a bond that holds them firmly in place, yet allows them to share experiences."

"Italian?"

"Sacri?" Antoine smirked sadly. "No. She wouldn't stop screaming when she was a baby and this French priest wandered on the tribe, lost, saying *'ça cri'*, which means 'it yells'. Well, her grandmother didn't know what he was saying and thought this strange white wandering man had been told her name from the heavens, and so they called her Sacri. I miss her a lot. I guess that's the price of love."

Doc gripped the cane and swung it with a flashing growl, shattering the lantern by the bed. Antoine didn't move. Now that the sorrow was gone, the anger would be intense.

It filled him, too, but they needed to use that anger to find Emma and Charlie. "The longer we wait, the further they get." He should have been protecting her. So many things he wanted to go back and redo.

If only he could forget.

Restart.

Antoine used a soothing tone, despite the panic gripping him. "Let's start from this breath. Now that we have the wisdom, we can fix this."

"Nothing to fix." Doc glared at the mess he made of the lantern. "They branded him."

"To mock *Cîpay* tradition. This is a message for me."

"No. This is a message for me. We've been living hell for a while now because of these so called ghosts. Myles said they were afraid of us but that makes no sense to me. Myles didn't deserve this." Doc touched Myles' lips, as if he might tell him what happened. Doc looked beaten, exhausted, and confused. "How do I fight fear?"

"Takes understanding. I know this guy, Franklin, he's afraid of snakes. Stupid really, because a snake is just a snake, it can't be anything else."

Doc tilted his head as he thought. "The fear comes from not understanding? So why direct it at the subject?"

"Because inside, we're all frightened boys who can't admit that something so simple frightens us. I don't think he should pick up snakes or anything." Antoine shrugged. "But if he learnt about them, he'd understand that his fear has nothing to do with the snake itself, it's all in his mind. Until then, I told him to just let me handle them."

"I've never had anyone make it so clear for me. So, you aren't afraid of me, right?"

"You? For real?" Antoine was surprised. "Why? 'Cause you hit me when I thought you were gonna hunt the pricks who did this? Why are we still sitting? This anger you feel, use it. Let's find Emma and Charlie."

"Doesn't anyone scare you?" Doc's voice was numb.

"Only person in the world who scares me is Emma. That's

not because she's scary at all, it's because I lose control when she's around. I turn into a moron who tries to pour himself all over her. If such a thing were possible, I'd have done it." He eyed Doc up. "Why would you scare me?"

Doc sighed. "I keep thinking about the guy I let go this morning."

"What about him?"

"He had a tattoo much like these burns on Myles. Is he telling me that he did this?"

Antoine ran his hand through his hair. He'd grazed Clement with that bullet? He told Doc about Clement. "Truth is, if Clement was here, it had nothing to do with Myles, but me."

"I should have left them to bleed to death." Doc was pale. "Emma said something about others vanishing." His jaw was tight.

"Priests know everyone's secrets. Where is the closest church?" Antoine demanded. "Anyone will do."

"Town not far to the north has a Catholic church, we'll start there. Father Kilby, I think. Myles went to pay him a visit after Emma left us. He said he was hiding something. Boy, does he dislike him. I mean disliked." He turned to Myles, as if expecting him to argue his case. "Dammit, I can't believe he's gone. Is it possible?" He sat on the edge of the bed and Antoine stopped in the doorway. "We had so many plans. So many things we were gonna do. We were going to Canada next month. Part of our yearly trips to search for his son. In case he survived. Funny how he held on to that hope after all these years." He looked up at Antoine.

"A father's love is that strong." Antoine didn't want to see him get lost in the grief again. He had to go, but he couldn't leave him like this. "Father Kilby is the one who landed me in your hospital. If I talk to him, he ain't gonna answer except to spit out teeth, so you'd better come with me, keep me calm."

"Now you plan to beat up a priest?" Doc glanced at him.

Antoine calmed instantly. "No. I suppose I could try and be nice." He took a deep breath. "I'm going." Antoine turned to leave, sure Doc would follow, but there, in front of the door was a shadow of a wolf. Cripes. Antoine stepped back.

Images of Josée's death flashed at him: the wolf attacking her, him hauling her tiny body back to Sacri, hunting the wolf.

Doc was talking but Antoine kept his eyes on the shadow as it paced in front of the door. "I'll stop by town," Doc was saying. "Tell his mother. We can bring Myles there. She'll want to see him. I think." Doc sighed. "Maybe not. You know, he said our soul was nothing but pure energy, light, and when we die that light merges with the world. If this were so, why can't I feel him around me? Sorry. I don't mean to burden you with my grief."

Antoine pushed up against the doorjamb as the shadow rushed past him on a mission to get to Doc. The wolf paced in front of Doc, eyes locked on Doc.

"I don't much care if you talk about it. I know what it's like to lose someone I felt the need to protect. My guess is that you don't feel him 'cause he went to shadow his son. What I would do, ya know, make sure he's safe." Antoine shoved his hand in his pocket so Doc couldn't see it shake. "When I lost my sister to a wolf, Sacri said death was a passage to a new life that makes us one with the world. Might be true, but I never found comfort in that. So I hunted the monster that took her life. Only... "Antoine stared at the wolf. Much to his surprise it growled at Doc. The sound brought back the horrible memories of their battle.

"Killing that wolf never ended the pain," Antoine admitted. "In fact, it deepened it. Sacri said I now have to live with his shadow until I learn what I did wrong. Perhaps, when someone becomes part of our journey then vanishes, we should miss them and not try to fix things. Not look for revenge. I'll bring you to town and you can grieve with his mother. We'll meet at Father Kilby's church in three hours. That work for you?"

Doc turned sharply and Antoine ducked as the wolf leaped at Doc and went right through him in a blur. At the same instant, Doc gripped a chair and threw it into the wall. It exploded into pieces. That's exactly how Antoine felt inside. Shattered.

Antoine approached Doc, quickly. He placed a hand on his shoulder, afraid to look for the shadow. "I promised Emma to protect her son as if I was his father and already, I failed. Twice now I lost the only woman I want to breathe with at a time when she needed me most. Doc, I need your help. We can't go back and fix Myles, but Emma and Charlie are in danger. You know this area, you know these people. I can't do this alone, but I will try."

"Antoine, you didn't fail them."

Feeling braver, Antoine searched the room for the shadow, but it was gone.

–Twenty-five–

Antoine rode out to the open prairie where Charles was born. The horse halted and Antoine dismounted. He walked the area, kicking up dirt. *Clunk*. His boot hit a wooden plank covered by loose soil and rocks.

More tunnels, hiding in plain sight.

Antoine shoved the board aside and dropped into the hole. He found a lantern. After he lit it, Antoine was surprised to see a narrow path under the earth. He'd have to duck, and he had no idea how a big guy like Clement had managed to fit through. The walls were made from light orangish clay that sprinkled itself all over him. It reminded him of Emma's arms when he'd washed her.

Holding the lantern in front of him, he pushed through.

The path split in two directions. With no idea which one to take, he studied the ground. Both paths looked well-worn so Antoine tried to sense which direction he faced, but he had no idea. Possibly north.

He was debating things when a warm body slammed into him. "Cripes Mister, is that you?" Hoolie grabbed him as he steadied himself.

"Hoolie?" Antoine was shocked. "What the heck are you doing down here?"

"Long bloody story that probably won't end well. But, you need to move. Take the right path, stay to your right at every turn. And I'm sorry, Mister. I really am. I didn't know that troublemaker was your sister, I swear. Once I found out I did everything I could." Hoolie took the path to the left and vanished in the dark.

His sister? "Is Marie down here?" Antoine called after him.

Antoine considered following him but then took his advice

and went to his right. He could always double-back. It didn't widen up and at some points he had to turn sideways or his broad shoulders rubbed the dirt walls.

When the path ended, Antoine moved the lantern around. The ceiling was solid, the walls firm. What the heck? He glanced at his dusty feet. Sure enough, a plank was there. He moved it aside and dropped into a second chamber. This room was clearly a basement. The walls were made of stone and scattered about were wooden crates.

He opened one of the crates and peered inside. Bibles. Confused, he shut the box and searched for a way out. A stone stairwell led up. Antoine rushed up the steps and stumbled into a church.

Sanctuary.

Yet why would a tunnel run from a church to... nowhere? He needed to go back, find out where the other tunnel led, where Hoolie had gone. He turned around and ran smack into Father Kilby.

Antoine clenched his fist and smoked him—instinct. His pent up anger flew out of him. Father smashed into the wall and rubbed his jaw. "I suppose I had that coming, and then some, but I don't have time for you. I need a doctor. A boy, he brought a woman in last night, beat and bleeding, she's in labour, and I'm not sure she'll survive. He said he was going for help, but hasn't returned."

"Yeah, he does that. Take me to her. Doc Williams will be here shortly."

Father Kilby rushed through the church, leading Antoine to a tiny room with only a bed.

"Marie." Antoine hurried to his sister.

Her beautiful curls were plastered to her sweaty forehead. "Eh-eh-hé," she mumbled.

"She needs water. A pitcher of cold and a pail of hot. Go," Antoine yelled at Father to get him out of his hair.

What was wrong with Marie? "Look at you." He bit his words.

She had a black eye, but even weirder, her eyes were over-dilated. It made him think of Sacri before she died. Was his sister dying? Antoine lifted her hair and examined her neck. It held a bruise in the shape of a large hand.

Everything in him exploded. He had to help her. She was all he had left. He couldn't lose her, too.

"*Moi?* Look at you. Antoine, you're a mess," she slurred.

He was filthy. "Can I slip behind you? You need support, and I want to feel what you're feeling, see how bad it is."

"I... I fell out of the wagon."

"Sure that's what happened." Just once he'd like her to be honest with him. He crawled in behind her and held her tummy as he'd done for Emma. She wasn't as far along as Emma had been.

"Breathe with me," Antoine said. "Focus on me, and we'll deal with your pains after."

"Things are swooshing. Swimming."

He didn't say what he wanted. Clearly, she was in no shape to hear it. "Breathe with me." Antoine sat with Marie for hours. She dozed off. "Marie. Stay with me." How could she sleep at a time like this? He needed help. Something was wrong. Unlike Emma's, her stomach was tight.

Doc Williams burst in the room. He paused when he saw Antoine holding her.

"This is my sister, Marie," Antoine told him. "Something's wrong."

Doc felt her tummy and checked her eyes. "She's drugged. Do you know when her water broke?"

"No. She's not making sense. Are you sturdy enough to help her?"

"Plenty of time for me to wallow in my own pity later," Doc mumbled. "Marie, can you hear me?"

She grabbed his jaw. "My own angel, about time you showed up."

"A doctor. I'll lift your blouse." Doc looked, then peeled it back for Antoine to see, while he listened for a heartbeat on her stomach.

Bruises screamed at him. With a few quick breaths, Antoine controlled his rage enough to say, "Can you help her?"

"I'll do my best." Doc rolled up her skirt and rubbed his chin thoughtfully.

Antoine saw the bruises on her legs. "Makes me want to kill him to see this."

"Him who?"

"Her husband."

"Consider what you told me about the wolf, because if you do kill him, be prepared, when the anger dies, you must live with that shadow of a memory. Seeing the fear in his eyes will remain with you in the dark, in your happiest moments, and locked in the eyes of those who love you. It cannot be forgotten nor can it be undone. Revenge is the breath before a damnation of regret, nothing more. So think before you proclaim yourself ready to judge who is worthy of this air you so selfishly breathe." His jaw was firm when he spoke.

"Damn. You went to the clinic and did them pricks in, didn't ya?"

"There are moments in a man's life that he hopes to forget, just let him forget, young buck. Think you can handle that? By the looks of you, I assume you found something."

"Tunnels." Antoine told Doc how he thought they were using the tunnels to get around. "Tell me, Doc, what do you see?"

"Judging by the amount of blood, the placenta came loose. She can't push with the amount of drugs in her and there's no activity. Yet she's in active labour and needs to push."

"No activity?" Antoine felt a lump growing in his gut.

"Doesn't mean the child isn't alive, could be weak, but be prepared. I have to operate and it might not be good for either patient."

"A caesarean?"

"Yes." Doc sounded so confident it gave Antoine the courage he needed.

Antoine rested his head against Marie's. "Tell me what to do. I only ever seen one done on a horse, and she didn't make it."

"First we need to put her to sleep and you need to wash up. I keep clean clothes in my car. Change."

~~

"Antoine?" Marie asked.

Two days later, Antoine was dozing in the chair at the church beside Marie and jumped to attention, reaching for her hand when she called out to him.

"Where am I?"

Antoine rubbed her hand. "A church."

"I feel weak. I burn everywhere." She felt her tummy. "My baby. Where is my baby?" She tried to sit, but couldn't.

"Rest, Marie."

"My baby?"

"Your daughter's soul has returned to dance among the spirits of the prairie. She was strong, but there is only so much an infant can do when her mother is breaths from death."

Marie let his hand go and stared at the ceiling. Not a tear fell. "You can't hate me as much as I hate myself."

"I wouldn't be here if I hated you. How could you let it get so bad, Marie?"

Father Kilby walked in.

"Get out," Antoine said without looking at him. "Get out. If you walk in here again, I'll run your damn fancy, ill-gotten car in a slough, I swear."

"Please." Father Kilby sounded sick. "What will it take for you to forgive me?"

"I'll meet you in your office," Antoine told him.

"Antoine?" Marie watched Father leave.

"Sleep. I'm handling it. Doc Williams has a car. He'll drive you to his place. It's not that far."

"The angel?" She relaxed. "You're coming, right? Please don't leave me alone with anyone."

He needed to find Emma. Antoine stood and Marie grabbed his arm. "Antoine, buried alive is how I see him."

"Probably not a good idea to say that about your husband in the house of God."

"Why not? He sees in my heart anyway."

~~

A week later, Antoine was back in the tunnel, exploring the other paths. Marie was still at the clinic, but she got along with Doc wonderfully. Besides, helping her kept Doc's grief manageable.

Much to Antoine's surprise, the tunnel came up not far

from Doc's farm and branched off to several farms along the way. This was of no help to him. Emma could be anywhere.

"Antoine, if you're sick of hunting gophers, why not make the gophers come to you?" Pa had been right about those gophers. It was time to turn the tables on Clement.

–Twenty-Six–

Antoine added wood to the stove in his storm cellar. It was a cold January, and Depaix Farm hadn't seen snow like this in years. He'd made himself a cozy nest. By day, he worked on his new house. Pounding nails. Nails. One after the other.

At night, he sat in his storm cellar, waiting for one of Clement's gophers, counting his nails for the next day.

His friends from town had been by to help, and his cousin Bernoit had spent a few weeks helping him. Henri's sister kept coming by. Despite the snow that layered the ground. Despite how he put her to work so she wouldn't freeze while she talked nonstop about things he didn't care to listen to.

Yet it was nice to have company, even if it was someone who made him feel guilty.

Henri's sister. He kept forgetting her name. Antoine was numb inside. Just doing what he had to.

He hung a cross on the wall over the bed with one of his precious nails and checked to make sure it wasn't crooked.

Suddenly, the door opened and a bundle fell down the steps into the cellar with him. "Damn. It's cold out." Hoolie shook himself off.

"Hoolie?" Antoine was surprised to see the boy in the middle of a snow storm.

"I'm frozen." Hoolie stretched and grabbed a blanket off the bed. "I'll be outta here by morning, just running an errand and got caught in that mess out there. Nice place you got. That you building the house? Is that your new home?"

"What the hell are you doing here?"

"Long flipping story that ends with me frozen on your bed. Is that your home or not?"

"It will be home, once I get my girl here."

Hoolie curled up on the corner of the bed. "Mind if I stay? I'm so blasted cold."

"I could use the company."

"The girl hanging around you all day today, the one with the brilliant light around her that dances when she talks, is that her? Is that your gal? I never seen light like that. It doesn't fit with yours."

Again with the light. "You mean you see her soul?" Antoine sat beside him. "Do you have the Sight?" Myles was gonna... Myles was gone.

"Shh." Antoine jumped up before Hoolie could comment. The shelf moved. He'd put a chair in front of it to slow whoever came by. Antoine dimmed the lantern and took out a knife. A long one so he wouldn't have to get too close.

"Door's stuck. Hold on," Franklin grumbled as he banged against the shelf from inside the tunnel.

In the dark, Antoine pulled out the ampoule that contained a shot of morphine and prepared the syringe. Then he stood off to the side behind a shelf and hid. He couldn't see Hoolie in the dark, but the boy seemed to take care of himself just fine.

Franklin stumbled in with Mable in tow, holding a lantern.

Antoine waited behind the shelf, pulling a towel from it. The lantern brought life to the room. Hoolie was nowhere in sight, the blanket he'd curled up in was on the floor.

"Place looks lived in. We'd better scram. Sit by the stove, it's warm. Here, give me the lantern. I'll make sure the coast is clear." Franklin left Mable.

Antoine was on her before she could pick up the blanket. He pushed the needle through the soft fabric of her jacket, hitting her arm muscle while covering her mouth with the towel. Then he hauled her into the tunnel.

Antoine moved quickly. "Shh. Not a sound. Close your eyes and let me do the running."

Antoine kept his hand on her mouth as he carried her off, but once her body went limp, he flung Mable over his shoulder.

Antoine didn't need a light in these tunnels anymore and he moved through them with ease. He carried Mable through Cross Passage and into the church. He still hadn't figured out why all tunnels led to a church. It was a curious thing. Maybe Clement was onto something. Maybe the church was corrupt. Or maybe they were sanctuary. Regardless, he brought Mable there and laid her in a pew. He'd lost her hat but she was in one piece.

Father Hillsdale came out with a washcloth, drying his hands on it. "Antoine? I thought I heard something. What are you doing out and about in this storm?"

"Cross Passage."

Father cleared his throat and glanced around, as if the walls had ears. "I see you've been exploring."

"Here, I brought you a package. Keep her safe. She's drugged."

Father Hillsdale glanced at her as if used to seeing drugged women in his church, hauled around in the heart of the night in a storm, no less. "Huh. So who's to claim this one?"

Antoine thought about this. "Me."

"How deep?"

"End of the earth if you can."

"I even have contacts that promise me hell. Get."

Antoine raised an eyebrow, curious what that meant, but Father Hillsdale went to the back of the church and opened the confessional. He pulled down a box, and went back for Mable. "You're still here?"

"Don't you wanna know what's going on?"

"I know all I need." The priest looked calm.

"I... I mean dang it, I don't know what I mean."

"Go."

Antoine rushed back to the basement and climbed in the tunnel that led to his farm. When the breeze from the main tunnel touched him, Antoine pulled back to listen closely.

Franklin searched one of the side tunnels, making his way back to the main one. He sounded like a bull on a rampage. His movements echoed.

In the dark, Antoine searched for the markers on the beams. When he was as close as he dared, Antoine pulled into a side tunnel and searched the ground for a nice size rock.

He waited.

Franklin's light approached.

Antoine whipped the rock low.

"Dammit!" Franklin cried out as the glass from the lantern exploded and Antoine got behind him.

Antoine slipped his hands around Franklin's neck, then yanking Franklin to his feet, he shoved him against the cold wall so his face was tight against it.

"Tell Clement I'll exchange his daughter in the same shape as I get Emma."

"Antoine? You're alive? Wait."

"I'm the only one who claims her. I die, so does Mable. Emma dies, so does Mable. My sister dies, so does Mable. He touches Emma, I touch his daughter. Think you can handle a message that bloody simple?" Antoine vanished in the darkness, eager to find Hoolie.

–Twenty-Seven–

September 1917—

Antoine was fretting as he finished his house.
  Stupid cowboy hat went missing.
  Hold nail. Pound it.
  Hoolie never came back.
  Another nail. Pound it. Put it home.
  Marie never came back.
  Nail. Pound it.
  Franklin never came back.
  And another. Pound.
  Only two left? Damn. Where did the last one get to? There should be three.

Antoine searched his pockets, the ground, but there were only two left. How could he make a mistake like that?

He grabbed the last two before they vanished, too. Hold nail. Pound. Put it home. Then the last.

Antoine was pounding his last nail when Doc pulled up in his fancy car. There was a warm breeze, but who knew how long it would last. Antoine planned to finish his house before another winter set in, before Clement decided to exchange Emma for Mable, and for that, he needed that last nail. He searched the ground again, this time on his knees.

Doc opened his car door. Then Marie's.

Why were they here and not Clement? It was taking him long enough, which had Antoine nervous. He needed more nails to pound. One more and he could stop for the day.

"Got a nail?" he hollered to Doc.

Marie jumped out. "The house is beautiful."

"It will be when I can afford more nails." Antoine got to

his feet to hug his sister while thinking about the nail bill he had in town. Would Gilles let him add another bundle of nails to that endless debt?

Marie pulled back from his hug and eyed him up, curious. "You're not taking care of yourself. You were hunting for her?"

"Worse—waiting. If I leave, they might miss me. I have to be here." Antoine rubbed his head, wishing to heck he could remember where he'd set his hat down. "I've been busy. Countless nails to pound. Help me search for the last one, it must have fallen."

Doc was still by the car, but he said, "Look at your sister. Forget the nails for a minute. Look at her. What do you see?"

Antoine *was* looking at her. She looked like herself again. "You better? Doc been good to you?"

"Hmmm. A little too good," she said it loud enough for Doc to hear and he chuckled.

"Leave him alone," Antoine snapped. "Besides, you aren't available, being a married woman and all."

"Don't talk about that rotten skunk. He's dead to me."

"I'm going to Eau Claire for a nail. You comin'?" Antoine asked.

"Let me check out this mansion you're making, first."

Antoine let her investigate the house and went to talk to Doc. "You survived my sister. I was expecting you much sooner than this. Thought everyone forgot about me. Beginning to wonder if maybe I was dead. A ghost just too stubborn to move on." Antoine gave Doc a quick handshake. Truth was, he was happy to be near someone he could trust. He was turning into a paranoid maniac. Nasties kept him busy at night, and during the day, he had too many nails to pound.

"Yeah. She is a handful," Doc admitted. "I see where you get it. Things have been crazy lately with this conscription. Everyone is heading off to fight, leaving farms even. You guys dealing with that up here in Canada?"

Antoine focused on him. "I ... fight? I actually forgot there was a war. I have no idea what conscription means."

"Over the summer, they announced that everyone between the ages of 21 and 30 had to enlist. Not sure what happened in Canada."

"Even farmers?"

Doc nodded. "They prefer that they find someone to care for their land and get their butts out there."

"Oh. Well dammit, I should go, I'll be twenty-one soon enough. Why didn't anyone tell me this?"

"I doubt you were listening. You're not looking well." Doc touched his hand to Antoine's head to feel for a fever. "I heal your sister, and find you... what's wrong with you?"

Antoine slipped his hand in his pocket before Doc could notice the shaking. "Hey! My nail." He pulled it out of his pocket not sure how it ended up there and rushed to bang it in. He wouldn't have to go to town today after all.

Doc followed him closely.

Antoine faced him once the nail was in place. He felt better. "Nothing is wrong, back off."

"If this is nothing, I don't want to see you upset."

"You were the one breaking shit. At least I build things when I lose it."

Doc rubbed his jaw thoughtfully.

"Just needed that last nail. Let me know if you see my cowboy hat, it vanished this morning."

Doc sighed, so Antoine added, "Thanks for taking care of Marie."

"I brought the bill in person." He handed Antoine a newspaper clipping. "It's interesting. Want me to read it to you?"

"I read fine, in three languages, thank you very much."

Doc waited while Antoine read it a second time.

"Okay. Maybe you will have to read it to me. What the heck am I reading? Some farmer lost a few cows. Happens."

Doc pointed to the clipping. "Read it again, Antoine. It's not a few cows."

"*Missing one cow. Reward even if found dead. X. Iapeda Farms.*" Things were clear all of a sudden. "*Ouais*, I see it, A. Depaix spelt backwards. That explains why I see men running around in sheets nightly. They even burned a bloody cross out front of my place. Symbolic, I suppose, since I refused to take my cross off on his ranch and it insulted him. He figures this will burn me." Antoine rolled his eyes. "No one saw it but me so it wasn't a big deal. I went out, collected the nails, and used them. They're in the door frame."

"Nails? Burning crosses don't scare you?" Doc asked.

"Just ticks me off," Antoine admitted. "I don't like people telling me what I can and cannot do."

"I'm seeing a man who's trying to forget something he can't face and he's using nails to do it. Trust me, I know. Talk to me. You scared you won't see Emma again?"

"Heck no. I know I will. The amount of happy I plan to be with Emma, I have a hell of a lot of earning to do. Magic like that, it just don't happen, you know."

"I should head back, but I'll be by to visit. You clearly need someone to talk to, so talk to your sister."

"You're not staying?"

Doc looked longingly at the house. "I'm petrified to go home to that empty house, and here you are building an empty one. Gives me courage I didn't know I had."

"Can't build nothing. I keep running outta nails. Stay for a bit. We'll annoy you enough you'll be dying to get back. I don't have much, just bread and brown sugar, but dipped in cream it kinda hits the spot. Lots of places to sleep on the floor if you spend the night. Nailed each floorboard down with four nails. I wanted to use five, but settled on four. One board only has three but it was happy that way so I left it alone."

Marie came toward them. "This house is nice. Simple. You do this yourself?" She examined Antoine.

"I needed something to do with my hands this winter, and come spring, it beat pacing a hole in the cellar. Hardest part was making sure I always had enough nails. Friends and family came out to help. One even showed me how to join beams together without nails, but I prefer the nails, feels sturdier." Faces blurred together. Yet... he knew each one. He remembered each one.

"You're clearly the type of guy who needs to do things," Doc agreed. "Waiting is going to kill you."

Marie sighed. "I'm going to town. We need a better table, chairs, beds, and food. What have you been eating? I'm tempted to go home with Doc. You're more broken than he is."

"I ain't got cash for things. I used my last nail. Did I say that already?" Antoine ran a hand through his long hair. It was a knotted mess. When was the last time he'd cleaned up?

"I eat what Henri's sister brings me. Jill. Her name is Jill. Don't know why I keep forgetting that." Antoine rubbed his forehead. Jill. Damn, the guilt was killing him. All of it. He needed another nail to pound. Just one more.

"Well, she's not doing a very good job snapping her apron around you," Marie said. "You're as thin as a post. Look how I fattened Doc up."

"Apron? What? No. She deserves a guy who looks at her and sees the beauty she is, not the failure he is." Antoine remembered her conversations, her endless chattering. "Damn, I know nothing about gals. Is that why she's always over here messing up my nails?"

"Well, if you don't produce a wife soon, she's gonna be bringing over a stuffed turkey this Christmas." Marie ran her tongue over her teeth. "So you want anything from town?"

"You deaf, woman? I have no money. Nothing. I only had enough cash to seed the land around Henri's home and a bit around here, but it's all ready to go."

"You broke the rest of Depaix land?" Marie looked stunned.

"A month back I ran outta nails and ploughed 'er all. Gilles came by with a case of nails, said the town bought them for me so I could finish my house. It was almost enough."

"I have cash," Marie said. "Just don't ask me how I got it. I'll grab you more nails, if you shut up about them."

"Money? Was it worth it, Marie?"

"You have no idea what I lived," Marie snapped.

"That was your choice. You ran from me," he reminded her. "All this could have been avoided."

"As if I ever ran from you, Antoine. I've been protecting Sacred Land. It's what *Cîpay* do." She stormed away, walking to town.

He let her go.

"The distance between us is sometimes too much. Do you know what she means?" Antoine asked Doc.

Doc watched Marie leave and shook his head. "She's troubled. Needs to make peace with what haunts her and she doesn't have nails to pound senseless."

~~

Later that evening, Marie jumped out of a black truck. A truck.

"You bought a truck?" It wasn't dark yet and the sun lingered on the horizon so Antoine went to investigate the pickup. "It's nice. Not as nice as a horse, but it'll do, I guess."

"It's yours, Antoine. I bought it for you. Your nails are in the back. I paid your debts around Eau Claire. Honestly. They had nothing decent so I'll go to Moose Jaw tomorrow. Got something sweet for Doc, too, but he'll have to wait for that treat."

Doc smirked when she marched past him and he joined Antoine while he checked the nails. "Your sister is a handful."

"You say that like it's a good thing." Antoine examined the nails she'd bought. *Wow. They were the best ones.*

"Sometimes it is. Keeps my mind off my own pains. Like you and your house. We tend to create blind work so we don't have to face what's eating at us."

"Keep her if you want her. I don't need the company." Antoine pulled the case out of the truck and left it in the kitchen so he could count them later, while he waited for ghosts and sleep to find him.

Then he returned to the truck to check it out. He had no idea how to drive one. "This might speed things up while I look for Emma," he told Doc.

"One day, you'll have to face the possibility that Charlie and Emma won't be coming home."

"I refuse to accept that."

Marie came outside. "Oh, and that cutie pie at the hardware store is coming to paint the place for us tomorrow."

"Paint?" Antoine asked. "You mean Gilles? Since when is he a cutie anything? What?"

She went in the house.

"Look at it this way, it'll protect the nails," Doc smirked.

Antoine studied the house he'd built this past year. The

door was slightly off but heck if he could straighten it. "You see how crooked my door is? It's those stupid nails I took from the burned cross. In fact, every time I touch it, it makes things worse."

"Take them out."

"Then what? Bury them? Screw that. That's a waste of good nails. Nope. I'm using them, even haunted." Antoine sighed. "Maybe paint won't hurt. Hide the mess I made of things. So, do you think Emma will like—" A scream from the kitchen cut him off. Antoine grabbed a good size rock off the path and bounded up the veranda steps.

The kitchen was a mess. Groceries were scattered over the floor.

"Move and I slice her throat." Mathew had Marie bent over the old wooden table Antoine had hauled in. He pinned her, a knife to her throat.

"Why?" Doc asked. "Why would you do that? Stop and think for a moment."

"I need this land. It's mine if I kill these two, but first I want my money. Where is it? I risked my neck for that."

"Little breaths," Doc said. "Stay calm. I'm a doctor."

"Ah cut the crap and kill her." Antoine rolled his eyes.

"What?" Mathew paused, confused.

"Kill her. I'm sick of her crap. I was gonna do it, but she's your wife so I'll let you. Come on Doc, I got better things to do than watch a gopher pretend he's a man. We'll share the money I stole from him while he handles her." Antoine turned to leave.

"Savage, if you got—" Mathew pulled the knife away from Marie to point it at Antoine, and that one moment was all Antoine needed. Antoine spun around and pitched the rock, smacking Mathew square in the forehead.

Mathew stumbled back and Marie rushed to Doc who whisked her out the door.

Antoine shoved the table at Mathew, hitting his gut. Mathew tossed the knife blindly. It caught Antoine in the left shoulder. Damn. It was just starting to feel better, too. Antoine pulled it out and flung it at Mathew who dodged it. The knife sunk in the wall as if it were butter.

Warm sticky blood spread through his shirt and Antoine

pulled his suspenders down so they wouldn't rub the wound, his focus tight on Mathew. "I told you. Every hit you gave her I would return. I decided to double it for my niece's sake."

Mathew glanced at Antoine's bleeding shoulder. "You don't know, Antoine. You don't know what it's like to marry a woman, then find out it's not even your child."

Antoine punched him with everything he had in the right shoulder. He would never be like this guy. Never. Everything inside him promised God that he would treat Charlie like his son.

Mathew's shoulder slipped when he slammed into the wall yet he threw himself at Antoine and they tumbled on the table. It shattered under them and they landed in a woody mess. With his left fist, Mathew hit the bloody shoulder.

Antoine took quick breaths, letting his muscles relax. His knee made contact with Mathew's gut. Mathew rolled out of the splinters and Antoine followed with a swing to the jaw. Sitting, Mathew shook his head. Then to Antoine's surprise, he used his head to whack him.

Everything went dark.

Swirled back in.

Antoine rolled off Mathew who lunged for him, but Antoine put up a leg and tossed him into the box of nails.

They poured from the box as Mathew stood, each one rolling across the kitchen floor. One escaped toward the bedroom.

Scattered nails.

It was exactly how Antoine felt inside. He wanted to collect them all and pound them in place. They each had a home, a purpose. Frantically, he gathered them.

Mathew pounced on him, interrupting his collecting, but Antoine shoved Mathew aside, hunting for the nails.

Six for the door frame to their room. Another six for Charlie's.

No logic was left in him. He needed these nails where they belonged.

Mathew came at him again, pointing a nail. *Was that the one for the pantry shelf?* Antoine stopped counting long enough to toss him into the wall. He broke through it.

Antoine went to collect the nail from him. "Stupid gopher. They aren't weapons, they have a purpose." Mathew didn't get up when Antoine took the nail and groaned at the mess. "Eighteen nails to fix a mess this big. What a bloody waste."

He gathered them in their piles, until a strong hand on his shoulder made him stop. "Antoine. Breathe." He shot Mathew a glare. No, he still wasn't moving. Doc knelt beside him. Doc. What was he saying? "Breathe."

Antoine did. One little breath.

"That's better, young buck. Tell me what you see when you look at these nails."

"They shouldn't be like this. They have a home. It's my job to get them there. I can't fail."

"I see." Doc turned Antoine's head toward Mathew. "He destroyed one of your dreams. Let's deal with him. You need to do something. Your sister tells me you've always had this problem, obsessing over things instead of facing your fears."

"I'm fine. It's not fear that triggers it. It's when I can't..." Antoine shoved his shaking fist in his pocket. "When I can't fix things. Drives me crazy to be powerless. How can I find them?"

"They might be dead." Doc's voice was gentle. "That might be why Clement hasn't showed. I want you to search for them. If they died, someone will know and you'll find closure."

"I can't fix that."

"Only thing to fix then would be you. These nails are distracting you."

Antoine didn't look at Doc. "You won't touch these nails, right?"

"They're yours, but I am going to clean them up. Enough of this. You trade these nails in first chance you get for something you don't need but you can't live without. Understand?"

Antoine took a deep breath and watched Doc put the nails in the box, one at a time.

"That one is for Charlie's room. I have a picture for him. Something I drew when I couldn't sleep."

Doc tossed it in the box and picked up another. "And this one? You see where this one belongs?"

"Of course, that is one of four that will hold the fixture in Emma's closet, to hang her dresses."

"You see this future in a nail?"

"*Ouais*. You can tell me any story you want about that nail, but inside, I know where it belongs, and that's all that matters to me."

Antoine dragged Mathew by the feet out the front door, down the steps, making sure his head caught each one.

"Where are you taking him?" Marie rushed to them. "You're bleeding. Let me wrap your shoulder."

"We're gonna have us some brotherly fun." Antoine dragged him to the barn. Doc followed, but Marie rushed off to find something for Antoine's arm.

"You won't kill him, right?" Doc wondered.

"Dying's the easy part, Doc. Watch him while I get a horse and paint."

Antoine could think of a thousand ways to make him suffer but none even came close to what he did to Marie and his niece so he'd let God deal with him.

Marie was shaking Mathew when he returned, waking him. Doc watched, silently.

"You judge me?" Antoine asked Doc while Marie dressed his wound.

Doc watched her. "Wait to paint him until you get him where you want so it doesn't get messed up."

"Ha. You always surprise me. Here, help me tie him to this horse."

"I'll grab his arms," Doc offered.

"No. No. You misunderstood. The horse drags him."

"He won't survive that."

"I want him to feel every rock on the land he tries to steal from us on the way to town. Is he awake yet, Marie? We don't go until he's awake. He can scream to everyone, telling them why this land is so valuable, why he beat his wife, why he deserves their sympathy."

Doc looked concerned even if he was silent, so Antoine explained, "It's called a shaming. I drag him through Eau Claire, tie him up, and accuse him of his crimes by painting them on his chest: ghost, thief, woman beater, child murderer. I might think of a few more on route. Then I walk away. Let God judge if he'll be cut down or left for the crows."

"This is justice?"

"Out here it is." Antoine studied the endless fields. A shadow dropped in the distance when he looked that way. Strange. Usually *Cîpay* stared back. Cripes. Was that Hoolie out there? Antoine almost ran to him, but Doc put a hand on his shoulder, bringing his focus back to Mathew.

The sun was leaving them, and a pink glow haunted the sky to the west. The moon was out, full and bright. "This is God's country. We live by one simple rule, respect others, respect yourself. You break that rule; a shaming is the logical solution."

"Call in the law," Doc offered.

"That what you did?"

Doc looked at the ground. "They were part of the problem."

"Hmmm. No law out here to turn to anyway. Just the priest, and he's welcome to cut him down and save his soul." Antoine smirked. "Somehow, I doubt that dirty bugger will."

~~

"You can't leave him here, Antoine." Doc rubbed his jaw. "I don't like this. You're as bad as them."

It was still night. Antoine swatted a mosquito. Marie was gone. She left about halfway. Didn't head home but to Eau Claire. She was probably in church and Antoine didn't want to face her.

"I don't like you like this," Doc said. "You've snapped."

"*Ouais.* Don't feel like myself these days. I see things differently. Breathing doesn't stop the panic I feel, either. Only thing that feels right is when I pound nails."

"And you did pound nails. You did good. You built her a house. Now go find her. I'll help."

Antoine looked at Mathew, bleeding and scratched up, tied to the cemetery post. His crimes painted on him. "On the way over, I found a nail." Antoine showed Doc the rusty nail he'd found. "I'll take it as a sign that I'm done pounding nails. Let's clean up. Put my nails away so they stop distracting me and I'll swing by later to see who saved his soul. If anyone should be that foolish."

~~

When Antoine returned to the cemetery at lunch, Mathew was gone. Cut down. No blood. No crowd. He asked around but no one saw him there at all.

Got away a free man.

Antoine went straight to the priest. Father Hillsdale met him at the door as if expecting him. He turned up Antoine's hands and studied them.

"What ya looking for?" Antoine asked.

"Just wanna make sure you had nothing to do with it. I made it clear that there was no shamings in my town."

"Missed that sermon, sorry. I've been busy getting my ass haunted."

Father was still studying his grimy hands, but Antoine pulled them away. "I came to fetch him so I can drag him through another town where the priest ain't so mushy. Where is he?"

"Buried out back."

"He's dead?" Antoine was surprised. "Who killed him?"

Jaw firm, Father Hillsdale said, "Didn't say he was dead, just buried. Your sister needs a ride home. And Antoine, I wouldn't check her hands if I were you."

"Cripes." Antoine backed out of the church and chills swept over him. The world suddenly came alive around him. He wouldn't tell Doc that part. He needed to forget, fast.

–Twenty-Eight–

December 1917—

Marie finished the Christmas prayer and started her soup. Antoine stared at his, not hungry.

"You have to eat," Marie said.

"I don't have to do anything." Antoine was frustrated that Mathew could come between them like this.

"It's not much of a Réveillon Supper, but I didn't feel very Christmas-y. Perhaps now is as good a time to tell you that I'm going overseas as a nurse. I hear the training isn't long. Wanna join me? A cause like that might do you good."

Antoine couldn't face his sister anymore. He used to see a woman full of pride and love; now when he looked at her, he saw Mathew struggling for life. She'd played God and that pain was etched into her soul, so deep it came through her every action.

"Why won't you talk to me?" he demanded.

"I am talking."

"About a war that's an ocean away, when right here, between us there is no peace."

"This wall is your fault, Antoine. I can't share my pain and I sure as heck don't want to know about yours. Let's sit in silence with our ghosts haunting us. Walls keeping us safe. Here, take the cross Sacri gave me for protection." She tossed it on the table. It was identical to his.

"Thank you." He smiled lightly. It was the first time she'd ever let him touch it. It was a simple cross with strange engravings like his. "I see my happy forever in it." He held it for a moment. It was warm in his palm and seemed to pulsate toward Marie. He handed it back. "Take this necklace as a gift from me. My sister gave it to me, and I give it to you, my sister. May it protect you until you find your happy forever. Merry Christmas."

She took it back. "This means yours is with her." She slipped it in her skirt pocket. "Isn't it? Why don't you talk about this wife of yours?"

"It hurts to breathe when I think about her so I try not to."

"You try not to breathe or think about her?"

"A bit of both," he admitted. Soon he'd have to accept that she was dead. If Franklin couldn't convince Clement to exchange her for Mable, there was no hope.

Marie put down her spoon with a clink. "You said she was sick. Why haven't you gone back for her?"

Antoine started to explain, then clammed up. "It's complicated. I don't even know where she is."

"Then rule out where she isn't. Is she hiding from you? Is she another man's wife?"

"She's to be my wife." His voice crackled, but he pulled out the marriage certificate Father Kilby had made for him. He had no idea if it was legal, but it looked real. "Got me a certificate that says she's my wife."

Her jaw clenched but she didn't reach for it. "This woman means that much to you that you'd risk this complication?" Marie looked in the soup she'd blessed as if expecting it to say something to support her. "Antoine, what you're not saying frightens me."

He picked up his glass and considered throwing it at the wall. If Marie wouldn't have been there he would have, but she'd seen enough violence in her life that he crisply set it by his soup, taking a little breath.

Then another.

Antoine dumped his food for the dog. Hardly touched.

Marie took in a couple deep breaths. "Walk away. Live a nice life. Marry that sweet Jill who thinks the world is wonderful. Innocent gal that one."

Antoine looked at his worn hands.

"There is no love. This is you being stupid. She's using you to get away from something. Wake up. This is how we women survive. We find a nice guy like you and bat our eyes until he rescues us from the maniacs on a rampage."

"So what, you decided to do the opposite?" Antoine didn't point out the scars on Marie's wrist, yet she pulled down her sleeves as if he had.

"Don't bring that son-of-a-bitch into this conversation." It was rare that Marie swore, but lately, Antoine noticed that she couldn't say Mathew's name.

"Your language, Marie."

"I'll swear if I feel like it. I don't tell you to clean things up. How much trouble are you in? Is this about the bootlegging?"

"What the heck are you talking about?" he asked.

"Rat told me that Depaix booze is a big hit down south."

"What? Ah cripes." Antoine felt like a fool. He explained what he kind of suspected to Marie; "This was never about me. It was about money. You see, Clement set up the prohibition and now he's supplying booze to the entire country. They make it in Moose Jaw, and use tunnels to get it around. And now, apparently, I'm gonna take the heat for it because if you ask anyone else, he's all for the prohibition."

Marie pushed her chair back but they were silent. The stove crackled and Antoine added wood to it while he thought.

Finally he asked her, "Nasties do more than smuggle booze these days, don't they? Tell me about Mathew. What were his beliefs? What did he do for Clement?"

Her index finger rubbed the table. "The prick searched for work in Moose Jaw and nothing was going his way. He complained openly about how there were no jobs when a gentleman approached him and asked if he thought the problem was that maybe immigrants stole his jobs."

Antoine listened carefully.

"Of course, that fired-up his over-inflated ego. Anyway, one thing led to another and before he knew it, he was underground, learning how to scare coolies back to their country."

Antoine felt Sacri reach out from the spirit world and whack Marie on the back of the head. Coolie was in the same list as slave. Forbidden words, yet Marie flung it on the table so casually.

"This is where I came in. As *Cípay,* we can't allow this."

Antoine was confused. "Allow what?"

"Slavery. It's not like it used to be, but it's going on all around us. In Moose Jaw I saw it with my own eyes. Chinese working underground in horrible conditions with no medical care and hardly any food. I had to get as close as I could, find out as much as I could and this guy was my way in. I did what I had to. This is about much more than us, Antoine. Like I said, there is no love, do what you must to survive."

Antoine knew better than to question *Cîpay* so he sat in silence, with a sister he thought he knew. She looked back at him, with all the wisdom of their ancestors. How had he missed the transformation in her? When had she become one? How? Sacri used to tell him that when he was *Cîpay,* he would know.

"His job was so simple that at first I didn't understand," she said. "The prick ran around, making them think the prairies were haunted. This was to keep everyone far from their operations. And oh yeah, while he ran around he might as well do a few errands for them. Little things at first, a message from this guy to that one, and they'd pay him, too. Then packages. Once they got wind that he liked the booze, they weren't paying, mostly feeding him the drink at each stop. The fool had potential, when he didn't drink. I better never catch you drinking." Then in Cree she said, "*Respect yourself.*" Reminding him of *Cîpay* law.

The posters. They were promising things people needed or wanted, to get them to run their errands. Then they would take the fall. So simple. But who were *they*? Was Clement behind all this? Was this how he made his money?

"Doc and I discussed this at length," Marie continued. "What happens when you give men a cause? They band together to make statements. What happens when you strip their identities and turn them into ghosts? It turns into riots. Veiled from society, freedom pushes them to the limits."

"Like *Cîpay.* They copy our beliefs, only they don't know *Cîpay* laws."

She ignored him. "Mathew brought me all over the province and I saw many gatherings turn violent." Marie paled. "My stupid husband said there was a certain power when he hid under a sheet. He could run wild, be someone he couldn't be in public." She smiled. "He knew nothing about being *invisible*. He slept beside his enemy every night yet chose not to see who I really was. Yes, Antoine, *Cîpay* are invisible, but not by choice. This is the world choosing not to see. Because here I am and no one knows it."

"How do I fight a ghost?"

"Face to face they are different people. Remove the sheets." Her index finger moved on the table wildly. A habit Antoine used to hate, but tonight that tic meant she was on his side.

"The money? *Cîpay* do not steal."

She glanced at the knife wound in the wall, and the smashed up section Antoine had repaired. "So I opened a few packages. The jerk was so drunk he had no idea."

"Why hasn't anyone come looking for Mathew yet? Do they even care?"

"I'm taking care of it. When a message comes for him to do this or that, I do it."

"Ah *merde*. You wear those sheets?" He understood what she meant about not needing to hear each other's secrets.

"You wear your own type of sheet, Antoine. Do you remember how obsessed you were with the wolf after Josée's attack? Days. You went days without sleep or food. And why?"

"Days? It wasn't that long."

"It was. And why?" she asked.

"So I could bury it with her. Justice."

"No. You did that so you didn't have to look Sacri in the eyes as a failure. She forced that invisible sheet off you with the *Cîpay* tattoo you refuse to acknowledge. You are a Warrior of God, a Teacher to Lost Souls. You are *Cîpay* because of your actions."

She was wrong. That tattoo represented his failings at protecting his sister.

"*Regardez-moi*," she demanded that he look at her.

Her brown curls fell loosely down her back. Once upon a time, he knew she was beautiful, but now Marie had deep scars on her face. It pained him to see who she'd become.

"I can't. I failed you."

"You are the opposite of failure. At least tell me this woman's name so I can help you look." She reached for the certificate but the way she said it made him nervous so he shoved it in his pocket.

"I love you dearly, Marie, but *Cîpay* don't steal, and they don't kill for revenge. I already told you too much. Now where is Hoolie? At least him I trust."

"He's gone, I sent him looking for your girl. He sees things others can't hide." She left the table.

–TWENTY-NINE–

May 1918—

The nightmares were worse. Antoine had to do something about them through the winter and took short trips in the States, searching for Emma.

He asked priests if they'd buried an unknown woman fitting Emma's description. No one had. He searched cemeteries for a mother and child. He found a woman with no name, and a child two towns away from her, but he refused to believe it was them. Doc was wrong. She was alive.

The sweet smell of spring lilacs invaded the house since Marie planted them everywhere, but when Antoine woke up sweating from a restless sleep, a rancid smell made him open his eyes.

Clement.

All the preparing he'd done, and the prick shows up in the middle of the bloody night.

There was a faint light in his room. "Rough nights." Clement sat in the chair, his feet on the bed, wearing Antoine's cowboy hat.

Slowly, Antoine reached for the knife he kept under his pillow.

"Looking for this?" Clement let the light catch it, then continued cleaning his nails with Antoine's blade. "I want my daughter. Took me time to calm Emma, but she's in one piece."

All the ache inside Antoine melted as relief washed over him. She was alive. "Charles too?"

"Is that the brat's name?"

"Watch what you say about that boy." Antoine sat up, ready to dive for him.

Clement looked about ready to smite him. "I want Mable back."

"Franklin couldn't find her?" Antoine was impressed with Father Hillsdale.

"Franklin is dead to me. He insisted I strike a deal with you but I was sure I'd find her. I practically raised that boy and the thanks I get? He cut off my finger in his madness." Clement showed him his hand and sure enough, he was missing the tip of a finger. "I won't tell you what I cut off him."

"You wasted precious time. Deal was simple. You hand over Emma and Charlie and get Mable in the same shape." Antoine felt around the bed for the marriage certificate. He'd fallen asleep with it in his hands. Clement hadn't taken that too, had he?

Clement glared at him. "I spend my nights with her. Every night, just to piss you off." Antoine dived for him but it was what Clement wanted and he snagged Antoine by the throat and tossed him against the wall. Damn. It always surprised Antoine how strong this guy was. Clement's arm pushed against his throat as he got in real close to Antoine's face. "She's at the ranch. I dare you to come and get her." Clement let him go and Antoine tumbled forward.

"Yeah well... I can't be responsible for cave-ins on your precious bootlegging project."

"You threaten me, mutt?"

Antoine shifted his eyes up slowly. "Acts of God are out of my control."

Clement set something on his dresser. "Emma gave up on you. Things like that are out of my control, too."

The ring he gave her caught the light perfectly, resting innocently on the marriage certificate.

–THIRTY–

Hoolie held the newest Wanted Flyer. Seems Mister was really in trouble this time. He couldn't understand anything on it. Not even one number. The Reward Hunter sat beside him and said in her happy-I-can't-wait-to-screw-you-over voice, "Train Station is busy today."

"What's it say?" Hoolie showed Marie the poster.

She snagged it. "Doesn't matter. Did you find this girl of his?"

Hoolie shook his head.

"Do you even know what you're looking for?" she demanded in her snide way.

Hoolie ripped the flyer in two. "Everyone's light is like half a flyer. All on its own it doesn't work. When you see the other half, it all makes sense, well, if you know how to read it. Kinda annoys me that I can read the light around people but a simple flyer I can't make heads or tails of."

"So you know what you're looking for?" she asked.

"No idea, but I'll know it when I see it."

"Well, Antoine left this morning to find her. This flyer says Clement wants my brother alive because one of his daughters ran off with him. I assume this Mable is who he linked to."

Hoolie sighed. Mister was in worse trouble then he thought. "Those boys call Clement the boss," Hoolie told her. "Everyone wants to please him 'cause not only does he have his hand in every politician's pocket, he has six daughters whose husbands will inherit more money than Satan could spend."

"Maybe you'll find one interesting," she hinted.

Great. Was this his new job? To get in the good graces of the boss. "I have my eyes on that girl out by Mister's, the one with the magical light."

"Jill will have to wait. I need you to deal with Clement."

"You want me to go back to that hellhole?" Hoolie wasn't sure that was a good idea. He really hadn't liked his last trip down south.

She handed over a bill.

"You don't pay enough." Hoolie leaned back and gripped his bag. It was time to ask for the payload. "I don't want money. I want a home, a real home, where I can raise a family and stuff."

"A home?"

"Yeah." Hoolie couldn't look at her. "You have all that empty land, tunnels. All these shadows haunt it that know interesting things. I...Think a guy like me could have a wife and a nice place to sleep above ground?"

She smiled. "Them dreams happen. Sure. But I'm the wrong Depaix to help you achieve those dreams, that's more an Antoine thing. Talk to him."

Yeah. He'd watched Mister build that house, even in the freezing cold. Antoine knew how important a home was. "Which way did he go?" Hoolie asked, determined to talk to him about it.

–Thirty-One–

Antoine was eager to get to Clement's Ranch but he was sick of the run around he kept getting.

"No tickets," the woman behind the counter said.

Antoine frowned. "You're telling me there isn't a seat left on any train going south? Not one?"

"For you? 'Fraid so, sir."

"Why not?"

"Um..." The ticket vendor, a large woman missing a tooth cleared her throat. "Acts of God are out of my control." Always the same answer he got, from every bloody person screwing him over. It was clear Clement wanted him to take the tunnels across the border, but he wasn't falling for that trap. He'd find another way.

"Wow. You're ruining my life for what? A few bucks? Whatever Clement paid you, I'll double. Double dammit."

"I... I have a daughter, sir, and my husband is fighting in this war. I can't sell you a ticket, end of story."

Antoine glared at her. "Never mind. I'll walk there."

Clement was a nuisance. Antoine leaned against the station railing, stewing. Tommy was probably following him. If he saw that prick—

"Pst."

Antoine glanced over. "Hoolie? Is that really you? You look... cleaned up."

"Shh."

"What ya doing above ground?" Antoine asked in French.

"Following you. What the heck do you think I'm doing? You know a Clement? Did you really steal his daughter?"

"You reporting to him which direction I'm going?"

"I'm not even sure God knows which direction you're

going."

Antoine pulled out one of the bills Marie had given him and dropped it. "That should keep you distracted long enough for me to steal your horse, *non*?"

Hoolie ignored the bill. "There's a horse at the livery barn, brown with white spots, that travels well in the dark, if you catch my drift. Only way you're gonna get across this border is if you hit the fields."

Antoine was starting to think the same thing. "You need a ticket back to Moose Jaw? I'll get you home."

Hoolie paused for a minute and looked Antoine over. "Like you, I ain't got a home, yet." He took off and Antoine picked up the five bucks he'd left behind.

–THIRTY-TWO–

August 1918—

Clement had many 'traps' for him and Antoine had detoured several times. He settled on travelling only at night, but a few months later, he was wrestling with the excited Beast on Clement's Ranch. He sneaked to the house and entered by the back door. Trying not to make a sound, he clicked the door shut. When he turned around, he was face to face with Emma.

"I missed you." His words just poured on her as she fell into his arms. She'd let her hair grow and it flowed loose into his hands as he gripped her. "I..." Antoine forced a swallow. He had so much to say, but the only thought pulsating in his brain had to do with ripping the flimsy nightgown off her. Her nipples were poking through it, and he couldn't focus.

"You're alive." Emma had tears shadowing her eyes and she touched him as if proving to herself that he was real. "How?"

His fingers ran over the ring on her finger and she pulled her hand away so he couldn't touch it. The ring he wanted her to wear was in his pocket.

His fingers slipped around her waist anyway and he pulled her as close as their bodies allowed.

"Where have you been?" she asked.

He put his head down. "I couldn't find you."

She ran a hand along his cheek. "We're here now. That's all that matters."

Already, his hands were out of his control as he touched her face, making sure she was real. "And Charlie? How is he?"

"I must learn to ignore the feelings I have for you. They got Charlie in trouble. He's safe here." Yet her hands never left his face, in fact, much to Antoine's bliss she pushed them into his hair and leaned into him. He felt her desire for him, as powerful as his was for her.

"He'll be safe with us on our farm. Promise." Antoine pulled the certificate from his back pocket. "I had a priest who owed me a big favour do it."

"I can't read well."

"See here, the date, it's the day I met you in 1916. We're married. I'm taking you home. Both of you." He bowed his head embarrassed that he was doing this all wrong. "If you want, I mean."

"Clement knows this?"

"He does. He doesn't like it but he knows."

"Come see Charlie." Emma led Antoine to the third door and rushed him inside.

Charlie slept peacefully. Healthy. Antoine checked every inch of him and pulled back shocked to see the teardrop tattoo on the back of his hand.

He couldn't even find the words to ask Emma about it. She'd had a hand on Antoine's shoulder but pulled away while he studied the tattoo. She placed her hands in front of her, covering the back of the left one. Antoine reached for her hands. Sure enough, she was marked, too. He traced it silently.

Antoine stood up and wiped her silent tears. So this was Clement's way to remind Emma of her place. He'd never fully believed in the power of these tattoos until this moment. This was clearly a message for him.

Well, screw him.

Antoine slowly took the ring off her finger and set it on the dresser, then he took out his and put it on her finger. "Only woman I want to see in it, only ring I want to see on you. Hope that works for you." He nudged her chin until she met his eyes. She was fighting back tears. He needed his hammer and nails. *Breathe.*

"I know my place, but I want a new place. Is this wrong?"

When she cried, even softly like this, her tears drove him crazy. "Depaix Farm is where we belong." He spoke between clenched teeth. "Is Clement home tonight?" *He'd kill him.* This thought triggered a breeze in the room and the familiar wolf-shadow appeared in the doorway.

"No."

"Does he leave you alone?" Antoine demanded.

The wolf growled, mocking his anger.

"Me, yes, he doesn't look at me, but he spends too much time with Charlie. He left weeks ago," she said. "He's trying to install telephone lines, but it hasn't been going well. He's frustrated all the time because not everyone speaks his language. He calls them horrible names."

"Only he would see it that way and not the other way around."

"What does that mean?" she asked.

"It's him who can't speak their language. He must be hunting for his daughter."

"Yes, Mable. *Cîpay* took her. Tommy knew of a boy who could help but he's slippery. Clement went to find him. He speaks many languages."

The wolf shadow curled up beside the bed. Antoine didn't like that. He wanted that wolf away from Charlie. "Let's go for a walk. Will Charlie be safe alone?"

"I'll let the girls know. They'll listen for him."

She left him alone with Charlie. Antoine sat beside him, coming between the shadow and Charlie. Antoine rubbed the teardrop on his hand. Marking a child with such a tattoo was unheard of. It was the saddest thing he'd ever seen.

The Song of Sorrow came to his lips. The melody washed over Charlie as he slept, filling the room with Antoine's grief, letting each breath pull the pain out and vanish it. The wolf-shadow faded into the dim light and was gone as he finished the song and sat in silence.

"Your song is magical." Emma rested her hands on Antoine's shoulders.

Antoine had no idea she'd come back. "I... it heals my soul when I can't pound nails. I hurt inside because I failed you both. This is not at all how I want things to be for us."

Antoine fondled the book by the bed. A Bible? Last thing he expected to see. "You read this?"

"No, I told you, I don't read well. It's Charlie's. He likes to hold it. The symbols in it mean things to him that he practises saying. He plays with it. I... I went to town not long ago to run an errand. Not normal for them to let me off the farm, but everyone is wound tight these days. Clement lost most of his workers to the war and it was urgent and well... I brought Charlie to the church there. He liked it. A minister gave Charlie the book and told him a story. Clement doesn't seem to mind, he even read to Charlie from it."

Antoine put it back and swept Emma out the door, eager to talk to her. The moon was bright. It was a warm August night. He settled under the trees where he'd left her the first time and she came beside him. He held her hand; sure he wouldn't let it go again.

Only way out was to kill Clement. He saw no other option. Again, the wolf-shadow appeared with this thought. He ignored it and focused on Emma.

She pulled her hand away and undid buttons on his shirt.

"What are you doing?" He watched her guilty hands, unable to stop them.

"I want to see you, my husband," she whispered.

He wanted her to see him. Softly, he pulled down the strap on her nightgown and kissed her shoulder. "How long have you been on this ranch?"Antoine took his time kissing her.

"Since after Christmas." Her hands were on his bare chest. "Can I tell you a secret?"

He nodded, unable to speak, but he wanted to know all her secrets.

"At first, every seven days I was given a chance to return and refused."

He frowned. "Where were you?"

"I can't say."

He pulled away and looked in her eyes. "Emma. We say everything between us, no matter how painful." His eyes bore into her as his hands slid around her tiny waist.

"Bad things happen in the dark." She held him tight. "It was so dark that Charlie learnt to see with his hands."

"Dark?" Antoine frowned.

"I thought he'd steal Charlie away from me, but when he saw him he sent us both to the hole. I was so relieved that he left me Charlie I never stopped to beg him to take him, to keep him safe. The hole is not a place for babies. I was glad you taught me how to strap him to me. He was safe and the others, they helped me with him."

"Others?" Antoine felt Sacri's warnings about secrets of the world. "Where is this hole?"

She glanced at the ground.

"Here? *Holy horses*. Show me."

"Please don't make me go down there." She panicked and Antoine instantly came around her, pulling away her fear. He wanted to go back and relive the bliss from a second ago. She stared off in the distance. "No days. No nights. Just one endless blanket of time. Food tastes like dirt and dust sticks to everything. The air is poison."

"Emma, if he gave you the chance to leave this hell, why didn't you?"

She met his eyes. So full of love. One single tear fell and he watched it roll along her cheek. Swallowing the lump in his throat he let it slide onto his finger and watched it melt into his skin as the truth sunk in. She thought he would come for them.

"What happened after Christmas to change your mind?"

Her chin quivered and she fell against him. "Your cowboy hat." Her eyes darted over his face. "I thought you were dead. I had no idea it was the thought of you coming for us that held me to this world. I fell ill and when I woke, I was back on the ranch, marked, and Charlie was calling Clement 'Daddy'. I asked him what my place was." She looked at the tattoo on her hand. "He said I was invisible to him, but I was safe as long as I let him talk with Charlie." She let go of his buttons, her head sagged in shame. "Charlie needed out of the hole. That was not a place for him and it seemed like such a simple promise to make." He felt all the hope in her die as her shoulders drooped. She turned to leave.

He grabbed her and brought her back beside him so they were sitting on the grass. "Nothing you can say will make me turn you away. You will never be invisible to me and I will love Charlie like my son, no matter. Emma, I was there when he was born. He's your flesh and blood. How can I not care for him as deeply as I care for you?"

Their eyes met.

"I can't even pretend to understand the things you do to survive or how you see the world. Since I made you feel vulnerable, perhaps you should know the truth about me," he whispered against her shoulder. "I've never been with a woman. Ever." He ran a hand along her cheek. "I don't even know where to start with you, but I really want to see more of you." He looked deeply into her rich brown eyes. Her eyelashes were so thick he had the urge to feel them against his skin.

He sunk back, beaten. Despite the emotions swirling in his brain, the idea consumed him. The more she breathed with him, the less real the outside world felt. He fumbled with her nightgown. The buttons were tiny, delicate. Like her.

She worked his shirt over his shoulder and paused. Her eyes read his body, taking in every detail as if she'd need to recall the image later. Her fingers travelled his scars, his wounds, his tattoo. She straddled him, exploring his chest with hands and eyes. Her breath warm against his skin in the cool air. Shoulders. Arms. Every muscle softened at her touch, leaving him at her mercy.

"Your body tells me stories," she whispered.

Eyes on her, he watched her slink against him, eagerly memorizing every inch of him. Dang. How had he lived without her?

Nails. That's how. He'd pounded nail after nail after nail.

He couldn't let her continue. Yet asking her to stop was impossible. "Emma, I built you a house."

She paused. "Show me."

His own hands started a journey out of his control, slowly working up her nightgown, around her thighs. Her hips.

Their lips touched. It wasn't planned or expected, a pull impossible to endure. Hands forgotten. Eyes closed. They rolled into the grass, locked together.

~~

"I feel so alive," Antoine mumbled to Emma's hair as he held her. "Alive. I mean... I don't know what I mean. Was I dead before?" Damn. Was this real? Their bodies, their souls, their entire beings connected in a way he had no idea was possible.

There was no other way to describe it. He was now alive, and it felt great.

Emma was safe under his arm. They breathed the same rhythm as if their bodies could no longer work without the other. Damp grass tickled them, and as the sun rose, a few birds unleashed his joy on the world in song for him.

"Will you vow before God with me in my church that it'll be only you and me until death finds one of us?" he asked.

"Clement says God cares not about such things," she mumbled against him.

"But I care. I want the strongest witness possible. Only God knows what's true in your heart. You can't lie to Him."

"So neither could you? I like that." She slipped over him. "I better get to my chores. Charlie's usually up with the sun."

Did it have to end? Antoine ran his hands down her body again, positive that he'd kissed every last inch of it, yet unable to let her leave.

"Antoine. We need to get back to the house. Breakfast..."

"The world can wait." He rolled her under him and eyed her up passionately.

"Maybe I shouldn't have..." She gently touched his chest, casting her eyes down. "My touch is evil."

He grazed her chin, bringing her eyes to meet his. "Your touch is warm and caring, so full of love it always takes me off guard. Things never felt so right. Besides, we can have breakfast right here, together." He pulled a fistful of berries off the plants around them and tossed them on her belly. Then he raised his eyebrows playfully and dived in.

~~

Antoine walked with Emma to the house. Everything looked new, different. He pulled a flower off one of the bushes and twirled it. Even the yellows in it were clearer.

He brought her to the side of the house so they weren't out in the open while they talked, and rubbed the flower along her jaw. "Tell me what you did in the hole."

"We worked. I am a slave-digger."

Worked? He dropped the flower, and his world returned to the one he'd always known, gloomy and clouded with grey anger. "You dug tunnels? Is Clement building his own tunnels to get across the border?"

"I only know what I saw," she said.

"I want to know what you saw. Tell me everything."

"One time, my friend, Rose, went missing, and we didn't find her for two days. By then, the rats had made away with most of her." Her eyes were so full of unspoken fear that Antoine felt it with her. "And Philip and Gracie showed, but Gracie is buried out back now. Clement said she died of not breathing and he had to take Philip away because he was dangerous. It was dark, but he sat with me while I prayed for her and he never said a word about my prayers."

"Ain't he the hero?" He ran his hands down her arm, wishing he could take away all her pain.

"Get Charlie. My horse is by the barn. I'll check if it's still safe. If not, we'll have to run." He squeezed her arm. "Emma. I'll bring you to a safe spot. If I die, there is a priest that passes by that church you went to in town, he goes there every month. Tell him my name. Tell him about those underground, he'll save them, too."

"A priest? Why would he do this for me?"

"Any good man would do this, *ma belle*."

"You mean... you'll free the others? All the diggers?"

"I need you and Charlie safe first, so Clement can't use you as an advantage." Antoine leaned over Emma. She smelled earthy, like he remembered, and it made him eager to hold her forever. When she rested her head against the house, eyes closed, he took it as an invitation and ran his jaw along her neck, while his hands slid down her nightgown.

When she moaned his lips were on hers, both of them forgetting the world haunting them.

–Thirty-Three–

The bed was empty. It was a wild mess. Emma knew better than to leave Charlie out of her sight. What had she been thinking? Charlie was too important. Clement would talk to him first chance he got, tell him things she hated. Already the twisted stories he told Charlie at night frustrated her. Stories to make him hate God. She was sure the Bible he read from didn't say such things.

Emma's stomach tightened while she raced the hallway, screaming silently for him, flinging door after door open. Everyone was gone.

She found Charlie in the kitchen eating his breakfast and her relief was so intense she fell on him with kisses. "Come Charlie, I have someone for you to meet."

The cook raised an eyebrow. "That what has everyone so crazy this morning? You up to no good? Why aren't you dressed? Your buttons are done up wrong. What's gotten into you?"

"I'll be right back." In her haste, she'd forgotten to dress. Emma did need clothes and went to find some before heading out.

With Charlie in her arms, Emma hurried to the stables. Lamenting winds shoved against them, telling them to return to the house. "Antoine is here. We're going with him."

"Papa?"

"He's safe. You be a good boy. Listen to what he says. I trust him."

Charlie brushed her face as she dashed across the lawn with him in her arms. He looked around, with his serious face. He didn't face the wind but away from it. His body tensed as if Clement was near. His little fingers tightened around her apron strings, but he didn't take his eyes off the field.

Her eyes weren't as good as Charlie's were, but she could trust his reaction. Clement was probably on his way home. That's why no one was in the house; they prepared for him.

It was now or never.

She rushed through the barn but it was empty. Not a soul. Not a horse.

Emma searched the grounds for Antoine. She found his horse out in the long grass by the shelter of a bluff of trees.

Antoine was nowhere in sight. Frantic, she went back to the stables. What was going on? Where was Antoine? Had he stolen Clement's horses and left? Why would he do that?

It felt like moments ago that he'd brushed his thick bottom lip against hers, so innocently. He was so gentle with her. She'd been sure this was it. The emotions in those kisses were a promise of safe.

But he left.

Gone.

She picked Charlie up. "Look around Charlie, do you see him? The man from the picture I drew?"

"Papa?"

Desperate, she scanned the prairies with a lost hope. Why did she keep putting all her faith in this man who kept leaving her?

The wind was strong, pushing against them but Charlie searched with her.

The wind ripped her of breath, snuggling in her soul.

Charlie squealed and gripped her hair, burrowing against her neck as if he'd seen... a ghost.

"Where Charlie? Point for me. Where did you see ghosts?"

He didn't look, just pointed toward the field. She set Charlie down and studied the field carefully as she went to get Antoine's horse, yet she saw nothing. The mare nudged her while they returned to Charlie.

How much did she trust those kisses?

Images flashed over her of Antoine gently exploring her, begging her to slow down, to relax. The way he'd tossed the berries on her belly and chased them over her skin to forbidden spots.

His strong hands full of safe.

His golden eyes.

A warmth grew inside that she didn't recognize but it made her want to fight with him.

"Come Charlie."

Charlie rushed to her and clutched her leg. He waited for her to tell him to hide. Trusting her to make the right choices for him. "Charlie, we do not hide anymore. We'll be happy."

Antoine had been sure.

His whispers.

His body warm with hers.

She'd been sure.

The wind calmed, as if debating which way to blow.

It's easier to give in.

Only she couldn't.

"We're leaving, Charlie." She placed Charlie on the mare and showed him how to hang on. "If something happens to me, find that big church I showed you. Every town has one. It's safe. And Charlie, don't let anyone ever tell you that giving in is easier. We're going to live with Papa Antoine."

"Papa?"

Emma nodded. "Yeah. Papa."

Charlie tightened his little fists. He was so small, yet he understood everything she told him.

-THIRTY-FOUR-

The man from the grocery store was slowly putting things on the counter for Emma. "Ain't seen ghosts here, Madame, and in a wind like this, I'd as soon they blew through." There were others in the shop, and he glanced at them uncomfortably, but Emma liked him; his accent was like Antoine's.

Emma was tired, windblown, and desperate. She'd rode for over an hour and had no idea where she was. The desperation showed in her voice. "My son saw them, I trust that. They took a good man."

"You're taking the word of a child. Better chance he got scared and ran."

She could still smell Antoine on her and refused to believe that he'd leave willingly. "They came through here. I know they did. Charlie saw them."

The clerk slid the things toward Emma.

She pushed aside the food, her stomach too upset to eat. Charlie grabbed the baguette and with big eyes, he chomped into it.

"Charlie put that back, I have no monies."

"I'll add it to your account. Got it recorded, I do. Let me carry this out for ya, Madame." He practically whisked Emma and Charlie back to Antoine's horse.

Charlie still had the breadstick and she hadn't the heart to take it from him. If this man gave them food, she'd take it. For Charlie.

He transferred things to the saddlebags while he whispered, "Dragging a man behind their horse through town about two hours ago. Making a statement known by the Natives as a shaming. We ain't seen one done in about ten years but their kind ain't welcome. Nope they're heading from town to town, burning fear into us, claiming to be the new bosses around these parts of the prairies. Watch who you talk to, what you say in the open. Trust no one. We're at war."

"Where will they go?"

"They went north, toward Pleti. Looked like a Cree they were dragging. I should know, being married to one myself."

"Antoine," she said as she put Charlie on the horse. "His name is Antoine."

"Papa," Charlie blurted out. It was a game to him. If someone said Antoine, he answered with Papa. If someone said dark, he answered with bad.

"Oh Gosh. I'm sorry. A shaming won't kill him. They'll make sure of that. It's up to God to decide if he dies. What can I do?"

"Well, either you know what you can do or you don't." She glared at the clerk who wrung his hands in his apron.

Charlie touched her hand, holding the reins. "Mad." His breath caught in the wind.

"Yes. This is mad I feel. Smart of you to notice. You are not growing up with this fear. Be like Antoine. He's not afraid."

"Papa brave."

She'd talked about Antoine enough to the boy, that Charlie knew him well, only... he didn't. He was a promise she'd made that Charlie might never get. "He's happy inside, Charlie. People can be happy, not scared like us, not mad either. Happy. With smiles they can't control and everything."

They rode and rode in the direction he'd pointed them.

She halted the horse to read the sign. P-L-E-T-I. It was familiar. She knew those letters in that combination. Myles. It said Myles. This was where Myles lived. He would help her. She couldn't wait to see him again. She rode as the wind kicked up dust.

Her horse needed to rest so she guided the mare to the barn and decided to wait there for Myles. The barn was open but dusky inside. Emma hesitated to go in, afraid of what might be hidden in the shadows. Where were the horses?

Charlie was slouched forward, fast asleep. Poor baby. He

was young to go through this. She rubbed his dark curls.

"Emma?"

She spun around, ready to run, but Doc stepped from the shadows. "Emma, my gosh." He rushed to her and wrapped her in warm loving arms. "You're alive. You're alive. I was sure you were dead, too." He buried her in his arms. "Antoine was crazy with worry."

She pushed away from Doc and returned to Charlie. "I was hoping I could leave Charlie with Myles."

Doc grabbed her shoulder. "What's wrong?"

"They're dragging Antoine around."

"A shaming?" He rubbed his forehead.

"You know what that is?"

"Did you leave Clement's Ranch?" Doc looked worried. "Just walked off? Can you do that?"

Emma frowned. "Where's Myles?" She had Charlie in her arms.

Doc looked around the barn, lost. "Gone." After a long silence he said, "Let me take the horse in. You go in and clean up, eat. I'll run to Pleti to see what I can find out."

"I'm coming."

"No. Hide."

Emma turned to him, anger in her eyes. She was sick of people telling her what to do.

Doc softened. "Antoine would kill me if I lost you. You have no idea how crazy that young buck was. How crazy I was. We searched everywhere."

"I was vanished."

"Vanished? Wish I could vanish." He closed his eyes.

"No, you don't."

"I meant my pain. You know, just deal with it in smaller doses. Make yourself at home. I won't be long."

"I'd rather talk to Myles," Emma insisted.

"You and me both. Think of Charlie and clean up. We have to return you to Clement's Ranch before he notices you're gone."

He was bringing her back? She'd been gone for a whole day. She couldn't go back. Inside the words screamed. She backed up, carefully.

Doc pulled the horse by the reins and turned from her.

She stood, not breathing. Not sure she understood anything Doc said.

Charlie's stomach rumbled, snapping her from her shock and pushing her into action. She was not going back to that ranch. That much she knew.

–Thirty-five–

A mob forced Doc to pull over before he made it to Pleti. He was moderately annoyed but needed to find Antoine, fast.

Doc climbed out of his car with his medical bag. Facing the blowing dust he tried to see around the crowd. Was Antoine among them? He approached the row of men wearing white sheets in even strides. The sheets clung to them as the wind fought for freedom.

Each step was forced, focused. Find Antoine. He'd know what to do with the girl. Doc couldn't make this decision alone. He wouldn't. He didn't trust himself right now, everything was clouding together.

On their horses, men in sheets looked down. The sight never got easier. And he was convinced they did this just for him. How did they know this was his weakness? That his greatest fear was to be invisible? A ghost of a man?

"Is someone hurt? I'm a doctor." They were silent so he said, "Let me through. I'm looking for a man, a Métis with long black hair, usually wears a cowboy hat with either bare feet or moccasins. I have something he wants." One of them pumped a shotgun. "You're gonna shoot a man who comes to offer medical attention?"

Still, the barrel remained in his face.

"Then shoot away. It's you who has to live with yourself when the sheet comes off."

"I will shoot you, Doc."

Doc closed his eyes with a painful sigh. He recognized that voice. He longed to forget that he knew these people. Forget it all. "After I helped your son when he returned from the war and no one dared operate on that hip? You have any idea the treatments Myles did with him so he could walk again? You could really pull that trigger knowing that I stayed up with him for three nights because I didn't trust anyone else?" Doc touched the horse gently and glanced up. Myles had told him to trust his instinct, that he had a gift when it came to getting inside people's minds. His instinct screamed to run back to... *where?* He didn't feel safe anywhere.

"You plan to shoot an unarmed man holding a healing kit? Is this how low you've sunk? I see the real you, despite that sheet, Jack. I see your children, your wife, your saddest and happiest moments. I see a free man who doesn't need a sheet. I wish you could see the real me from up there, because I used to be someone I was proud to look at in the mirror."

The shotgun vanished as fast as it had appeared and much to his surprise, two—Jack included—rode off without looking back. Huh. Maybe Myles was wrong and there was hope for mankind.

Other than that, there was no movement from the others. Doc pushed past them in case it was Antoine up ahead. He wouldn't let the young buck succumb to the same fate as Myles. He couldn't.

Doc scrunched up his eyes. The wind was fierce, but a crowd gathered around a wagon. Antoine was strapped to a post, unconscious in the middle of the wagon and men in sheets brought in kindling.

Doc ran up to them, his fear dropping as he assessed the situation in one fell swoop. Something was wrong with these people. Their movements were bizarre, slurred. *Drugs?*

To those not in sheets he yelled, "Stop them. What's wrong with you people? Stop them." Doc knocked the wood from one of their arms. "This is a human being. It's too windy for a burning. Stop." Doc climbed the wagon, frantic. Why did everyone look entranced? "A shaming allows God to decide and judge him for his crimes. What did this man do to deserve this treatment? Mob mentality is all this is." Doc felt Antoine's pulse. It was still strong. He was fine. *He was alive.*

"Don't touch me." Antoine breathed through tight teeth, head down, facing the wind. He was covered in scratches and bruises. Dust and dirt caked into his skin.

"Antoine, it's me, Doc. I found her. I found her. My God

man, what have they done to you?" With his knife, Doc started to cut him down.

They swarmed the cart and Doc was buried in a sea of fists and bodies.

"Enough." A booming voice came over the crowd followed by a gunshot.

Ghosts pulled away enough so Doc could see the source of the voice, sitting proud on his horse. It was the man he'd let go before Myles was murdered. Clement.

A deep anger burned, as if the wind suddenly ignited something in him.

"I see Tommy's been through." Clement glared at the crowd.

A man in a sheet held a golden chalice up and knelt before him. Without a glance, Clement hit him with the butt of his gun and he fell forward. Someone snapped up the chalice but let the man fall. Doc's breath locked in his lungs.

"The sacred Drink is out in the open." Clement ran the gun over the crowd as if ready to shoot them all.

Doc tried to break free from the man that held him. "Let me help that man. Let me go. He needs medical attention."

"Your education can be better wasted on real problems." Clement's eyes rested on Doc. "When will you learn not to meddle in my business, Doctor Williams?"

"I never..." Doc caught himself. Was this the man stealing his medical shipments right off the trains? Doc stepped back. Was this why Myles died? For drugs? The idea sickened him and his entire world swirled in and out. Of course it was. It always came down to money.

Clement ignored Doc and turned back to the crowd. "Clean this mess up. I see anyone consume the Drink from our sacred room again, I shoot their entire family. You have lost the privilege of such blessings."

"But this man—" someone started to say and again, without hesitation, Clement raised his gun and whacked him with it. The man fell from his horse into the crowd.

"Hoolie!" Clement demanded.

A boy rode up alongside of Clement. He adjusted his cap, and his fire-orange hair flew back. "Yes, boss?"

"Should I shoot this man they drag around?" Clement

rubbed the wound that Doc had stitched along his cheek.

"He knows where your daughter is," Hoolie said, so matter-of-fact. "I could talk to him, if you like. Men like that know things about what's going on. Might come in handy."

Clement let a smile creep up on his face but it vanished just as smoothly while his eyes fired over the mob. "Yes. You know more than you let on, Hoolie, and you honestly haven't let me down yet. Afterwards, find me Tommy. I want a word with him."

"I'll bring him to the meeting room, but you call these lunatics off. I ain't risking my neck for you." An eerie silence settled on the prairies when Hoolie ordered Clement around. As if to heighten it, the wind stopped dead and dropped a powerful heat on them.

Doc struggled to break free, sure Clement would hit the boy, but he nodded thoughtfully.

Doc's jaw throbbed where someone had hit him. His right side was on fire. Things never felt so unreal.

"I'm missing a dog dressed in rags." Clement's voice boomed over the crowd, while they listened intently. "She trucks around a small child and both are to be delivered to the fire chamber untouched. You ten empty the clinic and you six come with me, the doctor's farm needs another visit. The rest..." His eyes swept over the group. "The Catholic Church wants the Drink destroyed. Let's show them what you think of that. Focus on what is important and leave details like this to me."

Clement left. The crowd tightened around them. Doc curled up on his bag.

"Emma," Antoine mumbled and Doc snapped back to the real world. He had to get Antoine to her. He knelt beside Antoine and opened his bag. No time to move him. He'd have to give him something for pain.

"Back up." The redhead, Hoolie, got off his horse. "Help me get Mister on my horse."

"He stays with me." Doc was firm.

Much to Doc's surprise Hoolie spoke Latin. "Boss just saved your lives. These fools are lost. I can't make sense of their light when they're like this. Let's get him out before they snap."

His Latin accent was exactly like Myles'. He sounded so much like Myles that Doc spoke to him without thinking his question through. "Hypnotic drink?" Doc looked up at Hoolie and pulled back surprised. The boy... he had Myles' eyes. Identical, as if he seared into his soul, seeing the truth about the burdens he hid there.

"Yeah, Tommy makes stuff from my worst nightmares." Hoolie was already unbinding Antoine's hands. "You can come, but Mister comes with me."

He'd went with Myles to search for his son many times, but until this moment, Doc never actually believed he might be alive. Was this boy his son? Could it be? "I am not letting him go. You come with me." Doc held Antoine firmly. "Can you see souls, boy?" Hoolie, his name was Hoolie. Chinese?

"Yours ain't looking so hot. Blend in, just walk away. Let the Drink wear off. Any confrontation will ignite their rage."

Doc groaned when a knee caught him in the gut.

"Let him go. Bloody poof," someone said as they pulled his hair back.

"No, Hoolie! Wait!"

The boy was gone, lost in the sea of fists coming at him.

He swung. Doc was shoved to the ground. Eyes shut he felt them storm over him. He needed an escape.

Just forget.

Forget. Bring it back in smaller doses. Hypnosis, like Myles used to do. Maybe Clement was onto something. Self-hypnosis.

The song Antoine sang flashed over him and Doc let the melody carry his soul away, far far away to someplace safe, until he felt no pain, only the warm eyes of who he loved. Safe. He just wanted to feel safe for one moment.

–THIRTY-SIX–

Charlie ate and Emma washed him in Doc's basin with warm water. Snooping in the room where she'd stayed last time, Emma found a bunch of beautiful dresses. She picked out the most colourful one, not having ever seen anything so striking. Even Mable didn't wear dresses like this. A real lady wore this. She tried it on and twirled in front of the mirror while Charlie played on the floor with one of Myles' books. Where was Myles? Had Clement vanished him? If he left, why didn't he take his things? And who lived in this room now?

Bring you back.

She wasn't going to the ranch. Not ever. She'd die first. "Come Charlie, we're gonna take a walk."

"Papa?"

"Yup. Time to find Papa, but first, we let his horse go free. Everyone must think we vanished for good."

~~

Doc's car was turned over. Smashed. The windows were broken and glass was all over the trail. Emma checked inside to make sure he wasn't in it, but it was empty. Words were painted on the shiny black in white but they were too long for her to sound out. The paint was still wet.

Emma walked with Charlie. He touched her hand. "Bad."

"You don't say much, but your choice of words is powerful, little man. That's exactly how I feel—bad."

A body was on the road and she rushed to it.

Doc.

Emma pulled Charlie behind her and told him to turn around. He did. He always did as she told him. Such a good boy.

Doc's breathing was shallow. She looked around for help, but there was none. Only his kit along the road.

His kit. It would hold things to help. She retrieved it and opened it, not a clue what she needed. Doc bled under the ear. Too much. She wanted to stop that. Blood should stay inside not pour all over the road—that much she knew.

Emma found a clean cloth in the bag and put it on the wound. "Charlie, come here."

"Bad." He didn't move.

"No. Not bad, we help. Hold this cloth. We'll help. Myles said we could trust him. He's a doctor."

"Not bad. Help?"

"Yes, it's safe. He's hurt. We're helping. This is what good people do, no matter how afraid they are, they help."

Charlie ran over, his jaw tight. "Brave."

"Yes, you are very brave." She showed him what to do.

He touched her hand and she felt better. "Help not bad?" Charlie asked.

"Yes, Charlie. Helping is good." Emma found a flask and another cloth. She wet the rag and cleaned the dust off Doc's face. "Doc, wake up. Tell me what to do."

A shadow loomed over them and a woman knelt beside Doc, feeling his neck as if she'd done this before. Emma pulled back shocked; she'd been so distraught, she hadn't heard this woman pull up.

Her skin was pale like Doc's. Well, not as pale as Doc's; she had beautiful olive skin.

Emma looked at her own dusty skin. She was dirty from her travels.

"I... where did you come from?"

The woman pointed to her buggy with an annoyed frown.

It was fancy. Her bountiful blue dress was even nicer and her lacy hat... Wow. Emma had never seen anything so elegant.

"You're beautiful," she blurted out.

"What happened to him? Why are you in that dress?"

Emma felt foolish in the elegant rose dress. She should have never taken it from the closet. "I... I found it. It's my disguise. Can you help him?"

She stared at the tattoo on Emma's hand. Then she undid the ribbon on her hat. "Here, put this on. Don't say a word."

"To who?" Emma asked.

"Is that your boy? Hide him."

"Charlie, climb in the buggy and stay down." Emma tied the hat. She'd never worn one this fancy and it forced her head straight.

Charlie dashed off.

Doc moaned.

"Will hunny, it's Marie. Can you hear me? I need you on your feet. My buggy isn't far."

"Hey, beauty." A deep voice made Emma freeze and shots of panic sizzled through her.

Emma glanced up enough to see horse legs. She didn't dare look any higher in case it was a ghost.

"Don't let them take me," Emma whispered but Marie shot her a dirty glare that shut her up.

"Oh good, two strong men. About time. Get this scum in the buggy," Marie snapped.

"What you doing out by your lonesome, ma'am?" the deep voice asked.

"I'm not alone, stupid. I'm with my servant to pick up the doctor. Hoolie sent me to clean up, or are you so low on the food chain that you don't even know *that*?"

"You look lonesome to us." They got off their horses, and Emma knew that walk. She kept her eyes on their feet, ready to dash. If they were going to touch her, she would run far from Charlie so he couldn't see.

The thought made her panic.

She wouldn't let them touch her. She fumbled in Doc's bag for a knife.

The woman pulled the bag from her and frowned. "Stop drawing attention to yourself. You'll get us in trouble," she whispered, then turned to the ghosts. "If Hoolie even catches you not helping, he'll tell Clement. Now off with the sheets and be civilized. For heaven's sake, tell me your names. Didn't you learn to talk properly to a lady?"

"Yes, ma'am. Sorry, ma'am. I'm Stevie and this is Mitch." Much to Emma's shock, sheets dropped to their feet and they hauled Doc to the buggy.

"Now be gone with the both of you," Marie ordered. "Honestly, I don't need you fools hanging around me. I can manage fine myself. And take a bath. I can hardly stand the stink."

"Yes, ma'am. You be sure to tell Hoolie that we were helpful."

"Of course, Mitch. He'll be happy to know someone was useful."

They scurried to their horses and left their sheets behind.

Emma stayed by Doc's bag not sure what happened.

"Well, what are you waiting for?" Marie snapped. "Get in with your boy. We have to find a safe place before they grow a brain and come back for us."

Emma still didn't move. "How?"

"What?" Marie gathered their sheets and tossed them in her buggy.

"I... gee... How did you do that? We got away without them touching us?"

Marie marched over and touched Emma's chin. White gloves covered her fingers, and Emma had no idea when she'd put them on.

Emma met her eyes. They made her think of Antoine's golden eyes. Only his were much warmer. Emma stepped back from the woman. She didn't trust her.

"You're pretty. Radiant. Healthy. Need to get you cleaned up. You running from something? No, don't tell me. Get in. I'll teach you to talk to men. They're boys inside, just need to lean over them and mother them. The ones you can't slip under your thumb, you bury alive and let the earth deal with them."

Emma opened her mouth to argue this, thinking about what Antoine had said about being equal, then she thought that probably wasn't something a woman like this wanted to hear so she shut her yap.

"Nope. Won't do."

"What?" Emma asked, climbing in the buggy, checking for Charlie. He'd fallen asleep on the floor under some blankets. He was so tired lately.

"When you have a thought, say it. You wanted to prove me wrong yet bit your tongue. Why?"

"I..." Emma swallowed. "It's possible to be equal to men."

"Oh yes, you look like you've lived that several times, eh?"

"I have."

"Foolish notion that is. I'm Marie. What is your name?"

"Emma."

"No, Emma, men will tell you we're equal, we have a right to vote, and blah blah. They can blow it out their arses. It's a farce so they can get on top of us and it don't matter what race, religion, or nothing, they treat us like crap so you might as well be prepared. They make us do the damn dirty work so they can go off and fight in a blasted war that'll give us nothing but wounded men to nurse." The anger in her voice was so strong that Emma sat up taller. "Truth is, girl, I am petrified when they come near me. I want to curl up and cry, but I dig down deep and face them like the warrior I am. Know why?"

"No."

"Because I can."

Doc moaned in the back.

"Yet..." Emma glanced at Doc. "You're helping this one."

"Well, doesn't mean I don't have a use for a few of 'em."

–THIRTY-SEVEN–

Antoine woke with a splitting headache.

It hurt to breathe.

He wiggled his toes. Yup. Painful.

His fingers moved, but damn, they throbbed. His wrists. What was wrong with his wrists?

"Where is my daughter?" Clement hovered over Antoine with a fire-hot branding rod. Even in his worst nightmare, this wasn't possible.

Antoine's throat was parched but he croaked out, "My ugly mug gets her thrown at your feet and I won't do that until Emma and Charlie are safe at Depaix Farm. I told you this. Not my fault if you didn't believe me. I can't change that."

"Bloody *Cîpay* pricks." Clement pushed the branding rod into his shoulder and pain seared through Antoine's entire body, but he was too broken to defend himself. He tried again to swing. No, not broken, his wrists were tied down.

"Until you tell me what I want to hear, I find new spots to mark you as mine."

A light exploded around them and someone snapped, "What the hell!?!" Was that Hoolie who exploded from the sudden light? "I told you that a soul this stubborn won't respond to your dumbass ideas. If you want results you let me handle this guy. This won't get you nothing. Don't you learn? I am not working for you if you're going to be a moron."

The rod Clement held hit the cement floor with a clang.

Antoine felt weak. He closed his eyes as things swooshed in for him and dreamt of his happy forever. He imagined Emma twirling in the wheat, swinging Charlie. He could smell the peace of fresh turned earth as they danced in the field he'd planted. A cool breeze mixed with the warm sun. Happy. That's what happy felt like, and he might never get it, but he knew what it was. He let this image sweep him away.

~~

A damp cloth soothed his shoulder and he opened his eyes to Hoolie.

"Now I'm dreaming of a tunnel fox."

"Why not tell him what he wants to know, Mister? I never saw anyone as tough as you. You didn't even flinch." Hoolie moved the cloth to Antoine's neck. Every time he moved the cloth, he felt the fire in that new spot. "Can you teach me that? Your light merged with the earth. Just vanished, yet you stayed connected to it with this blurry energy, as if feeding it life. Clement called you a soulless demon, said you found a way to hypnotise yourself without the Drink. Drove him right crazy, it did." Hoolie smirked briefly as if proud of Antoine.

Antoine shifted his eyes to get a better look at the tunnel runner. "What for the love of these prairies are you doing here? I'm not back in Saskatchewan, am I?"

"Boss is searching for someone in other countries and he liked the fact that I know several languages, so he brought me here to get things rolling. Once he found out I see the light in people he's been treating me real swell. It was fun. I learnt two more languages while I was here. Met this really smart shadow that teaches me things. Besides, not many run his messages as fast as I do either. Earned me a bunch of cash, but I'd give it up to have courage like you."

"Takes only one thing to get courage, Hoolie."

"What's that?"

"A dream you can almost grasp. To be honest, Hoolie, the image I hold on to is Emma in the garden, Charlie chasing butterflies in the field, and me knowing they're safe. Maybe a friend comes over to borrow this or that. Ya know, simple. I'm not asking for much, just one happy moment. It's a dream of a home I might never get, yet it gives me the courage I need in moments of hell. Nothing secret about that."

Hoolie nodded. "Makes sense, but what if I ain't got a

home?"

"That's why it's a dream, Hoolie."

"Clement thinks you're hiding a couple of his girls. Are you?"

"I'd be home if I had Emma and all this would be over." Antoine focused on Hoolie, wanting to explain things to him, but a movement in the room made him think they weren't alone.

Clement appeared on the other side of Antoine. He reached over Antoine and handed a crisp bill to Hoolie. "Only thing Hoolie understands is money. You let him see that Mable is fine and I'll find Emma. You did well, Hoolie, now get me my daughter." Clement left them alone.

"So courage ain't something I can buy, eh?" Hoolie held the bill up so Antoine could see it, too, then he slipped it in Antoine's pocket before he left to work at the stove.

Antoine was spent. "Where are we?" He focused. A dim light from a fire warmed the room. He glanced at the dirt walls.

"Tunnels so full of life their stories scare me."

Antoine tried to sit. His wrists were free, but they still ached. He looked at his arms, the deep scars on them were already scabbing over. How long had he been out?

"Lay down, Mister."

"I have to get back to his ranch. He's gonna hurt my gal. Can't go home without my family."

"He wouldn't hurt a woman. Clement's a real gentlemen, he is. He says you plan to hurt them. He acts tough, but we all put on a show to hide the truth, don't we?"

"You need to pull your eyes out of his pocket and look around, Hoolie." Antoine tried to sit but fell back. Why was his body so tired?

"I see, Mister. Don't you ever worry about me. I see everything so clearly, it scares me sometimes."

"How so?"

"Sometimes, the sweet looking ones, they have light so contaminated it's nothing but mud. Guys like Clement act tough, but his light tells me something very different."

Antoine wanted to ask what, but the pain consumed him. He stopped breathing until he blacked out.

–Thirty-Eight–

September 1918—

Charlie was two today. Two, and Antoine still hadn't held him since the day he was born. Antoine smashed the wall making a deep hole in Emma's room. There. That felt better. Let Clement worry about nails.

"We need to scram," Hoolie said in French when he saw the hole in the wall. "*Vite.*"

Antoine wasn't going anywhere without Emma and Charlie. He picked up the Bible. It had teeth marks in it. Funny kid.

Antoine tossed the Bible to Hoolie. "Shove this in that bag of crap you carry around."

"I ain't hauling this around. Clement will kill me." Yet he didn't hesitate to slip it in his bag.

"I'm not done searching. You can go," Antoine told him.

"I don't leave your side until your debt is paid and I see the boss' daughter." Hoolie was ready to run. "They aren't here. Let's go."

"I've hidden on this farm for days, and no one's caught me. Stop being so nervous."

Hoolie studied his bare feet, like the rest of him, they were filthy. Antoine was sure the boy was afraid of water because he hadn't seen Hoolie swim yet. "The plans changed today," Hoolie finally admitted.

"Spill it."

"Well, for one thing, they know you're here. For another, I got this message today; they found his daughter in Tibet. She's married, apparently she had a baby and some bonehead registered her as the ma. Eyes everywhere I tell ya. I used to think that was swell, but since I've been hanging with you, it makes me nervous."

"I ain't forcing ya to stay. Go home to your mama."

Hoolie continued to study his feet while chewing on his lip. "I gave you the message first, but Tommy is going to give it to Clement. Should have been me. He already thinks I'm double-crossing him."

"You are."

"You know the tip that message would have gotten me? He checks ya know, to make sure I don't screw him over. Boss is more paranoid than you." Hoolie sighed. "We need to hit the fields, now."

Antoine rubbed his chin. "He'll kill Emma."

"Cook says she left on her own. Got on a horse and took off as Clement rode up. She ain't here for him to kill. So let's find where she hides."

"What if he finds her before us?"

"Cook says servants who run off end up in the hole, but she didn't know anything more." Hoolie stood in his sly way, giving Antoine a smirk that implied he knew about the holes.

"A fox like you would know what goes on underground."

"Bloody morgue under this place. Ground is putrid. Can we hit the fields?"

"Two years ago, Emma vanished from this room. What if there is an entrance that leads to this hole?"

"The one in Clement's room is quicker and easier to access than the one in this room."

"Show me." Antoine dashed upstairs and Hoolie was on his heels. "You know, Hoolie, I think you're right. Time for us to get home."

"Good."

"Hoolie, you really don't have to come with me in this hole, just point me in the right direction."

Hoolie smiled weakly at Antoine as he pushed opened the door to Clement's room. "I watched you crawl the prairies to stumble across your horse. Not someone else's horse, oh no, the one I gave you. Who has that kinda dumb luck? I mean man, that's better than cash. The richest man alive can't buy luck like that."

"God was looking out for me."

"God eh? I need me a friend like that. One who knows what I need and provides it, no questions asked."

"As far as friends go, your eyes come in handy," Antoine admitted. "But, I always feel like you're hiding things from me."

Hoolie nodded as he walked into the room. "I know more dirt than one guy can ever expect to report. I got nothing to hide from a guy like you, but I have to be honest, Mister, you wouldn't believe half the stuff I know is going down."

So far, Hoolie had kept him alive, he trusted that.

The bed in the middle of the room had a pink and purple floral pattern blanket that made Antoine smile. "Really not the room I imagined Clement snuggling up in with his wife. You?"

Portraits of Clement's six daughters lined the walls. Antoine pulled open a few drawers and glanced in them. In the nightstand drawer was a picture of Charlie. Antoine took it out. He snapped it from the frame and shoved it in his pocket.

"My guess is his wife vanished like everyone else who pisses him off. That hole must be huge, eh?" Hoolie had his head buried in a drawer and stuffed things from it into his bag.

"What you stealing? His underwear?"

"Hankies. Here." He tossed Antoine one as he climbed in the armoire in the corner, tying one so it covered his nose and mouth.

"You want me to use his snot rag to breathe through? No thanks." Still he shoved it in his pocket.

Hoolie climbed in among the suits. He poked his freckled head out and smirked. "I was hoping we were gonna scram, but if you want to check this hole for your girl before we go, let's be quick." He checked his pocket-watch. "I'd like to get out of this hole before two."

Antoine checked his own watch. That wasn't going to happen. He followed him, not sure if he should grab a lantern. The back of the armoire was missing. It led to a stone hallway where Hoolie felt the walls and came up with a lantern that he passed to Antoine. "If we take that path, it leads to Emma's room."

"You know your way around these tunnels?"

"Every one is the same. Grew up underground, Mister. Everything makes sense under the surface. Can you feel the life pulsate in the earth? Every wall has a story to tell. Trouble with you is that your home is all you focus on. You can't see the potential homes around you. A happy moment—that can be found anywhere, at any given time."

"Well, I lied to you. Anyone can be happy for a moment. I want to be happy forever. We've been together for two months, when you gonna call me Antoine?"

"Not today. I go around calling you Antoine, like you're my brother, and a mistake like that in front of the boss will cost me my life. I know how to survive, Mister. I won't call you Antoine until I'm prepared to die for you. Trust that, 'cause the minute I earn my pay—"

"Pay you? Every dollar I give you comes back to me."

"I don't take cash from guys like you. I figured if I help you save your gal and we get you that home you dream about, you can introduce me to that girl with the dancing light that hangs around your place and get me the home I dream about. Happy forever, like brothers or something."

"Jill?"

"Yeah." Hoolie's face reddened, even in the dim light. "And make me come off all heroic and stuff. Girls like that." Suddenly Hoolie stopped. "You hear that?"

They travelled the corridor until it came to a staircase. Antoine couldn't hear anything except Hoolie breathing.

Hoolie led the way, but never asked Antoine for the lantern. "Clement wants me in town by six with news about how you died down here. Think we'll be done messing around before then?"

Antoine sighed. "Probably not."

"You're not the best liar. You ever notice that about you? It might be a skill to master, if you're never gonna have good news for me. I like false hope when I'm feeling trapped."

A loud shriek made Antoine pick up the pace. "Head toward that sound."

Hoolie moved faster, as if he knew exactly where he rushed to in the emptiness that rolled out before them. Antoine grabbed Hoolie's suspenders so not to lose him.

"Don't touch the walls. Toxic. Smell it? If you feel lightheaded make sure you put that hanky over your mouth."

"Then here, take the lantern so I can tie my hanky." They stopped running for a moment so Antoine could tie his hanky, covering his nose and mouth. He looked around at the rough walls. Was this where Emma had worked and lived with Charlie for a year?

Hoolie handed the lantern back to Antoine and they were off again, almost running. Suddenly, Hoolie stopped. Antoine swept the lantern around. A girl was at his feet.

Setting down the lantern, Antoine picked her up. She was a child, about ten.

"Not good," Hoolie said, looking in front of him as if he could see something in the dark that Antoine couldn't. "Her light ain't in her body."

"She's breathing. Barely, but breathing. So calm down." Antoine walked with her, not sure where he was going. She needed sun, fresh air. Water. Food. She was skin and bones.

"You need this lantern?" Hoolie grabbed it and followed him. After another good walk, Hoolie stopped and opened his pack. He pulled out something wrapped in a hanky. "Goons just around the corner. I can handle this batch. Stay here."

Before Antoine could argue Hoolie rushed around the corner. "Hey. Came to see how things were going today."

"Hoolie. You aren't supposed to be down here." A rough voice crackled down the tunnel.

"Yeah, and I ain't supposed to be stealing you boys that whiskey either."

"Can I have some of that?" someone asked.

"I'm gonna eat it, thanks," Hoolie said. "Why? Aren't they feeding you?"

"Not cake."

"Ah hell. You know I hate them sob stories. Here take it. Why you doing this job when you boys could be freelancing like me?"

"You got us a job?"

"I always have work." Hoolie sounded smug and Antoine had to admire his way with people. He always knew exactly what to say to get what he wanted. "Two jobs today. I'm meeting some Antoine fellow in five minutes down that vein.

Now, if I could wait ten, he'd be stressed and pay me top dollar to get him out safely, but I don't have time to wait 'cause Tommy needs me pronto. So I have to move him around quickly."

"Um. Ah. Antoine?" Some papers shifted. "This one?"

"Yup. I do it right, I'll get a tip and reward monies. Pays the bills."

What reward money? Had Clement put a bounty on his head?

"We could do that so you don't keep Tommy waiting, couldn't we Mitch? I mean, we know these tunnels well and these bloody diggers aren't going anywhere but to bed. They won't miss us."

"Yeah, but I can't lose that money. Thanks," Hoolie said.

"Nothing saying we don't knock you out and..."

Antoine was ready to set the girl down and go to Hoolie's aid when Hoolie peeked around the corner. "Coming?"

Cautiously, Antoine made his way. The goons were in a heap on the ground.

"What the heck did you do to them?" Antoine kicked one gently. He was breathing.

"Something I borrowed from Tommy. Knocks them out like a baby. I was supposed to use it on you and blow one of these tunnels in on you. I still can if you think that would be better than the hell we're gonna go through."

"Thanks."

"Ah, they'll wake up feeling refreshed and ready to kick my ass." Hoolie chuckled. "Should be funny when I tell Tommy they stole it from me. He's gonna be fuming."

"Do you plan these things?"

"Nah, just let people make their own messes."

They had to duck to enter the large room at the end of the tunnel. Antoine stood taken aback by the sight before him. Several people sat on beds, talking, eating. They looked up at Antoine and Hoolie.

"What the heck?" Hoolie asked, shocked. "Mister?" He glanced at Antoine and set his bag down to dig through it. "They talked of diggers, but what the heck is this? These are dames and brats. We have to get them out. This is wrong, look at their light. No. No. We gotta move." He was frantic.

"Antoine?" One shot to his feet. "What the heck ya doing down here?"

Antoine was shocked to see Philip. "Emma was worried that you were dead."

"Might as well be." Philip tried to take the child from Antoine but Antoine shook his head.

"I got her. I'm taking her outta here. She needs fresh air."

"How the heck did you find us?" Philip asked. "Tunnels to the south are bad, tunnels to the north go in circles. Wise guys with pistols patrol the place."

Hoolie handed out the hankies from his pack and showed them how to tie them.

Philip hovered over Antoine, about four inches taller than him. He had a few more muscles than Antoine remembered.

"Another bunch that dream of home," Hoolie told Antoine when he handed Philip a hanky, glancing over his shoulder nervously. Even in the dim light, Antoine saw the desperation in the boy's look, and it reminded him of Philip's when he'd asked if Antoine would take Gracie with him.

Yeah. He was taking them all home. "Then home it is."

Hoolie sidled up beside him.

A woman put down what she was eating. It looked like burned rabbit or... rat? "Emma said you'd come."

"Let's go," Hoolie insisted. "We ain't got time for chatting. This has all kinds of me screwing up all over it. If the boss gets wind that I'm pulling a double-cross on him or helping his workers escape I won't ever see the light of day again."

The woman said, "If we're caught—"

Antoine flung around. "What? What can they possibly do to you that is worse than this? Screw them. We follow Hoolie, throw sheets over you, use Clement's own blasted horses to get you out of here. See how he likes that message."

"You sure we can trust this guy?" Philip eyed the hanky, skeptical. "This is Clement's."

"He sticks with me until I pay off my debt. That good enough for ya?" Antoine expected more arguments but they followed Hoolie.

A woman mumbled to Philip as she passed, "Emma was right, Philip. He did come. I wasn't wrong to believe."

Knowing that he was her hope, and he'd failed her tore at

Antoine. "Philip is right not to believe in me, it's because I convinced him to leave the ranch that he's vanished to this hole."

Philip placed a hand on Antoine's shoulder. "No. I'm here because I can't control my temper. Leaving was my choice. It's not you I doubt, it's that mousy one."

"Hoolie has the Sight. Means he knows a good soul when he sees one. I trust that."

Philip frowned.

Hoolie said, "Easy peasy, just follow the shadow through the tunnels of death."

Philip mumbled, "What shadow?"

Hoolie answered with his worried frown, "The one teaching me Latin."

"Don't ask," Antoine said. "Sometimes we have to trust blindly, Philip. You're welcome to stay." Antoine shoved the girl into his arms. "But you're responsible for her safety now." He turned to follow Hoolie in the dark. "Just don't touch the walls and do what Hoolie does."

Hoolie yelped as a hand reached around the corner and snagged him. "Mister, run." Tommy had Hoolie in a death grip, a knife to his throat. His feet kicked wildly as Tommy lifted him off the ground.

"You little shit. I told you to keep to the main vein. What if I would have gotten lost down here?"

Antoine didn't even try to reason with him. He snagged a stone and tossed it, hitting Tommy in the forehead. His grip loosened on Hoolie and he squirmed away.

"Cripes you could have hit me, Mister. What the heck you all waiting for? Run!"

"They need you to guide them out, Hoolie. Go."

Antoine charged for Tommy and rammed him into the wall.

Tommy swung and Antoine felt his shoulder weaken. Tommy's arms came up in a flash and Antoine was flying across the tunnel. Everyone was gone.

Tommy was on Antoine and shoved his face in the dirt. "That rat just left you for dead. He's gonna lead all that swine to their deaths and not a thing you can do about it."

Antoine felt the heat sear through his shoulder.

"Let the rats deal with you. Hell is what you are, mutt."

Antoine rubbed his hands into the dirt and rested into its comfort while he waited for death to find him.

~~

The ground rumbled. "Mister, come on. Come on, wake up. This place is coming down on us."

"Hoolie?" Antoine tasted dirt. He tried to stand but pain shot through him when he moved. His shoulder was on fire and like lightning it flashed through his entire body.

"Breathe through the pain." Philip helped Antoine to his feet. "I'll toss Antoine over my shoulder. Hoolie, you're gonna have to carry the girl."

"I ain't touching her, her light ain't in her body," Hoolie complained. "What if she dies and her shadow haunts me?"

"He ain't gonna make it," Philip said. "You wanna carry him?"

Antoine wanted to tell them he was fine but the words wouldn't come out. Was he fine?

"Oh crap. There goes his light again."

PART FOUR

A MONTH LATER

"No one deserves to breathe. We earn each breath until one day we earn one that never ends."

–Sacri

–THIRTY-NINE–

October 1918—

Hoolie sat on his heels watching Antoine pace the barn. They weren't far from Pleti, which is where the Reward Hunter liked to hang out lately. He'd spent all day searching for her but found nothing.

Whatever ate at Mister now, was like with the house. He fixated. Like some type of counting maniac, he counted the group on the run again as they crowded together. Hoolie wanted to scream, *Fourteen!* They were always fourteen, yet Antoine counted them every ten seconds like his gal might materialize among them and he might miss it.

"Counting again. Wow, when you obsess about things you do it well, Mister." Hoolie tossed Antoine a blanket. "Sleep. Do you even remember what that is? Cripes, it's cold. I need a little fox to warm me up. This travelling with you isn't good for me." He was eager to go home, too. Home. It felt weird, yet Eau Claire called out to him. It had everything in the world he wanted. Even a blasted girl he couldn't find the courage to talk to. Gosh. Could he talk to someone with dancing light? He felt his face warm with the thought.

Antoine said, "Every time I close my eyes I see Clement's ranch burning. They destroyed his home, Hoolie. What if Emma and Charlie were there somewhere? I should go back."

"No way in hell am I letting you go back. We go one way. Home. With or without your gal, we're going home. You know how bad Clement is gonna have it in for Philip? Clement saw him with you flung over his shoulder while he pulled you from that tunnel. I was in the hole trying to drag those goons out of a collapse when he found me, and he swore Philip was gonna pay. I am supposed to be hunting you right now. You know how messed up this is? Now sleep. I'm sick and tired of these games. I just want to go home."

Antoine studied the sleeping group, and Hoolie watched him count them again. He had no idea how to snap Antoine out of this obsessing. Hoolie pointed to the newspaper clipping pinned to the wall. "What's it say? Can you read that?"

"It's about the war. Feels like mine is just starting. We need to keep moving." Antoine counted the group again. "Twelve. Seven men. Four women and the child. You and me. Fourteen. *Quatorze.*"

"Argh. Stop it. Drives me crazy. She ain't here. She won't ever be. This woman you look for, she doesn't exist."

Antoine got right in his face. "Counting is the only thing I control right now."

Hoolie didn't back down. They were inches from each other, talking firmly, yet quietly. He could tell everyone was listening to them by the intensity of their light. "You aren't thinking straight. If you're gonna get us home, you need to breathe or something, geesh. Philip and I got us here, but from now on it's all you. I can't be seen with you if you expect me to work my magic."

"Breathe?" Antoine pulled away. It was so cold his breath made puffs. Antoine inhaled slower, longer, making the air white around him. "I promised them safety."

"Must have missed that."

"Not these guys," Antoine admitted. "My gal. Her son. It drives me nuts that I failed them."

Hoolie thought about this. "You ain't dead yet. Focus on what you can do."

"We need to keep moving. And Hoolie?"

"Yeah?"

"When we get home, I'll teach you to read."

Hoolie smiled. He really liked that idea. Did Mister even notice that he promised to take him home? "Why do freaks like me need to read? I see shadows and light, remember?"

"You might be surprised. Get them together, we're moving out."

"No. These guys are wiped and I'm sleeping whether you like it or not. Wake me up before I freeze to death." Hoolie snuggled into the straw until he could hardly see Antoine. It sucked. Straw sucked. He wanted a bed. "Besides, you told me this place was safe."

"I lied."

Hoolie waited for Antoine's earthy-light to surround them before saying goodnight to the shadow who taught him Latin. He was a nice warm shadow who seemed to like Antoine. Nothing was safe anymore, but with Antoine's light around them, really, it was home.

–FORTY–

Doc's house looked fine from the outside, but inside it was destroyed. Antoine couldn't tell Hoolie that the walls were painted up with words he knew would kill Doc to read. Scriptures taken out of context were written on his things. Everything was broken. Myles' books were thrown about and torn to pieces. Antoine thought about burning the place down so Doc wouldn't have to see the damage.

Where was Doc?

When he was sure Hoolie wasn't looking, Antoine undid his shirt and took a peek at his shoulder. It was festering. He took off the hanky and replaced it with a clean one he'd stolen from Doc's. He'd hoped to find something in Doc's office to help with the infection but there was nothing he could use so he'd cleaned it up and left.

Antoine counted them again as he did up his shirt and jacket. Twelve plus Hoolie. The girl, seven men, four women, one child. He was missing one. He counted again. Oh yeah, himself. Fourteen. It was fine. They were safe. He rubbed his head. He felt so hot.

Breathe in the cold.

Form a little white cloud.

Focus.

Antoine leaned against the door of the barn and stared into the night, just breathing. He took out the picture of Charlie he stole from Clement's nightstand and looked at it. He was getting big and this made him proud.

He wasn't about to fail this crew. He just wanted to wrap them in a safe blanket.

The moon was bright, and a man in a sheet stepped into the distance then vanished.

Antoine shoved the picture in his pocket. "Sheets on, let's go. Ghosts are out."

"Can I shoot 'em if I get close enough?" Philip asked. Antoine stuck close to Philip. He knew how to fight and he caught on quickly how to handle the shotguns.

"I ain't the boss of you." Antoine tossed him his shotgun. "Just make sure it's not me you shoot." Antoine threw a white sheet over himself then picked up the girl who needed a doctor. Not any doctor either. Only one he trusted, but where the heck was he?

Hoolie shot up and straw went flying every which way. "Hey, I'm up. Want me to count them again?" Hoolie was at his side. "Even under a sheet your light gives you away. That's kinda funny." Hoolie smirked.

"What? That's brilliant."

"It is? What'd I say?"

"A trick Sacri taught me so I wouldn't get lost. Find a trait that stands out. Like you and the six freckles on your nose." Antoine looked at the others. "I marked their hands, and it made them crazy because they couldn't live the double lives. What if we follow them home and expose them? Ya know? Steal away the invincible feelings they have. We can't let this madness continue."

Hoolie's eyes were impossibly huge. "I ain't following *them* home. I want my own blasted home. Besides, if they wanna dress up like idiots, I say let 'em."

"And what if they follow us home?" Antoine asked.

"Oh yeah. That would suck."

"There are too many," Philip said.

"Yeah," Antoine agreed. "I think they started using the sheets to scare off *Cîpay* but found something that empowers them. Still, if we focus on Pleti to the border and forget the others, I bet we're looking at no more than a few dozen fools in sheets. I mean, it feels like lots because they all look the same, but there can't be that many."

"There was more than that smuggling booze in Moose Jaw," Hoolie pointed out. "This idea sucks."

"We don't have to mark them, just identify them. This was your bright idea."

"I am not taking credit for stalking idiots while dressed up like one." Still, Hoolie tossed on his sheet.

Antoine took in a deep breath. Focused. "No more time to count. Keep tight and stay together. One of these fools might know where Emma is."

A shadow fell on them.

A shot echoed in the cold like a vibration in the air they couldn't absorb.

Antoine rushed out without looking. The others were tight behind him.

"Holy dirt. He got one. You turned out to be a good shot, Mister Philip. I taught him how to shoot, you know, Mister. I like his plan better, we could shoot them all. Do the world a favour and go home."

"No. There are good people under them sheets who forgot who they are," Antoine said.

"Can't be too good. Mister Philip ain't got one shadow following him, yet that's the third sheet I saw him kill."

They walked as a tight unit right through the ghosts coming at them, and vanished among them.

–FORTY-ONE–

November 1918—

Emma tucked Charlie in. The wind howled outside, blowing sleet at the window. She looked closer, sure her eyes were playing tricks on her. Were ghosts sneaking around in the snow? Could it be?

"How close did you say we were to Canada?" Emma asked Marie.

"Shut up about Canada. Why do you want to go there anyway? We're safe in this church. I like to hide right in front of them, confuses them, since they don't even know their own." Marie was in the doorway with that scowl on her face that never left. "They're up to something."

"How's Doc?" Emma asked, since it was the only topic that ever made Marie smile.

"He's good enough to travel so I'll bring him home. We have a tribal healer that might be able to reach him. He must have damaged his brain or hid a chunk of his soul. He can't remember anything."

"I wish I could forget." Emma hated the longing she felt inside for Antoine. Some moments it felt like he was so close she could reach out and graze him.

Marie was still talking about nothing.

Emma focused on her, her heart aching for Antoine.

Listening to Marie, Emma tried to remember her life before she knew about butter kisses. Had she been happy? Was she risking their lives for something unsure?

Where was Antoine tonight? Was he thinking about her?

"He's there but he doesn't remember much. You talk to him yet?"

"Who?" Emma asked, confused.

"Doc. What's wrong with you? Why are you always daydreaming like that?"

Emma bit her bottom lip and shook her head. She stayed hidden with Charlie as much as possible. Everyone was unsafe. "Thank you for keeping us safe. I shouldn't disrespect you by dreaming like that, it's just that sometimes, when you talk, you remind me of someone who changed my life."

"Change is necessary. You can't be a child forever. At some point, you need to stand on your own." Marie sighed. "I'll walk Doc across the border, but you, I can't. Since you're the one slowing us down and he's the one needing treatment, I'll go alone with him. I arranged for you to stay with a friend of my mother's, closer to Canada. You can rest there, then head where you want."

Emma nodded. It was what she liked about Marie, she didn't sugar-coat anything.

"Does it anger you when I say this? Would you rather stay with me?"

"No. Already you do too much. Plus, what you say is true. I haven't been well lately, but it's passing."

"Do you know why?"

Emma studied her ring. "I'm pregnant."

"Clearly. I meant do you know why I help you?"

Emma shook her head. This was how Marie always talked to her. Never about personal things, like babies or love, just about facts, about what she called the *real world*. She never asked Emma who she was or where she was going, which to Emma, meant she didn't want to know for a reason so she didn't volunteer this information. Marie could keep her and Charlie safe, but like Doc, Emma could see there was dimness on her life that meant she needed to get Charlie away from her.

"I wish for a moment I could be hopeful like you, but I have nothing to cling to, Emma. I have no idea where you get your hope but it makes me happy to be near you and that's more than I deserve."

Without warning, something exploded through the window, and the bed was on fire. Emma yanked Charlie from it and ran to Marie. She whisked Emma out the door, the cold slinking behind them.

"Get the boy in the cellar, Emma, there's a door that leads to the barn, take it. I'll put it out."

Marie left Emma with Charlie, alone in the stairwell. They had electricity in this place, but when Emma pulled the switch to trigger it, nothing happened. The cellar was dark. Too dark. It reminded her of Clement and she stepped back.

"Charlie, hide down there," Marie called. "Emma, you get Doc and follow the boy. We're under attack."

Charlie flew down the basement steps as fast as his little legs could take him. He knew better than to look back when told to hide and Emma watched the darkness eat him up. Bad things happened in the dark. She almost called after him to come back but her mother instinct told her that Marie was right, he would be safe there.

Rushing to the back room, Emma collided with someone hard and fell back, shocked.

Clement.

"The boy?" His voice chilled her more than the draught sweeping down the hall as he stepped closer.

It hurts less to give in.

Yet she screamed for Antoine when Clement touched her. His name tore right through her as if there was a chance he could hear her.

-FORTY-TWO-

"Why would they be attacking their own church?" Antoine asked, confused, as he looked out the window of the house they were camping out in. He could have sworn he heard his name. Was the wind playing tricks on his mind? "What a bunch of morons."

Hoolie had made himself a nest on the floor that made Antoine smile. The boy was funny.

"They think you're there, maybe?" Hoolie asked.

"You think they're still hunting us? In a storm no less?" Antoine studied the group. They watched him as if he was the only one with any ideas.

"Not us. You. They're hunting you," Hoolie reminded him. "Until you're caught, that won't end. I'm still on their side, remember?"

Six plus Hoolie. Four men, two women. They'd lost one woman, Tally, to a fight with a man in a sheet toward the end of October. The young girl, Loraine, was in some hospital in some town he couldn't remember. Three men and one woman went south when the snow flew. Home. He didn't stop them, just adjusted his count, and watched them leave.

Everything blurred together except his numbers. Eight left, including himself.

He could have sworn he heard his name a second time.

"Don't forget your bag," Antoine mumbled to Hoolie as he put on his jacket and fumbled with the sheet.

"No way. We're going out there? What the heck for?"

"If they knew we were here, they'd break windows on this house not the church across the street," Antoine said. "Something is happening and I want to know what."

"Good point."

"I'm comin'." Philip was on his feet, slipping into a jacket, too.

Antoine passed him gloves so his fingers would be warm enough to pull the trigger.

"Ah fine. I'll come. I wasn't gonna do nothing 'cept sleep anyhow." Hoolie joined them. Antoine was glad, because if he needed a quick escape, Hoolie was his guy.

He took one last look at the group. Eight minus three. Five were left looking at him in his sheet.

Antoine and Philip didn't wait for Hoolie and he dashed after them, doing up his jacket under his plain white sheet. "Holy dirt." Hoolie stepped back. "That's Clement's horse, it is."

"Got that paint in your bag?"

"Yeah." Hoolie never asked why Antoine requested anything in or out of the bag, he handed it over.

Antoine pushed through the wind and met the horse. Yeah. It was one of Clement's. "Hold still, beauty, I'm gonna bless ya." It hurt to lift his arm, but he tried not to wince. Hoolie was worried enough about him these days.

"You're putting a cross on his horse? Are you insane?" Hoolie asked. "You are. I knew it."

"Will you shut up? I'm listening. Do either of you hear the wind calling my name?"

"Oh great, now the wind is talking to him. I'm frozen. I'm going in." Hoolie turned around but didn't move. "Maybe not. Our safe house suddenly doesn't feel safe."

Philip ran after the two cowards in sheets who were on their way to the house they'd left. After tossing Hoolie the tiny can of paint, Antoine rushed to help him.

The ghost stumbled back when Philip threw a punch. "What the heck? Aren't we on the same side?"

"Looks like yer on the ground to me," Philip spat as Antoine took on the other ghost.

They rolled in the snow, buying Hoolie time to rush in the house and gather the others. Antoine had no idea where Hoolie would take them, but the boy was incredibly good at saving his own butt, and so, he was confident his numbers would be intact in the morning and the crew hunting them would be sent on another wild-goose chase.

Antoine ripped off their sheets. It instantly leveled the playing field and he stood a fighting chance. He was surprised to see Brute One and Brute Two. Somehow, they didn't seem so big out in the slushy streets.

"You left Canada?" Antoine pulled off his sheet, too.

"Savage? I almost didn't recognize you." Brute One flung icy water in his face, and Antoine let him fall to the ground. Brute One landed with a puff and tackled Antoine's legs, hauling him down.

They struggled in the slushy snow.

Brute One's focus was on Antoine's tender shoulder.

Bones snapped beside them as Philip broke Brute Two's leg. He screamed and Brute One pulled away when Philip dived for him, too.

"Shit man." Brute One's eyes flew over his buddy. "What ya do to him?" His pal was screaming like he was dying.

"Philip has an incredible strength in his hands, probably from breaking rock and hauling earth in the tunnels," Antoine told him, adding to his panic. Brute One ran off, leaving his buddy when he passed out from the pain.

Antoine lay back in the snow.

"You hurt?" Philip offered him a hand.

"I'll live, but I need you to pop my shoulder back in. They send out telegrams to everyone that they messed up my shoulder or what?"

Philip knelt beside him and unzipped his coat. Antoine took several breaths.

"You got a happy place? Ya might wanna visit it." Philip's large hands were warm against Antoine's skin as he examined the shoulder. Antoine let it fall limp, trusting Philip's strong hands.

"Breathe, one. Breathe, two—"

Antoine shot up as pain zapped through him, his breath catching in his throat. "Damn, that never gets easier. Thanks." Antoine stayed in the snow, as a wave of nausea swept over him. "You think we interrupted a deal or something?"

Philip shrugged.

Dizzy, Antoine waited for the throbbing to calm so he could stand. "Tell me why I'm doing this again?"

Philip traced a cross in the snow with his gloved finger. "Don't know about you, but I was happy with my life until some foolish cowboy showed up and told me that I could walk off should the fit take me. Decided I didn't have to wait for a hero to save me, when I was one."

"Sorry you ended up in that tunnel."

"Not your fault. I, apparently, think for myself. I had myself a paying job if you believe that. Pay sucked but I was impressed nonetheless, until I realized over half of that meager salary was for room and board. Well, it got worse quickly. I caught the boss with his no good paws on my Gracie."

"Oh, no need to say more." Antoine tried to stand but was too dizzy.

"'Fraid there is. I should have kept my nose outta it, ya know, but there are two choices in them moments and I made the one that broke his ribs. So no one believes me when the boss says I was the one who raped her, my own wife, and he caught me, brave lad that he is. Next thing I knows, I'm thrown in a pit that leads to a tunnel and told to dig my way out. He had oafs like this guy keep an eye on us and work us until we passed out. If I put up a stink, even sneezed near one the wrong way, they used it as an excuse to rape my gal in front of me." He showed Antoine his wrists and how worn down they were from the ropes he'd fought. "Not a blasted thing I could do except shut up. Yet when I thought about it, I was still free to make that choice. Then Clement got wind that I was digging tunnels for someone else and he bargains us all out. Tosses us in his pit. Tells me it's just to teach me a lesson for leaving and I can come up in a few months when I appreciate him a little more, but..."

"What happened?"

"We dug in earth that never sat right in my lungs. Clement lost dozens of diggers in a week, including Gracie." He sighed. "He moved us to another location with more food and water then we could ever consume, and he brought down those beds you saw so we didn't have to sleep on the floor. When he came to tell me he was sorry about Gracie, I promised him that I would make him pay. Stupid temper of mine. After that I was pretty sure I was never gonna see daylight again."

Antoine closed his eyes and breathed away the image tearing into him. He had no idea this was happening in the world. "I'm sorry."

"Ya ready?" Philip asked. "I'll take the back, you go around front."

"Front? I'm going right through that church. Clement's a dead man."

Instantly, the wolf-shadow was over him, growling, and Antoine leapt to his feet.

"Heh heh. Now that sounds fun. Want me to haul this fruitcake outta the snow or leave him?" Philip pointed to the Brute with the broken legs.

"Why would I care what you do with guys you beat up? He ain't my problem. I can't see ghosts." Antoine pointed to the side of the church where Brute One waited. "He'll deal with his friend."

Antoine was up and a scream made him break into a run through icy streets. He was sure a woman screamed his name.

~~

Antoine flung open the doors to the church and rushed in. He fought blindly, tossing aside anyone in his way. He found a man in a sheet pinning Marie to a bed in a back room, yanking her head back by the hair.

"Get off me," she screamed, kicking the attacker.

Antoine hauled him off her, ripped off the sheet to look at the prick: blue eyes that sparkled in the dim light, a tiny scar along the right one, dark hair, thin eyebrows—too thin. "Antoine?" Tommy looked at him shocked.

Antoine tossed him out the window like the sack of dirt he was while Marie pulled herself together.

"You hurt?" Antoine demanded.

She shook her head. "No. Shaken up a bit. Where did you come from?"

"My own hell." Antoine glanced around the room. It had two beds and not much more. "Let's get outta here." He tossed the sheet over his head and walked into the hallway.

Marie followed. "So what? You wear the sheets you hate?"

"I do what I have to, to survive."

"We can't leave Doc. I sent a woman with her son to the cellar. Get them, her name is Emma and she's afraid of men in general so don't be so in-your-face with her and please remove that sheet, you look like an idiot and will scare the boy. We need to hit the fields."

Antoine wasn't breathing.

Not moving.

Emma was here? Doc was here? He'd been this close to them and almost missed them. He pulled the sheet off. "Where's the cellar?" Antoine was already in the hall.

Marie chased after him.

He charged down the steps and searched the wall for a lantern. Why was it so dark in here? He found a lantern on the wall.

Marie's golden eyes were huge when he turned the lantern on her and the light made them appear that much angrier. "What's going on?" she demanded.

He glanced around the cellar. "Where are they?"

"How would I know? I was kinda detained, Antoine."

"Papa." A boy tumbled out of the woodbin, and crouched, ready to run.

"Gosh, Charlie." Antoine rushed to help him up. He dusted him off. "Are you hurt, Charlie? Look at you, you're big." Antoine touched his curly hair—like Emma's. "I missed you, little man. I can't believe how much."

Antoine scooped him into his arms, leaving the lantern on the ground.

Charlie touched Antoine's face as if memorizing it in the dim light. "Safe."

"Where is your ma?"

Charlie tightened up against his bulky jacket. "Bad."

"Let's find her. You'll help me find her, right Charlie?"

Marie rushed up the steps. "I agree with the boy, this is very bad, Antoine."

"Papa."

Eight plus one child and one sister. Ten.

Marie reached for his shoulder. "Tell me you didn't marry Clement's digger. Tell me you ain't that bloody stupid."

"Did you say Doc was here?"

"He's not well at all."

And one Doc, not well at all. Eleven.

~~

"I'll dress him while you prepare my sleigh." Marie held out her arms to take Charlie but Antoine didn't hand Charlie over. Instead he set him out of her reach, and snagged the jacket from her so he could dress Charlie himself.

Antoine undid his jacket and picked up the sheet he'd dropped earlier. Tearing it, he wrapped it around himself, making the familiar sling Sacri used. This way he could hold the child warm against him and not put weight on his sore shoulder. "Climb in, Charlie, we're gonna find your ma. I miss her, too."

Charlie nestled against him, and Antoine put his jacket back on after wiping the boy's tears.

"Kinda neat that he's not afraid of you," Marie said to Antoine.

"Why would he be afraid of me? We love the same woman. If you understood love, it might make a bit of sense to you. Besides, Hoolie says we can't always see who people are but we can feel it."

Hoolie rushed in. "They're gone. Last one rode off to the north. Whoa. What did she do to her light?" He pulled Antoine away from Marie.

"It's plus three. A sister. A sick doctor. A boy. That makes eleven."

Hoolie glanced around. "A boy? A sick doctor? Odd that I can't see them."

"Take Marie and Doc to the others. I'm going after Emma."

"Stay away from me, troublemaker." Hoolie chomped twice to warn Marie to stay back.

Marie twirled a curl but didn't try to get Hoolie on her side. She took off to get Doc.

Hoolie turned to Antoine and said, "Saw Clement heading north. He didn't see me though, busy wrestling this feisty fox, he was. He ain't gonna get far in this weather. I stumbled on this wild-looking sleigh. Philip was hooking up the horses so we should be good to collect the others."

Marie walked Doc out slowly. Antoine hardly recognized him. He was too slim, too pale, and his eyes were sunken. "Doc? What the heck happened to you?"

He studied Antoine with his eyebrows up. "Young buck."

"Oh sure, him you remember," Marie complained. "Yet me, nothing."

"Hmmm. I'm beginning to think I chose to forget you, Marie."

Hoolie chuckled. "Glad you survived, well most of you. Half your light went out. You need to light it back up."

Doc eyed up Hoolie. "How?"

Hoolie shrugged. "I just say what I see. Up to you to fix yourself, Mister Doc."

"Why do I keep thinking in Latin when I look at you?" Doc frowned. "Ever have something so important nag at you, scream at you, yet you can't put your finger on what you're forgetting?"

"See, him, I like," Hoolie said. "Plus one sick man. Got it."

"You look like hell, Doc." Antoine was disgusted.

"It's weird. I know your name, but all it does is make me angry. You piss me off?"

Antoine nodded. "Probably." Charlie shifted in Antoine's jacket.

"Holy dirt, Mister, you got worms flashing in your light."

"It's my boy. He's snuggling in."

Hoolie smirked. "Of course. Safest place I know, too, is bundled up in your light. Mind if I curl up with him?" He told Doc, "This is the guy to stick by. He has a friend who gives him what he needs to survive. He plans to bring his family home. Me included. You want in on a sweet deal like that?"

"Sure, I could use me some happy forever."

Antoine said, "Let's move out. I'll follow the tracks."

"Philip says he's riding with you, macho man. I have a few stops to make, had to spread us out." Hoolie helped Doc, so Antoine took off to the barn to find Philip.

Charlie clung to him, safe under his jacket, held tight against him in the sling. "You warm in there?" Antoine asked

Charlie.

Marie whispered, "Be safe, Antoine."

"Papa," Charlie blurted out loudly and ducked as if he might get in trouble.

Despite himself, Antoine smiled as he ran down the steps and out the back door of the church, looking through the falling snow.

A horse waited in the distance and he went to meet her. She was a black mare who nickered when Antoine rubbed her nose. "You ready to lead me to my girl?" Antoine asked her.

Philip came beside him—on a horse—and he waited, used to Antoine preparing his horse. Charlie peeked out and the mare sniffed at him, then nudged Antoine, ready to go. Antoine hoisted himself up and charged around in a circle scouting the area. He knew this area well. They'd visited every house this past month. The sky was cloudy and it was dark, but Antoine wasn't sure if he walked into a trap or if he set it. Finding Charlie changed things. Changed the rules.

Focus, Antoine.

"Which safe house will he go to?" Philip asked.

"Hoolie will know."

"Wish I could trust that boy as much as you. I keep thinkin' at any moment he's gonna switch sides."

"You're a free man, Philip. Trust who you want. I know a good soul when I meet one."

Antoine rode to Hoolie who made his way to the barn with Marie yelling at him, and Doc limping.

"I can't be running around in this storm all night," Antoine said to Hoolie.

Marie snapped, "Surely you're not going to trust this brat? He double-crossed me."

"Excuse me?" Hoolie glared at her and finally shook his head, giving his attention to Antoine. "Go to Finley. The big empty church we thought was new, turns out he built it. Some type of warehouse in disguise."

"He's building churches to hide in?" Marie rolled her eyes. "Don't be stupid."

"Not hide, store things," Hoolie corrected her. "I'm getting Antoine's numbers to safety and that's as far from Finley as possible. Don't bring your boy in that mess, Mister."

Marie nodded. "Rat, I like how you think." Marie reached for Charlie but Philip brought his horse between her and Antoine.

Antoine couldn't let Charlie go, yet he didn't need him seeing what he'd do to Clement either. "Keep him warm and safe. Charlie, Hoolie will take you while I get your ma back. You do as he says."

Hoolie reached out with a blanket and wrapped the boy in it. "Aw nuts." He looked up at Antoine.

"What?"

"Your son, he's..."

"What?" Antoine snapped. "He's what?"

Hoolie rubbed Charlie's tiny hand and looked up at Antoine, shocked. "He's marked as Clement's."

"Keep my count safe." It was so cold, Antoine's words hung in front of him, frozen.

"I got it. Eleven, minus you two. Nine including me. Not a problem. I count, too."

"I'm gonna add one more." Antoine followed Philip, his fingers numb.

–FORTY-THREE–

Doc was spent. He leaned against Marie. She smelled like lilacs, which relaxed him. He liked lilacs. They were travelling slowly. Two passengers were in the wagon with them. Hoolie never introduced them and they kept trying to hide their faces. Doc didn't have the energy to ask their names. He got the feeling there would be plenty of time for that later.

The winds were strong, but Marie pulled the blanket around them. "I don't trust that rat," she mumbled, so low, Doc wasn't sure he caught it all. "He's leading us south. We should head north. I'm going to talk to him."

Doc sat up. "Charlie?"

"I'll send him to sit with you."

Doc took in a breath. He couldn't look after a child. Everything in him was dying, he felt it. But something about Hoolie nagged at him, too, so he nodded.

"Where are we going?" Marie demanded to Hoolie, still beside Doc.

Hoolie glanced at them. "Got a few stops to make."

"Stops?" Marie said to Doc. "At the next stop we take over this wagon."

No sooner had she said it, the wagon halted. It was dark but Hoolie made a small yelping sound. Someone ran from the dark and rushed into the wagon. The pause was so brief, Marie didn't have time to get up.

They were on their way again, a new passenger on board. Doc looked at the shadow. It scurried to the back of the wagon, closer to the other passengers. Hoolie smiled over his shoulder and tossed a blanket to the group. The wagon halted again. Another body rolled in. A black woman.

"How many?" Marie demanded.

"What's going on?" Doc felt a spark in him. Hoolie was helping these people. He wanted to help, too.

"Last one." The wagon halted again.

Marie leaped up and jumped out of the wagon. Hoolie glanced at her. "I have no problem leaving your curls behind." He was already moving ahead.

"Hoolie come here, something is wrong," Marie said.

"What?" He scrambled from the wagon with the boy in his arms.

"Under the wagon."

"Who the heck cares what goes on under the wagon? Let's go."

"Give me the boy and check it out."

"I ain't giving you anything. If Mister knew half of what you did, he would have left you behind. You check it out."

"I did what I had to."

"You crossed lines you can't even tippy toe around and you tried to drag me down with you. No. Stay away from this boy, he's innocent."

The new passengers in the wagon talked low together, watching Doc.

Doc spoke up. "Hoolie, now is not the time to fight with her. I'll watch the boy while you two figure this out. It's cold, we need to get moving."

The silence was heavy, but Charlie scurried over to him and slipped under the blanket. "Dark bad," he told Doc as he hid beside him.

"Ghosts!" a man yelled.

"Dammit. They're coming this way. We need to get going west." Hoolie ran toward the horses but Marie shoved him into the side of the wagon.

"Bloody fool was leading us right into an ambush." Marie climbed into the driver seat and they left. Doc looked over the side of the wagon. Hoolie was face down in the mud. Not moving. Doc didn't like this. What the heck was nagging him about that boy? It felt important.

–FORTY-FOUR–

Antoine's face was frozen. His eyes burned, but he rode. Finley was visible in the distance. They circled the church and saw shadows walking inside.

They made their way to the livery barn. Antoine found the owner sleeping in the loft.

"Hey." He rubbed his eyes and looked Antoine over. "What ya doing out in this cold?"

"Searching for my wife," Antoine told him. "Some prick hauled her off."

"I don't want anything to do with that. We ask Natives to keep moving. This town isn't for you."

Antoine's hands were frozen, but as he talked, life tingled back into them.

"Christ!" The scrawny man almost fell over when he saw Philip. His eyes darted over Antoine and his horse. "This ain't good. I can't have you folks in here. Not tonight. His kind ain't welcome in here. Finley is ghost country. What ya thinking travelling with a black around here?"

"Just gonna save my wife, is all. Look after our horses while I search that church."

"I'd rather not." He swallowed. "I don't want trouble. This has trouble all over it." His eyes darted out the window and scanned the town.

Antoine peeked at the church. He had a perfect view of the stables behind it. Clement was smart to go there, it was the last place most would look for him. Good thing Hoolie was not like most.

The church door opened and a woman ran out.

Plus one.

–FORTY-FIVE–

Hoolie rolled over. Dang it. Stupid Reward Hunter would be the death of him yet.

One bloody job and he blew it. He should have gotten a better look at the picture Mister always sighed over. Then he wouldn't have been taken off guard like that. Never occurred to him that Mister's son was the golden child. Cripes. Clement told him that the boy was *his* son. What the heck was going on? How could a boy have two pas?

Mister was in a heap of trouble, he was.

"Don't move," a ghost on a horse ordered.

"It's me," Hoolie glared at them.

"Hoolie? Christ man, you look like hell." He recognised Mitch's voice.

"I'm working. What the heck you guys doing?"

Hoolie reached in his pack and filed through the Wanted flyers. He thumbed past the one for Doc, the one for the diggers, and he hesitated on the last one but finally pulled it out. He stood in the wet cold mud, showing them the flyer. "Had my hands on this one. Bloody Reward Hunter got him. A dame, you get your hands on her you bring her straight to me."

"You gonna tell Clement we were helpful? We're looking to marry his girls," Mitch said.

Everyone wanted something impossible. Still, Hoolie liked Mitch. "Honestly Mitch, the secret to win Clement over is to tell him to go to hell."

A hand reached down to help him up. "Yeah right," Mitch said.

With his bag over his shoulder, Hoolie tossed the flyer aside and held on tight, smearing cold mud against the sheet.

"I just call 'em as I see 'em. I mean really, Mitch, have I ever been wrong?"

The horse stepped on the Wanted flyer, pushing the picture of the golden child deep in the mud. One little boy who he swore to one man to protect and another to rescue. Yet he just let him ride away with a troublemaker. Cripes, this sucked.

~~

"There." Hoolie could make out the wagon in the distance and pointed Mitch in that direction.

The wagon wasn't moving. Had that crazy woman made them walk? He scanned the area, looking for signs to tell him where they were. It was easy to get lost on the prairies, especially in the dark.

A pile of rocks. One of his markers. He counted them. Crap. They were in Finley. Last place in the world Hoolie wanted to be right now. "Leave me. I want to scout out that wagon. See if they left any change. Tell the boss I'm coming with his package."

"You sure you don't want help?"

Hoolie ignored him and slid off the horse. He rushed toward the wagon. It was parked right over his marker for danger. He glanced up at the livery barn shadowing it. Sleeting rain pelted him. This wasn't good at all.

Someone whimpered from inside the wagon.

Hoolie peeked over the edge and was surprised to see everyone intact. "Where's that lunatic?" Hoolie asked Doc.

"Marie? She went to get medical supplies. I'm..." Doc closed his eyes. "We were attacked. Marie used up all the ammo she had." Doc placed his gun on the sheet beside him. "She was shot, but pretends it's nothing. My back is warm. I think maybe I need stitches."

Of course they were attacked. They walked right into Clement's trap for them. Idiots.

A loud explosion made Hoolie duck. He opened his pack and took out all the weapons he had except one grenade so he could make it home.

"Fight," he told the others. They looked like they went through a war, but they were all here and Hoolie was starting to think of them as family. Best crew he ever had, that's for sure.

Plus, he had to give the dame some credit, she knew how to save her hide. "Wagon will be in the safe zone just outside of Finley. What the heck were you fools thinking letting her park here? Speak up. You all know better than to set up behind this livery barn. I went over this with you before. I can't protect you if you don't listen. Don't come back to this wagon unless I'm counting heads. Piss me off, the lot of you. Now get."

"We should run," Jerome said, helping one of the gals up.

"Oh now you speak." Hoolie glared at him, but truth was, he was more frustrated with himself. "You could." Hoolie watched Jerome's light as he handed him a grenade. "Or you could blow their bloody distillers up. I don't much care either way, got my own job to do. Think for yourselves."

Jerome's light exploded at the idea and he hopped out of the cart with new energy.

"I can't walk," Doc told him after the others left. "I'll need a hand."

Hoolie looked around. "Then hide. See those bales? Let's get you to that sucky straw."

Charlie kept nodding off.

"I'll come for you when the coast is clear. Unless your bloody haystack is on fire, you don't move. Got it?"

How had Antoine tied Charlie inside his jacket? Could he do that? He couldn't afford to lose him again, and he wasn't letting this boy get caught up in some war between those two idiots.

–FORTY-SIX–

Antoine ran to meet her in the cold. "Emma," Antoine shouted, his words blowing back at him.

It was her.

Emma stumbled in the snow. She wasn't wearing a coat or shoes. When she looked up, the blood on her chin made Antoine push harder against the blowing snow.

Her lips. Her beautiful lips were swollen and raw from the cold. Possibly a fist.

"Antoine," she hardly breathed the word as he knelt beside her. His hands ran around her freely, feeling her stomach, her back, pulling her out of the slushy snow and onto his lap.

Blood streaked down her leg and around her ankle.

"I fell off the horse."

Please God. Antoine's hands took in the bulge under her fancy dress. *Please protect this child.* The wind was stolen from his lungs as he tried to speak. He kept his eyes on hers, promising her this would work out fine. Hanky in hand, he wiped her chin tenderly.

Emma winced but reached for him.

"Charlie is safe, far from here." He knew this would be her only concern so he didn't waste a breath on anything else. There was so much Antoine wanted to say to her, yet as usual, the look they shared said enough.

Sheets crowded them but Antoine's energy was on Emma as he cradled her on his knees in the snow. She wrapped her arms around his neck and held him tight.

From his pocket, Antoine pulled a knife and tossed it, hitting one. There were too many, appearing out of nowhere. He drew the gun Hoolie had loaded for him and fired toward them, but he wasn't good with a pistol this small, even this close. It felt foreign to him, and he had no idea how many shots he'd have. He needed rocks, but there were none around. Nothing but snow.

Antoine tossed the gun like a rock, hitting one square in the forehead.

He gathered Emma in his arms. Then he stood to face them.

The livery barn was swarmed, and when he glanced over, Philip stood as a prisoner with a knife to his throat.

His count went up one and down three within moments. At least he could trust that Hoolie had the other nine safe.

Antoine carried Emma to the church. He didn't have much choice, she was freezing. She rested against him, too weak to fight.

"Antoine," she mumbled. "Don't take me back to him."

He didn't have any choice. She was bleeding, it was cold and she wasn't dressed for it.

Clement sat on a chair in the back of the church and watched Antoine walk her through the hordes of crates to the front.

"Tempting to shoot you, Antoine. You're a real pain. Almost makes me wish I had gotten rid of you the same night I watched your old man walk into our cave-in."

He's trying to get a rise. Focus, Antoine told himself, yet the words stung.

"You have no idea how much I'd like to." Clement had his eyes on Emma. "Someone, get me Hoolie," Clement snapped. "I need to know what he's found out about the boy."

Hoolie? Antoine's throat tightened and he forced down a swallow.

"Put me down, Antoine," Emma mumbled. "Go. It's easier to give in. Go. Protect Charlie." Even though she said this, she clutched him tightly and Antoine refused to let her go. Instead he carried Emma to the altar and took the tablecloth off it to wrap her in. She was frozen. He turned his attention on Emma, yet he'd taken in the entire church with one quick sweep. Barrels and ghosts. A few chairs, but no pews, no religious statues or photos. Just barrels and ghosts mixed among the odd crate.

"Where does it hurt?" Antoine asked her, his voice almost locked in his throat.

"I'm fine."

Antoine kissed her forehead, afraid to touch those damaged tender lips. "You're cold. Come into my arms."

Antoine heard a gun click but he kept his lips tight against Emma and whispered against her hair while he held her, keeping her warm, "I'll tackle Clement, and you get on a horse. You go west." He showed her the direction while he rubbed her belly. "Charlie is with a young boy. Hoolie. He has six freckles on his nose, other than that, he fits in anywhere. Have him lead you to the safe place. I'll meet you there, but Charlie needs you. Go to him."

She clutched his arm, eyes closed but didn't agree.

"For Charlie. Can you do this for Charlie? He needs you."

She pushed him away and got to her feet. Antoine helped her up and took off his jacket to wrap her in it, but she shoved it off. "Keep Charlie away from him," she said.

He held her steady as she walked to Clement, taking tiny steps. He had no idea what she wanted to do. She wasn't going to go with Clement, was she? Emma stumbled and fell against Antoine. Clement moved to catch her and both men were eye to eye, Emma between them.

"You hurt her," Antoine accused him.

"She was safe with me, mutt. You're the one who hurt her. What are your big plans? To bring her to your country of unfamiliar things? She won't fit in there. At least with me, she knows her place."

"She's my wife, back off. Stop harassing her."

Clement gripped Emma's arm. He wouldn't let go either. Could it be that this was what it was all about? Clement fell in love with one of his diggers and had no idea how to cope with that?

With a deep breath, Antoine changed his approach. "Clement, Emma's hurt. She needs a bed. Let's put her first. This spitting match between us can wait until we're alone."

"I don't care for her." Clement let her go.

"She's weak and tired. I'm leaving with her." Antoine would not discuss this.

"The place is surrounded. Put her down in the side room,

but you and me, we end this tonight."

Out of the corner of his eyes, Antoine saw men in sheets swarm in, hovering along the walls of the church. Antoine counted them. At least twelve. Sometimes, a dozen was too much.

With no option, he carried Emma to the side room. With her safely out of the way he could face Clement and his goons.

The room had a bed and a door with a ghost standing in it, gun in hand.

Six freckles were visible through the long eye hole.

Hoolie stepped back as Antoine burst into the side room with a woman in his arms. The normally safe earthy-light that pulsated around Antoine was crimson and the wolf that hovered around him was wild, growling, ready to eat his soul and haul him to hell. Anger, rage, very, very, bad.

"Cripes, I just about shot you, Mister." Hoolie yanked off the sheet, dropping his gun as if Antoine caught him doing something wrong. "You know I ain't good at this knocking people out, and I feel so bloody guilty every time I slip on a sheet, it makes me jumpy."

Antoine kept his eyes on Hoolie, ignoring the body at his feet. "I thought nine were going west. What are you doing in Finley? Where's Charlie?"

Hoolie stepped back and unzipped his jacket to show him Charlie, sound asleep. He hid him away again. He was not handing this boy over to Antoine while his light looked all wild like that. "Don't you worry about this boy, he's easy to look after."

"You work for Clement behind my back?"

"What ya giving me grief for? You know I work for Clement. We wouldn't be here if I didn't, Mister. What you see is what you get. Breathe."

Antoine kept his eyes directly on him. "I'm going back to deal with Clement. Find Philip. I need him to take Emma."

"Already ran into him." Hoolie signaled to someone and Philip appeared. He took Emma from Antoine.

"Livery barn's in flames," Philip told him. "We stumbled on barrels of gunpowder from their ammo shop." His eyebrows went up playfully. "Kaboom."

"Philip shot a few too many. I kept mine alive." Hoolie

glanced at the body at his feet. "This one just fell over on me. So this your gal? Phew. That makes more sense."

"How so?"

"She looks like your son which is a bit of a relief. I was worried there for a minute that you kidnapped this one from Clement. He is your son, right?"

"Keep him safe if I don't survive this."

"I got a soft spot for brats without a pa, but don't make him fatherless."

"Plus one. I'll buy you time," Antoine promised. The red in his light actually deepened.

"Then you might need this." Hoolie dropped his bag on the brute at his feet and vanished him and Charlie under sheets. "We're headed to Prairie Burrow North. Follow the markers if you get lost, and take the time to read the flyers in my pack, because that's what I gave up. Can't put a price on home, it's just a happy you earn."

Much to Hoolie's relief, Antoine's light returned to normal in a sweep.

Yup, home was his weakness.

–FORTY-EIGHT–

Gone. Antoine was trusting them with everything.

Antoine went to tie up the brute with ropes from his bag, but he was dead. Had Hoolie killed him? Antoine found that hard to believe. Hoolie didn't even eat meat because he said animals had light around them that creeped him out.

He checked the body and found a tiny silver arrow in the neck. Silver?

It tempted him to run with Hoolie and his family, but he agreed with Clement; this had to end. They couldn't keep running.

With the bag over his shoulder, Antoine walked to the main part of the church. A sheet was on his way to collect him, but retreated.

There were exactly twelve nasties hovering around the edges of the room, behind the barrels.

Someone screamed outside.

"You gonna shoot me?" Antoine asked as he sat on the altar and opened the bag Hoolie trucked around. Wanted flyers he shoved aside. Seems Hoolie was in deeper than he let on. How the heck had he ended up working for Clement? He paused at the one for Emma and pulled it out.

Clement held a knife. "I'm not above scalping you for what you did to my house."

"You burned mine first. Sounds fair to me. The problem between us is that we both love the same gal. You're even offering a reward for her." Antoine set the flyer with her picture down beside him and returned to the bag. "So what we gonna do?" Antoine palmed the grenade he found in the bag.

"I don't love that dog any more than you do."

"Then why the fuss?"

"She has something that is mine."

Did he mean Charlie? Was this what it was about? A boy? A son. "How about, if she picks you, I won't stand in her way."

"Yet you just did." Clement tightened a fist. "Your tunnels—"

"Belong to *Cîpay*. You should have never pushed them, Clement. You thought because they took slaves from your family that you could show them who was boss."

"They do owe me. I saved them."

"And in turn, they are trying to save your soul. You might not understand how that works just yet, but one day you will. They won't kill you, just take everything from you until you face God, a barren soul, with nothing but humility. Then you can tell Him what you learnt."

Antoine felt confident he'd buy Hoolie and Philip enough time to get Emma and Charlie to safety even though bodies closed in on him. Some had beating rods, others blades. He wouldn't survive twelve men thrashing him. Antoine looked at the back of his hand holding the grenade. He was filthy. Slowly, he turned up his hand and showed them the toy.

"Donkey has a frigging grenade in a hot house," one sheet said as he stumbled on his way out, but Clement forced him in front of him, like a shield.

Antoine took a closer look. Scuffed shoes. Untied. Frayed pant seams. "You're gonna use the owner of the hardware store as a shield against a grenade? Who will sell these morons booze? Not that they should buy it after Philip pissed in his distiller last week." An explosion outside shook them. "Gee. Maybe someone shut down your production."

Another explosion.

Antoine had no clue if the grenade was real, or if it would even work, but he was left with few options as they got tighter around him. "I'm a desperate man with nothing left to lose. I want to walk away with my wife and yet you want a war."

"Aye, she's black," one of the ghosts shouted in a raspy voice. Tommy Smyth.

Antoine rubbed his dry dirty hand against the arm clutching

the grenade.

"I say we string him up outside and let him freeze to death," Tommy said.

Through the open door, Antoine saw nasties dragging Philip to the church. Following were others, on their feet, guns pointed at them. Marie. Doc. He counted. No Emma. No Hoolie.

Clement glanced out the door, too. "You thinking about leaving? Because I doubt that's an option."

There was more at stake than his life. "Your dark deals are ruining this country."

Clement put out his hand to hold Tommy back. "And you are ruining my life. You think that boy will fit in that tight town of yours? Emma won't see invites to the quilting parties, mutt. What will you do when your precious church refuses to marry you? Open your eyes, this is the real world and I run it. Not because I'm smarter than you but because I have the means. She's better off with me and if you cared about her like you say you do, you'd be begging me to look after her."

Antoine faced Clement. "Here." Antoine pulled the pin on the grenade, placed it in Clement's hand, and shoved him into Tommy and Eddie, then he made a mad dash for the door.

Much to his surprise, the men in sheets ran with him.

"You idiot! This is a hot house," Clement shouted.

He wasn't surprised when nothing happened, but he headed toward Philip, determined to get his numbers back to safety and fight as long as he could.

Bodies were inches behind him. As they reached the door, an explosion propelled them into each other. Clement slammed into Antoine's back and they crashed into the snow.

The hot, silent eruption was not what Antoine expected.

Blew him right off his feet.

Wood flew through the air. Windows popped out. Dark black smoke puffed. Yet... he couldn't hear any of it. Sound was sucked from his world.

Clement said something. Antoine watched his lips move. *Gunpowder.*

Rumbling. Antoine felt it deep in his soul as if it was him

blown to pieces. He glanced at the church he blew up, shoving Clement aside. Men were still inside, trapped under falling beams. Antoine rushed to help.

Clement grabbed his arm, yelling something Antoine couldn't hear. Lips moved. *Save her before the gunpowder blows.*

What the heck did that mean?

Barrels.

"You store gunpowder in a church?" Antoine's voice was distorted. The words were a deep echo inside him. "Another front. Only you'd be that stupid."

Ground vibrated. Shook. Antoine stumbled over Clement.

The entire back end of the church collapsed and Clement cinched his eyes in pain and dropped to his knees.

Damn. Could one grenade mess things up like this? Would the others survive under that rubble? Antoine knew from experience that gophers fared well in explosions.

Clement was on his knees in the snow, catching his breath.

Focusing on the living, Antoine searched the crowd for Emma.

He shook his head to clear his ears. Sound returned, but distant. Echoes.

Flames came up behind him and another explosion.

Clement's pleas were distant even though he got to his feet. Antoine glanced at him. Their eyes met.

Antoine scrambled toward the fool holding Philip face down in the sloppy snow but Clement hung on him. Antoine shoved him off. The force of the explosion flung a chunk of glass, catching deep in Clement's right shoulder. Clement dropped. A woman screamed from under one of the sheets. Women joined them? Great.

He still couldn't hear right. Bloody annoying.

Clement checked his shoulder. Prick would probably outlive them all. Antoine swung, catching his jaw and stormed off to deal with the nasties who held his crew in the sleet.

The others fought as well as they could, and the explosion divided the nasties in sheets, giving Antoine and his crew an advantage. Not much, but he'd take it.

Winds were strong and flames from several of the buildings danced in it.

None of his numbers were free to move. Antoine couldn't help them all.

Sometimes you only have to save one.

Antoine veered for Philip. He was the strongest and could help him eliminate as many as possible. Help him find Emma.

Antoine ploughed into the jokers who had Philip pinned. A knife slashed at his shoulder while he tackled him.

"*Cîpay*," someone yelled, and the sheet on top of Antoine fell with a squeak that reminded him of a gopher in pain. Dead instantly. Antoine shoved him off, prepared to fight a fleet of men in sheets but it was Hoolie helping him.

"Don't you ever pull dirt like that again, Antoine." Hoolie was panicked. "You don't blow up churches filled with gunpowder. You have some type of death wish?"

"Hoolie, did you call me Antoine?"

"I thought you were dead. Don't you ever do that to me. I can't do this alone. None of it. All of it scares me. It's all just an act so I don't get dead. Despite my better judgement, Antoine, I would die with you. You are the only person alive with light that makes me feel safe."

Despite the frozen rampage around him, Antoine felt warm inside. "That's what makes you a warrior, little brother." Antoine got to his feet. Wet snow clung to him but he surveyed the mess in front of him. Those holding their ground fell without a warning as if the hand of God passed over them casting judgement.

"So what's *Cîpay*?" Hoolie was breathing normally again. "I imagine it has to do with them forgetting about us and dropping like flies."

"Ghosts of the Earth, my mother's tribe."

"They run from ghosts?" Hoolie glanced around. "Aren't they ghosts? Or are you talking real ghosts? Because they don't usually fight back, just scare the bee-gibers outta me."

"All this is a war over Sacred Land. Use this distraction to help me find Emma."

"That way." Hoolie pointed toward the livery barn. Thanks to the flames, Antoine caught sight of Emma running with Marie.

Emma held Charlie in her arms. She ran. Not fast, but

moving.

Antoine shifted his course, his focus on her. He tackled anything and everyone in his way. When someone touched Hoolie who was tight by his side, Antoine spun to help him.

"Whoa. It's me. Doc. Breathe."

Antoine had Doc's frail arms ready to toss him and stopped.

Six freckles stood beside him, steadying him. Family.

"We have to get Mister Doc outta here," Hoolie said. Doc leaned against him.

"Philip," Antoine called.

Philip was buried in a pile of ghosts, but when Antoine called to him, he leaped up and dished out swings as if they might leave him behind. Philip pulled a shotgun from one of them and took down one after the other with the backend of it as he made his way toward them.

"Glad that beast is on my side," Hoolie mumbled as they ran toward Emma and Marie who were on their way to the burning livery barn. "You got that God-friend handy? Maybe ask Him for a favour."

"It don't work that way."

"It's gonna take us a bloody miracle to escape," Hoolie said.

Too many stood between him and Emma. "Speaking of miracles, don't you have a shadow? You ask for help."

"Don't work that way, they have to offer."

"Where is Silver?"

"Who?" Hoolie asked.

"*Cîpay*. He killed that guy for you in the church."

"He was dead? Cripes, I was touching a dead guy? You sure? I whacked him on the head. He didn't look dead to me. You sure? I ain't got a shadow behind me, do I? I hate that."

Philip joined them. A wall of nasties blocked their path.

"We're gonna have to fight our way through this, Philip," Antoine told him.

"Only one bullet. I'd like to save it for Clement."

"Doc can hardly stand. I tell ya, Antoine, we need that Friend of yours to pull a miracle. I'm starting to doubt here."

The ground shook with a brief explosion that came from everywhere yet nowhere.

Slowly, painfully slow, the steeple from the church's shadow grew as it toppled over. Ghosts scattered as it crashed into them.

Hoolie had big eyes while they ran in the sleeting snow and had to climb over the cross to get to the other side. "Damn. Now you're showing off, Antoine."

FORTY-NINE

Hoolie took the reins. Counted the heads. "Twelve. Holy dirt. Twelve. We all here or is this a different twelve?" he joked.

"Don't matter, twelve is the count. Go." Antoine was tight beside him.

The wagon was already moving, taking them to the North Prairie Burrow. Closer to the border. By the large oak, Hoolie stopped and looked at the shadow in the distance. He sure wished he knew whose shadow that was. Was that guy just a prairie ghost, too stupid to move on?

"*That* is Silver." Antoine nodded to Silver as he vanished in the snow. "Ghost of the Earth. *Cîpay*."

"You see him?" Hoolie glanced at Antoine and back to where Silver had been. He didn't know Antoine saw shadows, too.

"Of course, that's my uncle. That is *Cîpay*. I hope to be a warrior like my uncle one day."

Should he tell Antoine that his uncle was dead? Or did he know that? He did call him a ghost of the earth. "He's just a shadow. A ghost walking the prairies."

"That's what *Cîpay* means. It's what we all study to be. One day, if I should be so lucky, I could be like him."

Hoolie thought about this as he climbed out and lifted the two large doors. A ghost of the earth. Wonder what a guy had to do to get their light to merge with the earth like that when they died.

Antoine brought the wagon underground into a storm cellar that was built to hide horses from prairie storms back when the land was first settled. A forgotten paradise for a guy like Hoolie.

Hoolie shut them in and everyone sat in silence, waiting.

The air hummed, or maybe it was his ears. That was way too many explosions.

"Nowhere to run if they find us." The stupid Reward Hunter pointed out. She really liked to get under Hoolie's skin. He snapped his teeth at her.

"We can fight," Antoine told her, his arms around his girl.

Hoolie smiled when he saw the picture their light made as it blended together warming up the area. His other half, she fit perfectly against him and already Hoolie forgot what his soul looked like without her. This was the real Antoine. "At least someone has confidence in my plans." Hoolie hadn't survived all these years because he walked into dead ends. Only a fool did that. "We can vanish from here. Tunnels all under this area, but they're not the sturdiest and I'd much rather we drive out." Hoolie passed out weapons. Rods, pistols, things he'd stored.

No one spoke. Antoine held Emma against him. Charlie crawled on his lap, adding to the light with fun colourful explosions. Hoolie liked rugrats, they always let their light rub off like that.

"You hurt?" Antoine whispered to Emma.

"I'm fine."

She didn't look fine to Hoolie, but what did he know about dames?

"It won't be long. We let them get ahead of us, and we sneak up behind them. Hoolie's idea. Guy is as sneaky as a fox."

"Shh." Hoolie whacked Antoine on the back of his head to shut him up so he could listen. He counted the hooves as they passed overhead. The ground over them dropped dirt in the wagon. Only three.

Snuggled and warm, no one breathed until the shaking stopped. Hoolie let out a long breath. "Anyone got sandwiches? I'm starved, and we're only gonna wait an hour, any longer they might double back." He checked his pocket watch. Well, Clement's, but he'd earned it.

—FIFTY—

When the wagon stopped, Hoolie leaned over the edge and met Antoine's eyes. "Got an accident back there. Thought it was a trap at first so I went around it, but I'm going back, in case someone is hurt. It's a car, and Clement usually sticks to his horses so we should be fine. Anyone wanna come?"

"What d'ya see?" Antoine asked.

"Just a car skidded off the trail and flipped in the water. It's as icy as a skating rink. Horses are the way to travel this muck."

"I don't like this." Antoine eyed the others. "Anyone think that's odd?" They sat silent, waiting for him to cast judgement. "You guys are gonna have to learn to speak your mind. It's annoying to talk to you."

Philip chuckled as he aimed the shotgun over the wagon toward the car.

"You still got one bullet you're saving?"

Phillip nodded.

"Well. Philip don't need to speak, but the rest of ya should." Antoine stood and said to Emma, "I'm gonna go with Hoolie to make sure no one's hurt."

Emma nodded, but it was hard for Antoine to jump out of the wagon.

"Go, Antoine," she said.

"Papa."

"He obsesses like you," Hoolie mumbled.

"We all obsess. You do it too, with these escape routes you're always planning. What happens when you can't run, Hoolie?"

"Can't wait to find out."

"I won't let anyone near them," Philip pumped the shotgun.

"Promise."

Antoine followed Hoolie. The car sank slowly in the icy slough. Accident must have happened moments ago.

The sun was rising, and they found a dead deer on the path. "Looks like they hit this poor thing," Antoine said.

"Is there anyone in that car?" Hoolie stopped by a body on the road.

Antoine knelt too. "Geepers. This is Tommy. From Clement's Ranch."

"Tommy Smyth," Hoolie nudged him with his foot. "Yup. He's got a sad story. Was a hero, you know."

"Tommy a hero? I doubt that."

"He was. Fought a stint in the war and came back crazy, afraid of everything, and meaner than heck. Lots of shadows next to his light. When he got back, his wife had died from that strange coughing disease, both his children died of a pox. This guy, he's the one making magic with the opium he pulled out of Saskatchewan. Guy will try any drug in any combination just for kicks. Clement said he needed a father figure and made it his mission to teach him."

"Clement said that, did he?"

"Sure. Why he likes guys like me and Tommy. He just wants to have a son and treat him better than his pa treated him. Pretty simple goal, kinda like you and your home."

"Well, you ask me, this guy got what he deserved."

"Yup, his stint in hell is over. Not a shadow. Funny, even jerks find peace when they die."

Antoine felt for a pulse while thinking about what Hoolie said. Tommy did look peaceful. His usual scowl was gone, as if he'd welcomed death.

"Gross, don't touch him." Hoolie shoved his hand off Tommy. "He's dead."

"What if he's not? Think."

Marie pointed Philip's shotgun between them. Hoolie and Antoine fell back when she pulled the trigger and blew Tommy's head clean off.

"That's how you check for life in a dirtbag like this," Marie snapped.

"Cripes, Marie. He was dead. Ain't you got enough shadows?" Hoolie turned his back on her. "That car's sinking outta sight. Think anyone is in it?"

"Go see."

"I ain't going in that freezing water. It's probably too late anyway."

Something moved in the car. Antoine stepped in the water. When he saw it a second time—a hand—Antoine shoved Hoolie aside and sloshed into the water. He glanced back at Hoolie. "Coming?"

Marie had run off.

Hoolie was on the bank and he shook his head fearfully.

Antoine splashed to the window of the car, the water was only chest deep, but the car shifted as a body smashed against the door. With freezing hands, Antoine pulled on the handle. The door flew open and Antoine grabbed the man by the neck and hauled him up but he wouldn't come.

He was stuck. With his knife, Antoine dived under the water. The victim's pants were stuck on something so Antoine used his knife to cut them. The man gripped Antoine's shoulder. His bloody sore shoulder.

Cold, in pain, they broke through the chilly water. Antoine could hardly feel his frozen legs.

The body against him clung for dear life.

Antoine gripped his hand to pull him to safety but dropped it as quickly. A teardrop tattoo. He lifted the man's hand unbelieving.

Clement.

Antoine shoved him back under the water, his anger exploded in him.

"Your Friend delivers again," Hoolie said from the slough's edge, but the shake in his voice was familiar. It reminded Antoine of how he'd talked to Marie after she'd buried Mathew. That shake made Antoine release Clement and he glanced at Hoolie.

Beside Hoolie, ready to leap was a shadow of a wolf. Hoolie kept his hand on it.

Then you shall bear the weight of his schooling until you find your way.

He needed to breathe. To focus. Antoine filled his frozen lungs. Burning.

Clement didn't deserve his breaths. All the forces of the

universe told him this. He could save so many from his evil deeds.

Yet.

Even jerks find peace when they die.

Hoolie looked concerned, wading out to get him.

Clement surfaced and sucked in air as if his lungs were frozen. Antoine saw all the pain he'd caused Emma and dunked him again, holding his head down. Clement's arms flailed. Fighting. *He acts tough, but we all put on a show to hide the truth, don't we?*

The tattoo flashed before his eyes. This was a man who had saved his mother.

He pulled Clement to the surface, seeing him with clear eyes.

Hoolie splashed toward him in a panic and the wolf jumped for Antoine.

The wolf.

He'd been blind.

Antoine let his sight guide him, not the cold that had him petrified as he yanked Clement forward with him.

Hoolie stopped and stood in the water, up to his waist, pale, as the wolf vanished mid-flight.

"Was there anyone else?" Antoine demanded.

"No. Thought I was dead. My eyes are frozen. Where did you come from?" Clement's teeth chattered. Antoine shoved him back to shore. Rage exploding in him until he no longer felt the cold.

Hoolie helped Antoine and they let Clement crawl through the reeds.

Together they collapsed on the bank.

Clement fell against him. "I thought you were gonna kill me for a minute there. Saw my entire life flash before me."

"Bet that was a blast." Antoine lay in the snowy mud, too angry to feel the cold. He'd hauled Clement out of the water. Clement.

Fists clenched, he breathed.

"Your wolf vanished," Hoolie whispered. "What happened out there? I didn't know we could get rid of shadows."

"I trust My Friend has a plan I don't understand."

"Looked pretty bloody clear to me."

Philip pulled up in the wagon and Emma jumped out with a blanket. She wrapped it around Antoine. "You're frozen. Get out of those wet things. Marie is gone to get you dry clothes at that farm."

"Ah Emma. I thought you were dead. Thank goodness. I'm hurt. Help me up." Clement reached for her but Emma pretended he wasn't there. All her focus on Antoine, she moved out of Clement's reach.

Antoine swung and smoked him. Clement tumbled into the weeds. "You talk to her again, I break your jaw." He'd probably broken it anyway, he'd hit him hard enough.

Clement gasped for air.

Emma was so warm, Antoine melted against her hands while she checked him for injury. "I'm fine, just frosty and annoyed that it was Clement. I should have trusted Hoolie and let God deal with him. Serves me right for sticking my nose in His business."

"Nah," Hoolie whispered, "I expect a guy like you to help everyone. Truth be told, I would have been mighty disappointed to see you walk away. We can't all blow dead people away like your sister. Some of us have souls to worry about."

"Get Hoolie a blanket, he's cold," Antoine ordered no one, yet everyone as he walked with Emma back to the wagon where Marie stood with Charlie and a pile of dry clothes. He didn't question it, just changed and handed Hoolie dry slacks.

"Wait. Help me. My leg," Clement called after them.

"Yeah, like that's gonna happen." Hoolie chuckled, slipping his pants on in the cold.

Someone else would probably be along to help him. Yet when Antoine looked up, Charlie watched with those green eyes and that serious face.

Doc was still in the wagon, but he mumbled, "That man will freeze to death before anyone finds him. At least give him dry clothes."

There were no clothes left. Antoine took a breath. And another.

What he did would forever affect Charlie's life. Charlie had to understand how to live a decent life. Antoine couldn't leave the boy with the image of him walking away from a dying man. A man Charlie called daddy. No. That wouldn't do.

"Marie, grab blankets for Clement. Get him out of these wet things. We'll drop him off at that farm."

Marie objected, but Antoine glared at her until she got the blankets. She tossed them on the ground and turned around in her annoyed way.

Hoolie smirked. "You set her light straight."

Antoine ignored him. "God knows we're the last crew who should help this devil, but," Antoine surveyed the crowd, not sure any of them would understand this, "they can save him if they want. It's the most we gotta do."

"He'd have left you," Hoolie mumbled but he was helping Clement up. "I am taking whatever he has for cash. Just so that's clear."

"Difference between men who live outside a sheet and those who live under one, Hoolie, is that one has earned a home and the other has lost many in the yearning for one."

"Annoying is what you are, Antoine." Still, Hoolie didn't go through Clement's pockets. Clement did whisper something to Hoolie though, but Hoolie ignored it.

When he put weight on his leg, Clement crumpled, bringing Hoolie down with him. "I'll need help. He's heavy."

The men carried Clement to the wagon. Philip looked at his leg and rolled his eyes. "Baby. You'll be up and running around in no time. Maybe I should break this properly. Too bad my gun is outta bullets."

Everyone pushed against the one side of the wagon as if Clement might attack. Even Emma kept her eyes on Antoine. He scanned her face, reading those eyes. They pleaded with him to listen, yet she didn't speak.

Antoine wiped snow from his face. It wasn't sleet anymore but large white floating flakes.

How did things get so confusing?

Yet, Antoine was seeing things clearly. He was right, and they didn't have to understand.

"Charlie. Come to Daddy. I'm hurt." Clement reached for the boy.

Charlie squeezed deeper between Emma and Antoine.

"Tell that dead man to shut up, Antoine," Marie said. "Or

I'll shut him up."

"Papa." Charlie pulled a blanket over his head.

"He is not your old man." Clement reached for Charlie again. "And speak English. Where did he learn that?"

Marie grabbed the shotgun from Philip and fired but it was empty so she turned it around and used it like a bat, knocking him out. "Works without bullets."

~~

Later that day, Emma wouldn't look at Antoine as he returned to the sled. The others were gone.

Hoolie fell in step beside him. "Nice jacket. I got gloves, and a sandwich, but don't ask how, it's sad what a guy has to do to eat around here." He handed the sandwich to Charlie who grabbed it with both hands and took a huge bite.

"Where's Marie?"

"Took off across the border, said she'd find her own ride. She'll bring Mister Doc home and wait for you where the crows fly. She'll be there in one night's time, every night until you show. So don't leave her hanging out there alone."

"Where are Philip and the rest of our crew?" Antoine asked Hoolie.

"Took off when this Native priest showed. My guess is they figured he was more trustworthy than you. I mean, what the heck were you thinking back there? Don't give me that dirt about trusting it to God. God trusted you to do what was right."

Philip was gone. Free. Antoine would miss him.

"I... You gonna leave too?"

"Depends what you say about it."

Antoine checked on Charlie, who offered him a bite of his sandwich. "You eat it, little man."

Emma was silent, snuggled into the blankets. The sun was out, warming her cheeks, but she kept her eyes down.

How could he explain this so Hoolie would understand? "I didn't want to change the way you look at me, if that makes sense."

"Me?" Hoolie cleared his throat. "I guess you have to think of things like that when someone who can see your soul stops calling you Mister, eh? Still."

Antoine climbed in the sled wagon.

"So you think vanishing a prick is murder?" Hoolie asked.

"Not if God does it. Last time I checked, I was only his warrior." He rubbed his band tattoo that identified him as such. Now, he'd earned it. Letting Clement live was the hardest thing he'd ever done and this act made him *Cîpay*. He felt it. Revenge wasn't fighting, but guiding a lost soul.

"So we trust Your Friend, do we? Fine, He ain't let us down yet. Four, all aboard." Hoolie knocked on the side of the wood and got ready to leave.

"Am I still welcome to sit beside you, Emma?" Antoine felt the imaginary door between them and knocked gently. Emma kept her eyes down. "Emma?"

She pulled her knees in and wouldn't look at him.

Antoine snuggled in beside her as the sled pulled out. "Let me tell you a story." Charlie snuggled up to him. "It's a sad story. My sister Josée was attacked by a wolf when she was four. I was fishing in the creek, about fourteen-years-old. Worst day of my life. I hunted that wolf. The wolf fought hard and when her soul left, she met my eyes with accusation. I made an unbearable situation worse with that one act of vengeance." Antoine couldn't look at Emma but he felt her come in beside him.

"How? You were protecting your sister." Her voice was full of love again. He wrapped an arm around her.

"Protecting my sister should have happened before the attack, with me showing her how to avoid situations like that and not goofing off when I should have been alert for danger. Protecting someone is not the same thing as revenge. That wolf was not a cold monster, she was a mother protecting her pups and we were fishing over her den. See the difference? I thought I knew everything about her, yet I didn't know a blasted thing. I was blinded by my rage, only seeing what I wanted."

She rested against his shoulder and reached for his hand.

~~

Antoine watched Hoolie drive. He leaned forward, squinted

and pulled to the right, taking them off the path and toward a farm. Antoine shot up. "What's wrong?"

"That ghost of the earth, he wants me to ditch you." Hoolie shook his head. "You sure your uncle ain't dead?"

Antoine thought about how Silver always happened to be there when he needed him. "He might be. With Silver, who the heck knows?"

Emma climbed out with Charlie and waited for him to join them.

Antoine looked north. Hoolie was leaving them not far from the cemetery that led to Depaix tunnels.

Hoolie pulled away without even a good-bye, and headed east at full speed.

"Bad," Charlie said.

It was exactly how Antoine felt as he hurried them to the cemetery.

PART FIVE

1918-1919

"The nice thing about the prairies is that everything you don't want to keep close, the wind blows away. Not many friends that understanding."

–Sacri

–FIFTY-ONE–

November 1918—

Antoine ran his fingers along the last marker of the tunnel under Depaix land. No one had spoken since Marie's scream shook them up.

"It's too dark. Say something to make me laugh." Emma was right, he needed to say happy things, yet he couldn't think of one thing to say. The walls crowded out his happy thoughts.

"Me laughed." The little one in his arms was alert.

"What made you laugh, Charlie?" Antoine was curious.

"Hoolie."

Despite the cold, despite his fear for his sister, Antoine smiled and it warmed his entire frozen body. "That brat made me laugh a few times, too. Did you like to laugh?"

Charlie touched Antoine's cheek and ran a finger over his lips to feel his smile. "Happy. Papa happy."

"Yeah. I like the idea of Hoolie making you laugh, Charlie. Makes me warm inside."

Charlie clutched Antoine around the neck. "Happy. Me happy, too." Antoine felt him smile against him, and the action shook off the last of the chills as he placed the boy down so he could open the trapdoor.

~~

"Marie." Antoine rushed to her. The snow hadn't started on this part of the prairies. The ground was chilly but there was only a sloppy wet that made things frosty.

If Marie had come by sled or wagon, it was gone. A fire

burned beside her, and Antoine tossed dirt on it. They'd used it to brand her. He knelt and touched her face. Blood. The moon shone on them, making it glimmer. Blood everywhere.

"Charlie, I have to carry my sister. It's far. Can you hold on tight if I need to run?" Antoine's shoulder throbbed just thinking about lifting her. "I know you're tired but we're close. We can do this."

"I can carry him." Emma used her torn dress to clean Marie. "Not many wounds. This isn't her blood. Look at her nails. She fought hard." Emma pulled down Marie's skirt, and straightened her up. "Give me a knife."

"What?"

She didn't repeat herself, just set to work. Antoine handed her his knife while Charlie crouched beside Marie. Antoine met his eyes and Charlie said, "Help."

Antoine nodded but he had no voice to say anything else. He couldn't lose his sister. He couldn't. Not like this. Not to them.

With the knife, Emma cut a long strip from her skirt and wrapped it around Marie's thigh, then wrapped another around her right arm. "Done. Only two wounds to worry about."

Antoine looked at Marie, then Emma. "That's it? Who taught you that?"

"Doc. He showed me things he remembered about healing. I let him talk and watched what he did." Emma touched Marie's face. "Marie was protective of him so she doesn't know I talked to him. She would have sent me off."

"Will I hurt her if I pick her up?" Antoine wished Hoolie was there. He understood what Hoolie meant about how it was impossible to do these things alone.

"No. She's too weak to feel the pain."

"You say that like you know."

"I do."

Antoine brought Marie's frail body into his arms. She was much heavier than Emma. He wouldn't be able to carry her all the way home so he switched directions. Town was much closer.

It would be a long walk in the cold, without the horse and buggy, but Emma used the sheet to tie Charlie to her back.

"You shouldn't carry him, you're hurt," Antoine said.

"I'm fine. How far is your home?"

"Our home." He sighed. "Emma, I hope you'll be happy here."

"This is where your mother and father lived together. Is it not?"

"Yup."

"And they were happy."

Antoine nodded. "Very."

"And you have skin the colour of your mother, and your sister does not. Does this mean your parents were like us? Two colours?"

No mixing on my land. Would Clement haunt them forever? "Sacri was Cree and Pa was a French Catholic settler. Each one brought a rich culture to my life that feeds my beliefs. Each one was special to me and made me who I am. It's not how they looked that made them happy, it was their love."

"How we look matters more than you think. Marie taught me this. I could blend in or stand out, depending on how she dressed me."

Maybe she was right. Charlie's green eyes bothered him, even though he would never admit that to anyone.

"Clement said it's wrong for us to be together. Why would he say such things?"

He hated that she cared what he thought so he ignored her question and said, "Charlie and I are lucky. We look like our mothers. Nothing wrong with that. Right, Charlie? Are you cold, Emma?"

"I'm too angry to be cold."

Antoine didn't have the courage to ask who she was mad at.

–FIFTY-TWO–

It was a few days later when Antoine woke in Charlie's bed with the sun in his face. He wasn't sure why, but they were all camping out in Charlie's room. He had his family with him in a house he built yet nothing was right. Emma kept avoiding him. She hadn't said a word when she saw her new home, just escorted Charlie inside, and found the bed. She'd kept to herself since then. Not opening closets or touching things. She was a stranger in her own house.

Charlie wrestled with Hoolie's bag and he let it go and hid under his pillow when he saw Antoine watching him.

"What ya got there, little man?" Antoine sat up and opened the bag for him. "There might be something of yours in here. Shall we look?"

Antoine pulled the Bible from Hoolie's bag and laid it by the pillow Charlie hid under. "Yours."

Charlie exploded from under the pillow. The green in his eyes alive, energized as he ran them over the book.

"You know that book? It's yours."

Charlie pulled it to himself in a big hug and brought it to the pillow to play with it. Antoine watched curious. Charlie took off his necklace and matched it to the cross on the front. "Papa," he announced with a shy glance at Antoine. Then he opened it, looking for more signs he knew. "Ghost."

"I'll teach you to read, Charlie. I promised to teach Hoolie, too. You'll learn together."

Charlie smiled.

"For now, I'll read it to you. There are fun stories in there."

Charlie returned to his book. "Baby." He turned the page. "Bad Papa."

Bad Papa? Antoine peeked over his shoulder. Abraham

held his son, who was tied up, and Abraham had a knife.

"Ah, it looks bad, but it turned out fine." Charlie watched his lips, as if what he said next was crucial. How much did he understand? "Did someone tell you this story?"

"Daddy."

Daddy? Antoine fumbled for his words. *Daddy?* "You want to hear Nukum's version of this story?" Charlie brought the book to Antoine and they snuggled together. "You like horses, right? Well in this story, a stallion—"

"Papa horse."

"*Ouais*, the stallion is the papa horse. So, he is led to a field he doesn't know with his foal, his *petit*."

"*Phe-tee?*"

"*Ouais, petit* means little one."

"Baby."

Antoine nodded. "The papa didn't want to go there, but he had no choice, his master brought them and he trusted him. But once in the field, the master took out his knife." Antoine pointed to the knife in the picture. "He went toward the baby with the knife."

"Bad."

"It did look bad. Yet the papa stallion, he nudged his *petit* toward his master. You know why? Because he trusted his master completely. A stallion has to have faith in his master, right? How else can they work together? They have to trust that both are good."

"Good." Charlie frowned. Antoine gave him time. "Not bad. Help."

"That's right, the master brought the knife up and cut off a thistle trapped in the baby's mane. If the stallion had interfered, he would have hurt them all. By trusting that his master knew what was good for them, he saved his son pain. So it's a partnership of give and trust from both sides." Antoine pointed to the picture. "Good papas know when to trust and when to protect. That's what makes them safe."

"Me like."

"I like that story, too. Here, find another picture you like and I'll tell you and Hoolie the story tonight. I'm gonna find *Maman*."

Antoine left Charlie in his room and peeked into the room

he wanted to share with Emma, if she ever told him what exactly was bothering her.

Emma stood in front of the looking glass, holding the dress he'd bought her. She tilted her head this way and that. Then she leaned in and closed her eyes as if kissing him. Antoine rested against the doorjamb amused. Suddenly, she twirled, making the dress dance with her.

She dropped the dress when she saw him, cleared her throat, and went back to the laundry.

"I take it you like the dress then. I wasn't sure, since you didn't say anything."

"I..." She clammed up.

"Emma, talk to me."

"I never owned anything so beautiful. Why would you buy me this?"

"It's just a dress." Antoine walked in and helped her fold the laundry so he could be closer to her.

She pulled the shirt from him. "You shouldn't be folding laundry."

"I can fold just fine." He sat with a heavy sigh. "I wish I could shower you in things that make you twirl, but I traded half a box of nails for it."

"I'd look horrible in nails."

He chuckled and picked the dress off the floor. "*Ouais,* you can't wear nails to the dance tonight."

She grabbed the dress from him and clutched it.

"I have no idea what you're thinking. Please say your thoughts."

"Mable went dancing. It always made her happy."

She looked so sad and troubled, happy was exactly the result he wanted. "Well, that twirl you did was perfect. Put the dress on and do that in my arms."

"I can't leave Charlie."

"Hoolie showed up yesterday morning. He agreed to watch Charlie, well, if I ever get him out of those tunnels. He's the safest guy I know. Marie wanted to come, she's bringing Doc. They could use some happy, too."

Emma swallowed but still didn't answer. He craved words from her.

"So?" he asked.

"I do not know what you ask, Antoine."

"You see, there's this dance in town tonight. I thought we could go. You and me. Dancing." He felt like an idiot. Why was he talking in circles?

Emma met his eyes. Antoine smiled, instantly lost in the deep beautiful brown. "What ya think?" he asked.

"A date?"

He let out a breath and nodded, not realising he held it. Gosh. What if she said no? "We don't have to. I thought it might be fun. A date."

"I'll be ready by seven, will this do?"

That simple. Not a pause, not a debate. It was the best yes he'd ever heard. "Have you ever danced?"

"No."

Antoine ran an arm around her. "Then let me show you how."

Emma slipped against him and her sweet bread-like fragrance drew him in until he forgot about dancing and kissed her neck, his hunger for her deepening. He took the dress from her hands and his head spun while their lips danced and their bodies teased each other.

More kisses.

Her lips were his entire focus.

Emma pulled away, but he twirled her back into his arms so their heads touched and they could breathe together.

"A date." He let out a long breath and backed up to get a better look at her. "Sounds perfect. It'll be fun, *ma belle*. They have a band that plays swing music." His hands were still on her and he slipped them along her back, around her bottom, and pulled her in so their bodies kissed. "I can't wait for you to meet my friends tonight."

"I would like to come to this bed tonight, but you said we were to vow in your church before we shared it, and I... I really don't understand my place."

Her words flashed up another door between them, as anger blazed over him, and it hit him that this door between them wasn't her doing but his. He should have told her what the priest said yesterday. He opened his mouth to do exactly that but all he could form was, "Plans change." What angered him the most was that Clement had been right.

~~

Yesterday, Antoine almost bounded into the church he was so excited. He had it planned. A wedding, dancing—the best night of his life. Hoolie agreed to watch Charlie so he could have Emma all to himself for one night. Everything was perfect.

"Father." Antoine could hardly breathe as the joy exploded from him at the idea of vowing to the woman he loved in his church. "I hoped you'd still be here. Emma and I will swing by tomorrow to say our vows before the dance. Marie said she'd witness things. She's up and about and frantically wants to do something."

Father Hillsdale didn't lift his eyes from loading a shotgun. "Antoine, I went over this with Marie. The answer is no."

"No?" Antoine pulled back, shocked. "Why the heck not?"

Father hid the gun in the confessional. "Didn't Marie talk to you?" he asked in the dark of the chamber.

"She said you needed to see me."

"Well, I don't. This conversation is over."

"I... I mean... I don't understand what the heck you mean. Why can't you marry us? We can wait if tomorrow isn't a good day for you."

"No." Father Hillsdale faced him, but didn't meet his eyes, instead, he looked toward the confessional that led to his tunnels. "There won't be a good day. Not anymore. I don't even want to know where that woman came from, but I will not be a part of it."

"Why not?"

"You have different upbringing."

"*Quoi?*"

"Your children will be confused."

"Our children will be loved. Stop for a minute and back up. Are you telling me that I can't marry in this church? Ever?"

"Of course you can marry in this church. The young Levigne girl asked about you, perhaps you should talk to her mother—Jill, I believe is her name. Sweet girl."

"What? No. I plan to marry the woman I love." Antoine pulled out the marriage certificate. "I long to make a home with her and it starts right here." He waved the certificate in

Father's face. "I want to make this real."

Father turned away from him. "I have no cross in my church, Antoine. Very bad ghosts hauled it off last night. Does it mean I am not in a church? Symbols are things we carry with us to show others what we believe. That certificate doesn't make your marriage any more than a cross makes a building a church. Marry Jill, it's easier."

Antoine's fists clenched up and his body tightened. This was not what he expected. He thought this priest was on his side.

Breathe. Just breathe.

"Easier is not always right," Antoine said.

"You have no grasp of the real world, torn between different cultures. This is not—"

"Now *my* upbringing is a problem?" Antoine glanced at the confessional. "Look around, moron, the real world isn't one race or one religion. Outside the walls of this church you preach in, there is a blanket of cultures woven together and God is in all of them. I'll go elsewhere," he lied, because he had nowhere else to go. If a priest with a blasted shotgun in his confessional wouldn't marry them, no one would.

Father sat in one of the pews and invited Antoine to sit with him, but he was too wound up and paced the aisle.

"Each religion has clear boundaries to guide mankind. God has chosen me to stick within the confines of this one religion. I have no need to see outside this. I am here to share these teachings in a specific way, to reach as many as possible. You know the lengths I would go for you, but do not ask me to do something that does not need doing. It's like asking me to stop calling this place a church now that the cross is gone."

Antoine marched to the door too ticked to debate this.

"Marie stormed out, too, not hearing me."

Antoine paused with his hand on the doorknob. Marie stormed out—for him? Antoine pointed to where the cross should hang. "Your missing cross pisses me off."

Father looked at the empty altar. "We'll be fine."

"Yet it really, really, pisses me off that someone took something this important from me."

"A symbol was important to you? Why?"

"It'd be easy to walk away and shrug. Make you another cross, right? But deep down, I want the cross that was there because I made it while I watched my mother die. My friends sat with me, drinking all night, cheering me up. I carved in all sorts of names on the back. Names of people who did something for this town in the hopes that one day, a cross would hang at its heart. I don't expect you to understand why I would do such a thing or why I would carry around a marriage certificate that doesn't have the power behind it of spoken vows. But it means something to me."

"Then it has served its purpose, and I have done my job." Father swallowed, his eyes where the cross should be. "Think about what I said."

Despite the cold, Father was almost arm and arm with him as he walked out. "Leave me alone, we're through," Antoine snapped.

"No. You're walking away from a church you helped build and I should be honest with you. It has nothing to do with Emma but *her* son." Father stretched the word *her* as if telling him something.

"*Our* son. So choose your next words carefully, because I have no problem hitting you. The mood I'm in, I might hit you twice."

"I told you there is good in everyone, Antoine, but I was wrong. The boy you claim is yours, he has the same green eyes as the devil and a mark on his hand that matches. He—"

Antoine swung. It was instinct, but Father slammed his arm aside with his left hand before he made contact and his right rammed Antoine in the ribs. Antoine caught his breath, surprised, and stared intently, waiting for an apology. Too shaken to demand one. Too flustered to use his legs to walk away.

Yet the priest looked back at him as if nothing had happened. "That cross is missing because you took another man's son as yours. You see how this works? You see why there will be no marriages in my church that don't need doing."

Dammit. Antoine glanced around. Was Clement here? "Trading a cross for a boy. Is this how you work?"

"This won't end well. I'm preparing you."

"And to think, Pa called you *Cîpay*."
Father bowed his head as if Antoine had slapped him.

–FIFTY-THREE–

Clement crossed his arms as he leaned against Antoine's stupid rundown barn, watching them. Tonight there was supposed to be a dance, and everyone in town was a busy bee. His breath formed little clouds. He pulled out his cigarette case knowing it was empty. It had been empty since the day Emma told him he tasted like ashes, yet at times like this, he still wanted it to be full. Why did he care so goddamn much what she thought?

He just did.

He'd planned to storm in while Antoine was out but then... Emma twirled. She actually twirled in front of the window and scooped Charlie up, dancing. He was enthralled with them as they paraded around, giggling. Passing by each window.

He should have danced with them. Why hadn't he? Guilt. Always guilt. He hated that. Every time he looked at her, all he felt was guilt and nothing ever appeased it. He really needed a smoke.

"Antoine must have forgotten something. He's on his way back." Some idiot slapped a hand on Clement's shoulder and Clement glared at it, as if considering breaking it. "He just walked in the field, talked to nothing and came back. Think he knows we're here?"

Finally, Clement tossed off the heavy hand. "Give me a minute. You got a smoke?" He glanced at the man at his side, surprised to see it was his future-son-in-law. "You shouldn't be here, Mitch. I told you to stay at the ranch to watch my girls." One simple order. He couldn't even follow one simple order. What was wrong with guys these days? Didn't their fathers teach them anything?

Before Clement could send him home, Antoine ran down the path and burst into the house. He'd only been gone all of ten minutes.

"Papa, we dance." Charlie rushed to him and the door slammed shut as Antoine scooped him up.

Clement grabbed the cigarette he was handed. As he watched Emma rush to Antoine and twirl with him, he snapped it in two. Dammit.

"What's wrong? Let's go. We'll come back later, there's a dance tonight."

No hesitation. Not a breath of guilt when Antoine scooped them up. He could accept he'd failed her, but how could Clement look at his son and not feel the overwhelming guilt he normally did? Was it possible to look at the boy like Antoine did? There was a secret. He knew there was.

"Look at them dancing together, like idiots." Mitch chuckled. "That pansy should be easy to whack, eh?"

Clement turned around and walked away. "We're done here. Nothing left for me."

"We're leaving?"

"Soon. I have to pay the priest another visit. Next time I ask you to stay home to watch my girls, you do it, or you're out. I won't have a son who can't follow simple orders. They're for your own safety. Understand?"

"I make my own rules, and I keep my own gal safe. You understand, Pop?"

Clement paused and faced the boy. He smirked. Finally, a worthy one.

–FIFTY-FOUR–

Antoine barged into the house, after his search for Silver. Silver had agreed to keep an eye on things while they were at the dance, and this made Antoine feel much better. He didn't like the idea of leaving the boys without surveillance.

Hoolie paced the kitchen while Charlie ate at the table. "About time you got home, bunch of women showed up, and I don't like this, they have shit-disturbers written all over them. Listen to them yapping their gums." Hoolie pointed to the salon. "I never liked me a bunch of foxes huddled together like that. Made me nervous how they came bearing gifts and baking."

Antoine walked up to the salon and before entering, he stopped to listen.

"How far along are you, sweety?"

"Baby should be here in the spring," Emma said.

It pleased him to hear her fitting in with the others. It would take time, but she was talking to them, they were talking to her. Antoine smiled, relieved. She'd make friends.

"Antoine sure looks thrilled."

"Did he tell you about Jill yet? Hear he gave her a horse. They've been quite the thing this past year. Was sure they'd get married but he shows with you. Imagine our surprise."

Antoine groaned and walked in before they told her more lies. "Good day, ladies. Mind if I steal away with my wife before the dance?"

They walked past him, mumbling their hellos.

Alone, he waited for Emma to say something. Silently, she rose and walked past, too.

"Emma. Emma. Look at me."

"You don't want me to say my thoughts."

"I do."

Her eyes bore into him. "I never lied to you."

"I…"

Emma pushed past him when a knock at the front door made him glance that way.

"Dang it, Emma. I never lied either. These are just women gossiping."

She shut herself in Doc's room.

Antoine went to answer the door, no idea what to tell her anyway.

Jill smiled back at him. "I heard you found your gal. Can I meet her? Are you taking her to the dance tonight? I have no one to go with. Sucks."

"Not today. She's not in the mood to see you. Met a bunch of crazy women who told her I was in cahoots with you."

"Who cares what they think?" Jill rolled her eyes.

"She apparently does. She doesn't understand gossip and believes what she hears."

"Aw, I just came to meet her. Don't be grouchy." She walked in but Antoine wouldn't let her in the kitchen. Jill's eyes were huge with worry, but he was used to her.

"I have to fix things with Emma. You'd better scram."

"Oh I can help." She pushed past Antoine and went toward the voices in Doc's room. She walked in without knocking and Antoine followed.

Doc drew Myles as he chatted with Emma.

"Emma," Antoine interrupted. "This is Jill."

Jill pushed past Antoine. "So you're the gal Antoine would not shut up about. Gosh. You're as pretty as he said."

Emma sat stone silent. So Antoine talked, telling her the story about Henri. "Jill is a sister to me, Henri's sister. Because of her I was able to breathe without you."

Emma stood and looked at the portrait Doc worked on. "Myles helped me like that." She smiled at Antoine and he felt the wall between them come down enough.

"This Myles?" Doc pointed to the portrait. "Wish I could remember one thing about this haunting image that won't leave me." He sighed, frustrated. "I messed it up, too. For some reason, I keep drawing in Hoolie's eyes."

"It looks very much like him, Doc," Emma encouraged

him. "He did have Hoolie's eyes. He talked like him, too."

Jill sat. "I have this trunk of baby things I made last winter, and I bet you can use most of them. Oh my, and I just about forgot but when Antoine seeded our land..." She went on in her way.

"Do I know this one?" Doc asked Antoine.

"No, Marie kicked her out when you showed up. Said she talked too much."

Jill was still blabbering and Emma hadn't said a word.

"You coming to the dance?" Antoine asked Doc. "You look better today. Marie could use fun and she won't go unless you do."

"Well." Doc pulled the picture from his notepad. "I suppose I will." He rolled up his drawing. "I should probably talk to her. I don't know what to wear to a dance."

Emma pushed passed Antoine. "I need to find Charlie." She rushed to her room.

"He's with Hoolie," Antoine called after her.

"Who's this Hoolie?" Jill looked confused.

"Me. What's up?" Hoolie sidled up to them, holding Charlie. "Hey." Hoolie went red the minute Jill glanced his way. "I mean, hey. Um. Gee hey. I..."

Antoine rolled his eyes as Hoolie's face got redder and redder. All his big talk, yet the guy was shy around Jill? Cripes. "Jill, this is Hoolie. He's seen you around and believe it or not, he goes red like that every time. Tonight, he's watching Charlie and could use a hand. They'll pick you up after six, since you got nothing to do anyhow."

"Yeah, what he said. Sound like fun?" Hoolie gave her his half smile.

Jill nodded. "I am great with little gaffers. I used to be one, you know."

Hoolie chuckled. "Me too. Maybe we have a few things in common. Charlie knows the best hiding holes. Maybe we can show you a few, if you're into that type of thing."

They talked but Antoine was off searching for Emma. She sat on their bed. He walked to the window and leaned against the wall. "We talk about everything," he reminded her.

She twisted her skirt. "Jill says you looked after her and her mother. Must you help everyone? Is this what I must do? The women talked of things we have to do as a group in town. Am I supposed to go there and do this on top of the things you need me to do?"

"I don't need you to do anything. This is your place. Emma, everything you see is yours. Yours. Touch these things, make them yours. Move things, use things. If you want to help in town, go for it. If you don't have time, skip it and catch the next thing. We do what we can. Friends and family helping each other. Does that make sense?"

"Mine?" She glanced around and her eyes grew wider. "I don't know what that means. Why would these things be mine? You can't give me your things. I don't know my place."

"This is your place, all of it. These are our things. We share them, like a family or something. My things burned. I bought each thing in this room while thinking about you." Antoine sat on the bed, air rushing at him. "Truth is, this place feels empty to me. There are no stories in these walls, Emma. My family home, the one with the warmth and love in it, the one I couldn't wait to show you, it's gone. So I built us another, but we have a lot more dancing to do in these walls before it feels like home."

"You built this? By yourself?"

"That board you're standing on only has three nails. Others have four. I know that because I pounded in every single nail. Gilles tried, but I wouldn't let him. I wanted it to be ours. I thought of you while I pounded each nail. The fourth nail went there." Antoine pointed to the wall. "For you to hang a picture. Not sure why, but I thought you might like that."

"Me?" She ran her hand over the wall as if seeing a painting there then she looked at Antoine and smiled. "No one ever gave me a nail before."

He chuckled. "Welcome home."

—FIFTY-FIVE—

Hoolie was a nervous wreck. "How do I look, Charlie?"

Charlie was playing with his new toque. He pulled it on and giggled.

"That bad?" Hoolie ran his hands over his shirt, trying to get the wrinkles out of it. "Now you gotta help me with this gal, she's so..." He let out a long puff of air, at a loss for words. She was just perfect.

"Help?" Hoolie asked. "Brave."

"Yeah, I'm trying. Let's go." Hoolie threw on his jacket and scooped up the boy. They stood on the steps and a ghostly earth shadow rushed at them in the dark. He was getting used to those coming at him. All this land was haunted something fierce.

The shadow came at them again.

Hoolie searched the dark. Several lights were heading his way on foot. Great. He knew that orange-guilt-stricken light. Clement was here.

"Bad." Charlie shivered.

Hoolie pulled out his pocket-watch and glanced at it as he calmly stepped back into the house. Hopefully Jill would understand. He slipped out the back door to the cellar and tossed up the trapdoor.

"It's gonna be dark, but don't worry, I got it covered."

Charlie clutched onto Hoolie's jacket, his eyes wide. "Dark good?"

"Yup. Dark means I can see the light before they can see us."

–FIFTY-SIX–

Antoine and Emma walked into the dance hall together. Arm in arm. After Antoine took her coat, she kept smoothing out her new dress as if it scratched her. "You're beautiful," Antoine whispered to her neck and escorted her to the dance floor.

Silence fell on the partying room. Even the band came to an abrupt halt.

"Marie isn't here." Emma curled up tighter against him. "You said Marie would be here."

The familiar faces blended for Antoine. It never occurred to him that Emma wouldn't know anyone. With all eyes on them, he felt like he should say something, but the words were locked in his throat. This wasn't how it was supposed to go. He couldn't introduce her to everyone at once.

His cousin Bernoit approached. "Antoine, what are you doing?" His voice was a whisper, as if even talking to them would get him in trouble. He kept glancing uncomfortably at their joined hands.

"Bernoit, this is Emma. We came to dance. What's going on? You guys forget how to party while I was gone or what?"

"Antoine, you need to go. I mean get far from here. What the heck did you do?" He glanced at Emma's rounding belly. "So it's true. No wonder you were crazy." Bernoit ran a hand over his face.

"We don't want trouble." Gilles stepped forward.

Emma slipped out.

Before Antoine stormed after her, he faced the crowd and said, "Nails. Bloody nails." These folks brought him nails so he could build his wife a house yet when he gets her here, they shun her. Made her feel unwelcome. He felt betrayed.

Antoine found Emma frozen on the steps to the hall. Her eyes were on a sheet who walked out of the church and stopped to stare at them. Antoine wrapped her jacket around her and put on his own. "Cripes." He pulled her behind him. "What the heck is that moron doing in our church?"

"Hey some idiot got lost," Bernoit said, having followed them outside.

"Don't they know where they are?" Gilles chuckled. "Well, let's introduce them to your pa, Bernoit. See how they like Silver."

A few guys gathered behind them, and one even whispered to Antoine that Emma should go inside. Antoine stood, fists clenched, staring at the ghost in his hometown as it stared back at him. "I brought them to Eau Claire," Antoine told them.

"Argh, we ain't afraid of a loser walking around in a sheet. Are we boys? Maybe he brought back our cross." Gilles pushed past Antoine and others followed.

The man in the sheet ran and they chased after him. Half of them weren't even wearing coats.

"That was him," Emma whispered, a ghostly cloud formed with her words.

"Just a fool in a sheet. Emma, please come back in with me."

"I imagined laughing and fun. That was neither. I want to go back to your place."

"Our place."

She winced. "Those women said the priest wouldn't marry us. Does Clement still own me? Is that what everyone is afraid to tell me? Is he coming for me? If he does, will you keep Charlie safe?"

Without realizing it, he ran his hand along her cheek. Her skin was warm against his chilled hand. "We are married." He pulled out the marriage certificate and studied it. It felt real even if he knew Father Kilby only whipped it up out of guilt.

She kept her eyes down.

The group of guys charged up the steps excited and energized. "Caught a glimpse of Silver in the distance. Coming in?" Gilles nudged them as he flew past.

Emma caught her breath. "Look, Marie is coming."

Antoine could tell Emma wanted to run to Marie. A familiar face in a crowd of faces that blended together. He understood that. "Go on then, I'll wait."

Emma flew down the steps and rushed to Marie who walked leisurely with Doc. Emma twirled in front of her, showing off her dress and new jacket. Even her scarf was up for discussion and Antoine had pulled that out of a trunk in the barn. It didn't take much to please Emma and that made Antoine happy inside, despite the fear that crept up on him.

"Dang, you found yourself one hellofa dame." Gilles was beside him, doing up his jacket and slipping on his gloves. Antoine hadn't even heard him, he'd been so lost in thoughts of Emma.

"I should beat the nails right out of you. Her first date, in a town full of strangers no less, and you monsters treat her like the outsider she's afraid to be." Antoine shook his head. "Gilles, I expected better of my people. She deserved to be welcomed as one of us. She belongs here."

Gilles took in a deep breath. "No offence, Antoine, but your gal is not like us at all."

"How can you say that garbage?"

Gilles lowered his voice. "For starters, she's got a tattoo of judgement on the back of her hand. You can't marry someone marked for judgement. You're *Cîpay*. Aren't you? I mean, damn, I saw that tattoo on your arm. You are a Warrior of God, like Silver. I can't even imagine the hell you suffered to earn *that* symbol."

"Some prick marked her so he wouldn't have to face judgement alone. A message for me that is none of your business."

"Oh. Not my business. That's different. I guess I'll welcome her then and ignore those teachings your mother drilled into me, ignore the rumours flying around about you stealing some boy."

"Any other problems I should know about?" Antoine adjusted his Sunday cap, his eyes still on Emma while she walked, her arm slung through Doc's other arm.

"I assume you have eyes, and see she's much too beautiful for the likes of you, so I'll shut up, but you should have warned us or something."

"Warned you?" Antoine turned to Gilles, anger making him clench his fists. "That I was coming out to dance with my girl? You knew I was bringing her home. You helped me build our son a room for Pete's sake. You even listening to yourself?"

"I meant that she was... ya know..." Gilles swallowed and looked out at Doc with the two gals at his side. Doc was hardly limping and stood tall and happy.

"Is that your baby in her belly or you stealing that one, too?"

Gilles ducked, missing Antoine's first swing but his second one caught him in the gut, and he bent over catching his breath.

"She's my wife." Antoine shoved the marriage certificate at him, not sure why he was still carrying the stupid thing around, yet he had no idea what to do with it.

Gilles pushed it away. "Oh good then, glad I cleared that up. Damn. Did you have to hit me?" Gilles took in a deep breath. "We're just on edge. Antoine, what did you do? I mean, damn, I heard rumours she was a slave-digger. I thought those were horrible legends meant to keep guys like me in line."

"Legends are always based on truth."

"Well... Not a chance in hell some asswipe is coming in here and taking a cross from our town because he doesn't like one of our dumb ideas." Gilles looked at Marie coming down the path and back at Antoine. He sighed. "Is that your sister? Is she with that guy? Damn. I was giving her widow time and already I missed my chance."

"That's Doc. She's showing him around."

"So I stand a chance?" Gilles' words made a cloud of smoke as he straightened up his jacket and tried to act the hero.

"After tonight, I wouldn't welcome you in my home, a home you helped me build."

Gilles stood beside Antoine so their shoulders touched. "Thing I like about you is how you take swings without swinging. That one hurt, Antoine. Just about as much as the nail comment. Bring them in and we'll show them how we get down and dusty here on the prairies. I'll even be nice to that chump on your sister's arm, especially if he's a doctor you brought us. Where'd you dig him up? Will he work with *Cîpay*? Want a drink? We got ourselves the best booze in Saskatchewan, and since there is a nasty prohibition going on, you know how we got our hands on that, eh? Busted up a few ghosts we did." Gilles slapped Antoine's shoulder and Antoine winced. It was still tender. "Set me up with that sister of yours before she realizes she's too good for me."

"You should know, she called you a cutie pie."

"Urgh. For real? Here I was trying to come off all warrior-like." Gilles shrugged. "I guess I can play that card." He vanished inside.

Within moments, Antoine heard a jig start up.

~~

"You look much better," Antoine said to Marie as she approached. "Doc, too. Pretty macho looking in your three-button vest, but you should do up your jacket, it's mighty cold."

Doc chuckled and adjusted his new grey cap. "Marie picked it out for me. Told me I was charming."

"Did you see her dress?" Emma's eyes lit up as she slipped her arm through Antoine's. "Your sister is so pretty."

"Hmmm." Antoine only had eyes on Emma. "The music is playing again, and I can't wait to twirl you on the dance floor like we did this afternoon. One dance and we'll check on Charlie." He didn't like the idea of ghosts in town and those boys alone on the farm. The sooner they returned, the better.

"I'm not going in there."

"You'd let me dance by my lonesome on our first date?"

"Come on." Marie took her arm. "If I have to have fun, so do you."

Emma pulled away. "I hate it here."

Antoine stopped breathing and met her eyes.

"Breathe, Antoine." Doc was in his face.

"No reason to if she won't breathe with me. I can't fix this, everything I try is wrong. I have nothing left to offer. Clement was right. She was happier with him." He dropped the marriage certificate and stormed off.

Doc chased after him. "She said she hated it, not that she didn't want to be here. Antoine, stop and look at this." Doc shoved the picture of Myles at him. "I don't remember Myles... yet how did I draw this if I don't remember him?"

Antoine grabbed the picture. Emma had been right, it was good. "Don't know, I guess a guy can't forget who he was, it's a memory edged into his very essence."

"Yet here you are, asking Emma to do this. She isn't the problem, you are. You have to accept her as is, with Clement haunting her and all. Of course she hates it, you haven't made her feel at home. You can't just force someone to be at home, they have to settle in themselves."

Oh. That made sense.

"Thanks, Doc." Antoine glanced at her. "Emma, come. I'll show you around." He didn't wait to see if she'd follow, just made his way to the school and leaned against it, looking toward his farm. It was desolate but he knew his home was close. Was Charlie already asleep? Jill had better behave with Hoolie. He wasn't sure who he was more concerned for, but he was leaning toward Hoolie getting more than he could handle.

Emma appeared in the darkness and leaned against the building beside him. Far enough so he couldn't touch her. "You dropped this," she said.

"A butterfly is just a caterpillar."

"What?" She asked.

"My mother used to always say this, but I never understood until just now. You see, the problem is that no matter what a butterfly says, it can't convince a caterpillar that it was once one, too. The change is too much, yet inside, it feels like a caterpillar."

"Sometimes, you say things that are so stupid they're smart. This is how I feel."

"It's how we all feel." Antoine edged in closer and took her hand in his. He was happy to see that she wore the gloves someone from town brought her. "Look around, what do you see?"

"I hate the dark."

"I was thinking about how I knew our house is straight

ahead, even if I can't see it, even if all around me I feel hopelessness, the pull of home is still there, inviting. I know those boys are safe in a place I built. That makes me feel warm inside."

"I never had a home." She shoved the certificate in her jacket. "People normally tell me what to think."

"People tell me what to think all the time, too. You're not alone."

They stood, enjoying the silence.

"My pa said, a smart man knew when to take orders and knew when to think for himself."

"Tell me about him. I love your stories."

"Imagine open prairies. Bison running free. The creek, rocks in the fields. A few bushes here and there. When my pa came to this area, there was nothing as far as he could see. He set up camp for the evening and planned to continue, but..." Antoine smirked. "He saw strange things in the shadows that kept him an extra day. He was sure he'd seen a ghost. His companion thought him crazy, but Pa was determined to catch a glimpse of this shadow again. The second night, his supplies and his companions vanished, forcing him to search the area. What he found was perfect land where he felt at home. He called it a peaceful possibility—Depaix Land. Despite the bad omens, he decided it was worth the fight. And fight he did. Some invisible force tried to tell him to leave. One night they even threw him in a canoe and sent him down the creek. Shown the door, so to speak."

Emma chuckled lightly.

"Pa swam back with the canoe. All the way. Exhausted he crawled to shore on what was to be Depaix Land, and standing there with his gear was a goddess. After they had it out, each in their own language, she marched off and he followed. Pa discovered that an entire tribe lived here, at one with the land. They protected this land from settlers. Yet he refused to leave. He was home. He couldn't explain why, he just was. They reached a compromise, their own treaty, so to speak. If he insisted on staying, it would be on their terms, and he would have to learn their ways and live by their rules. Pa was all for that, if it meant he could be closer to Sacri. So you see, he gave up one life for another. A choice he made.

At first, he was lost in this new way of life, but much to his surprise, he ended up teaching them how to blend into this new world, and slowly the two lived in harmony. After making Sacri a home, Pa became the spokesman for the ghostly tribe. He vowed to keep settlers off this land if they didn't follow *Cîpay* law; respect others, respect yourself, and respect nature."

Emma glanced around as if she might see them. "Is this tribe still here?"

"Of course. When I told you that Charlie was safe, I meant it. Silver is my uncle, and I made sure he was watching those boys tonight. He'd even shoot a priest to keep them safe."

She looked relieved.

"Come see how well they evolved together. It's sometimes hard to see where the tribe begins and the settlers end." She followed Antoine into the school. "Our school. Everyone pitched in. Not one piece of wood or even one nail was supplied by anyone except these settlers and the *Cîpay* they chose to live with." He ran his hand over the wall and lit a lantern so she could see. "We have two teachers. One is paid with our money and it's this teacher who lives here. She follows provincial teaching laws. The other is *Cîpay*. A *Cîpay* teaches survival in Cree and it's for those classes that I went to school. They were the best. You never knew who'd stop by or why, but it was always an earthy adventure."

Emma studied a calendar with writing on it.

"Every night a different family makes sure the paid teacher has food and fire. Our day is the 16th of every month. The calendar is where we write our name on the date so she knows who's coming. She's young, and easily frightened so we'll keep it down. She sleeps up those stairs. The wives keep it clean and when we go to the hills for firewood for winter, we bring extra wood for the school." Antoine showed her the woodpile and the wood stove.

Emma took off her gloves and warmed her hands in front of it. "A fire made possible by everyone. I like that. It's... homey."

Antoine dropped in a log.

"That's... not at all what I thought happened," she said. "Your world is different than the ranch."

"We do this so our children have an education, yet have the chance to become *Cîpay*. They read and write, add, and learn about places other than what they see on these prairies, yet live in harmony with the earth that feeds us."

"All this sounds perfect. Too perfect."

"Well, it's not. You know what we get for our efforts?" She shook her head, her eyes sparkling in the dim light, so he continued, "Now we're told we must teach only in English."

"Why?"

He closed his eyes. "Because they don't know that we were caterpillars, and it scares them to see butterflies. I learnt English in this classroom because it was all my teacher spoke and I wanted to read. I spoke French at home and with my friends. Cree was saved for times when I wanted to feel closer to the earth. Today, I received a telegram from the superintendent that says Charlie isn't allowed to come here because he has no birth certificate. Which Doc says is a lie, he filed it with us as parents. His name is Charles Depaix. What bothers me the most, is how the heck did he even find out about Charlie so fast?"

"What?" The fire in her voice made Antoine proud. She was home.

"You have nothing to fear, Charlie will be welcome. I know this." Antoine opened one of the desks and passed the lantern over it. "Here's why." Antoine lifted out two books and pointed to the bottom book. "A French book, despite the new law that says this is illegal. This is what you find when you stop to see the world around you. No one in this town cares what caterpillars say."

"Show me your church."

"I'm not welcome there anymore, even if I can access tunnels that run directly to it. More people telling me what to do."

Antoine brought her there anyway. "I have a sad story about when this church was built. If you want to hear it?" he said while he lit the lantern.

She sat in a pew and he snuggled up to her.

"There was a point where we ran out of wood, and had to haul it from Winnipeg. Pa brought me along for the ride and it was the first time I watched someone die."

"What?"

"I was chasing my friend, Mit. We played in the field while our pas set up camp for the evening and Mit tripped in a wasp nest. They swarmed him. The more Mit screamed the more they filled his mouth. The men ran with a bucket of water and they tossed it on him, but it was too late. He was swollen. An image I'll never forget. I never understood why it wasn't me. Why Mit? We were both not paying attention. Why did he die and I got away with a few bites? How could I have helped him? I felt responsible for his safety, but for the love of these prairies, I had no idea what I did wrong."

Antoine took a deep breath. "Sacri promised me that one day I would understand and when that day arrived, I would be *Cîpay*."

"Do you understand?"

"I do. God judges who returns to Him and when. All I do is run happy in the field until it's my turn." He brushed her chin with his bare finger, studying her features in the dim lantern light. He felt the imaginary door between them open a touch. "Once you see the world as a butterfly, you can only remember how innocent you used to be."

Before he knew it, he was kissing her. Slow at first. He could stay lost in her sweet tasting mouth forever, but she pulled away. "Antoine, as I sit here, God sees in my heart and knows I am home."

"Feels kinda nice, eh? Almost... happy."

–FIFTY-SEVEN–

The next morning, Antoine went straight to Gilles' hardware store and pinned him in the corner. "I thought you chased that ghost out of town last night." Antoine wanted to beat the nails right out of someone.

"You have blood on your hands." Gilles tried to shove him off.

"Charlie is missing." Antoine took two quick breaths. "Pricks left me an interesting message."

"Whose blood?" Gilles paled but Antoine relaxed his grip.

"They slaughtered the horses. I promised one to Jill and the other was Hoolie's."

"Gosh." Gilles glanced at Marie who'd come with him.

"Blood everywhere. Even killed the dog." Antoine clutched his fist and banged it into the wall. Emma was gone, but he couldn't say that out loud. "Hoolie's missing, too. Jill said she waited for him to pick her up but he never showed."

"Double-crossed," Marie said.

"We don't know that," Antoine snapped. "What if Hoolie is in trouble?" He refused to believe that Hoolie would turn Charlie over to Clement.

Marie unfolded a paper she'd been holding. "That boy would sell his soul for a few bucks." Antoine glanced at the flyer. It was a Wanted flyer for Charlie. Nine hundred dollars. Exactly what he'd been offered for his land.

"Hoolie is a butterfly who keeps his wings tight against him so no one notices. He would never offer Charlie to a life of slavery."

Gilles raised an eyebrow. "You sound like Sacri sometimes."

"Ask me, the rat already sold his soul to the devil." Marie

tossed her hair over her shoulder.

"Gosh, you're pretty. You sure you don't want to go out with me?" Gilles asked dreamily.

Antoine smoked Gilles on the back of the head. "Focus. I need your help. What did you learn from that idiot last night? Did you talk to Silver? Is someone hiding Clement? I received an interesting letter from the superintendent that made me think someone is double-crossing me. That storm blew in fast last night, they couldn't have gone far."

"You think one of us is a moron?"

"Gather those you trust," Antoine ordered.

"Cripes, Antoine. I trust everyone around here."

"Then take Silver with you."

Gilles swallowed. "Silver? No way, the guy is see-through."

"Any *Cîpay* will do to sniff out a gopher. I'll talk to the priest."

"Talked to him last night. He said he was leaving, said his job was done. Told me to keep an eye on the confessional for you."

"For me? What the heck does that mean?"

Gilles shrugged. "No idea, but you look sick."

"Emma is gone," Marie spoke for Antoine as he stormed out. "She made a choice and Antoine can't accept that."

He wouldn't accept that. Never.

-FIFTY-EIGHT-

Emma held her hands firmly in front of her as she sat on the bench waiting for Doc to return with the tickets. The train station by Eau Claire was actually someone's farm. Things were strange here. She couldn't imagine living in a house where travellers were in and out. Yet... she looked at the woman watching her from the parlour. It would be an adventure every day. So different.

"Two tickets to Pleti." Doc showed her the tickets. "From there, we'll go by buggy. You sure you want to do this, Emma?"

"He took Charlie."

"We don't know that."

"I have to go back with him. I can't leave Charlie alone with him."

"Well." Doc handed her a pistol. "I want you to hold on to this. Might make you feel safer."

"I am sla..." She touched it with her gloved fingers and pulled away quickly. "I am not allowed. I mean... I cannot. I must not. It is forbidden."

He showed her how to use it anyway. So simple.

She squinted her eyes as the rising sun greeted them and grabbed the gun without looking at it. It was heavier than she'd imagined. Perhaps if no one knew. Gracie said at night Philip would touch Clement's guns, and nothing bad ever happened to him. She slipped it in her jacket pocket.

The storm tapered off, but the wind was still cold. She'd helped Antoine search all night for Charlie and was too numb to feel the sting of the icy air. Actually, she didn't even notice it anymore.

Suddenly, a tall man wearing a jacket, much like Antoine's,

was in front of her. His bow was tied to his back and his grey eyes swept over her and settled on Doc.

Doc stood but didn't pay him attention. He rubbed his forehead, upset. Doc was taller than this man, yet they seemed to be eye to eye, not seeing each other.

He reminded Emma of Antoine, yet not in a good way. As if this was who Antoine could be, if he didn't have the safe side she loved fiercely.

"Emma?" Doc followed her gaze and took a step back.

The man's eyes were still on Doc. "*Antoine owes his life to the magic of this medicine man. Cîpay need this man yet you steal him from us.*"

"Emma?" Doc asked.

She sat silent. She didn't need to explain herself to this stranger. She ignored him.

The man continued talking, "*The one marked for judgement talks to God. I let him be, figured they had a wagon load of things to discuss, but I thought you might want to talk to him yourself.*"

Clement was still here? Talking to God? Emma shoved past Doc and pulled out the gun he'd given her.

"Where are you going?" Doc chased after her. "You can't march the mile back to town in the blowing freezing wind." Doc tried to stop her.

"Watch me."

-FIFTY-NINE-

Antoine burst into the church. After lighting the lantern, he went to the confessional and pulled down the box he'd seen Father handle when he'd brought Mable here.

The box was empty, except for a brown envelope with *Marriage Certificates for the Stubborn* written on it. Antoine tore into it and a few papers fell out. He read the note first.

I am not really here, a ghost passing through until my time is done, a Warrior of God on my own in a world that no longer makes sense.

The copy of his marriage certificate had a note attached. "I filed it for you years ago. Didn't trust that fool to do it."

Along the bottom was Cree writing: *How do you see in the dark?*

Candles? Lanterns? He glanced around. There were plenty of those.

Why the games? Antoine looked around the simple church. How many secret passageways were in this place? Henri and him used to explore it when they were younger and he knew of at least two.

"Charlie. Hoolie? Are you boys here? It's safe." Antoine grabbed the candle holder on the altar, the one his pa had made from cedar. It was the only one with *Cîpay* symbols on it. Not any symbols, either; Sacri had carved in a symbol for Warrior of God along the one side. He tried to pick it up but it was attached to the altar. Hmmm. He removed the candle and felt inside the base with his finger.

His finger caught on a piece of wood. He was about to wiggle it when a gun clicked behind him.

A voice behind him said, "Go on, finish what you were gonna do."

–Sixty–

The storm blew in fast, and Clement had held up in the church overnight. He hated that. These places always creeped him out. Going through the good Father's things, Clement found a letter he'd received that promised him the package was in Tibet. Meant this was the prick who'd vanished his Mable. He'd planned to wait to set that debt straight but much to his surprise, Antoine had walked in, looking for Hoolie. Another debt he needed to right and so here they were, Clement with a gun on Antoine but he had no more reason to pull the trigger.

"You healed quickly. Guess it wasn't broken after all, eh?" Antoine backed up, removing his finger from the candlestick. "Clement, you the one who took the cross?"

"I said finish it." He kept the barrel of the rifle tight against Antoine's chest. He'd never in his life pulled a gun on a man, but he had to admit, the thought pulsated in his mind.

Antoine looked down at the rifle on him as if it were a twig and not a promise of death. "Bring that cross back. You'll apologize to my neighbour for killing her horse as you replace it, and whatever magic you pulled with the superintendent, I expect you to undo so Charlie can get a proper education."

Clement tried not to smile. Damn. He just loved this guy's audacity. "Oh, so you don't like me making your life hell, Antoine? Welcome to my world. Every breath I take, you bloody *Cîpay* sneer down my neck. Why would I ever do this for you?"

His jaw clenched. "You got what you wanted. Emma chose you." The pain in Antoine's eyes was deep. Clement stepped back.

Why would she choose him when she had looked so happy? "I don't want that tramp," he lied. Just once he wished he could say what he really felt, like this guy glaring back at him. "She's yours. Where is he?" Clement meant the priest but it was clear Antoine thought he meant the boy when he hurled the lantern at him, ordering him to leave his son alone.

Clement ducked and the lantern exploded on the tapestries behind the altar. In a flash, Antoine shoved the barrel aside and dived for Clement, tackling him clear across the altar. They landed in the front pews and Antoine flung a right and another.

Clement took the hits well and shoved Antoine off. His right got Antoine in the left shoulder. Antoine dropped with a moan.

Smoke filled the church so Clement left Antoine on his knees, fighting the pain while he went to check out the candlestick. Already the flames ate the wall behind the altar, yet he rushed to it and felt inside like Antoine had done. He found a slight rise and pushed it. A panel on the side of the altar fell open and Clement slipped in as a bullet exploded in the church. He didn't look over his shoulder to see who was firing at him.

–Sixty-One–

The church door opened, filtering light into the cloudy mess. Antoine coughed as smoke filled his lungs. The pain searing through him was so intense it was an effort to get to his feet. Was he dying?

He walked slowly toward the front of the church, not sure where Clement vanished to. A woman stood with the sun behind her in the doorway.

Antoine's eyes burned. Was that Emma? His Emma? Had she come back to him?

Wind blew in and flames exploded around them.

The smoke made it hard to breathe, to see. He coughed, but a terrible echo that reminded him of a gunshot muffled it.

A sharp twinge in his sore shoulder pushed Antoine to his knees. Slowly.

Why was the world moving so slow?

Breathe.

Silver was beside him with his hanky. "*Use it to breathe.*" How had Silver got his hanky? Why was he talking so slowly anyway? Who talked that sluggish?

"Charlie," Antoine said as he fell, but much to his surprise, Silver caught him.

"*I'll be with you, Antoine. Just breathe.*"

Antoine felt his body move toward the door as if he fell. Did Clement shoot him? He looked up toward Emma. She came back.

A gun in her hand gleamed, catching the light. It fell from her hand to the church floor.

Emma screamed. Far away. An underwater echo he wanted to capture.

Why scream? What did she mean she was sorry? She came

back. Nothing to be sorry about. He'd understood that she was looking out for Charlie. He knew what it was to protect someone. He understood.

Antoine watched Emma shove past Doc to get to him. Fast. How was she moving so fast in a world that had almost come to a stop?

Antoine wanted to rush to her without Silver but he kept falling. Her name was on his lips yet he was too weak to speak it. He touched his shoulder which was hurting more than usual. Blood. He was shot.

Emma.

Doc took him from Silver, moving too fast. Air rushed at him. Cold wind hit him as they dragged Antoine outside. But he couldn't go outside. Those boys might be in the church. Where was Clement?

A sea of people crowded him. Faces blurred together. He hated that. Why did all of him hurt? A fiery blaze locked in his shoulder, yet pain was everywhere. As if something in him had blown apart.

"Antoine. Breathe with me." Doc held him up. Were they walking? He felt himself moving.

It burned to breathe. Antoine tried to say this but a gurgle surprised him instead of words. Was he dying? He looked around for Silver but he was gone.

-Sixty-Two-

The tunnel was chilly so Hoolie did up Charlie's jacket. "That's just a line, Charlie. I can draw that, you have to give me a challenge. Antoine said to put the lines together like this for the letter A." In the dust, Hoolie made lines but joined them together to make a mountain. Charlie chuckled as if he was hilarious and copied his lines.

A shadow swept down the tunnel and Hoolie leaped to his feet. "The shadows are nuts this morning." He dimmed the light so he could see them more clearly. "It's almost like they're getting ready for a celebration."

Charlie grabbed his leg.

"I smell smoke. You?"

"Bad."

Hoolie reached for his hand, then thought twice about it and scooped Charlie up. He wasn't sure which way to run. He'd picked this spot to camp because he had several choices. Right would bring them to the altar in the church. Left would lead them to the livery barn. Both paths had two holes they could hide in. He'd stored water and things in each, 'cause really, it was only a matter of time before he'd need them.

The ground shook. He hated that feeling. Heat poured on them from the right and a strange glow was coming at them fast so he turned left. He reached for the beam to find the marker that would tell him how far until the first safe exit, but pulled back shocked. It moved toward them.

Hoolie tossed Charlie forward and reached for the beam, trying to push it back where it belonged. He'd survived a few cave-ins but not in tunnels made by God. These were made to crumble on themselves when He was pissed off.

Hoolie felt the weight as the earth came down on him. "Run, Charlie." Hoolie dropped between the beams, close to the wall, and curled up the best he could. Eyes shut tight, he waited for death.

It didn't come. Not death. No pain. Just weight, trying to merge him with the dirt he loved. Then suddenly it stopped.

"Dark, Daddy." Hoolie heard Charlie. He couldn't be that far under if he heard him.

"Son." There was a long silence. Was that Clement? "You're safe now. Who brought you down here?"

"Hoolie."

"You alive, Hoolie? It's just a bit of rubble. Hear me?"

Hoolie groaned into the ground, but he pushed upward with his back. Things shifted.

"Hoolie? Is that you?" The weight lessened on his legs. "Christ boy, you got twenty-five lives or something?"

Hoolie pushed up and gasped for fresh air. Clement held the lantern on him while he caught his breath.

"You took that cave-in to save my son?" Clement's eyes were so full of admiration that Hoolie almost forgot to watch his light. Thing with Clement was that what he said never matched the light around him. He was one big lie, only... not this time. He really meant it. "That's probably the most heroic thing I ever seen anyone do. I mean, I was a ways back, but that's what you did, wasn't it? Why? You hardly know this boy."

Hoolie shook the dust from his shirt. "Ain't something I can explain, moron." For some reason, Clement's light always beamed when Hoolie snapped at him.

Clement let go of Charlie's hand so he could climb the pile of dirt and join Hoolie. A loud boom vibrated through the tunnel from the right and Clement shoved Hoolie out of the way of a ceiling beam.

Hoolie dived for the boy, aiming for his light. Together they rolled down the tunnel toward the livery barn.

The explosion left them in the dark. Where was Clement's lantern? His light?

"You hurt, Charlie?" Hoolie asked.

"Ouch," he said, rubbing his head.

"We'll live, eh? Clement, you there?" His light was gone.

Cripes.

Everything in him ached but the earth grumbled, forcing Hoolie to his feet. "Don't look back, Charlie. Hold on to my neck inside my jacket. We have to run, God is not happy about something." Hoolie dashed in the dark toward the cool breeze coming at them and away from the complaining sounds following them.

-Sixty-Three-

Emma watched her guilty hands as she clutched Antoine on the floor of the livery barn. Her entire world collapsed in one crazy moment. She'd wanted to end this. She'd seen a way out.

Now it was over. She'd shot Antoine instead of Clement.

How could she hit Antoine? "Don't you die on me," she screamed frantically at him. How could she touch a weapon? She knew this was forbidden. What had she been thinking? She was a digger. She always would be.

Doc ordered people around, but Emma had Antoine's head cradled on her lap in the livery barn. They were sheltered from the wind and the horses added warmth, but he was cold. Why was he cold?

She ran her hands over Antoine's face. Doc had undone Antoine's jacket and checked his shoulder. Blood. So much blood. Too much. Blood should be inside.

Antoine tried to say something, but only gushing came out.

Emma's vision was blurred from tears she had no idea existed in her. She couldn't catch her breath. First Charlie and now Antoine. She was alone. Clement would walk out of that church and still own her.

She'd shoot him.

Doc had taken the gun away from her. *God judges who returns to Him and when. All I do is run happy in the field until it's my turn.*

"Save him, Doc. This can't be his turn."

Doc met her eyes but spoke to the others around them. Why were they standing there?

A trapdoor to her left opened and without thinking she reached for the blade Doc held.

–Sixty-Four–

Normally, Hoolie was very careful when coming out of a tunnel, but there was no time for his paranoia. He exploded out of the tunnel and fell at the intense light of a mob. As he dropped, a knife blew past him, just grazing him. Cripes. What the heck was going on?

Jill's hand grabbed his, shouting his name. He squinted, trying to make out her light as it merged with the light of others around her. Was he dead?

No, not dead. There were just too many people, and the light he normally saw in each one was all smeared together, as if they were one unit.

He focused on Jill who stared at him deeply. Her normal happy light was swirling with brown clouds he wanted to wipe out. Hoolie met Jill's big accusing green eyes as they brimmed with tears, and he scrambled to his feet.

"Why are there so many people feeling the same thing?" he asked her, afraid to look at the group again. He wiped his sleeve on his face, smearing the dirt around.

"Antoine has been shot."

Even as she said it, Hoolie saw him lying on the dirt floor of the livery barn. "Antoine?" Hoolie went toward him and knelt at his feet.

Jill was at his side "Doc says he won't make it."

"Doc? What the heck happened? You're gonna fix him, right? You gotta."

Doc glanced up and pulled back. "You. I knew something about you nagged at me. Myles' boy. I knew your father. Gosh, he searched everywhere for you," Doc talked while he worked. What was he saying?

Emma took his hand and held it against Antoine. Everyone

seemed to blur together. Antoine couldn't die, could he? He... Hoolie just couldn't accept that.

Emma tried to speak but her questions caught in her throat. "Charlie?"

He felt the boy's grip around his neck. "In here." Hoolie pulled away and unzipped his jacket. Charlie tumbled out. His head had a huge gash on it so Hoolie used his hanky to wipe the blood, but it just smeared dirt into it. Dang.

The church made a loud cracking sound behind him. When the wall fell in, the light surrounding the crowd flared out in pain. It all felt unreal. He'd never seen a crowd breathe as one.

Doc did things to Antoine that Hoolie couldn't watch. He tried to pull Charlie away from him but the brat was pushing the light back into Antoine's body. That probably wasn't a bad idea. Hoolie didn't want to see that light step out of his body and turn into a shadow either, yet it was slowly blending into the earth. Greying.

Another wall of the church fell in.

–Sixty-five–

Tiny, warm hands touched his face, but Antoine couldn't see them. He didn't have to. "Help," Charlie repeated. It felt nice to have Charlie near him. Where had he come from?

Before him was the open prairie. The snow was gone. It was spring, his favourite time of year.

Emma hummed softly beside him, the song Sacri used to sing. Her hands were warm on his cold skin. Why was he cold when the sun was warm? Antoine rested against Emma while she sang The Song of Sorrow. Why was she sad? The wind swirled around them, cool, yet peacefully warm. Her belly rubbed life against him. So hopeful. Nothing to be sad about.

Love filled the song as it swept over him. She was always full of love, even sad like this.

Then heat. Hot, hot. Like the sun warming him, only stronger. The sun was never this hot.

He gazed out to the open prairies at the setting sun that had been coming up only moments ago. So bright along the horizon it hurt his eyes to look at it. Yet he had no choice, for in the light was Sacri.

"Sacri." Antoine shot up, surprised to see her so alive.

Not alive.

A ghost.

She stood in her serious way, watching him with Emma. *"You have to let her go, Antoine."*

Eyes wide open, he looked at Emma, clutching him. Why wasn't he in his body? The body she held for dear life.

"Am I dead? Really? This is dying?" It was easy. "I want to stay with Emma."

"Why must you fight every little breath, even your last?"

"I don't want to fight. It just happens that everything is worth the fight."

Doc was there. So smart, telling him to breathe.

Antoine studied the crowd. Endless faces, yet he knew them all. He liked that. Hoolie held Jill's hand. Hoolie? Where had he come from? The brat was dirty, but he looked well. It made Antoine smile to see him safe. Marie picked up Charlie, explaining something.

Could he fight this?

"Where is Clement?" Antoine asked Sacri as she stood beside him watching the chaos.

"*Judgement has been issued and he passed.*"

Antoine glanced at Sacri. He'd forgotten what she was like. "Why would you let him pass?"

"*I do not decide these things. He chose to pass.*"

Clement walked toward them from the flames of the church. Antoine stood between him and Sacri—instinct. "Devil, go back."

"*Antoine.*" Sacri held his shoulder. "*He is at one with the earth.*"

"He's a jerk."

"*You cannot judge people for fighting for their own beliefs when you yourself do this.*"

Clement stood about ten yards back.

"We're dead. Happy now?" Antoine glared. "This is where your stupid beliefs got us. We had it all and now we have nothing."

"*Au contraire. Now we have it all. Before, all I had were walls, mutt.*"

"What?"

"*All I saw—walls,*" Clement complained.

Antoine turned to Sacri. "Any idea what he goes on about?"

Clement answered, "*Tramp of a wife is sleeping with the farm hands. Wall.*" A brick wall shot up behind Clement. "*Don't need to deal with that, not when I have my pick of gals, right?*" Clement smirked weakly. "*Then... I found one who understood me. But she's black and gives me a goddamn black son. What the hell am I supposed to do with that? Wall.*" A flimsy wall flew up to his right and Clement stared at it longingly. "*No idea why* that *wall exists. That's what drove me crazy. I put up that wall because my old man said this was how things were done. Yet inside, I know how important that boy is to me. I don't give a rat's ass what colour his skin is.*" He punched the wall and it toppled. "*Should have done that a long time ago. Maybe Emma wouldn't have left me for the likes of you.*" He looked to his left. "*Everyone builds walls around me. Friends, people I trust, all of 'em using me, telling me what they think I want to hear. You know how rare it is to find a guy who tells me to go to hell?*" A rock wall blurred to his left.

Sacri said, "*Judgement comes from within. We welcome home a lost soul who has found self-acceptance and is prepared to teach others.*"

Grey shadows exploded from the earth and twirled around Clement, pushing away the walls.

"*Before you stands a soul who sees beyond walls. He feels worthy, and therefore, he is.*"

A door appeared and Clement opened it and stepped closer to Antoine.

The snow was trampled by the mob, but Antoine saw no people, just Clement and Sacri. They left together, talking like old friends. Clement glanced over his shoulder once and shook his head.

Still no people.

Not one ghost.

Antoine glanced down at himself.

Well. Maybe one.

The world came back, loud and confused.

Emma sang the melody he'd taught her. Word for word, her soul called on the chords.

Antoine leaned against the imaginary doorjamb of the door that linked them, watching her sing to his body. Her love was clear. Why had he let fear build this door between them?

"*You gonna fight, son?*"

"Pa?" Antoine almost fell over. His pa looked so... alive.

"*Walk with me. We have much to catch up on.*"

Antoine smirked at his pa. "You think I should walk away?"

"*Up to you. What do I know about your fights, really?*"

"I can't leave her."

"She told you this was a journey she planned to take alone, yet you want to stay for her? She'll be fine without you. Look at her. She's tough."

"I didn't get my happy forever."

"So this is about you then? You earned it?"

"No, Pa. She deserves her happy forever. This is what I want to give Emma and Charlie." Antoine bowed his head. "This would make me happy, too. But what if Clement was right? What if she won't fit in here?"

His pa studied the crowd, all the town was there. His friends, his family. People who grew up with him. *Cîpay* and settlers from every walk of life. They were together because his pa fell in love with the land, with Sacri, with a way of life he didn't fit into.

"Look who I'm talking to."

The church burned, but it wasn't what he saw. Antoine saw possibility in the finer details. Silent looks of support. Already, they crowded around Emma and Charlie, the pain in their eyes as deep as hers. Hoolie watched him, his hand clutching Jill's. Not the Antoine on the ground, no, Hoolie saw him talking to his pa. He looked from one to the other with worried breaths, waiting for something.

"Think she'll be fine without me?"

Sacri was beside them again, and Antoine had no idea where she'd come from but it was nice to have his parents on either side of him.

"So you'll come with us then?" Pa looked relieved.

"Ya know, Pa, I might stay for a bit. Help get this town back on its feet. I'm kinda attached to the place."

Sacri took his hand. *"Sing with Emma. Your soul must heal. Put your hands in the dirt and feel the healing energy of your ancestors."*

"What dirt?"

"It's there, you just aren't seeing."

The air burned his lungs. "It hurts to breathe."

"Yeah, sometimes it does." Pa nodded so matter-of-fact.

Antoine still wasn't ready to go back in that body she held. It looked painful. What was Doc doing?

Besides, he had so many questions. "What if I fail her?"

"Either you come with me or you breathe. Failing her isn't a choice you make, it is one she makes." His pa had a troubled look on his face. *"You don't have much longer, Antoine."*

Again, Antoine sucked in a deep breath. It wasn't as painful as the last one. It went in smoothly, easily, giving him energy, as if someone else was breathing for him.

"Each breath, Antoine, each one has a past, a reason, and leads to the future." Sacri's voice was distant, even if she was right against him.

Light blinded him and burned him so hard that sounds rushed together.

"Emma," Antoine mumbled and his body responded.

"Antoine."

He opened his eyes. Emma was inches from his lips.

"Hurts to breathe."

"Then I will breathe for you."

He focused on her breaths, watching her eyes. So full of love.

–Sixty-Six–

Dear Antoine,
Really, you should have taken the easy way. I'm just saying.
I'm sure Doc healed you up nicely. Funny how seeing you die triggered something in him and he came back to us. Maybe he was hiding under his own sheet. Protection from the pain. Regardless, it was nice to see him.
Don't bother coming for me, Antoine. I have my own journey to make. Just let me go.
Hoolie needs to burrow somewhere, so teach him, you owe him. Good brat you found there.
Emma's courage inspired me.
If you see Silver, tell him thanks for the things I don't know he does.
–Always, Marie

"What does it say?" Emma was curled up beside Antoine and he gripped her tightly, no barrier between them, just pure free air for them to enjoy.

"It says..." Antoine watched Emma, her deep brown eyes so trusting. He didn't want to disappoint her. "She asked me to let her go."

"Will you?"

Antoine stared at the ceiling. His place was with Emma, yet Marie had the right idea. Something in him wanted to fight. "I'll miss her."

Doc took his pulse. "She didn't say anything about me, did she? I mean. Not that I care or anything, just... Well, did she?"

"It's fine to care, Doc. It's what makes us human. The problem is when we stop caring." Antoine folded the letter and handed it to Doc. "Keep it. You know," Antoine said, "you're welcome to stay with us. Your house is kinda trashed and this town needs a doc opened-minded to other healing techniques."

"Fresh start with new friends sounds about right." Doc smiled his sad smile as he left them.

Emma brushed Antoine's arm. "I hung a picture while you slept."

Antoine was curious what she'd pick and sat to look at the nail he'd left for her. He chuckled when he saw the marriage certificate he'd carried around.

"Figured if God saw in my heart, he'd make that real. I am home. Clement can't take this feeling away from me, not ever. It confuses me, and I don't fit in at all, but it seems everyone feels that way, so I kinda fit in after all."

"Clement is no longer a problem. Promise." Antoine pulled her toward him for a kiss he wasn't ever going to let end.

–SIXTY-SEVEN–

June 1919—

Charlie raced after a butterfly. The boy laughed. He actually laughed, and it was the best thing Antoine ever heard on the prairies. It echoed forever.

Hoolie even stopped to watch his antics.

Not far off, Emma worked the garden, little Sacri strapped to her back. Their daughter looked so much like his mother, no other name fit.

They were living the happy moment Antoine dreamed about but over the past months, ghosts erupted in Saskatchewan. He didn't really know what they were up to yet, but someone else was leading them, firing them up.

Antoine continued to the wagon with the rock, waiting for the right moment to talk with Hoolie.

"Damn, your fields look good. Let me carry the big ones," Hoolie said, taking it from Antoine. "So, who taught you to do these things?"

"Pa."

"Oh. He the one who showed you how to build a house?" Hoolie asked. "Because I might need one and I don't have a pa."

"These aren't my fields we're clearing. I was thinking the same thing. Ya know. So you can bring your family here."

"My family?"

"Yeah, you told me you worked the tunnels to feed your family," Antoine reminded him of their first conversation in Moose Jaw.

"Oh sorry. I meant my family of runners."

"You have no family?"

Hoolie frowned and for a minute, Antoine thought he was gonna yell at him. "I got you. And Charlie. And Emma. And Jill. Even Doc. What more do I need?"

"So what you need a house for then? I have one big enough for you." Antoine waited.

"Jill."

"Oh? So you plan to make a home with her?"

"She says we can't live in my den and we can't live with you. You giving me this land? For real? I don't have cash or anything. I sorta spent it getting here, but I like the idea of owning dirt."

"You got hands. You help me. I'll help you. Like a family or something. But Hoolie, we don't own the land, we owe it."

Hoolie squinted as if the sun was too bright. "I like that. Honestly, Antoine, you have no idea what you owe this land and I don't ever want to have to explain it to you." He looked off in the distance. "Nice tunnels. I might stay."

Antoine's chuckles were cut off when Charlie stopped running in the long grass.

"What ya see, Charlie?"

"Ghost."

Sure enough, Uncle Silver pointed to the horizon.

"Hide, Charlie," Hoolie said.

Charlie stood by Antoine, his tiny hands clutching Antoine's pants.

"We don't hide on land we work, Hoolie."

Antoine hollered at Emma and she went in the house. Then he searched the ground for a rock and waited. Sure enough, on the horizon they appeared. Two ghosts on horses.

"You tempted to hide?" Antoine asked Hoolie.

"Heck no. Safest place in the world is when your light wraps around us. I'm staying beside you. Even the boy knows that." Hoolie stood at his side, as if Antoine was a shield.

Antoine glanced back. Emma was on the steps with the rifle. He'd taught her how to fire properly, but he hated to see her holding that weapon.

The men in sheets didn't slow, just rode past at full speed and dropped a sack of flour at his feet.

Emma fired off three warning shots, to alert the

neighbours, but the ghosts vanished as quickly as they appeared.

On his knees, Antoine prepared to open the bag. "Charlie, search the fields for Silver while I look in this bag."

Charlie turned around but his shoulder rubbed Antoine's as he untied the bag.

Marie.

His sweet Marie.

Cradling his sister in his arms, he tried to decipher her last moments. Around her neck was a golden cross, like the one Charlie wore. The one he'd given her back. Antoine took it off and clutched it in his hand.

"Take this necklace to your sister." Antoine handed it to Charlie. "It matches yours and I gave it to my sister so that will mean something if you give it to yours."

Charlie took off as fast as his little legs could go, without a glance at the bag.

"Gosh. I'm sorry. She looks peaceful," Hoolie said as he brushed the curls from her face, unafraid to touch her. "Hard to believe this woman had shadows around her."

"Hoolie, how many did she have around her?"

"They're gone. She's at peace."

It was how Antoine felt as the sun warmed his skin. Peaceful. He knew what that meant.

Silver rushed toward them.

"Clement? Did he have any?"

"Only a few people have shadows, Antoine." Hoolie knelt beside him. "No. Clement was caught up in bad choices as he desperately searched for truth." He looked at Antoine's tight fists. "Does this mean another fight? Because I was kinda hoping for some peace myself."

Emma ran to him with his horse and gun, scooping up Charlie along the way. This peace he felt was worth the fight.

Elsewhen Press

an independent publisher specialising in Speculative Fiction

Visit the Elsewhen Press website at elsewhen.co.uk for the latest information on all of our titles, authors and events; to read our blog; find out where to buy our books and ebooks; or to place an order.

Elsewhen Press

an independent publisher specialising in Speculative Fiction

The *Royal Sorceress* series
by
Christopher Nuttall

The *Royal Sorceress* series will certainly appeal to all fans of steampunk, alternative history, and fantasy. As well as the fun of the 'what-ifs' delivered by the rewriting of our past, it delights with an Empire empowered by magic – all the better for being one we can recognise.

The Royal Sorceress
Book I of the Royal Sorceress series

It's 1830, in an alternate Britain where the 'scientific' principles of magic were discovered sixty years previously, allowing the British to win the American War of Independence. Although Britain is now supreme among the Great Powers, the gulf between rich and poor in the Empire has widened and unrest is growing every day. Master Thomas, the King's Royal Sorcerer, is ageing and must find a successor to lead the Royal Sorcerers Corps. Most magicians can possess only one of the panoply of known magical powers, but Thomas needs to find a new Master of all the powers. There is only one candidate, one person who has displayed such a talent from an early age, but has been neither trained nor officially acknowledged. A perfect candidate to be Master Thomas' apprentice in all ways but one: the Royal College of Sorcerers has never admitted a girl before.

But even before Lady Gwendolyn Crichton can begin her training, London is plunged into chaos by a campaign of terrorist attacks co-ordinated by Jack, a powerful and rebellious magician.

ISBN: 9781908168184 (epub, kindle)
ISBN: 9781908168085 (400pp, paperback)
For more information visit bit.ly/TheRoyalSorceress

The Great Game

Book II of the Royal Sorceress series

After the uprising in London, Lady Gwendolyn Crichton is settling into her new position as Royal Sorceress and fighting the prejudice against her gender and age that seeks to prevent her from fulfilling her responsibilities. But when a senior magician is murdered in a locked room and Gwen is charged with finding the culprit, her inquiries lead her into a web of intrigue that combines international politics, widespread aristocratic blackmail, gambling dens and personal vendettas... and some of her discoveries hit dangerously close to home.

Continuing on from the end of *The Royal Sorceress*, *The Great Game* follows Gwen's unfolding story as she assumes the role formerly held by Master Thomas. A satisfying blend of whodunit and magical fantasy, it is set against a backdrop of international political unrest in a believable yet simultaneously fantastic alternate history.

ISBN: 9781908168375 (epub, kindle)
ISBN: 9781908168276 (400pp, paperback)
For more information visit bit.ly/TheGreatGame

Necropolis

Book III of the Royal Sorceress series

The British Empire is teetering on the brink of war with France. A war that may, for the first time, see magicians in the ranks on both sides. The Royal Sorceress, Lady Gwendolyn Crichton, will be responsible for the Empire's magical resources when the time comes. Still struggling to overcome prejudice within the Royal Sorcerers Corps, she has at least earnt the gratitude of much of the aristocracy, if not their respect. Just when Gwen needs to be firmly focussed on training new sorcerers, her adopted daughter Olivia, the only known living necromancer, is kidnapped. Her abduction could signal a terrible new direction in the impending war. But Intelligence soon establishes that it was Russian agents who took Olivia, so an incognito Gwen joins a British diplomatic mission to Russia, an uncertain element in the coming conflict. Once she has arrived in St Petersburg, she discovers that the Tsar is deranged and with the help of a mad monk has a plan that threatens the entire world.

Immediately following on from 'The Great Game', 'Necropolis' sees Gwen thrust into the wider international arena as political unrest spreads throughout Europe and beyond, threatening to hasten an almighty conflict. Once again Christopher Nuttall combines exciting fantasy with believable alternate history that is almost close enough for us to touch.

ISBN: 9781908168726 (epub, kindle)
ISBN: 9781908168627 (416pp, paperback)
For more information visit bit.ly/RSNecropolis

Elsewhen Press

an independent publisher specialising in Speculative Fiction

TimeStorm
Steve Harrison

In 1795 a convict ship leaves England for New South Wales in Australia. Nearing its destination, it encounters a savage storm but, miraculously, the battered ship stays afloat and limps into Sydney Harbour. The convicts rebel, overpower the crew and make their escape, destroying the ship in the process. Fleeing the sinking vessel with only the clothes on their backs, the survivors struggle ashore.

Among the escaped convicts, seething resentments fuel an appetite for brutal revenge against their former captors, while the crew attempts to track down and kill or recapture the escapees. However, it soon becomes apparent that both convicts and crew have more to concern them than shipwreck and a ruthless fight for survival; they have arrived in Sydney in 2017.

TimeStorm is a thrilling epic adventure story of revenge, survival and honour. In the literary footsteps of Hornblower, comes Lieutenant Christopher 'Kit' Blaney, an old-fashioned hero, a man of honour, duty and principle. But dragged into the 21st century... literally.

A great fan of the grand seafaring adventure fiction of CS Forester, Patrick O'Brien and Alexander Kent and modern action thriller writers like Lee Child, Steve Harrison combines several genres in his fast-paced debut novel as a group of desperate men from the 1700s clash in modern-day Sydney.

Steve Harrison was born in Yorkshire, England, grew up in Lancashire, migrated to New Zealand and eventually settled in Sydney, Australia, where he lives with his wife and daughter.

As he juggled careers in shipping, insurance, online gardening and the postal service, Steve wrote short stories, sports articles and a long running newspaper humour column called *HARRISCOPE: a mix of ancient wisdom and modern nonsense*. In recent years he has written a number of unproduced feature screenplays, although being unproduced was not the intention, and developed projects with producers in the US and UK. His script, *Sox*, was nominated for an Australian Writers' Guild 'Awgie' Award and he has written and produced three short films under his *Pronunciation Fillums* partnership. TimeStorm was Highly Commended in the Fellowship of Australian Writers (FAW) National Literary Awards for 2013.

ISBN: 9781908168542 (epub, kindle)
ISBN: 9781908168443 (368pp paperback)

Visit bit.ly/TimeStorm

Elsewhen Press

an independent publisher specialising in Speculative Fiction

Jacey's Kingdom

Dave Weaver

Jacey's Kingdom is an enthralling tale that revolves around a startlingly desperate reality: Jacey Jackson, a talented student destined for Cambridge, collapses with a brain tumour while sitting her final history exam at school. In her mind she struggles through a quasi-historical sixth century dreamscape whilst the surgeons fight to save her life.

Jacey is helped by a stranger called George, who finds himself trapped in her nightmare after a terrible car accident. There are quests, battles, and a love story ahead of them, before we find out if Jacey will awake from her coma or perish on the operating table. And who, or what, is George? In this book, Dave Weaver questions our perception of reality and the redemptive power of dreams; are our experiences of fear, conflict, friendship and love any less real or meaningful when they take place in the mind rather than the 'real' physical world?

Dave Weaver has been writing for ten years, with short stories published in anthologies, magazines and online in the UK and USA. Jacey's Kingdom is his first published novel. He cleverly weaves a tale that takes the almost unimaginable drama of an eighteen year-old girl whose life is in the balance, relying on modern surgery to bring her back from the brink, and conceives the world that she has constructed in her mind to deal with the trauma happening to her body. Developing the friendship between Jacey and George in a natural and witty style, despite their unlikely situation and the difference in their ages, Dave has produced a story that is both exciting and thought-provoking. This book will be a must-read story for adults and young adults alike.

ISBN: 9781908168313 (epub, kindle)
ISBN: 9781908168214 (272pp paperback)

Visit bit.ly/JaceysKingdom

Elsewhen Press

an independent publisher specialising in Speculative Fiction

The Lost Men
An Allegory
David Colón

In a world where the human population has been decimated, self-reliance is the order of the day. Of necessity, the few remaining people must adapt residual technology as far as possible, with knowledge gleaned from books that were rescued and have been treasured for generations. After a childhood of such training, each person is abandoned by their parents when they reach adulthood, to pursue an essentially solitary existence. For most, the only human contact is their counsel, a mentor who guides them to find 'the one', their life mate as decreed by Fate. Lack of society brings with it a lack of taboo, ensuring that the Fate envisioned by a counsel is enacted unquestioningly. The only threats to this stable, if sparse, existence are the 'lost men', mindless murderers who are also self-sufficient but with no regard for the well-being of others, living outside the confines of counsel and Fate.

Is Fate a real force, or is it totally imagined, an arbitrary convention, a product of mankind's self-destructive tendency? In this allegorical tale, David Colón uses an alternate near-future to explore the boundaries of the human condition and the extent to which we are prepared to surrender our capacity for decisions and self-determination in the face of a very personally directed and apparently benevolent, authoritarianism. Is it our responsibility to rebuke inherited 'wisdom' for the sake of envisioning and manifesting our own will?

David Colón is an Assistant Professor of English at TCU in Fort Worth, Texas, USA. Born and raised in Brooklyn, New York, he received his Ph.D. in English from Stanford University and was a Chancellor's Postdoctoral Fellow in English at the University of California, Berkeley. His writing has appeared in numerous journals, including *Cultural Critique, Studies in American Culture, DIAGRAM, How2,* and *MELUS. The Lost Men* is his first book.

ISBN: 9781908168146 (epub, kindle)
ISBN: 9781908168047 (192pp paperback)

Visit lost-men.com

ABOUT THE AUTHOR

Born and raised in Saskatchewan, Tanya Reimer enjoys using the tranquil prairies as a setting to her not-so-peaceful speculative fiction.

She is married with two children which means among her accomplishments are the necessary magical abilities to find a lost tooth in a park of sand and whisper away monsters from under the bed.

As director of a non-profit Francophone community center, Tanya offers programming and services in French for all ages to ensure the lasting imprint and growth of the Francophone community in which she was raised. What she enjoys the most about her job is teaching social media safety for teens and offering one-on-one technology classes for seniors.

Tanya was fifteen when she wrote her first column. She has a diploma in Journalism/Short Story Writing. Today, she actively submits to various newspapers, writes and publishes the local Francophone newsletter for her community, and maintains a blog at *Life's Like That*.

Ghosts on the Prairies, a Sacred Land Story for adults, is her debut novel.

www.ingramcontent.com/pod-product-compliance
Lightning Source LLC
Chambersburg PA
CBHW050612170726
48283CB00001B/209